By Raymond E. Feist

The Chaoswar Saga
A KINGDOM BESIEGED • A CROWN IMPERILED

The Demonwar Saga
RIDES A DREAD LEGION • AT THE GATES OF DARKNESS

The Darkwar Saga
FLIGHT OF THE NIGHTHAWKS • INTO A DARK REALM
WRATH OF A MAD GOD

Conclave of Shadows
TALON OF THE SILVER HAWK • KING OF FOXES
EXILE'S RETURN

Legends of the Riftwar
HONORED ENEMY (with William R. Forstchen)
MURDER IN LAMUT (with Joel Rosenberg)
JIMMY THE HAND (with S.M. Stirling)

The Riftwar Legacy
KRONDOR: THE BETRAYAL • KRONDOR: THE ASSASSINS
KRONDOR: TEAR OF THE GODS

The Serpentwar Saga
SHADOW OF A DARK QUEEN • RISE OF A MERCHANT PRINCE
RAGE OF A DEMON KING • SHARDS OF A BROKEN CROWN

The Empire Trilogy
(with Janny Wurts)
DAUGHTER OF EMPIRE • SERVANT OF EMPIRE
MISTRESS OF EMPIRE

Krondor's Sons
PRINCE OF THE BLOOD • THE KING'S BUCCANEER

The Riftwar Saga
MAGICIAN • SILVERTHORN • A DARKNESS AT SETHANON

Other Titles
FAERIE TALE

RAYMOND E. FEIST

A CROWN

BOOK TWO OF THE CHAOSWAR SAGA

IMPERILED

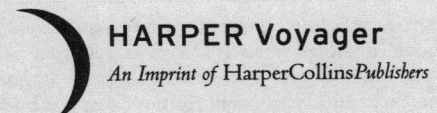

HARPER Voyager

An Imprint of HarperCollins*Publishers*

HARPER Voyager

An Imprint of HarperCollins*Publishers*
10 East 53rd Street
New York, New York 10022-5299

Copyright © 2012 by Raymond E. Feist
Map designed by Ralph M. Askren, D.V.M.
Cover art by Steve Stone
ISBN 978-0-06-146842-1
www.harpervoyagerbooks.com

First Harper Voyager mass market printing: March 2013
First Harper Voyager hardcover printing: March 2012

Harper Voyager and ⟩ is a trademark of HCP LLC.

Printed in the U.S.A.

10 9 8 7 6 5 4 3 2

THIS ONE'S FOR DIRTY ROTTEN SCOUNDRELS;
YOU KNOW WHO YOU ARE.

CONTENTS

Prologue	Awakenings	1
Chapter 1	Warning	7
Chapter 2	Raid	28
Chapter 3	Attack	48
Chapter 4	Isle of Snakes	67
Chapter 5	Fugitive	89
Chapter 6	Conspiracies	108
Chapter 7	Alarm	126
Chapter 8	Assault	143
Chapter 9	Evasion	166
Chapter 10	Wilderness	186
Chapter 11	Treachery	200
Chapter 12	Onslaught	216
Chapter 13	Search	237
Chapter 14	Escape	251
Chapter 15	Exploration	266

Chapter 16	Journeys	289
Chapter 17	Reunion	308
Chapter 18	Mysteries	328
Chapter 19	Conflicts	353
Chapter 20	Manoeuvres	371
Chapter 21	Destruction	389
Entr'acte	Awakenings	403

ACKNOWLEDGMENTS

As is always the case, I must begin with thanks to the original mothers and fathers of Midkemia, who generously gave me permission to use their playground; I trust I haven't abused it too much.

As always to Jonathan Matson, my thanks for being more than a business partner, but a friend of the very best kind, one who puts up with you with humor and affection just because that's the kind of person he is.

To the brilliant ladies at HarperCollins, on both sides of The Pond, for making me look good.

I would like to take a moment to thank all of you who have written me over the years, to tell me something I wrote made you think, helped you solve a problem, or endure a trial, or gave you comfort. It is my intent only to entertain, but if I somehow move you beyond that point, it is an unexpected blessing and I thank you for letting me know.

Lastly, to my kids who keep me tuned into what is really important in life and make so many things that otherwise would confound me bearable.

Raymond E. Feist
San Diego, CA

A CROWN IMPERILED

PROLOGUE

AWAKENINGS

Mighty dragons raced through the skies. Hurricane-force winds struck his face, yet the rider sat confidently astride the neck of his scaled ebony mount; his to command by will alone. Arcane arts kept him firmly in place, and exultation energized every fibre of his being as the Dragon Host rode out in search of conquest.

Never in the long history of the Valheru had the entire Dragon Host risen united.

The entire Host, save one. Dark emotions

turned quickly to rage. The white-and-gold rider was absent. Ashen-Shugar: the only dissenter within the Host.

But the absence of the father-brother did not signify. The Valheru had answered his call, and Draken-Korin had taken his rightful place as leader of the Dragon Host.

He watched mad energies race through the skies above the dragon riders, flashing colours of blinding brilliance as energy vortexes and tears in the fabric of space and time exploded into spectrums invisible to mortal eyes, but perfectly clear to his Valheru vision.

His vision shifted; memories fading as others resurfaced. The cavern, once the Lord of the Tigers' seat of power, was dark. That didn't concern him since his vision was far sharper than any mortal's, but he missed the warmth of torches and . . . Where were his servants?

He tried to lift his left arm and pain tore through his shoulder. He had not felt pain like this since . . .

Images cascaded through his mind as he relived the memories of ages past.

He felt his first breath and heard a contemptuous mother curse him as her servants carried him away. Elven slaves brought him newborn to a clearing in the warm, damp forest, and without any tenderness left him on top of a large rock. To live or die by his own strength.

He remembered extending his infant senses, a primitive assessment of danger and threat; he felt no sense of fear, only compelling need. His instincts emerged at need, drawing upon ancestral memories shared since the dawn of creation. The forest was deep, and he sensed predators on every side. The most dangerous, now receding, were of his own race.

Valheru.

A pack of golden jackals sniffed the air, seeking the source of the tempting hint of birthing blood, their heads up and their senses alert. They had left their den as the sun set in the west, to hunt.

The child felt them move closer, the scent of his birth

summoning his death. He reached out and sent a blast of hate and anger at the troop.

The jackals stopped, and cringed. Then, ears flattened, they continue to skulk towards the architect of the mental assault, hunger outweighing their fear.

Another presence . . . nearby. He reached out and instantly recognized the massive predator. But this time instead of danger he discovered contentment there, a warm, nurturing feeling that felt alien, but also compelling. He reached out once more and formed a simple command.

Come.

The tigress leapt to her feet, ignoring the plaintive mewing of her cubs, and bounded down the hill towards the tiny thing that coerced her.

The jackals approached the exposed infant cautiously, knowing that it possessed dangerous abilities, yet driven by the need to feast. Then another scent arrived on the wind and they halted.

The massive tiger charged into the clearing next to the infant and roared a challenge.

The baby might be an unknown threat, but the tiger was all too familiar to the pack hunters, and to be avoided at all costs. Turning tail, the jackals ran, opting to survive and hunt elsewhere.

The tigress lowered her head with a snarl, but the thought emanating from the infant was clear: *Protect me.*

A mortal child would have perished had it been seized and lifted in the tiger's mouth, but he was not a mortal infant; he was Valheru, and his small body was far from delicate.

The great cat returned to her den and deposited the infant next to her own pair of cubs, barely three days old, and still mewing with their eyes closed. She lay down on her side to let them nurse, and watched as the man-thing reached out and gripped her fur. Somehow, it managed to pull itself to her teat where it began to nurse alongside her young.

His eyes opened and he struggled to breathe. 'I'm dying,' he whispered to no one.

You are being reborn, came a distant voice.

He felt feverish and his entire body was in agony. He could no longer feel the separate pain of his wound, for he was consumed by a throbbing, burning ache. Every particle of him hovered at the brink of death, for only at the edge could the transformation be completed. He tried to move and couldn't. Just opening his eyes was a trial. He let them close. Death lingered seconds away, beckoning him with promises of relief and rest.

Something else called to him now: the dreams. He knew the dreams contained madness, but they were vivid and compelling, filling him with a sense of triumph and power. And as much as he longed for relief and rest, the consciousness within the dream was growing in strength, singing of power and control, lust and conquest, blood and victory.

The man who had once been Braden of Shamata felt his will fading.

He remembered joining a band of mercenaries in the Vale of Dreams, and sailing across the Endless Sea to distant lands, where weapons smuggling was a hundred times more lucrative than at home. One last caravan and he'd have enough gold to retire. He'd return to the Vale as a man of means, find a talented, young apprentice weapon-smith and make him a partner. No one knew more about weapons running than a Vale mercenary! He would sell to both sides of the Vale, and run his goods all the way from the foothills of the Grey Towers in the north, to reach the dark elves and goblins, to the Confederacy in the south . . .

His ambitions faded as that old identity gave way to one that was more powerful, more commanding.

The mercenary's faint memories seemed so petty: now he could remember what it felt like to command his dragon, to destroy his enemies, to mate with his own kind when the breeding frenzy seized him. Now he knew he was one of the paramount beings on this world.

He was Valheru! He had no choice. He turned away from death and embraced the dream.

It is not a dream, whispered a distant voice that sounded like his own. *It is an awakening, Lord of the Tigers.*

Tomas awoke, his body bathed in perspiration, his heart pounding. He blinked in confusion for a moment, before recognizing his surroundings. The body lying next to him stirred, then his wife returned to her slumber. Rising slowly, he moved to the large window carved out of the trunk of the massive tree that held their quarters. The soft, ever-present glow of Elvandar entered the bedchamber as he drew aside the curtain and gazed upon the forest that had been his home for most of his long life.

The sheen of that glow made of his body a study in shadows and highlights. Muscles still tight beneath youthful skin marred only by a few battle scars, Tomas's appearance had remained unchanged for more than a century. Even when unarmed he was among the most dangerous beings on this world, for his power was far greater than physical strength: it came from the dark energies that lived at the heart of a race vanished centuries ago. The Valheru.

A soft hand touched his back, familiar; affectionate. The Elf Queen spoke softly, 'What is it, my love?'

Tomas's blue eyes continued to stare into the glow of Elvandar, where most of his wife's subjects lay asleep. Softly he replied, 'It was a dream. Nothing more.'

She leaned against his back, her cheek resting on his shoulder. 'You are troubled.'

He said nothing for a moment, then repeated, 'It was only a dream.'

Sighing slightly, she returned to the bed and slid back under the covers. 'Sleep, Tomas,' she said.

He could tell that she was already drifting back into slumber by the time he came back to the bed.

For a long time he remained silent, even as the sun rose in the east and the sky began to brighten. The dream had been unlike any he had known since that time of madness, when he had first donned the white-and-gold armour of a Dragon Lord. Tomas had wrestled for years with the internal struggle, as the human and Valheru within him strove for dominance. But once he had gained control, he had reclaimed his humanity and found love, both in the woman who slept next to him every night, and deep within his own heart and soul; and since then the dreams of madness had left him untroubled.

Until tonight.

Once again, he had flown on the back of the mighty Shuruga, greatest of the golden dragons, above the lost city of Sar-Sargoth. But this time he had seen his greatest enemy, astride the neck of a massive black dragon.

Draken-Korin.

1

WARNING

Shouts rang across the plaza.

Moredhel warriors gathered in the large square below the palace steps, ignoring the biting chill of the twilight wind off the mountains as they waved their fists and bellowed threats at their enemies. Clans that would otherwise be at sword-point observed the truce, content for the moment to exact revenge on some future day.

The city of Sar-Sargoth had been built hard against the foothills of the Great Northern Mountains. To the north of those mighty peaks stretched the vast icelands where summer never

came. Even as spring presented herself to the rolling Plain of
Isbandia to the south-west, winter lingered in Sar-Sargoth,
only reluctantly releasing her icy grip. The stinging cold did
nothing to alleviate the frustration of the assembled chieftains as they waited for those who had summoned them to
council.

The rising volume of their simmering rage was enough to
move the more cautious of the moredhel chieftains to note
the closest escape route should frustration build to bloodshed. Too many old rivals had been forced together at this
council, and for too long for the truce to last more than
minutes.

Arkan of the Ardanien surveyed his surroundings, then
nodded once towards a side street that he knew led straight
to an old farm gate several blocks away. Arkan was the
model of a moredhel chieftain, with strong, broad shoulders
and a narrow waist. His dark brown hair was cut short at the
front to ensure that his vision was never impaired, and left
long to flow past his pointed ears, down to his shoulders.
His dark eyes were set in an almost expressionless mask.
Arkan's reputation was impressive: he had shepherded his
troubled clan through more than thirty perilous years. Despite having many rivals and sworn enemies, the Clan of the
Ice Bears had grown under his leadership.

His companion returned his nod and glanced around to
assess where trouble would most likely originate. Morgeth,
Arkan's self-appointed bodyguard, let his hand stray to the
hilt of his sword. 'Those damn southerners,' he said at last
to his chieftain.

Arkan could only agree. Their cousins from beyond the
Teeth of the World were an agitated bunch, forced to dwell
as their guests in ancient homelands where they had sought
refuge during the Tsurani invasion. 'Well, they've been here
for a century; they're starting to get restless.'

'Who's keeping them here? They can go home any damn
time they want.'

'Some have tried.' The Chieftain of the Ardanien spoke

quietly, with the thoughtful candour that those who knew him had come to expect. 'It's a difficult trek past those damn Kingdom defences at the Inclindel Gap.' He paused. 'On through Hadati country, skirting the dwarves and Elvandar.' He glanced around as the volume of voices rose again. 'I'd not attempt it with less than the entire clan—'

The sounds of struggle became more urgent.

'Narab better get on with this or we're going to have more than a little bloodshed,' Arkan added.

Morgeth said, 'And then we use that street?'

'Yes,' the chieftain said. 'I wouldn't mind breaking a few heads, but I don't see any point in starting new feuds when I haven't put paid to the old ones.' He looked around. 'If fighting starts, we leave.'

'Yes.' Morgeth gathered his woollen cape around him to ward off the biting wind. 'I thought it was supposed to be warmer down here on the flats.'

Arkan laughed. 'It is warmer. That doesn't make it temperate.'

'I should have brought my bearskin.'

Glancing at the sea of dark cloaks around them, Arkan said, 'If things turn ugly, you'll be glad not to be clad in white fur.'

A shout went up, but this time it wasn't a brawl, but directed instead at a group of figures standing at the top of the stairs at the crowd's edge.

Morgeth said, 'Who are those two on the right?'

'I've never seen them before,' said his chieftain. 'But from the look of them, I judge them to be our lost cousins, the taredhel.'

'Tall bastards, aren't they?'

Arkan nodded. 'That they are.'

The two elves they referred to were indeed a full head taller than those who had led them to the top of the staircase. Behind the group rose the maw of the palace, the large entrance to the empty throne room that no chieftain had dared to occupy since the death of the true Murmandamus, the only moredhel in memory to unite all the clans **under** one banner.

A moredhel dressed in ceremonial robes raised his hands, indicating the need for silence, and the cacophony of voices fell away. When it was quiet, he spoke. 'The council thanks you for attending,' he began.

Muttering answered this, for the council's message had been clear: to ignore the request would have invited the ire of the most powerful leader among the moredhel, the man who now addressed them: Narab.

'We also welcome our distant kin, who have returned to us from the stars.'

The chatter rose; rumours about these elves had been rampant in the north for the last few years. One had whispered of their alliance with the hated eledhel in the south, so it was something of a surprise to see them standing next to Narab.

'What is this, then?' asked a chieftain standing nearby.

'Shut up and find out,' answered another.

Arkan glanced towards the voices to see if trouble was about to erupt, but both warriors had returned their attention to the top of the palace steps.

One of the taredhel stepped forward. 'I am Kaladon of the Clan of the Seven Stars. I bring you greetings from your cousins in E'bar.'

Several of the chieftains scoffed and snorted in derision, for the word 'E'bar' meant 'Home' in the ancient tongue. Others strained to listen, for the wind was blowing hard and this star elf's accent was strange to the ear. No matter what blood history tied them together, these beings were far more alien than even the hated eledhel.

Kaladon continued, 'I bring greetings from the Lord Regent of the Clan of the Seven Stars. We are pleased to be returned to our homeland.' He paused for effect. 'Yet we see much has gone amiss since our departure.'

The murmuring took on an angry note and Narab raised his hands for silence.

Morgeth muttered, 'This is going to turn ugly.'

Arkan whispered, 'It already has.' He motioned for his companion to follow him as he edged towards the side street. A few others were also moving quietly towards the escape routes, but most of the chieftains stood silently waiting for the strangers' next announcement.

The other figure who wore yellow armour trimmed with purple and gold, so garish compared to the dark grey-and-black of the moredhel fighting garb, stepped forward and announced himself. 'I am Kumal, Warleader of the Clan of the Seven Stars.'

That brought total silence. Despite his advancing years and colourful raiment, the speaker possessed a warrior's carriage and visible scars, and his manner communicated a kinship to the moredhel chieftains that they recognized. A few chieftains shouted out traditional words of greetings to a fellow warrior.

If the warleader was pleased to be received in such a fashion, he showed no sign of it but simply nodded once and continued, 'The Regent's Meet has elected to recognize your independence.'

Instantly the mood of the gathered chieftains turned ugly once more. 'You recognize us?' shouted more than one chieftain.

'Quiet!' shouted Narab. 'He brings news!'

'The humans war among themselves,' Kumal went on when the noise had died down. 'Their Empire of Kesh has marched against their Kingdom of the Isles, and much of the land to the south lies covered in smoke and blood.'

This brought a mixed reaction, for as much as the moredhel hated humans, dwarves, and the eledhel, war in the south meant trouble for the southern clans. The leader of one such clan shouted, 'What of the west?'

'Kesh has taken Crydee,' returned Kumal, 'and is driving over the northern pass in the Grey Towers to Ylith.'

'What of the Green Heart?' shouted another voice.

'Kesh ignores all but the human towns and cities. The

dwarves stand ready at the borders of Stone Mountain and the Grey Towers, but will act only if their lands are threatened. The Green Heart and the mountains to the south of E'bar are untroubled.'

One of the southern chieftains cried, 'Now is the time to return to the Green Heart!'

'As to that,' said Kumal, 'the Regent's Meet has decided that we shall welcome any of our kin who venture south of the river boundary . . . as long as they recognize our rule over all lands south of Elvandar. You must pledge fealty to the Clans of the Seven Stars.'

Instantly, furious shouts rang out. 'That is *our* land!'

'We bow to no one!'

'Our ancestors died there!'

Arkan turned to Morgeth. 'It's time to leave.'

Morgeth nodded and the two of them quickly made for the sidestreet and gate beyond. As they entered the dark lane, the sound of approaching warriors made Arkan motion for Morgeth to stop. He pointed to the door of an abandoned building and they ducked inside, crouching down beneath broken windows.

A moment later, they heard the sound of a large band of armed warriors passing by. The two warriors from the northern mountains kept silent until the sound of boot heels on cobbles was replaced by war-cries and the noise of steel ringing against steel. Arkan touched his companion and signalled, and they ran from the abandoned building towards the distant gate.

'Narab seeks to be king, then?' asked Morgeth once they were clear of danger.

'Since killing Delekhan.'

'A hundred years of hunger is a long time.'

Arkan nodded, then pointed to the distant gate.

Morgeth frowned. 'What do we do if it's guarded?'

'Talk first, then fight.'

They reached the gateway and found a company of guards waiting: a dozen warriors stationed in front of fifty or more horses. Even before the warrior in charge could challenge them, Arkan waved and shouted, 'Hurry!'

'What is it?' asked the leader.

'Take your detail up the road, and go north at the first cross street. Cut off those trying to escape behind the palace! Hurry!'

'The horses—'

'We will take care of the horses, now go!'

The twelve warriors hurried off and Morgeth shook his head. 'Clan Bighorn always were a little thick.'

Arkan said, 'Our horses are on the other side of the city.' Looking at the large selection of mounts they had to choose from, he added, 'Seems a fair trade.'

Picking a handsome gelding, Morgeth said, 'You can't possibly think of taking them all?'

Getting into the saddle on a bay mare, Arkan said, 'I was thinking of it, but we have more pressing business. We should hurry back to camp before word of this fighting reaches them.'

'Should we break camp?' asked Morgeth.

'That would draw too much suspicion. Narab has been planning this for a while, I think. He's made arrangements: Bighorn is not one of his usual allies, which means he has added new ones. No, have our men stay close to the tents and tell my sons to be ready to fight, but we should keep our swords sheathed unless attacked first. No one is to look for trouble. Anyone who starts a fight, answers to me.' He grew thoughtful for a moment as he gazed into the distance. Then he said, 'I don't think Narab is ready to crown himself yet. Tonight he was merely showing the unallied clans who held the most power here by breaking a few heads. I doubt more than two or three warriors will die before morning.

'Tell Goran that if I discover his sword has been drawn before I get back I'll personally make him eat it.'

'Your son won't like that,' observed Morgeth with a wry, half-smile.

'He doesn't like a lot of things, which is why Antesh is my

heir,' answered Arkan. 'Make sure Cetswaya stays close to my sons.'

Morgeth nodded. Cetswaya was their shaman and always a calm voice and wise counsel.

'If I don't return by sunrise tomorrow, have Goran and Antesh take the men north, then west. Find the rest of our people and take them back into the icelands, then wait until it's safe to return to our normal range.'

'And how will we know when that time arrives?'

'That will not be my problem, for if you must flee tomorrow, I will likely be dead. If I don't find you in the north by next spring, I will certainly be dead.' Arkan put his heels to his horse and shouted, causing the other mounts to shy. Some pulled up stakes.

As Morgeth watched his chieftain ride off into the deepening gloom of the hills around Sar-Sargoth, he said to no one, 'They're not going to like this much.'

Then weighing Clan Bighorn's ire at finding their mounts scattered against the wrath of Narab discovering that Arkan wasn't among those chieftains in the square, he decided his chieftain had the better bargain. He shouted at the horses nearby without enthusiasm, then turned his mount down towards the plains. There, twenty thousand moredhel warriors awaited the return of their chieftains, and he wondered if it was possible for the Ardanien to somehow get away intact.

Arkan rode for more than an hour, circling the vast array of camps outside the walls of Sar-Sargoth. A thousand fires or more burned as the main host of the moredhel nation had gathered outside the walls of the massive city.

Despite being the closest thing to a moredhel capital, the city was deserted for most of the year. Delekhan, the last moredhel chieftain who had attempted to occupy the city as a symbol of his supremacy, had been killed by Arkan's father, Gorath, during the second abortive attempt to seize the Kingdom city of Sethanon.

Since then, Delekhan's heir, Narab, had occasionally moved his clans into the vicinity, but had avoided the vanity of occupying any of the palaces scattered through the city. Today, it appeared, was to be the day he decided to advance his claim to pre-eminence, if only symbolically.

And so Arkan rode through the night, seeking the one leader among the moredhel with enough power to balk Narab's ambition for a crown one that no moredhel in history had dared to wear. The Ardanian chief hoped what he saw tonight was just another tribal conflict, one quickly resolved, rather than the beginning of a true dynastic struggle. For in the first instant he had seen them, Arkan knew that the true threat came from the elves from the distant stars.

Their presence beside Narab told the chieftain all he needed to know: Narab would rather stand in good stead with them than confront them as enemies, so they were powerful and very dangerous. Arkan knew it was Narab's nature to plot, but he was clearly overmatched if he thought he could court them and make them serve his ends, or even count them as true allies. The taredhel might be content to allow those living north of the Teeth of the World to think themselves free, but eventually they would seek to put their boot on the necks of the moredhel. The strange elves wanted to claim all of Midkemia as their own: of that, he was certain.

Not for the first time in his life, Arkan wondered if his people weren't their own worst enemies. Beyond the constant bickering and occasional bloodshed, there was an underlying drive for supremacy between rival clans . . . but for what? It was as if struggle itself was the point of existence, rather than as a means to achieving some higher goal.

Not usually reflective by nature, Arkan had been forced by the exigency of leading his clan on more than one occasion to weigh what he felt was an obvious truth against a more ambiguous, less easily understood reality. The world was not a simple place and life was never effortless, especially when most of one's day was filled with the struggle merely to survive, but few of his people considered the world beyond their daily needs: hunting, eating, defending their lands and raising their families. Peace had made that so much more probable, yet his people still had an appetite for bloodshed that ran counter to their own best interests.

Why was that? Arkan wondered. Struggle as he might, he had never come close to an answer. Every time he pondered it, he was left to concede he lacked the mental gift of some-one like Cetswaya, his shaman. In the end he shrugged off the question, accepting that it was simply their nature.

Still, this was not the time for abstract musing. He had a real problem to confront and his experience told him there were two things he must now do quickly. The first was to get his people back into the high mountains to the north. Almost two generations before, his father had been the first to lead the tribe into the vast frozen peaks and the glaciers beyond. In doing so he had saved the Ardanien from obliteration at the hands of their ancient enemies, and had given them their new name, the Ice Bears. Part of the once-powerful Clan Bear, most of their kin had been obliterated by the mad prophet, the false Murmandamus, during his war against the humans to the south.

His second task was to seek out the one person who could be termed an ally, albeit loosely. She might make the dif-ference between his people's survival and their obliteration.

Arkan eased his horse down a dark trail. His night vision was better than the horse's, so he had to carefully manoeu-vre his mount to keep them both from stumbling.

At last, in the distance he saw the campfires that marked his destination. As he neared the edge of the encampment a voice called out his name. Slowing his horse, he approached the fire's glow. 'Greetings, Helmon.' He glanced around the sentry camp and said, 'Are the Snow Leopards ready for war?'

'No more than usual,' said the warrior in charge of the post with a wry chuckle. He extended his hand. 'Good to see you, cousin.'

'Let's hope our aunt feels the same,' answered Arkan, taking his arm. Each gripped the other's wrist.

'She's expecting you.'

Arkan didn't try to hide his surprise. 'Really?'

With a slight smile the broad-shouldered fighter nodded once. 'Head straight to the split in the trail, then right to the small clearing above the main camp. You'll have no trouble finding it.'

Helmon was correct: Arkan found the pavilion he sought with ease. A great tent had been erected on a plateau overlooking the largest encampment in the area. A guard signalled for Arkan to leave his horse with him. The Chieftain of the Ardanien dismounted, tossed the reins to him, then paused for a moment, looking down at the massive encampment below.

The Snow Leopards.

The most significant single clan among the moredhel, they had grown steadily in size and power over the last century. Their leader was Arkan's aunt, Liallan, widow of the notorious Delekhan. It had been Delekhan who had tried to invade the human Kingdom of the Isles; an invasion based on the lie that the humans had imprisoned Murmandamus during the moredhels' first invasion of the south years before. Delekhan had been second among those who had served Murmandamus, only surpassed by Murad, the shaman-chief of Clan Raven. Delekhan had also been among the maddest of those servants. Much of the truth about that struggle was hidden, but Arkan knew that his father, Gorath, had killed Delekhan. And it had been Narab who had killed Delekhan's son, Moraeulf, seeking to gain control of the Delekhan's Clan Badger and the rest of his alliances. That would have made him king a century ago.

But Delekhan's widow, Liallan, had kept control of the Snow Leopards and Badgers. Their clans had never merged while her husband lived, but with Delekhan's death she had deftly integrated the Badgers into the Snow Leopards. She was now the only force among the moredhel with enough power to thwart Narab.

A warrior motioned for him to dismount as he reached his aunt's tent, a sprawling thing divided into several segments by cleverly hung curtains.

Inside, across an expanse of fine wool rugs, Liallan reclined on a pile of furs wearing travel garb made from the costliest of materials. No tanned leather breeches and home-spun tunic for the mistress of the Snow Leopards; her riding trousers were cut from the best woollen weave, dyed a midnight blue, and her open-collared shirt was white silk laced with loops and frogs carved from ivory over which she sported a dyed red leather vest with a soft sheepskin lining. Arkan had hunted the massive ice walruses and so had some sense of what those buttons alone had cost her.

He bowed slightly. 'Aunt, are you well?'

Liallan's appearance had changed little throughout Arkan's entire life. Her hair was still dark, though shot through with grey streaks, and there were now fine lines at the corners of her eyes and mouth. Years of riding horseback in the sun had given her whipcord toughness and her movement was lithe as she stood to greet her great nephew.

'Well enough, Arkan.'

'Regal' was the only term to sum up her carriage and manner. If the moredhel were ever to have a queen, she would be the perfect exemplar. Arkan was always struck by her vicious combination of seductive beauty and unconfined ruthlessness. It was reputed that when Arkan's father had killed Delekhan, Liallan had poured wine and toasted Gorath. She was without a doubt the single most dangerous woman in the history of his people.

'It is good to see you, nephew,' she said as she indicated a place for him to sit.

A young female servant brought over a tray and from it Liallan took a small sliver of spiced sausage and placed it ritually between Arkan's teeth. It was a formal acceptance of him as her guest, and under the laws of hospitality meant that no harm would befall him while he was in her tent.

'So, you managed to get here without incident. Good.'

He gave her a slight smile. 'Those who might cause me trouble were otherwise occupied, Liallan.'

She inclined her head. 'Narab?'

'His warriors were breaking heads when I left the council.'

She sighed. 'Narab is prone to impatience. The Southern Clans are not loyal to him, although they reside within his traditional territory. And given my unwillingness to ally with him, he's been unable to press his claim to supremacy. He'd provoke rebellion among his own subjects if he tried to move in a more overt fashion. So he must contrive a way to have leadership forced upon him over false protests.'

For a moment, Arkan wondered if inviting the Star Elves into Sar-Sargoth was as foolish a move as he had thought mere moments ago. 'Aunt, do you think he's found a common enemy to unite the clans of the north under his banner?'

Liallan waved her hand dismissively and reached for a flagon on a low table just behind her. Filling a cup, she handed it to Arkan then poured one for herself. 'Even the real Murmandamus after he had united the clans was clever enough not to claim the title of king. Had he lived another fifty years, perhaps he might have. His rule was the greatest in the history of our people.

'At the time of his death the true Murmandamus waited for the clans to endorse his rule, and had he been victorious in his assault on Elvandar, they almost certainly would have.' She sighed. 'My grandfather told me of that time. We have never known like times since. The false Murmandamus made no attempt to rule: he merely offered portends and signs to persuade us that it was time to march south.

'The chieftains were ready for a fight and by routing the Kingdom at Highcastle, he gathered many to his banner.' She smiled at her great-nephew. 'Drink.'

He took a sip and found the ale bracing and nutty. Smiling

he said, 'Cetswaya will be pleased to know there's still some winter ale around.'

Her smile broadened and he could see genuine amusement in her expression. 'How is he?'

'Well, enough,' he answered. He was a little surprised at her interest in the heath of his clan's shaman, but then he considered that at their age each had few other contemporaries left alive. 'He worries, as always.'

'It's his place to worry, as it is yours to be cautious or bold as the situation merits. And now is the time for you to be worried, cautious *and* bold.' She studied his face when he didn't reply. 'What do you know of the story of your father and Delekhan?'

Arkan shrugged. 'Only what is commonly known.'

'And what is that?' she prodded.

'That my father learned of a plot by Delekhan and a band of magicians known as The Six. They sought to unite the clans, move south and rescue Murmandamus—'

'The false Murmandamus,' she interrupted.

'Yes,' he amended, 'the false Murmandamus.

'For reasons I do not understand, the plan unravelled, but my father is reported to have died killing your husband while the clans retreated north, back across the Teeth of the World.' He looked away as if thinking for a moment, then added, 'My mother never wishes to speak of it.'

'If you take your people north, Arkan,' said Liallan, 'it will be their second trek across the mountains. Gorath married my sister as a means to save what was left of the old Clan Hawk, and my father grudgingly gave permission. But rather than bend his knee to my father, your father took my sister and his remaining retainers into the distant icelands, to nurse his wounds and grow strong again.' She indulged in a chuckle. 'My father was livid. Gorath had outsmarted him, using his relationship to the Snow Leopards to ensure that the Ice Bears endured, while not surrendering any authority to him. It was a lesson I remembered when I was forced to wed Delekhan. I always admired your father and envied my sister in some ways.'

Arkan raised a curious eyebrow.

'Not the life Clothild endured: frozen lakes, barren ice floes, living on fish, walrus, and seal flesh. But she bore him three strong sons and when the Ice Bears came south thirty years later, they were a small but solid clan, one to be treated with respect.'

He listened patiently, but had so far heard nothing he hadn't already known.

'My father – your grandfather – had died by then, and I ruled the Snow Leopards. My marriage to Delekhan strengthened my position. It was his choice to make me an ally or his enemy. He wisely chose the first.

'Yet I would not merge our clans, to his everlasting ire. There was never a hint of love in our marriage, my nephew.' She sipped her ale. 'But here's the truth,' she said flatly.

Now Arkan was attentive.

'Your father was counted a traitor by many, even by my sister, his wife, because he did something that ran counter to our every belief and history: he bargained with our enemies.'

'Bargained?'

'He had been captured by Delekhan's agents while fleeing south—'

'Fleeing?' echoed Arkan.

She waved at him to be silent. 'Your father chose to carry warning to the humans in the south. He had been the first to recognize the danger Delekhan and The Six were to our people, but knew he could not find allies enough among the clans to oppose them. So he sought those to the south who might be able to stop Delekhan. And he found them.'

Arkan wanted to ask a question, but he remained silent.

'He spoke with human nobles, spent time in Caldara, home of the Dwarven King of the Grey Towers, and even paid a visit to the Queen and that abomination she sleeps with in Elvandar.'

Arkan stared at her. None of this was widely known. Finally he asked, 'How do you know?'

'Narab,' she said. 'When Narab killed Delekhan's son and rose to take command of Clan Badger, he needed to make peace with me. For once in his life he made the right choice and told me the truth.

'The trap that was laid during the second attack on the Kingdom city of Sethanon was aided by eledhel and dwarves as well as humans. The secret Narab would happily kill you to hide is that he was the one in league with the eledhel, dwarves and humans. He used them to lure Delekhan's son, Moraeulf, to his death and then solidify his hold on Clan Badger and their vassal clans.'

Arkan sat back and drained his ale. 'If the clan chieftains knew of this, Narab could never claim supremacy over the clans.'

'It is a secret worth killing over. If he could will me dead, I'd be dead. And that's why he chooses the path of patience on his journey to the throne.' His aunt looked solemn.

'Why tell me this?'

'Because Narab is close to claiming supremacy.'

'Unless Narab has more swords than we know of, he may have already set what will become a full-scale bloodbath in motion, with his rough treatment of the clan chieftains down there.'

Liallan shook her head. 'It won't come to that. By now he will have subdued the "council" without killing any but a few bodyguards. We can be certain that if any chieftain perished tonight, he was no friends of Narab's. He'll send them home like whipped dogs in the next hour.'

'The Star Elves?'

'They have magic beyond our understanding, beyond even that of the spellweavers down in Elvandar.' She fixed her nephew with a steady gaze. 'Unless something changes quickly Narab is only a year or so, away from entering Sar-Sargoth's throne room and putting a crown on his own head.'

'Even the false Murmandamus didn't dare that, and he was mad.'

'And he was mad,' Liallan repeated. 'I think holy men are more dangerous than ambitious ones, Arkan. The false Murmandamus was content to just lead the nation on a pointless invasion of the human lands.' She sipped her ale. 'Give me an ambitious murderer over a fanatic every time. The first will only try to kill you for your position, the second will destroy everything and everyone you love.'

This took Arkan by surprise. His people were not especially demonstrative when it came to feelings and his aunt was perhaps the most ruthless a person he had ever encountered. The dark elves understood desire, but love . . . that was rare and usually reserved for children or, occasionally, siblings. To hear the word 'love' come from Liallan's mouth was something he had never expected.

She smiled. 'Yes, there are things I love, nephew. Mostly my clan: I have nurtured them as if every warrior, every woman, each child were my own.'

He nodded. As chieftain of his own small band he understood this feeling. 'It is more than mere duty.'

'Indeed,' she agreed.

'So Narab seeks to make himself king and we are to just sit here and let him?'

She shook her head and smiled. 'No, to both. He will not make himself king . . . yet. Tonight is merely an abject lesson. If you head back down into the valley you'll discover that most of the broken heads belonged to those in open opposition to Narab. His allies and those uncommitted to his cause were, perhaps, jostled a bit, but for the most part remain unharmed. He will claim he was merely restoring order and protecting his guests.'

'Not all the clans were in attendance. I saw Clan Blood Elk heading west a few days back.'

She looked contemptuous. 'Those primitives are of no importance.'

He knew she was right politically. 'But good to have on your side in a fight.'

'No doubt,' she agreed, 'but this time we struggle to avoid a fight.'

'I noticed no Snow Leopards at the gathering,' he said in a neutral tone.

'Why would I go? I knew what was going to happen.'

'Spies?'

'I have many . . . friends. And Narab doesn't have as many as he thinks he does.'

'Well and good, but that still leaves me up here with you.'

She stared at him, but said nothing.

Finally he said, 'You knew I'd come tonight.'

She smiled. 'As I said, this time we struggle to avoid a fight. Had I been in attendance tonight, Narab might have let his ambition overrule his better judgment, but if he knows I'm up here with my Snow Leopards . . .' She left the thought unfinished. 'He knows that even now he cannot attack me.' Her smile broadened. 'Again, he doesn't have as many friends as he thinks he does.'

'Which brings us to me.'

'If I were to count all the relatives I have through marriage and by blood who are smart enough to recognize a futile fight, and then invite them here . . . well, let's just say you and I wouldn't have a lot of company.' She paused. 'What orders did you give your men?'

He shrugged. 'If I'm not back by sunrise take the clan into the high mountains. If followed, journey further north to the ice floes.'

'Just like your father,' Liallan said with a sad smile. 'Do you welcome another twenty years hunting walrus and seal?'

'Not particularly, but I welcome the obliteration of my clan even less.'

'Then let us speak about what will preserve our clans.'

'Our clans?'

'The Ardanien and Hamandien are kin, even if some of my chieftains would wish it otherwise.'

Arkan understood what she meant. The Ardanien and Hamandien were allies through blood and necessity. Had it not been for Liallan's power, the Ice Bears would have been obliterated after Gorath's defection to the Kingdom. No matter that he had saved the moredhel from being dominated by a madman, and aborted the attack on the Kingdom city of Sethanon, thereby saving hundreds of lives; he was still seen as a traitor. He waited.

At last Liallan said, 'Even as Narab unfolds his schemes, and thinks he's gained the upper hand, there are other forces that may consume us.'

'Those Star Elves?'

'Among others. The humans war among themselves as well.'

'So Narab stated; what has this to do with us?'

'Ah, that is what must be discovered.' She studied his face for a moment, then asked, 'What does Cetswaya tell you of his dreams and visions?'

'He speaks little. He claims he puts little faith in dream-lore.'

'Still, he has said something.'

Arkan remained silent.

'Then I shall tell you of my shaman. Arjuda dreams of dragons.'

Arkan's face became an unreadable mask.

'Dragons on the wing, with riders on their back; a host mighty enough to blot out the sun.'

Almost whispering, Arkan said, 'So do I.'

She nodded. 'Then there is something you must do, for yourself, for me, for our clans, and ultimately our people – perhaps even our entire world.'

Surprised by the fervour of his aunt's words, he said, 'Tell me.'

'Who among your sons is fit to lead in your absence?'

He thought about this. 'All three, although Antesh is my heir. I have taught them to be ready, but he is the most level-headed.'

'Good.' She sighed. 'I've lost sons, Arkan. It is most bitter. Your father lost two, making you his heir.' She took a long moment to study Arkan. Her nephew had been as young as his father had been when the responsibility for his people fell to him. After a while she said, 'Very well. There is something you must do. It will most likely get you killed, and even if you survive you may never be able to return to your clan. Are you willing to risk everything to save your kin?'

Without hesitation he said, 'That is a chieftain's burden, and his honour.'

'I'd expect no less an answer. Then come, Arkan of the Ardanien, this you must know: a conflict that will engulf our world is brewing, and without your help we may all perish. You must travel south, where the humans make war, and possibly beyond.' She fell silent.

'What must I do?' he asked.

Liallan looked him in the eyes, then motioned for him to stand. Once again she studied his face before speaking. 'I do not know.'

'So, I am to leave my home, place the care of my people in my sons' hands, and . . . do something; but you do not know what it is?'

'You must go south. You must disguise yourself as an eledhel, since few humans would notice the difference, and you must seek someone out.'

'Who?'

'Again I do not know. But I am certain you will find that person and then your next path will be made clearer.'

Arkan was silent for a time, then said, 'I respect you as much as anyone does – and you are my kinswoman – but you ask much and give so little.'

'Should you survive, nephew, should all of us survive, I will give Kalina to your eldest son.'

Arkan was rendered almost speechless. 'Why?'

'Your sons are closer to the soil of this world than my chieftains. They are true sons of the moredhel, warriors without dishonour, strong without being overly ambitious.

Should I name any of my chieftains my heir, the bickering
and rivalries would tear the Hamandien apart within hours
of my death. But if I name your son my heir, not only will he
bring a small but powerful clan into the fold, but it will also
prevent such a falling out. Clan Ardanien would serve as effective a personal bodyguard as any chieftain could desire.
My chieftains would bend their knees and accept his rule to
keep the clans intact. The Snow Leopards grow stronger and
survive for another generation.'

'You'd do that?'

'If you go south and find this man you're fated to meet.'

'How do you know I'm fated to meet this . . . human?'

'In my dream I see dragons flying; and upon a mountain
peak two figures, one a man in a black robe, and the other is
you. You protect him while he wields great magic. You are
destined to save our people, Arkan.'

He had no words, so he merely sat in silence. Then he
rose, nodded and left the light, warm pavilion, and returned
to a dark, cold, and windy world.

2

RAID

Bugles sounded the warning.

Martin conDoin, son of the late Duke of Crydee, dropped the spoon carrying the first bite of food he'd had in hours and was nearly out of the door of the inn he was using as a forward headquarters before his chair hit the wooden floor. He hurried to the south-western gate. 'Report!' he shouted as he ran from the harbour to the city's entrance.

Sergeant Magwin looked down from his position on top of the tower, a small figure at that distance, but his voice carried. 'Scout's returning, sir!'

'Open the gates!' shouted Martin.

An exhausted rider wearing the tunic of the garrison of Crydee came cantering through the partially opened gate and pulled up before Martin as it was slammed shut behind him. He was covered in road dirt and sweat, and his horse was near collapse. He saluted and said, 'Found the infantry, sir.' He held out a folded parchment.

Martin read the report. 'Is he seriously refusing to return?'

The scout dismounted. 'Yes, sir. The captain of the column is from LaMut. He said, "I've got my orders, and they are to go to Sarth and meet the Duke; no lad from Crydee is telling me otherwise."' He lowered his eyes. 'That's when he wrote that and gave it to me, sir.'

Martin fumed silently, then said, 'That's . . . perfect.'

Brendan, Martin's younger brother and his adjutant, had hurried from the heart of the city, dodging through the press of people who were waiting nearby to hear what news the scout might bring. He was almost out of breath when he stopped and gasped out, 'A small band from LaMut has arrived.'

'Some good news,' said Martin, looking around. The two young men looked like twins, both with long brown hair to their shoulders and slender, agile bodies. Being only one year apart, the differences between them were growing smaller with each passing month. 'How many?'

'Forty,' said Brendan. 'Mostly men over fifty, but they seem fit: farmers and millers, loggers and the like. Twenty or so are bowmen.'

'Good, we can always use more archers on the wall. See to their quarters.'

'They've got this old—' He laughed as he spread his arms widely, as if describing a fish he had caught. 'A ballista that big . . . Maybe a bit bigger, but I've never seen its like. Said it's been on the top of the gate in LaMut since . . . well, since anyone can remember. Some of the retired soldiers who came south thought it would be useful.'

Martin tried to be amused, but failed. 'Have them bring it

here.' He glanced around and saw a small patch of earth between two buildings, perhaps once a garden in better days, and pointed at it. 'Move the wagon there. We might need to put the ballista up on the wall.' He scanned the entirety of the battlement above, then said, 'But I have no idea where.'

Ylith held a unique position in the Kingdom. It was nestled in the north-eastern corner of a near-perfect but tiny harbour. Given the city's position, the massive harbour gates were its main entrance. Away to the south-east, there was a small beach running barely a quarter of a mile between the southern edge of the city docks and the rocks along the quickly rising headlands. From there the coastline reared upward sharply to the promontory called Questor's View, two days' ride on a fast horse. A small village occupied the flat top of the promontory, and a small garrison was stationed there. The Duke had stripped it of soldiers as he marched south, leaving the village protected only by its surrounding terrain. From there, no safe landing existed until one was deep within the principality, near the town of Sarth, which currently was expecting the muster from Yabon.

Shoals and rocks hidden just below the surface, to the south-west of the harbour, provided a natural defence against any nearby landings. The shallows created a tide race, and every experienced captain gave that part of the coast a wide berth lest they be swept onto the rocks and wrecked. It was over half a day's ride by swift horse before a safe landing south of the city could be found.

Between the city walls and foulborough beyond was an open plaza, giving archers on the wall a field of fire. The booths and stalls that on market days and holidays traditionally stood against the wall had been removed even before Martin and the Crydee muster had arrived.

Three roads intersected at the centre of the plaza southwest of the harbour gates: the highway to the Free Cities and Natal ran south along the bay; the road to Crydee moved away to the north-west; and a small road led east, which rap idly turned into a farmer's track. Here lay the heart of Ylith's commerce, the busy port that was the gateway to Yabon.

The city of Ylith had been seized by invaders once before, when the general leading the invading army of the Emerald Queen had set himself up as King of the Bitter Sea. Only a betrayal by one of his southern commanders in exchange for consideration from the Kingdom had allowed the tyrant to be dislodged. Martin had read the history of the Emerald Queen's invasion and knew the vital part played by this city in protecting the principality, Yabon, and the passes to the Far Coast. The Kingdom might lose Crydee and recover, or even lose control of the eastern shore of the Bitter Sea between Ylith and Sarth, but if Ylith fell, all would be lost.

'What news from the south?' asked Brendan.

'It's bad,' said Martin, handing over the message.

Brendan quickly read it. 'Is he serious?'

'Apparently.' Martin threw the parchment into the dust and looked around. 'If I were in his place I would not wish to explain to my duke where his infantry was, if he was expecting them to arrive in Sarth next week.'

'Would you rather explain how you lost all of Yabon?' countered Brendan.

'Just following orders,' said Martin dryly. 'Well, the pirate we hired should have delivered my message to the Duke by the time the infantry reaches Sarth.' He calculated. 'If the Prince hasn't commanded him to continue on to Krondor or stay in Sarth, he could be back here with his cavalry and light foot regiment in ten days.'

'Lots of ifs,' said Brendan.

'I know,' answered Martin. 'Where are we now?'

His brother knew exactly what Martin was asking. 'Our men at arms number three hundred from Crydee, plus the fifty irregulars the Duke of Yabon left here with Bolton.' Captain Bolton was the nephew of the commander of the Earl of LaMut's guard. The brothers were convinced that he had been left behind in the hope that no attack would ever reach this far north. Once he had been taken down a peg or two by Martin, the earnest young man had turned out to be completely out of his depth, which was the reason for all his bluster when they first met.

Brendan continued, 'About two hundred men and boys have trickled in since you sent word north, but they're the ones who were too unfit to answer the Duke of Yabon's first muster: mostly old men, a few former soldiers, and eager boys, for the main part under fifteen years old. And too few damn weapons.'

'Well, set them to making arrows. They'll be slow at it at first, but if there are enough hands put to the task we should do well. I'd rather the archers had too many than too few.'

'Wood is no problem, and the smiths here can do the broad-heads, but we're going to have a problem with the flights: not enough feathers.'

'Use chicken feathers if you have to. Set snares for pigeons and seagulls,' snapped Martin. 'I don't care.' Then he closed his eyes and said, 'Sorry. I'm . . .'

Brendan put his hand on his brother's arm. 'I know.' He indicated with a nod of his head that the scout was still standing nearby.

Martin dismissed the man with thanks and ordered the gates of the city sealed. He looked towards the heart of the town and said, 'How are the provisions?'

'Enough,' said Brendan as they started walking back to the mayor's house, which was being used for local headquarters. 'With most of the fighting men down south, the local farms can provide enough for a siege, as long as we keep the north gate and road clear.' The old baron's castle on the hill to the north-west of the city was far enough away. Martin had done little more than give it a quick inspection, but it would serve as a last resort for defence if the entire town fell to the Keshians. It was his purpose to see that didn't happen, for even if they held the keep above the town, Kesh would have achieved their purpose: bisecting the Western Realm. If that happened, no aid could flow in either direction. Not only would this region be lost, the entire Western Realm would be left vulnerable.

Martin glanced around as if seeking inspiration. His home of Crydee was already crawling with colonists from the far south of the Empire, the region known as the Keshian Confederacy, and they were aggressively driving out whoever occupied the farms and mills, mines and lumbering villages. Herds had been seized, as had anything else of value, and a steady stream of displaced Kingdom citizens entered Ylith on a daily basis.

'You look lost in thought,' observed Brendan.

Martin smiled slightly at his younger brother. 'Just trying to imagine what I'd be doing next if I were the Keshian commander in Crydee.'

Brendan shrugged. 'It would depend on what his orders are, right?'

Martin nodded. 'We've not seen any Keshian ships this far north. Queg must be keeping them busy to the south.'

Brendan knew his brother meant that Queg was keeping Kesh from sailing west of their island kingdom. While no formal treaty existed between Queg and the Kingdom, they were effectively allied against Kesh's northward expansion in the Bitter Sea. The part of the Kingdom fleet that wasn't stationed down in Port Vykor and Krondor would be hugging the coast of the Principality, freeing Queg from the need to protect their eastern coast. 'Even if they bottled up all of the Prince's fleet at Krondor, some Kingdom ships had to sortie out of Port Vykor and would have been out on the water when this war started. Most likely, there's a line of ships between Vykor and Sarth, enough to hold the Keshians in check.'

Martin nodded. 'Which means Kesh is not reinforcing her armies by sea.'

'So, the only large force they have in the region is the one that drove us out of Crydee,' finished Brendan.

Martin squatted. 'Let's assume for the moment that whatever ships Kesh have are down south supporting the land assaults against Land's End, Vykor and Krondor. So how does that leave us here in the north?' He pulled out his belt knife and drew a half-circle in the earth. 'We're here,' he said, sticking his blade point into the ground.' He motioned towards what would be the west on his makeshift map. 'If they bring those forces here, we can face them along one or two walls at most, without support and not worry about the rest of our defences.' He motioned to the south of the harbour gate. 'Out there is a natural choke point between the docks and gate.' He stood up. 'Unless they mean to swim across from the western shore then attack up the road . . .' His expression changed and he motioned for Brendan to follow him as he hurried over to the steps leading up to the ramparts.

At the top of the wall he could see the handful of men stationed along the battlement, all trying to appear keen and ready, but really just hiding their boredom. Martin knew the tedium of the watch only too well as he and his brothers had served more than their share; their father had ensured that his three sons understood every aspect of the soldier's trade. There was an old soldier's saying: *War is protracted periods of boredom punctuated by short bursts of violence and terror*; and so far, Martin had found that to be entirely true.

Scanning the docks below the wall and the foulborough between the city walls and the docks, he said, 'How would you attack this city?'

Brendan moved to one of the crenels and leaned out slightly, his hands resting on the merlons to either side. He said, 'I'd not wish to.'

'I know, but if you did, how?'

His younger brother was silent as he continued to survey the landscape beyond the wall. His attention lingered for a moment on the keep high above the city and then dropped to the road from the west, across the harbourage and then the road to the south. Finally he said, 'I'd come at the city from the east. It's the weakest part of the defence.'

'But to do that means you'd have to get your forces across the water to the western coast of the principality. No ships, remember.'

Brendan said, 'The Free Cities have ships.'

'But to turn south and move on Port Natal leaves your rear exposed to . . . well, us.

'And even if you get past the Rangers sniping at you from behind every tree, win past the city defenders, and get your hands on enough ships, you've still got to sail back north and get past Queg's patrols.' He stopped, thoughtful. 'But your instincts are right, I'm certain. We just have to figure out how they intend to do it.'

'Which brings us back to a raiding fleet from the south,' said Brendan.

Martin shook his head. 'Let's leave the problem of how they do it to the Keshians. We must assume they can get to the western shore of the Bitter Sea. If I were their commander, I'd make straight for Questor's View and come ashore on that beach to the north of the town.'

'Which would put you only a day's forced march south of that old fortification there,' said Brendan, pointing across the water.

'That would be a fine staging area. Leaving out the part about swimming across, invisible ships, or other magic as beside the point of having soldiers there, let's assume the Keshian commander is as intelligent as you are.' Martin turned. 'Sergeant Ruther!' he shouted.

'Sir!' came the answering reply from below.

The old sergeant might not always be in sight but he was always near at hand. Martin motioned for him to come up and despite his age the old soldier took the steps two at a time as he hurried to his young commander's side. When he reached Martin, he said, 'Sir?'

'What can you tell us about that old fortification?'

'Been abandoned for nearly a hundred years, I've been told. Built as a buttress against some nasty raids over the mountains and down along the coast. Seems things got calmer and one of the old barons decided that paying for a second garrison wasn't necessary.'

'How long would it take to ride down and have a look around?'

'An hour to get there. It's farther away than it looks from here. That's no hill overlooking the beach and the road bends through the woodlands. Another hour to inventory, and then an hour to return. Be back by supper, sir.'

'Get to it,' said Martin.

As Ruther headed down the steps bellowing orders to form a detail to ride with him, a sentry at the far western corner shouted, 'Patrol coming in!'

Martin turned to see four riders coming in at a canter; an urgent enough pace to indicate that there was news, but not fast enough to signal immediate danger. 'Open the gates!' he commanded.

Four riders entered, as grimy as their horses. The sudden early summer rains had quickly dried out and mud and dust covered both mount and horseman. The leader of the patrol, a newly promoted corporal named Jackson, dismounted and said, 'Saw 'em, sir.'

'Where?'

'Their vanguard is about half a day's ride the other side of the pass.' The rangy, sandy-haired young man stopped and calculated. 'Saw them at dawn yesterday, Commander, so they must be a day and a half, perhaps two days at the most, behind us.'

'How many have they brought?' asked Brendan.

'The whole bunch, sir,' said Jackson. He thanked the guard who handed him a water skin. He took a long pull from it, then said, 'Seems like they don't feel the need to leave much behind. It's as if they don't care about any attempt to retake Crydee from the south.'

'Odd,' said Martin. 'So what numbers do you think we'll see, and when?'

'Five hundred horses, if I judged rightly; a bunch of those

desert fellows with the leopardskin trim on their helmets, maybe three hundred; and what looks like heavy cavalry: lancers with baggage wagons. And infantry. At least a thousand Dog Soldiers, and twice that number of irregulars.'

'Siege engines?' asked Brendan.

'I expect they took 'em apart after we left Crydee, and will be dragging them along, sir. Didn't stay around to see if they were in the rear with those leopard fellows getting close. A couple of them gave chase, but they didn't last long once we turned and ran.'

Martin studied the distant road through the gate. He had ordered entrapments and barriers erected, knowing full well they were more of nuisance to the enemy than a real deterrent. Still, anything that kept the Keshians from swarming over that hill and coming straight at the gate was to be earnestly wished for.

His eyes returned once again to the old keep on top of the hill overlooking the road. He had conducted a quick inspection of their defences a week earlier when he had first arrived. Now he wondered if he had been overly hasty.

'Find Bolton,' Martin said softly to his brother.

Captain Bolton appeared at a run behind Brendan less than five minutes later. He was a slender young man, the same age as Martin. He had been left in charge of the city's defences by the Duke of Yabon, and until now, his only practical experience had been overseeing a squad of the Earl of LaMut's personal guards, of which his uncle was commander. To the brothers' surprise, he had turned out to be a willing worker and a quick study; his arrogant manner as defender of the city had been a mask to hide his uncertainty. But once Martin had defined his duties, Bolton had thrown himself into whatever task had been given him. Even Brendan had come to like him despite the fact they were both smitten by the mayor's daughter, Lily.

Martin said to him, 'What I need to know is if there is any sort of sally port or secret exit from that keep.'

Bolton said, 'I don't know, but I'll find out.'

Martin nodded and Bolton ran off towards the stable nearest the gate.

Brendan smiled at his retreating back. 'He's still eager.'

'He's just like a lot of men,' said Martin. 'A total waste until you give them something meaningful to do, then you see the man's true measure.'

'What are you thinking?' Brendan asked with a twitch of his head in the general direction of the keep.

'If that Keshian commander can get control of that ridge up there,' he pointed to the crest of the road and the clearings on either side, 'he can erect those trebuchets and just pound this wall until it's rubble. Then a single charge down the hill and he has this city.'

'So you want to hit him in the arse?' said Brendan, but his expression was serious.

'If I can get a big enough company behind him, yes; but he'll have pickets stationed a quarter of a mile out on either flank. If there's a tunnel or an old escape route, or a sally port with a road downhill . . .' He shrugged. 'It's worth a look.'

'Yes it is.'

Martin motioned for the gates to be closed and said, 'If I was that Keshian commander, I'd be sending scouts south of the pass road to seek out game trails and old farmers wagon paths, so I can infiltrate as many men as possible south of here without being seen.'

'Should we send a patrol towards Natal?'

'The Free City Rangers should be able to annoy the Keshians and prevent them moving too far south, so we can guess where they'll pop up if they do infiltrate.'

Brendan said, 'I'm glad it's you having to puzzle all this out, brother. I'm a bit out of my depth.'

'You'd do fine, I suspect,' Martin said with a tired smile. Then he stared at the closed gates as if he could somehow will his sight through them, over the mountains and to the Keshian camp. 'It's just the waiting that tires me out.'

'And a lack of sleep.' With the evil grin of a younger brother Brendan said, 'Besides being up all hours getting our defences in place, Bethany—'

Before he could finish, Martin raised a single finger before his brother's nose. 'Don't!'

Stepping back, Brendan put his hands up, palms out, in a supplicating gesture. 'I was only going to say that you spend a great deal of time talking to her after supper.'

Martin fixed his younger brother with an expression that meant he found his brother's claim to be dubious, but he let it go. 'She's a wonder,' he said in obvious admiration. 'She's done amazing things with the women and children in this town: about two-thirds of the women and almost all the children are leaving tomorrow for the north, to seek shelter in Zün. The women who are staying behind will cook, wash clothing, and care for the wounded.'

'They will no doubt make good account of themselves if the Keshians do get over that wall.'

Martin nodded. 'Kesh is never gentle with those they conquer. Rape and slavery is the best to hope for beyond a quick death.'

Both young men had read the histories and accounts of wars in the past. No nation could claim virtue in the throes of struggle; the Kingdom had been as brutal as anyone during the conquest of their neighbours as they extended their borders in ages past, but those had been wars of expansion and those who had been conquered were now considered as citizens as much as the first raiders who left the island Kingdom of Rillanon.

Kesh's wars were of subjugation. Only 'Truebloods' were granted full citizenship. Those who served the Empire and had lived around the massive lake known as the Overn Deep for generations were counted as lesser citizens, though some had risen to high office. Everyone else was regarded as a subject. Even colonists who had moved to distant lands, like the Far Coast and Natal – the ancient province of Bosania – and the Island of Queg, became lesser subjects. And as a result, Kesh's Legionaries and Dog Soldiers had been putting down rebellions for centuries.

The results were uniform. When Kesh conquered, she occupied: indigenous people were driven out, killed or enslaved.

It was that knowledge that kept Martin from feeling like a total failure. He had abandoned his family's castle, but had he remained he would be dead, or perhaps an object of ransom. There would be no truce with Kesh. Their only hope was to withstand whatever assault came this way, and hold out against the return of the Duke of Yabon's forces. When they arrived, he would lead his men of Crydee home and drive the Keshian trespassers from every mill, farm, mine, and fishing community within the Duchy.

Brendan saw his brother's expression and said, 'What?'

Letting out a long breath, Martin said, 'Nothing. Everything. Just a lot of thoughts.' He glanced around as if he might find one more task that needed his attention.

'Go back to the mayor's house and get some rest. Talk with Bethany now and get some sleep later.'

Martin let his shoulders slump as he relaxed. 'I just—'

'I know,' said his brother putting his hand on Martin's arm. 'If anything needs to be done, I'll do it.' Then he grinned, and said, 'Or I'll send for you. Is that all right?'

'Yes,' said Martin. 'I'll never admit it to anyone else, but I couldn't have pulled this together without your help, little brother.'

Brendan said, 'I would be lost without your leadership, Martin. But I would give all of my inheritance to have Hal here.'

Martin nodded in earnest agreement. 'I, too.' Their brother had been groomed to rule, and was a far better leader than his two younger siblings. 'He has a definite knack for this sort of thing.'

'You're not doing badly, honestly.'

'I wonder what he's up to right now?'

'Probably trying to find a way to get home,' answered Brendan. 'Little chance there, I should think. Kesh probably has Roldem bottled up, or Roldem's now allied with Kesh and Hal's been arrested or is in hiding.'

'You think like Father,' said Martin. 'I never gave a thought to what might be occurring in Roldem.' A moment of sadness passed between them: they'd had little time to truly mourn the loss of their father.

Finally Martin broke the mood and said, 'Come, we have work to do.'

'Raiders!'

The warning echoed across the silent square behind the harbour gates and was repeated by every sentry along the wall. Martin was dressed and out of the door of his room in the mayor's house before the alarm bell stopped. He was joined by Brendan as the two brothers nearly collided at the top of the stairs.

Two young women were waiting for them as they reached the main floor of the house: Bethany, daughter of the Earl of Carse, and Lily, the mayor's daughter. Bethany was sharing Lily's room at the back of the house and both women were wearing heavy robes over their nightgowns.

Before either could voice a question, Martin said, 'Get dressed and be ready to ride north if I give the order.' He kissed Bethany absently on the cheek and was quickly away while she stood there for a moment.

She looked at Lily and shook her head. 'Be ready to run? I don't think so.' She turned towards her host's room and said, 'Are you coming?'

'Where?' asked Lily. She and Bethany had taken an instant liking to one another, but Lily was often amazed at what she thought of as Bethany's rough ways. She rode a horse like a man, wearing trousers! She was practised with weapons, and thought nothing of fine clothing, jewellery, fragrances, or cosmetics. Still, the younger girl liked Bethany a great deal and because of her rank the mayor had been reluctant to stem her more outlandish behaviour; a condition Lily exploited at every chance. Bethany's expression was one that communicated the answer to where was obvious.

Lily's eyes widened as she realized Bethany was going to ignore Martin's orders, then she nodded and grinned as she shouted, 'Wait for me!'

The raid was well under way by the time the young women had changed into something more appropriate. A few inhabitants still ran northward, many carrying their most precious belongings in sacks over their shoulder or in packs on their backs, but at the foot of the city's wall, no other civilians were in sight. Columns of soldiers were lined up on either side of the street, awaiting orders to mount one flight of steps or another, flank either side of the gate, or be ready to repel invaders should the gates fall.

Flickering light in the sky above the gate was a sign of fire, and Bethany ran up the right-hand steps to the top of the wall.

Martin and Brendan stood talking as Captain Bolton pushed past them, 'Excuse me—' He stopped. 'Lily?' He glanced at Bethany and added, 'My lady?'

Bethany wore her travel clothes: riding breeches, a linen shirt under a leather tunic, and riding boots. She was also sporting her composite bow and a hip-quiver full of broadhead arrows.

'Ah, I don't think you should be here—' he started, but Bethany planted her left hand on his chest and gave him the slightest shove.

'Don't let us keep you from carrying out your orders, Captain.' She swept past the wide-eyed young man.

Lily shot him a quick smile as she also darted past him to follow Bethany.

Martin turned just as Bethany arrived, and if he was surprised to see her there, he didn't show it. A quick play of expressions across his face betrayed his internal debate about what to do with her, but he finally decided that telling her to do anything was futile. Without her asking, he said, 'Raiders.'

She glanced over the wall, and despite the night's gloom could see the dark figures carrying torches down near the docks. 'What are they doing?' she asked.

'I don't know, but I'm not about to risk men tonight to find out. The docks and foulborough are deserted and anything worth saving was fetched inside the city walls days ago. Besides a couple of rotten fishing boats at anchor, there's nothing there of value.'

'They're setting fires,' said Lily.

Brendan leaned back a little, looking behind his brother and Bethany so he could clearly see the girl. 'Lily,' he said with a nod. 'You shouldn't be here.'

Her eyes got wide and, feigning surprise, she said, 'Oh?'

Brendan smiled. 'My brother won't say it to her,' he nodded at Bethany, 'so I felt the need to say it on his behalf, even though I know telling Bethany to do anything is a lost cause.'

Martin ignored their banter. He looked up to the sentry on the closest tower and shouted up to him, 'What do you see?'

'Just what you do, sir. They're setting fires all over the docks.'

Brendan said, 'What are they up to?'

Martin glanced at the bow in Bethany's hand and said, 'If you're staying, you must do two things: follow my orders exactly and don't get killed.'

She kissed him. 'Tell me what to do.'

He glanced around and said, 'Stand over there,' he pointed to a crenel, 'and watch for anyone coming along the wall opposite you. You'll have to lean out a bit, so don't overbalance. I don't want to open the gate and come out to fetch you back in.'

She smiled and said, 'But you would.'

He ignored the flirting, knowing she was hiding her own

fear at possibly being under enemy fire again. 'Shoot anything on that side of the wall that gets close to the gate.'

Martin turned to the general assembly of soldiers gathering in the square and shouted, 'Sergeant Magwin!'

'Sir!' came the instant response from below.

'Archers to the walls, and form a flying company opposite the gate!'

'Yes, sir!' shouted the old sergeant from Crydee.

'Sergeant Ruther,' said Martin in a lower tone, knowing that his most senior officer from Crydee would have by now found his commander on the wall.

'Sir?'

He turned to look at the grey-haired fighter. 'Archers are to shoot anything that crosses the outer killing ground, especially anyone carrying torches or oil near the gate.'

'Sir,' he said and set about at once relaying Martin's orders.

Ancient cities often outgrew their walls, especially during times of peace; a foulborough grew beyond the outer precincts of many of them, such as Krondor, LaMut, and all the great eastern cities. In some cities like Salador, the inner walled city was the smallest quarter. But the barons of Ylith had been cautious men, who knew how easily the invaders under the Emerald Queen had swept in through the foulborough and over the walls. Since then, no building had been permitted against the city wall behind the fishing town and docks area, creating an effective bailey where archers could punish any attackers.

While a long peace had existed between the invasion of the Emerald Queen's army and this Keshian attack, vigilance had been bred into the rulers of Ylith. Moreover, the natural slope of the landscape and the curve of the harbour caused the main gate to the city to be set at an angle unfavourable to attack. There was no easy way to bring a ram to bear on the gate and move it into position for a run. Unlike Crydee, the city gates of Ylith were massive, their huge hinges had knuckles the size of a small tree bole, with three foot leaves on each side held in place by massive iron bolts driven through the foot-thick hardwood. They were as stout as steel after years of drying in the sun, being oiled and tended with preservatives. The Keshians would have to stand on the crest of the road and hurl stones at the gate with their trebuchets, to see how long that portion of the wall could take a pounding. Martin knew they could take weeks of damage before giving out, long enough for relief to arrive from the south.

As he thought of that, he understood. 'I know what they are doing.' Brendan and the girls looked at him as Martin explained, 'This isn't an attack on our gates. They are trying to prevent any Kingdom fleet from landing.'

Brendan appeared confused, then comprehension dawned. 'The piers!'

'Burned to the waterline,' Martin said, nodding.

'The underwater pilings would stove in any hull that got near,' finished his brother.

They thought of the three long piers that extended out from the quayside and imagined the tree-sized wooden supports jutting just below the surface.

Bethany said, 'The tide would carry any ship right into them.'

'They would have to anchor off shore and row men in to land!' added Brendan.

It was Lily who said, 'I know that slows things down, but they'd still come ashore to relieve us, right?'

Martin scanned the tableau before him; the flames had begun to take the buildings nearest the docks and the scene below was quickly growing clearer. 'Not if they have to withstand . . . The old fortress!'

'What about it?' asked Brendan. Sergeant Ruther had inspected it the day before on Martin's order, and had reported back that it was run down, but the walls were still stout; with a little work it could easily be made defensible.

'Sergeant Ruther!' Martin bellowed.

'Sir!' As ever, the answer came at once from below.

'Open the sally port and get a detachment of cavalry down to the old fortress! Round up a company of foot soldiers and send them on afterwards. At first light I want carpenters and stonemasons down there starting repairs!'

'Yes, sir.'

'I thought we weren't going to utilize that fort,' said his brother.

'We wouldn't if we were only facing an assault from one quarter.' He paused and let out a slow tired breath. 'We have to deny them any possible foothold on the eastern shore.'

'Do you think they mean to seize it?' asked Brendan.

'It's what I would do if I was going to attempt a landing,' said Martin. 'If they get a foothold on that side of the harbour mouth, install some catapults or trebuchets into that fortress, they can deny any reinforcements a safe landing, and when they're ready to attack they can hit us from two sides at once. We would not only have to defend this gate, but the eastern gate as well, and that would spread our archers too thinly. We don't have enough men to deal with an assault from two sides.

'And if we were forced to sally against an eastern assault, we'd have to ride out of the north gate and circle through miles of pasture lands and hedgerows, with no clear line of attack until we reach that beach—'

'Where their archers would cut us to pieces,' finished Brendan.

Martin considered the possibilities for a moment, then shouted, 'Sergeant Ruther!'

The old soldier reappeared at Martin's side. 'Sir?'

'Where do we now stand with archers? How many do we have?'

'Those who can fire a bow, sir, or those who can actually hit a target?'

Martin hesitated, then said, 'Fire a bow.'

'A hundred and fifty, give or take a few,' answered Ruther.

'Take thirty of our best and that flying company, and occupy the old fortress to oversee the refitting personally.

Build a fire under the carpenters and masons if you must, but I want it defensible by yesterday.' Suddenly a thought came to him. 'And take that miniature ballista with you.' He pointed to where the portal ballista rested in the wagon that had carried it down from LaMut. 'Aim it where you think you can do the most damage to the Keshians if they try to seize that emplacement. I have a feeling,' he added in lower tones, 'that they're going to try to ferry men across and hit us from the east as they assault this gate.'

'Sir!' said Ruther. 'May I suggest that we might do well with some oil, sir?'

'Take what you need, but if you use it, try not to burn the place . . .' Martin stopped. For a long moment he was silent. Then he said, 'No. Take as much oil as you need, and if it comes to it, burn that fortification to the ground. If we lose it, we'll deny the Keshians its use.'

Martin glanced at his brother and the sergeant, and then turned his gaze back to the harbour and sea beyond. 'Kesh won't try to land troops in small boats if they can't gain a foothold. If we place archers in the trees on the hills above the harbour, there's no safe place for them to muster for an assault. More than half would be dead before they got to the road.' He nodded.

'Well done, sir,' said Ruther with obvious approval. He turned and ran off.

As flames leapt skyward and the entire foulborough became consumed, Brendan said, 'What do we do next?'

Martin glanced west, then towards the fire, and then eastward, as if trying to see something in the distance that might be approaching from any side of the city. Finally he rested against the stones, already feeling the heat from the fire behind and looked northward. 'We wait, and hope the night holds no more surprises for us.'

3

ATTACK

Miranda pointed towards the smoke in the sky.

'Fires,' said the being once known as Child.

Belog, who now called himself Nakor, nodded. 'Big ones.'

They were riding in a wagon towards the north gate of Ylith, having discovered in LaMut the single most frustrating fact of their new identities: they might have had Miranda and Nakor's memories imposed over their own, but they didn't possess their abilities.

Two days of trying to reassert their human abilities, one aggravating attempt after another, had left them both exasperated and at a loss. It was as if they knew the language, yet when they spoke only gibberish emerged. They still possessed their demonic abilities, despite their human appearances, but no hint of the prodigious power that Miranda once possessed now remained. Even in her human guise she was physically more powerful than the strongest human warrior many times over, as well as being faster than the swiftest elf. Her magic was what it had been in the demon realm: an ability to inflict destruction at an astonishing rate. But even the most meagre of Miranda's human magic remained beyond her reach.

Her first thought had been to find Miranda's husband, Pug, for while she knew she was not really his late wife, she still possessed all of Miranda's memories and emotions. For the very first time, a demon appreciated the concept of love as mortals understood it, and felt the pain of separation from her husband and sons; or rather Miranda's husband and sons.

The demon in Miranda's form knew the memories had been grafted on to its own, and how: another ploy by the Trickster God, Kalkin. Yet they were so vivid, both the good and the bad, that it was impossible to remain objective about the life imprinted over her own. Child possessed mere days of memory, while Miranda's stretched well beyond a century. Her false human identity overwhelmed her true demon consciousness. The same held true for Nakor, as the demon known as Belog now thought of himself, although his demon memories were years longer than Child's. But while Nakor had possessed abilities, Belog had only possessed knowledge, so his inability to access Nakor's 'tricks' was not a particular source of frustration to the demon-turned-human.

He found it amusing that Nakor was by nature far more patient and content to accept things as they were than Miranda; if a woman over a century old could be called 'youthfully impetuous' it was Miranda.

One thing became truer by the day: their human consciousnesses were slowly displacing the demonic, and both had begun to feel as if they had somehow simply died human and reawakened in these new bodies. If anything had eased Nakor's annoyance at his changed status, it had been the wry amusement he felt watching Miranda's complete frustration over hers.

Lacking the ability to transport themselves to Sorcerer's Isle magically, they had been forced to seek another means of conveyance. So a ride on a supply wagon had been purchased, allowing the former demons to discuss their situation as they slowly wended their way southward. To the others travelling in this tiny caravan they looked like nothing out of the ordinary, no more unusual than any pairing of an attractive middle-aged woman with an odd-looking old man, Keshian by his garb and complexion. With the war under way, there were many people on the road, some moving northward, away from the pending Keshian assault, others south, towards potential riches.

Nakor and Miranda had both lived a very long time, and had known many wars, and so neither was surprised by the flow of people towards the coming bloody conflict. There was always a direct relationship between risk and reward in wartime.

Over the years both of them had witnessed wars fought by armies outnumbered by their camp followers: prostitutes, gamblers, weapons sellers, armour makers, tailors, skinners, bowyers, food suppliers, all willing to risk harm, even death, in exchange for a possible windfall of gold. Miranda's memory even recalled one bold and enterprising farmer who had rushed his small herd of cattle to an invading army's quartermaster and sold it for gold, mere hours before the commander ordered his riders out to forage for food; he had managed to sell what they would have pillaged anyway. Miranda had always wondered what had become of that farmer.

Despite the odd musings created by memories that were at once familiar yet new, the attention of the two demons-turned-human was drawn to the south, where the afternoon sky was thick with smoke clouds above the city.

The wagon slowed and the driver turned and said, 'Looks like Ylith has fallen.'

Miranda said, 'There may be fires, but that doesn't mean it's fallen. If the gates had been breached, we'd see a flood of retreating people streaming past us now.'

'Well, I'm going to wait and see. No risk in pausing,' said the old teamster, 'but a lot of risk in blundering forward.'

Miranda jumped down from the back of the wagon and saw that the other teams in the small caravan had also pulled over to the verge of the road. 'I'll tell you what,' said the demon in human form. 'We'll wander down and take a look and if we don't come back . . .' She saw the face of Nakor grinning. 'Assume the worst.'

They set off down the road at quick pace and when they were out of earshot, Nakor laughed loudly. 'Assume the worst?'

'Well, I wasn't going to tell him we weren't coming back, and if he wants to sit there waiting for someone to blow the all-clear, he's picked the wrong trade.'

They moved rapidly, their demonic strength and endurance extant under their human appearance. Miranda and Nakor, as they now thought of themselves, had no idea why they were here, even if they knew Kalkin was behind their existence. But they trusted that it was for a reason and an important one, and they knew that to uncover that reason, the most logical place to begin was where the most powerful practitioners of magic resided: Sorcerer's Isle.

Moreover, though she said nothing to Nakor, Miranda ached to see her family. In her memory she had just withstood a brutal demon attack on her home and had successfully driven them off with her husband, son, and the other magicians when a wounded demon had leapt from feigned death and ripped out half of her neck, causing almost instantaneous death. The shock of the attack had made the details vague and since Nakor had died before the invasion, she had no witness with whom to speak. She didn't know if her husband had survived, though she counted it likely, nor how her children fared. She needed to know, and it was slowly becoming an overwhelming urge.

Within minutes of leaving the woodlands, they started down a gentle sloping road and could clearly see the city. The fire appeared to rage beyond the city, perhaps on the docks or through some ships near the quayside, for although a canopy of smoke hung over Ylith, no pillars of soot and ash rose within the walls. Still, the defenders of the city were vigilant, and as Miranda and Nakor approached the gate, they were challenged from the wall.

'Who's there?' The voice sounded very young and not terribly confident.

'Travellers,' answered Miranda. She glanced at Nakor who grinned at her statement of the obvious. 'Who seek shelter.'

'The gates are to stay shut. Commander's orders.'

'We're hardly an invading force from Kesh,' said Miranda.

'He looks Keshian,' said the owner of the high-pitched voice, now obviously a boy wearing an ill-fitting helm as he leaned out between two merlons to point at Nakor.

'I travel a lot!' shouted Nakor, his grin widening.

Miranda said, 'This may prove difficult.'

'You want to just leap up there?' asked the short gambler.

Miranda looked dubious. 'I might be able to, but could you?'

'I'm more nimble than I look,' said Nakor, his grin fading as if she had hurt his feelings. Then the smile returned. 'Besides, it would terrify the boy.'

Looking up at the downturned face above them, Miranda shouted, 'When will the commander order the gates open to travellers?'

'I don't know,' answered the boy. He kept glancing over his shoulder as if expecting someone to arrive and tell him what to do.

'Why don't you run off and find someone to ask?' said Miranda, and the boy nodded and vanished from sight.

'I was about to say that,' said Nakor with a relieved expression.

Glancing around, Miranda wrapped her arms around her as if chilled, though the air was balmy. 'It's so difficult at times.'

Nakor nodded. 'I think the longer we abide in this realm, the more these memories will begin to feel like our true ones, and the memories we have of our home realm will fade to nothing.'

Miranda nodded. 'I sometimes struggle to remember being Child.' She looked for a moment at Nakor, once Belog the Archivist of King Dahun, Demon Lord of one of the five most powerful realms in the Fifth Plane of existence. 'My earliest recollections of my mother, and even those of meeting you, are fading and becoming dream-like.'

Nakor grinned. 'One thing remains constant: no matter the realm in which we find ourselves, or what manner of being we become, life will be a struggle.' He shrugged. 'That, in its own way at least, is reassuring.'

'What you told me—' She shook her head as if struggling to find the correct context. 'What Nakor's memories . . .' She sighed in resignation. 'What *you* told me in the Dasati realm about Miranda's father, do you think that will happen to us?'

Nakor cocked his head slightly as if pondering the thought for a moment, then said, 'If you mean do I think we shall die once our purpose here is over . . . ?' Again he shrugged. 'I can only speculate. There are differences. From what Pug and I surmised, Macros's memories were overlaid on a dying Dasati, and his life extended through the Trickster God's intercession, but the Dasati was verging on death already. We on the other hand, despite our appearances, are still demons in the prime of our power, thanks to your generosity in our home realm.'

'You mean in not devouring you?'

'Among other things,' said Nakor with a widening grin. 'It is the nature of our race to view most things as a struggle, combat or a transaction, but now that we have all these human memories and emotions . . . I remember . . . The last thing Nakor thought was how interesting his life was.' The grin broadened. 'And that, I must say, was an understatement.' For an instant the grin faded. 'If only all of these humans understood how wondrous their lives could be . . . This being that I'm becoming, this Nakor, had amazing travels and experiences. The people he knew and . . . loved.' He was silent for a moment, then said, 'What a powerful thing that is: love. I think Dahun attempted to engender that in our people; I think that is why your mother gladly gave her life for yours.'

Miranda's head tilted to one side slightly, the one remaining gesture that was purely Child's.

'From my – Belog's – point of view, I have been given the gift of another's lifetime, the feelings, experiences, knowledge . . . From Nakor's point of view, his life just got more interesting. I'm sure we have a purpose.' He narrowed his gaze and said, 'Kalkin may be many things, but even the gods have their limits, and for him to take the trouble to "cheat," as he called it, and play hob with what is and is not permitted across the realms . . .' He nodded once emphatically. 'No, we are not here because of a whim. We are here to do something vital.'

'Love is one of the reasons I must find Pug,' said Miranda. 'Just to see him . . .' Her eyes welled up with tears and she wiped them away. 'Damn, I know these aren't my memories, but they feel like they are.'

Nakor said, 'So many questions.'

'You seem delighted about that,' she said regaining her composure.

'Always. Learn a simple answer and, well, it's over; but a really good question,' he winked, 'now, that's worth something.' Then his expression darkened. 'We need to find out why Kalkin did this to us, changed us and gave us those memories.'

Miranda looked surprised. 'I thought that was obvious.'

'Few things really are.'

'We need to warn Pug about the Dread.'

'Pug is very smart. He should have figured that out by now. There is something else.'

'What?'

'I don't know. But Pug will know of the Dread by now. He's the smartest man I ever met.'

Miranda smiled slightly. 'He used to say you were the smartest man he'd ever met.'

With an evil twinkle in his eye, Nakor said, 'That's why I know he's the smartest man I ever met.'

Miranda was about to say something arch, when the small door set into the large city gate opened and a man wearing an old, ill-fitting tabard over simple work clothes appeared. 'Who might you be, then?' he asked.

Miranda said, 'Two travellers trying to find a safe place to rest.'

The old man said, 'This city is hardly that, or did you miss the blaze to the south? We're at war.'

'Which is why we wish to get inside,' she said.

The old man looked tired and his expression revealed his unhappiness at being roused from his rest by the boy who had fetched him to the gate. If he wanted to know why this unlikely pair was on the road alone after dark, he put the question aside and said, 'Well, you two don't look like a Keshian assault brigade, so I guess there's no harm letting you come in. There's an inn a bit further down this boulevard, the Black Ram. Travellers are being housed there until we can sort out who's who.' He hiked his thumb at the boy who stood behind him at the door. 'Teddy will see you there.' He moved aside, motioning for them to enter.

They passed through the gate and followed the eager boy down the street. This portion of the city was shuttered and for the most part had been abandoned, though signs of a few determined souls lingered: a blacksmith's furious hammering echoed from a nearby street, and one family had obviously kept their home; the windows were open to the warm afternoon air, despite the acrid smoke which gave a bitter tang to the air. A wagon rolled down towards the city's southern wall in the distance, but otherwise most of this quarter of the city was still. The boy moved at a good pace and soon he indicated an inn on their right. They nodded their thanks and entered the great room.

As inns went, it was one of the biggest either Nakor or Miranda had seen, and they had seen quite a few. 'I don't remember this inn being so large,' said Miranda as Nakor peered around the room for someone in charge.

'When was the last time you stayed at an inn in Ylith?' he asked, spying a serving woman bringing ale to a table in the back room.

She calculated. 'About thirty, to thirty-five years ago.'

'Things change,' he said with his usual grin and motioned for her to accompany him through the crowd. 'Lots of travellers from the Free Cities, Krondor, and Queg must come through here on business in LaMut and Yabon. It was already pretty prosperous when we . . . left.' He waved around the room. 'Lots of business for an enterprising innkeeper.'

About thirty people cluttered the hall, occupying every seat and every table; they even stood along the walls, which were blessed with a series of waist-high shelves. At the rear of the room they found a servant who looked cheerful despite being nearly overwhelmed by the demand for her services. A plump woman of middle years, she turned and said, 'I'll be with you good folks in a moment.' Then she returned her attention to the four young men she had just served. 'That's a silver for four,' she said.

'Why don't you wait until we're done?' asked one of the young men sitting at the tiny corner table. He was obviously a labourer of some kind, a stonemason's apprentice, given his large arms and shoulders and the covering of stone dust on the apron he wore over his heavy woollen shirt. His three companions were likewise scruffy and ill-kempt; none of them appeared to have shaved in a week.

The woman laughed. 'As crowded as it is, I might not get back here until an hour after you left.'

'Where would we go?' He waved towards the door. 'We step outside and one of those watchmen will fetch us back.'

Trying to keep the tone light, the woman laughed again. 'Those silly boys?' Her expression turned serious. 'I'm sorry, lads, but I have my instructions. Pay as you go.'

Miranda could smell trouble coming and glanced around the room. The bartender looked burly enough to handle two, even three of these boys, but he was on the other side of the room. She glanced at Nakor, who nodded. The room was packed with people who were tired, bored, irritable and drunk. It was ripe for a brawl or a full-on riot.

Miranda gently pushed the serving woman aside, leaned over and said, 'Pay up, that's a good fellow.'

'I am not your good fellow, woman,' said the young man with a defiant sneer. 'I'm a mason from Natal trying to get home after a long job away. I'm a man whose ship was heading south before we reached this miserable city.' His voice rose. 'I'm a man who has been shut up in this inn since then, with no way to get home, and I'm in no mood to argue with whores!' He took a drunken backhanded swing at the serving woman who nimbly stepped aside.

Her eyes widened and she shouted, 'Whores!'

The man was half-out of his seat when Miranda reached out, put her hand on his shoulder, and shoved him back into his seat so hard he cried out in pain, the pop of his shoulder joint loud enough to be heard. She continued to squeeze and the effect was instant: his eyes widened and he opened his mouth, but was unable to make a sound save a slight whimper. Colour drained from his face and tears started streaming down his cheeks.

She released him and turned to the serving woman. 'You all right?'

The dumbfounded woman could only nod, and the mason's three companions backed their chairs against the walls in a futile attempt to put more space between themselves and this insane, but obviously powerful, woman.

Miranda stared at them. 'Where do you idiots sleep?'

One of the gasping man's companions said in a terrified whisper, 'Basement.'

Miranda simply said, 'Go!'

All four men struggled quickly to get out of their seats, two of them helping the injured man away. Nakor laughed as they vanished into the crowd. 'Well, now we can sit down,' he said.

As they did so, the serving woman said, 'Thank you.' She blinked for a moment like a barn owl caught in lantern-light, then her happy expression returned. 'What can I get you?'

'What have you to eat?' asked Miranda as the famished Nakor nodded enthusiastically.

'I've some mutton on the spit that's edible. We've almost been eaten bare by this lot. It's lovely to make coin, but when there's nothing to buy . . .'

Miranda beckoned her closer, then spoke softly, 'There's a wagon train from LaMut parked outside the city walls waiting for someone to let them in. Good, fresh food, flour, butter, everything you need. You might want to tell your employer and have him send someone down there to make a deal before the other innkeepers in town find out.'

The woman brightened and said, 'Thank you, I'll tell him straight away!' Then she leaned over. 'Got some stew about to finish, and there are a few hot loaves of bread left.' She gestured over her shoulder. 'My dad is trying to keep 'em drunk enough to be happy, but not so drunk we can't keep them in line. Those four from the Free Cities have been complaining all day and most of yesterday, like no one else here is suffering.' Her smile returned. 'Drink?'

'Two of whatever you think is best,' said Nakor.

'Two dwarven ales it is, then,' she said. 'Back in a moment.'

As the serving woman vanished into the crowd a tall figure made his way through the press until he stood before their table. He was blond with pointed ears and broad shoulders and was clad in a dark brown leather tunic, trousers, and boots. He held a long bow which he now placed butt end on the floor in front of them. Smiling quizzically, he said, 'You always did know how to make an entrance.'

Both Miranda and Nakor glanced up and then broke into broad smiles. Miranda said, 'Calis!'

The son of the Elf Queen and Warleader Tomas of Elvandar leaned forward slightly and said in a lower voice, 'Aren't you two supposed to be dead?'

Nakor laughed, and Miranda motioned for Calis to sit. The blond half-elf, half-human, part-Valheru had been a close friend of both Nakor and Miranda, and for a time much more than friends with her. Nakor had sailed with Calis on a voyage to Novindus in the early stages of the Serpent War, the invasion of the Kingdom by the demon possessing the body of the Emerald Queen. In an odd twist of fate, the Emerald Queen had once been married to Nakor and later became Miranda's mother.

Calis sat down and Miranda leaned over to give him a hug and a kiss on the cheek; then Nakor shook his hand.

The serving woman returned with two flagons of ale. 'Sir?' she asked Calis who shook his head.

When she had departed, Calis said, 'A story, then?'

Miranda reached out and put her hand on his. 'I am not who I appear to be.' She felt a strong sense of affection for this being, and remembered that Miranda and Calis had been lovers for a time before she had met Pug.

She could feel his fingers tense ever so slightly under her hand, and pressed down lightly in a gesture of reassurance. 'It is not deceit, nor trickery, but a strange twist of fate which brings us here.' She glanced at Nakor who nodded.

'If you are not two of my oldest and dearest friends, returned to me, then . . . ?'

'It's a long story and hard to believe,' said Nakor. Grinning, he added, 'Then again our little band of desperate men saw some things terrible and wondrous to behold on our travels, didn't we?'

Calis nodded. He gave Miranda a pointed look. She returned a sad smile and said, 'I remember everything.' She gave his hand another slight squeeze. 'But those memories are not mine.'

Calis said nothing.

Nakor asked, 'When was the last time you saw Pug?'

'A year or so ago. He came to visit my mother and Tomas.' He looked at Miranda. 'He was still saddened by your loss, as well as Caleb and Marie.'

Miranda couldn't help but gasp, and tears gathered in her eyes. 'Caleb? Marie?' She tightened her grip on his hand; a lesser being would have endured broken fingers. Caleb had been Miranda's youngest child and Marie, his wife.

Calis softly said, 'In the attack that took you.'

Miranda looked away for a second, then finally she composed herself and asked, 'The boys?'

Calis squeezed her hand in return and said, 'Tad, Zane, and Jommy are well. There were other losses when the demons attacked your island, students and two of Pug's teachers, but given the severity . . .'

'I remember.' She said nothing for a long moment, and then lowered her eyes. 'I will tell you everything, but not now.' A sad sound, barely a whisper of a breath, was followed by silence.

Nakor said, 'Not that I'm unhappy to see you, old friend, but what coincidence brings you here on the very day we arrive?'

'Not such a coincidence, I'm on an errand for my mother. I carry word to young Lord Martin that those sent to us from Crydee to care for are safe in Elvandar.'

Composing herself, Miranda asked, 'Why come this way? Why not take the straighter course south across the River Boundary to Crydee?'

'Because Martin is not in Crydee, he's here in Ylith.'

'They have kept you waiting here?' She indicated the inn with a quick wave of her hand.

'They haven't,' said Calis. 'I saw Martin yesterday and paused here on my way north.'

Miranda said, 'Because you had never spent a night in an overcrowded ale house with too many strangers who haven't bathed in weeks?'

Calis grinned and Nakor laughed. The Prince of Elvandar said, 'Whatever you may be now, some things about you are exactly as I remember them.' He looked across the room to the far corner. Where the bar ended, a small additional room had once been added; there was a step leading down to a pair of tables that had been placed together for a large group. All of the chairs had been moved to allow a band of workers to sit together, save one. A figure wearing a dark cloak sat in the corner, his arms crossed over his chest, surveying the room. He was staring directly at Calis.

'Ah,' said Miranda taking in the figure's hair and ears. 'One of yours?'

'Hardly,' said Nakor. 'So, you were curious about that dark elf and decided to linger?'

Calis nodded. 'I was curious to see what a moredhel was doing in Ylith.'

'And no doubt he's curious to know what a prince of Elvandar is doing in Ylith,' said Nakor.

Miranda glanced at the figure half-hidden in shadows and said, 'How did you know he was moredhel?'

'It's in our nature to recognize our own kind, and those who are not. He travels as an ocedhel, one of the elves from across the sea, but his disguise is flawed.'

Nakor peered at the figure for a bit and sat back. 'I can see nothing.' He squinted, then shook his head. 'Under the table?'

Calis nodded. 'The boots.'

Nakor laughed. 'Trust a moredhel to be unwilling to sacrifice his boots.' Then the little man's expression turned serious. 'Or his sword, I expect. Though I wager you'll have to kill him to get a good look at it.'

'How do you know so much of dark elves?' Miranda asked Nakor.

'I travel,' was his answer.

Again Miranda was struck by the absurdity of their two sets of memories. Belog had never travelled further than the distance from the archivists' quarters to Dahun's palace and back, until he had left the city and encountered Child. Nakor had travelled to every distant part of Midkemia and worlds beyond.

'He does look like a traveller from across the sea, like Calis's wife,' granted Nakor. Miranda had rescued Ellia and her sons during the war of the Emerald Queen, across the sea in Novindus and had taken them to Elvandar, where they had met Calis.

Calis said, 'His tunic, trousers and cloak are simple enough, and he wears no armour, but that's a bad bow: it's cracked and has been re-glued and banded with leather, so he's no archer. And he wears fine boots of a craft common to the Dark Brotherhood.' He used the human name for the moredhel. 'Those are unmistakable, and from what I can see, well-made. He's important, perhaps even a clan chieftain.'

'Well, that does raise the question of what he's doing here,' said Miranda.

'Renegade?' asked Nakor of Calis.

Calis shrugged. 'Rare, but not unheard of, although they rarely venture this far south; there are too many places between here and the northland for a moredhel to die alone. The few who are expelled from their clans are usually found in the east, among humans who traffic in weapons, drugs, and slaves.'

'A spy, then?' said Miranda, obviously intrigued by the speculation.

'If he is, he's a bad one,' said Nakor, standing up. 'Well, the best thing to do is ask him.'

Before either Calis or Miranda could utter another word, Nakor had worked his way through the crowd to stand before the dark-haired elf in the corner. With as friendly an expression as the demon-in-human form could manage, he said, 'Excuse me, but my friends and I were wondering what you are doing here?'

Dark eyes regarded Nakor for a long moment, before the dark elf spoke, not in the King's tongue but in heavily accented Common Tongue, the trading language of Triagia. 'Go away, little man.'

Nakor's grin broadened even more. 'We could have some fun. I could tell this crowd exactly what you are. Many are from the north and have no love for your people; and then we can see how long you survive. Or, you could simply answer my question.'

Lowering his voice so those at the next table couldn't overhear, Arkan of the Ardanien said, 'Or, I could simply ignore you until you go away!'

Nakor kept grinning. 'I can be very persistent and patient.'

'And annoying, apparently.' Arkan stared Nakor in the eyes, then suddenly stood up and pressed past the little man. With no apology, the moredhel chieftain pushed his way through the crowd eliciting complaints and muttered threats.

Reaching Calis and Miranda, he spoke in a language only Miranda and Nakor could understand. It was High Elven, the common ancestor language of all branches of the elves. 'Had you wished to know my reason for being here, Prince of Elvandar, you could have simply asked, rather than send over that annoying little human.'

Miranda tried not to chuckle.

Calis said, 'You know me?'

'By reputation,' said Arkan. 'You are eledhel, but you are not. There's something about you that is . . . human.' He said the last as if it was an insult. 'There is only one being like that: the son of the Queen of Elvandar.'

Calis raised his eyebrows slightly and tilted his head, as if what he had heard was of little importance. 'It is true, I was curious.'

'Which is why you followed me into the inn when you were obviously about to depart this pest hole of a city.'

'So, are you going to tell us why you're here or do I send for the city watch and begin some carnage?' asked Calis.

Arkan studied the Prince of Elvandar. Like others north of the Teeth of the World, he had heard of the bastard son of Aglaranna and that abomination in the garb of the Valheru. Yet Calis wasn't anything like he had imagined him to be. Save for his ears, which were less pronounced, more human-like, and the faint sense of power that emanated from him, he seemed surprisingly ordinary. His plain garb was that of a hunter or traveller, his bow was superbly made, but otherwise of simple design, and he wore no jewellery or badges, no bracelets or hair ornaments. With his traditional grey armour and black cloak he could have passed for a member of one of the moredhels' southern bands.

Finally Arkan said, 'While I would happily kill everyone in this room, given the opportunity,' he fixed his eyes on Calis, 'and finish with you, Prince of the Light Elves, I am forbidden from such sport. I am pledged to a quest.'

'Now, this is getting interesting,' said Nakor. 'What sort of quest?'

'I'm to find a man, a human. That is all I know.' Arkan briefly told them of his mission and saw that, while the humans were ignorant of Liallan, Calis was not. Finally he said, 'It is simple. I am to find this human no matter what the cost.'

'And then what?' said Miranda having already formed an opinion on who Arkan was seeking. 'Kill him?'

Arkan smiled and for the first time Miranda, Calis, and Nakor saw a genuine expression of humour in the demeanour of a moredhel. 'Actually, quite the contrary. I am to protect him with my life if needs be.'

'Now that was unexpected,' said Nakor with glee. 'I do so love surprises!'

'I think you'd better sit down with us,' said Miranda. 'I think we have a great deal to talk about.'

Arkan hesitated, finding the situation as absurd as Nakor,

he nodded once and sat in the empty chair, while the others retook theirs.

Arkan retold his story briefly and when he was finished, he said, 'And that is why I am here in this pest hole of a city.'

Nakor grinned. 'If you think this is a pest hole, you should visit Durbin!'

Miranda put her hand on Nakor's and said, 'Enough.'

Calis said, 'You said you are of the Ardanien. You knew Gorath?'

Arkan looked surprised for the first time. 'He was my father.'

Calis nodded. 'I see the resemblance. I met him when I was young. You had a remarkable father, Arkan. He was the first moredhel I had ever spoken with and he bore a terrible burden.'

'He is counted a traitor by most of our people.' He glanced at the three faces confronting him and felt reluctant to discuss family history, but he was surprised to discover that Calis had met his father. 'I know there are rumours and some, like Liallan, think him a saviour, but the truth of those days is shrouded by lies and rumour.'

'Perhaps Pug can shed some light on that time?' said Calis.

'Pug?'

Nakor said, 'The man in black, in your aunt's vision, is almost certainly Pug or perhaps his son Magnus. Both are given to wearing black, and both are great sorcerers who struggle to protect this world. If the vision of dragon riders is more than mere metaphor, they would be the Valheru's most powerful opposition.' He glanced at Miranda.

She looked deeply troubled. 'We know things,' she said to Arkan. 'Some of which are best discussed after we find Pug. We seem fated to travel together. If we can contrive some way to get past this invading army and navy blocking our way!' She sat back in her chair with an audible sigh and said, 'If there was some way I could contact Pug, reach out with my mind and tell him . . .' Tell him what? she wondered silently. That his dead wife's memories had been attached to a demon queen, who under any other circumstances would happily rip off his head and devour his brain; but who would now like nothing more than for him to hold her? Tears threatened, and she willed herself away from that emotional trap.

'Pug,' she said softly. 'I wonder what he's doing this minute?'

4

ISLE OF SNAKES

Pug signalled.

Sandreena and Amirantha moved out from behind the large rock where they had been waiting. She was clad in the traditional armour of her order, the Shield of the Weak, and he had forgone his usual finery to don a more appropriate outfit: heavy woollen trousers, a dark green flannel shirt, and stout black boots. His attire made the staff he carried look almost gaudy. It had been created that way for theatrical effect, to help gull potential victims into his confidence scheme – summoning relatively harmless demons then banishing them for reward – but was a powerful magic artefact in its own right.

They were tired and dirty from their journey down to the region where Jim Dasher had encountered what he thought was a Pantathian Serpent priest, and it had proved far more problematic than anticipated.

Reaching a safe house in the Keshian city of Teléman had been simple enough, since Pug's orb had taken them there. But that was as far south as the Conclave had established any permanent stations. Like almost everyone monitoring Kesh, the Conclave had considered the nations of the Keshian Confederacy barely worth consideration. They were universally regarded to be nothing more than an annoyance to the Empire on her southern boundary, and not an area noteworthy enough to warrant the Conclave's continuing surveillance. The Conclave resources had limits, and Kesh was a vast land. Most of their intelligence gathering had been focused on the City of Kesh, heart of the Empire, and key population centres along the borders with the Kingdom, as well as major sea ports. None of Pug's agents had travelled below the Girdle of Kesh, as the two ranges of mountains that divided the Empire from the Confederacy were called. Which made it the perfect place to organize the major undertaking of subverting the Empire's rulers and launching a wholesale invasion of the Kingdom.

And it made it impossible to reach by the magical means at Pug's disposal.

So, more mundane means of transport had been required. Pug had the ability to transport himself magically to any place in his line of sight, and to the places he knew well, but he was limited in how far he could transport himself and two others repeatedly. Still, the occasional sorcerous jaunt was handy for bypassing certain obstacles and to avoid roving bands of raiders, bandits, and what passed for the local militia, but most of their journey had been made by horseback, small boat, and foot.

The weather was chilly, as it was now early winter in the southern hemisphere. A misty rain had been falling intermittently since dawn and the three travellers were just damp and cold enough to be irritable. Sandreena in particular was beyond patience, as she had been forced to leave her horse stabled in a tiny village on the mainland coast with the other mounts. As a Knight-Adamant of the Order of the Shield of the Weak, worshippers of the Goddess Dala, she found that being on foot was like having to fight with one hand; something she was able to do, but would rather not.

Pug had secured a boat but the owner had refused to row them over to the large island, and at last Pug understood why. The maps that Macros had drawn years before and left behind in his library were full of errors and inexactitudes, one of which was sloppy translation. After speaking to the locals on the far shore of the mainland, Pug now realized that this was not the 'Island of the Snakes,' but rather the 'Island of the Snake Men.'

Apparently, he had found the Pantathian homeland. Which puzzled him, as he had thought the heart of the Pantathian murder cult had been located near the foothills of the mountain range named the Pavilion of the Gods. Legend said many of the Valheru Dragon Lords had resided in that region as well.

The Pantathians were an unnatural race, distorted by a Valheru by the name of Alma-Lodaka, Mistress of Serpents, who had created them to serve her. She had bred them, then evolved them into intelligent beings and granted them magical abilities. It was conceded that while the Valheru could not create life, they could manipulate and distort it.

One unintended consequence had been the creation of a death cult who worshipped the long-departed Mistress of Serpents as a goddess, longed for her return, and who would stop at nothing to bring it about. Much of Pug's personal history was intertwined with these snake men: upright serpents who were human-like in form, but who were more alien than any other race Pug had encountered on Midkemia. He understood the Dasati, a race from another plane of reality, better than he understood the Pantathians.

Pug and his son Magnus had been instrumental in destroying the Pantathian crèches in what they had thought to be the final blow against the lizard race, but apparently there had been more than one enclave of the creatures. As disgusting as it might have been to obliterate every egg and spawn they had encountered, Pug had at least found some solace in the knowledge they were not natural creatures, but twisted parodies of intelligent life focused only on one purpose, and that purpose entailed the annihilation or enslavement of all other races on Midkemia in service of their 'goddess.'

Pug surveyed the landscape and sniffed the air. There was a burnt wood tinge in the heavy damp air. He motioned for his companions to follow him and led them up a small rise to a ridge overlooking a shallow valley. In the distance they could see what looked to be a community, but even at this distance it was clear that it had been burned to char.

Pug motioned for Sandreena and Amirantha to stand close, and they stepped forwards to flank him, and put their hands on his shoulders.

In an instant they were standing at the edge of the town. Signs of battle were evident in all directions. 'Looks like whoever did this wasn't willing to let anyone survive,' observed Sandreena.

'They were making a point,' said Pug.

'Point?' Amirantha looked at the short sorcerer.

Pug nodded. 'I'm not entirely sure of what the point was: vengeance, perhaps. This wouldn't be the first time an army destroyed every man, woman, and child of an enemy. You don't slaughter those who farm and raise livestock if you plan on occupying a land and ruling it.' He looked around. 'The dead pay no taxes, either.'

Pug silently turned in a full circle. 'This valley runs to the south from here.' He pointed to a nearby stream. 'If we follow that stream I suspect we'll find more villages.'

'We walk?' asked Amirantha.

'Most of the way,' said Pug and he set off. After a moment, the other two followed.

By the time they found the fourth village, Pug was perplexed. 'This was no small raiding party.' He pointed to several locations around the area where they stood. 'This was a coordinated attack. I've seen enough battlefields over the last hundred years to recognize that.'

The one unexpected factor had been the corpses left intact enough to recognize: they were Pantathians. They had all been Pantathian villages, and the bodies which had not been literally torn to shreds, or incinerated, were lizard men, women and children.

Sandreena said, 'You're right. There's no sign of anyone fleeing.' She pointed behind them and said, 'If it was merely a raiding patrol, those fleeing the first onslaught to the north of here would have warned those in the south. By now we'd have seen abandoned wagons along the way, or more dead . . . people,' she shrugged as if unable to think of a better word to describe them, 'with bundles of precious belongings. There's none of that. This was a coordinated attack, as Pug said. Several elements support a military strike.' She looked at Pug. Then she faltered, pausing as if she heard a distant, faint sound. 'Do you feel that?' She looked at Amirantha.

He said, 'I've been feeling something for a—' His eyes widened. 'Demons!'

'Someone sent a demon army here, Pug,' said Sandreena.

Pug sighed as if it was the last thing he wished to hear.

'It's as if the gods can't find enough grief to visit on this world,' said Amirantha. 'I can no longer control one demon, so they send an entire army . . .'

Pug slowly let his gaze wander. 'It's the gods who are trying to stop this. That is why we are here.'

'I'm a woman of faith,' said Sandreena, 'but these are the moments when that faith is tested.'

'That's odd,' said Pug.

'What?' asked Sandreena.

Pug pointed to the recently-dead corpse of a Pantathian.

He approached it, ignoring the stench of decay, and said, 'Whenever we encountered the Pantathians, even when we raided their crèches in the mines below the Ratn'gary Mountains, we saw no soldiers.' The corpse was dressed in a full open-faced helm, a cuirass of steel, a chainmail kilt and heavy leather boots. It still clutched a blood-caked sword in its dead fingers and nearby rested a distorted round shield, rent with talon marks. 'We saw a few guards, but they were mostly workers, priests, and the female breeders.' He knelt beside it. 'There were no soldiers.' He looked around, seeing others garbed in similar fashion. 'These Pantathians have hidden an army.'

'It's smaller than a few days ago,' quipped Sandreena. 'The demons did thorough work here.'

'What should we do now?' asked Amirantha.

'If this Pantathian society remotely resembles ours,' said Pug, standing, 'these farms and villages support a city somewhere, or at least a fortress.'

'If there's a fortress full of snake-men, I doubt we would be welcome,' observed Amirantha.

Pug nodded, continuing to look around. 'Something here feels . . . right.'

That statement brought puzzled looks from both his companions and he went on, 'I have been battling Pantathians since the Great Uprising. They played a key part in the invasion of the Emerald Queen's army.' Both Sandreena and Amirantha were aware of the role the demon Jatuk had played in that war, using powerful magic to disguise himself as the Emerald Queen. 'The Pantathians were duped as much as the Saaur and many of the humans loyal to the Emerald Queen. But there was even more in play than was apparent.' He looked down at the dead Pantathian again. 'I know there are others; the Shangri, also called Panath-Tiandn, are strange, nearly mindless creatures that have been twisted by dark powers to manipulate magic energy.' He pointed to the dead soldier. 'But it seems that there may be a third type of Pantathian we've never encountered before.' He bent and took a small pouch that had been wedged into the soldier's sword belt and pulled it free. Inside he found small objects. He tossed one to Amirantha. 'What do you make of this?'

It was a tiny spinning top. Finally, the Warlock of the Satumbria said, 'It's a toy.'

'A child's toy. The sort of thing a boy or girl might give to their father to bring him luck. Or as a remembrance of happier times.'

'He had a family?' asked Amirantha incredulously.

'I tend to be sceptical as well,' said Pug, 'but whenever I've encountered Pantathians before, the miasma of their magic is palpable, almost a stench if you will.'

Sandreena said, 'That's how demons make me feel. It's how I know there's one nearby without having to see it.'

Amirantha could only nod.

'I sense none of that here. Granted, this is an alien place, but I've been to many such and this city and these lands, scarred by war as they are, still do not offer any hint of that black evil that usually surrounds the Pantathians.'

'You want to go find them, don't you?' asked the warlock.

Pug could only smile. 'I think we need to. I suspect the three of us are powerful enough to protect ourselves, and at worst I can transport us back to this place.' He took a moment to grab some rocks and make a rough pattern, all the while studying features and details, etching them into his mind as he had been taught while studying with the Tsurani magicians over a century before.

'Ah, could you perhaps make us invisible, or something like that?' asked Amirantha, obviously unhappy with Pug's conclusion, 'While we traipse around looking for a snake-man army?'

Sandreena couldn't help but laugh. Amirantha smiled at the sound; he hadn't heard it often in the last year.

Pug smiled. 'I could, but you would have to remain motionless. Not very helpful in a search, I'm afraid. If Laromendis were here, perhaps he could mask us as Pantathians, but that's problematic, as well. Three Panthathians unfamiliar approaching a fortress, camp or village, are just as likely to cause a stir as three humans.

'Amirantha, have you any shielding magic at your disposal?'

'Against demons? Certainly. Against arrows . . .' He shrugged.

'Then if we encounter any Panthathians, stay close by my side.'

'Or stand behind me,' said Sandreena with a sour, mocking look.

'Back to your old self, I see,' he said.

She elbowed him playfully in the ribs and said, 'Still can't stand a jest, can you?'

'Oh, that was a jest?'

She frowned. 'If you—'

'Children,' Pug interrupted. 'If you don't mind; resume your fighting when we're back home, though how you two can find any humour in the midst of this carnage I can't imagine.'

The former lovers were embarrassed and both fell silent as Pug said, 'Let's begin.'

They made their way south for more than an hour, down through the heart of the small valley. Cresting a rise they found themselves within sight of a small stream that ran through its centre. Pug glanced around then pointed to the north-east. 'Remember that range of low mountains we saw from the boat as we looked for a landing?' They both nodded. 'That must form some type of rain shield, and the stream has cut this valley over the ages.' He looked at the relatively bare landscape above the valley. 'Constant water, shelter from harsher weather; this may be as close to an ideal habitat as you'll find on this island.'

They trudged along, wending their way through battle-scarred villages and farmsteads. Everywhere they looked they saw charred ruins. Amirantha paused several times to examine a blackened spot on the ground and indicated it was where a major demon had died. Pug was uncertain how he could know from the size of the burn mark; several of the minor demons were an impressive size, but as the taredhel magician possessed more knowledge about demons than anyone else he knew, save perhaps the star elf demon master, Gulamendis, Pug deferred to his superior knowledge.

The valley deepened as the day grew longer.

Sandreena held up her hand and said, 'Do you hear something?'

Amirantha glanced around and said, 'Yes, off that way.' He pointed to the top of a ridge a few hundred yards to the south of where they stood.

Pug said, 'I can get us that far.' He held out his hands and they each gripped his shoulders, and suddenly they were standing on the southern ridge.

Below them was an unexpected vista. The winding river valley they had followed had opened up and the river course turned to the south-east. Along its banks were more sheltered farms, unremarkable except that these had been more recently sacked. The pungent aroma of wood smoke still hung in the air, a legacy of rain-damp, burnt timbers.

Pug motioned for the others to accompany him one more time and suddenly they stood on the other side of the river, about a dozen yards north of a burned-out, skeletal house. It had stone foundations – necessary this close to the river if you didn't wish to sleep on a damp muddy floor for half of the year – but its timber siding was gone, as well as whatever type of roof it had had.

Amirantha pointed to what appeared to be a mound of burned scraps and singed rags.

Pug knelt beside it and discovered the remains of a corpse. Little was left but blackened bone. 'Magic,' he said. 'A fire blast of some sort.' He moved his hand in a small circle, indicating the untouched ground nearby. He gently lifted some of the shreds and studied the upper half of a man-sized torso and skull. 'Pantathian. Whatever happened here was only two, three days ago at most.' He stood and pointed to a small pass running through a range of hills to the south. 'There's a road. Well-travelled from the look of it.' He looked in all directions. 'I'll wager that there is a river or swamplands at the end of this river, at this bend, all river traffic . . .' He looked towards the course of the river and again pointed. 'There! Can you see?'

Sandreena peered in the direction Pug indicated and said, 'Piers. Large enough to unload barges and small boats.'

'Logic would suggest that there's a city nearby, it's likely to be defensible, so . . .' He motioned for them to come close. 'Let's take another jump to that ridge up there.'

They instantly appeared on the southern ridge and below them lay a sight to make even Pug feel wonder. A small city rose in the distance, surrounded by white walls perhaps covered in a wash or pale plaster, gleaming in the sunlight. Behind it, towers and the tops of building were visible.

'Well, that's not good,' said Sandreena.

They had materialized behind the ragged remnants of a demon army that had obviously fought their way down the river valley, up the hill and were now advancing upon the walls of the city.

A circling flyer spotted them and dived. Only years of battle-trained reflex kept Sandreena on her feet. She raised her shield above her head as she ducked and the lightweight creature bounced off it, rolling across the ground in a tangle of wings, arms and legs. The stunned monstrosity skidded across the ground, sending up a spray of dust. Amirantha, who had begun an incantation the moment the demon struck Sandreena, pointed at it, and it vanished in a cloud of smoke that carried the stench of sulphur.

'That tears it,' said Amirantha as the rearmost demons turned around to see what the fuss was.

Pug didn't hesitate but unleashed a blast of white-hot

energy through those standing directly before him. Instantly they were vaporized in an explosion of foul steam and sparking metals, as armour and weapons turned instantly red-hot then exploded. Many of the demons near the blast caught on fire and screeched, racing in random directions and colliding with their companions.

The advancing demons were thrown into disarray as those in the vanguard heard fighting from behind before they had even crossed half the distance between the walls and their starting position. Some turned, anticipating an attack from the rear, while others continued to advance.

Pug shouted, 'Stay close!' and Sandreena was at his right side in a single step, Amirantha appearing to his left a moment later. He held his hand high above his head and made a circle with his index finger. A line of red-orange flame seemed to erupt from the tip and arced until it hit the ground, then followed the circular path his finger had made. A spiral of flames started to spread out from their location and each demon it touched screamed or bellowed in pain. Most retreated before it, but a pair of especially aggressive ones tried to push through and fell at Pug's feet, their corpses rapidly consumed in a flaming burst that left a stinking, blackened mark on the ground.

'These are not like the soldiers we saw in Kesh,' Amirantha said.

'No,' agreed Sandreena. 'They're undisciplined and disorganized, but they are definitely battle demons.'

Amirantha knew she was correct. They were confronted with a mixed group of bull-headed, ram-headed, and lion-headed figures: fighting demons. They were accompanied by others that bore some resemblance to animals, monstrous boars or massive dogs, but with scales instead of fur, horns in multiple locations on their heads, nasty dagger-like fangs and talons the length of swords.

The advancing spiral of flames caused the demons before them to retreat, while those nearing the city walls were being greeted with a hail of arrows and stones. The presence of the three magic-users was beginning to turn an already disorganized assault on the city to complete chaos.

Pug lashed out with every imaginable form of destructive magic he could conjure. A scintillating wave of silver energy rippled outwards, and those demons it struck stopped in their tracks, their bodies shaking violently as if gripped by a sudden palsy. Several fell over and thrashed on the ground, while others eventually shook off the shock and continued to advance.

Pug pushed his hands in front of him, palms out, and a huge blast of wind swept dozens of demons backwards, some of the lighter creatures being picked up and tossed yards to the rear. But still the others came on, heads lowered in a charge.

Amirantha picked his targets. If he couldn't banish them instantly, he confined them until Pug's magic or Sandreena's mace dispatched them properly. The demons threw themselves at the three humans mindlessly and furiously for nearly a minute. Then a pause came as the creatures who had pressed into the battle saw the carnage before them.

'This lot aren't terribly bright,' shouted Sandreena, 'but they're smart enough to see this isn't going their way!'

Amirantha yelled back, 'Agreed!' then lashed out with a punishing blow of his staff, spinning around a stocky, ram-headed demon that had ventured too near.

Pug unleashed another wave of magic. Crimson flame washed along the ground everywhere he pointed, a fountain of mystic energy that caused demons to collapse and writhe in agony on the ground until suddenly vanishing in an explosion of black, sulphurous smoke.

The gates of the city opened and a company of Pantathian foot soldiers raced out. Each wore armour identical to that which Pug and his companions had seen on bodies strewn around the valley. The warriors looked tired and battle-scarred, and their armour showed newly hammered out dents and tears repaired in a makeshift fashion, but despite their ragtag state, they seemed determined to help end this struggle, sweeping into the milling demon forces that staggered under the new attack. Brutal hand-to-hand fighting ensued.

Pug cursed silently, for now he was prevented from unleashing more spells of wholesale destruction. He was no friend to the Pantathians, but at that moment they both struggled against a known enemy, which made them temporary allies. He would not mourn their dead, but he would not create any more of them.

So, each of the three magic-wielders used their arts and strengths as they best knew how: Pug and Amirantha with magic, and Sandreena with both magic and mace.

Despite being assaulted from two sides, the demons were unrelenting. Without magic, the Pantathians were no physical match for any demon; but they had larger numbers on their side: two or three fought against one demon.

Pug now used his arts to distract, trip, or otherwise confuse the demons, and in surprisingly little time, the battle was over. A dozen dead Pantathians bore mute testimony to their sacrifice as the last demon body vanished in flame and smoke.

Pug said to his companions, 'Stay close. I have no idea what comes next.'

Sandreena moved slightly ahead of the two men, prepared to take on any physical assault from the soldiers so the two magic-users could bring their arts to bear.

One of the soldiers was looking around the field, and Pug noticed that his armour was more ornate then the rest, his helm bearing a small set of metal horns on each side. He assumed it was a mark of rank, for the soldier began to issue orders and those around him moved smartly despite being exhausted. They inspected each of their fallen comrades and two were picked up and carried back into the city.

Finally, when it was apparent that all the survivors were standing, the higher-ranking soldier stood looking at the three humans, then turned his back and issued an order in a language Pug had never encountered before. The soldiers turned their backs and began walking toward the city.

After a few steps, the officer stopped, turned, and looked at the three humans for a moment. He made a small gesture with his hand, then turned away.

Amirantha said, 'If I'm not mistaken, he just asked us if we're coming or not.'

'I think you're right,' said Pug as he stepped around Sandreena and began to follow the soldiers. His two companions fell into step behind him.

They walked slowly down the sloping hillside, and onto the flat ground around the city. The area had obviously been cut back recently as a few sapling tree stumps were visible, as was a large patch of burned grass. 'Torch rather than the scythe,' said Amirantha.

'If there are no buildings close by, it's easier,' said Sandreena. 'If these people aren't constantly plagued by demons, then they have other enemies they worry about.'

Pug said, 'Perhaps. But it looked to me as if those communities along the river were relatively peaceful until the demons showed up.'

'Old habits?' suggested the Warlock. 'Maybe they just keep the plain around the city open because they've done it that way for years?'

'Again, perhaps,' said Pug.

As they neared the city Pug thought he detected movement on the wall, but by the time they neared the gate no one could be seen. The massive city gates had been left open.

'Be ready,' said Sandreena, then she realized that was an obvious thing to say. 'Nervous, I guess.'

'As are we all,' said Pug, reassuringly.

They entered and saw three Pantathians waiting for them, not armoured warriors, but wearing robes unlike the ritual dress of any Serpent Priests Pug had encountered before. Their clothing was colourful and made of a fine weave and intricate design, decorated with fancy thread and bead-work.

Pug came to a halt a few feet away from them. These three were like the dead Pug's party had encountered in the river valley, and the soldiers who had sallied from the city; they bore only a superficial resemblance to the Pantathians Pug had encountered years before. These people had more pronounced foreheads, and their skulls were less reptilian.

'Can you understand me?' Pug spoke in the common trading tongue, assuming it would most likely be the only human language to have reached this remote island.

'We do,' answered the serpent man in the centre. His accent was odd, but not impossible to comprehend. 'But I find common speak a bit cumbersome, and prefer to use Keshian,' he said in perfectly unaccented Keshian.

Pug couldn't hide his surprise. He, Sandreena, and Amirantha to a lesser degree, all understood Keshian; the Sergeant-Knight Adamant had lived in Kesh for years and the dominant language of Amirantha's homeland was closely related to that tongue.

'We come seeking answers,' said Pug.

In a remarkably human-like change of expression, the speaker said, 'Is that not true of us all? Come. You do not find us at our best. We've struggled for a long time against those you banished.'

'Demons,' said Sandreena.

The speaker turned to regard the armoured woman. 'You have knowledge of the creatures, I assume?'

'More than I would like,' she answered.

'Well, then we have a great deal to discuss; until a few weeks ago, we were ignorant of them. Please, follow me. I am Tak'ka, elected Autarch of Pantathia.' He and his two companions turned and led Pug and his companions deeper into the city.

'Is this place Pantathia?' asked Pug as he walked beside Tak'ka.

'That is what you humans call it. It's a variant of the Lower Delkian dialect, meaning "Home of Snake-Men." You could not pronounce our name in our own tongue, so Pantathia will serve.' He motioned for them to follow. As they walked, he glanced sideways and at last asked, 'You are the one they call Pug?'

If Pug hadn't already been surprised by what they had encountered, he was now openly taken aback. 'Yes,' he said.

'I thought you'd be taller,' mused the Pantathian. 'My people have very strong feelings about you, and they are not all good, I'm afraid.'

As they reached the centre of the small city, Pug was astonished by the scene before him. Like many cities in Kesh and the Kingdom, the main plaza was large and square with a fountain at its centre. Stalls stood against the buildings around its edge, and free-standing booths completely filled the rest of it. Only two paths permitted easy passage through the area.

'Usually, we only have this much clutter on market days, but with the coming of the Hell-bringers many farmers, traders, and woodsmen have been forced to come here. It's more of a refugee camp now than a market.'

Pug marvelled at the people with every step. Every eye turned on them and many voices fell silent as they walked past. The people whispered in their sibilant language and Pug suspected that the Autarch was right; it would indeed be too difficult for human vocal cords to master their language. He used more than a century of observational skills to assess the scene as they made their way through the crowd. Rather than animalistic creatures, he now saw them as a crowd of people no more or less diverse and threatening than the population of any small human city on market day: females with wide-eyed children in tow, vendors displaying their wares, and refugees trying to find a space to settle as comfortably as possible.

Once through the press, they mounted a series of steps to a terraced portion of the city upon which several larger buildings rested. There was nothing remotely like a palace within sight. Behind the buildings rose a wall, high enough to conceal any hint of its purpose. Whatever lay behind it felt oddly familiar to Pug, but there was nothing alarming about the sense of familiarity; instead he found it oddly comforting.

They entered the largest of the three buildings on the plaza, and were led into a hall. Five empty chairs stood behind at a table on a dais near the far wall, but the rest of the room was lined with benches able to seat perhaps as many as two hundred Pantathians.

'This is our seat of government,' said Tak'ka. He motioned for them to sit on the bench closest to the table, and rather than mount the step and take one of the chairs, he sat on the bench next to Amirantha. His two silent companions sat on the next bench directly behind them. 'As Autarch, I preside over Pantathia and the surrounding communities.' He motioned to the two other Pantathians and said, 'This is Dak'it and Tov'ka, fellow Presidents of Pantathia.' He pronounced the names with a sharp-pitched tone and a closing of the throat in the middle, and again Pug doubted he could duplicate it.

Tak'ka sighed in a very human fashion. 'There are usually five of us, but two of our members gave their lives during the last defence of the city.' All three bowed their heads slightly, as if honouring the memories of the fallen; then Tak'ka looked at Pug. 'As I said, we have very strong feelings regarding you, Pug of Stardock.'

Pug said, 'Tell me, please.'

'You've killed many of our people,' said the Autarch, flatly.

'And you have killed many of mine,' said Pug. 'It was war.'

Tak'ka lowered his head slightly. 'True; and to our everlasting sorrow.'

'You find me at a loss, Tak'ka.' Pug knew he was not doing justice to the pronunciation of the Pantathian's name, but the leader of the lizard men took no offence. 'We first encountered your people during the Great Uprising, when the moredhel clans swept down from the north and threatened the Kingdom of the Isles.' He chose not to mention their goal, which had been to seize the Lifestone hidden under the city of Sethanon. 'An imposter, who claimed to be the incarnation of a great moredhel hero, was revealed to be a Pantathian priest, disguised by very powerful magic.' He paused, and his shoulders sagged.

'We are a deliberately created race; bred to serve a long departed mistress.'

'Alma-Lodaka,' said Pug. Tomas had shared much of his memories of Ashen-Shugar, and had told Pug all he knew of the Pantathians, as had Macros and others over the years.

'Ah,' said Dak'it. 'You know our history.'

'A bit,' admitted Pug. Glancing around the room he said, 'Obviously not as much as I thought. From my previous encounters with your race, this city is completely unexpected.'

'Then there is much history that you do not know,' said Tak'ka. 'Many of those known to us as the Ancient Ones—'

'The Valheru,' Pug interrupted.

'Yes, though we were forbidden to use their names. She who was our mistress raised us up for her amusement and to serve her. Others of the Ancient Ones did as well, though to the best of our knowledge, only the Tiger Men in the Great South Forest also survived the centuries since the Ancient Ones rose to challenge the gods.

'Centuries ago some of us began to change. There had always been a caste among us who were talented magicians. Those you may know as the Panath-Tiandn are our most talented forgers of magic, but also our least intelligent brothers and sisters. When one is hatched, the child must be constantly watched and cared for, as well as protected from harming himself or others. It is a difficult responsibility for the parents.'

'Parents?' said Pug. 'I thought I saw families huddled together in the square, but in the mines under the Ratn'gary Mountains I only saw breeding crèches.'

An expression suggesting sadness crossed the visage of Tak'ka. 'So much to explain.' He shook his head. 'We began as a single race, a priesthood created to worship our creator. We have had centuries of debate as to our state of being, for we were not created out of the primal matter of the universe, in the fashion of humans, elves, and others, but rather we were lesser creatures—reptiles yes, though strictly not 'serpents,' yet that name has remained. Our creator took a particular breed of lizard found only on this island – ironically that creature is now extinct – and created those beings with whom you are most familiar.

'When the Ancient Ones departed, and we were told we were a free people, we had little choice but to continue in our duty. But then some of us began to change. We became more . . . Intelligent sounds boastful, doesn't it? But we did. And as that happened, two other changes occurred. We lost our ability to construct magic devices and create spells. And we lost our drive to serve our creator, She Who is Not Named.'

Pug sat back. 'I'm amazed.'

'Our evolution continued until there were three distinct, perhaps "tribes" is the best word, of my people.

'Those you know as the Serpent Priests are in the middle, I suppose you could say. They have magic ability but they are single-minded in purpose and of all of us, they most resemble those creatures created by She Who is Not Named. They are not critical thinkers or creatively intelligent, but they are very clever.

'The Panath-Tiandn are the savants of magic, but need others to care for them in the most basic way.' Looking at Amirantha he said, 'It was such as they who fashioned our magic wards against such an attack as we've endured recently. But the priesthood removes them as soon as they can, for they have their own uses for them. We are at the other end of this spectrum, those who can think for themselves, have put aside the mindless service to She Who is Not Named, and we do what we can to have full lives.'

'Astonishing,' said Pug.

Sandreena said, 'You mentioned a debate over your state of being?'

'Ah, yes.' Tak'ka nodded. Large black lidless eyes regarded her as he said, 'We wonder if we have become true beings.'

'I do not understand,' said the Sergeant-Adamant.

'We speculate on the question of souls and whether we possess them.'

Pug turned to Sandreena. 'I would think that is more in your area of expertise, serving your temple.'

Sandreena could only shake her head. 'I'm a warrior, Pug, not a philosopher. I know many in the temple who would enjoy the debate, but it is outside the scope of my knowledge or wisdom.'

'Of little matter,' said Tak'ka. 'We may have time in the future to discuss this.' He stood up and motioned for his silent compatriots to depart and as they did, he turned to the three companions. 'We have had a fair amount of contact with humans over the years. We have, or rather had, a trading post on the north shore. It was the first place the demons attacked, and all trace of it was obliterated.'

Pug glanced at his two companions. They had seen no sign of such a thing when they had landed.

'But given that our brethren in the Priesthood are frequent callers here, we always dissuaded visitors who attempt to travel farther south. Only one other human has ventured to this city and survived to leave.'

Sandreena and Amirantha tensed at the suggestion they might not be allowed to depart peacefully, but Pug raised his hand slightly, palm downward, and motioned for them to relax. 'Macros,' he said softly.

'Why, yes. You knew him?'

'Yes,' said Pug. 'How long ago?'

'More than a century. His name is recorded in our annals. He stayed with us for a short while, then departed. He was persuasive. Though I suspect had my ancestors tried to prevent his departure they would have been unsuccessful.'

'You have no idea,' Pug said with a hint of humour.

'Well, it is of little import. Other humans have reached here despite our warnings, having passed through the villages to the north. We assumed they meant ill and dealt with them harshly.' He shrugged in a very human fashion and said, 'Or there were priests visiting here and they dealt with them. Either way it's of little importance now.' He motioned for them to follow him.

'With the advent of those creatures you call demons, it's clear that we are in a situation far beyond our abilities to endure. I think we would have repulsed that last contingent of demons you so conveniently destroyed, but should another such band arrive . . .' He sighed. 'Well, I think it safe to say we would eventually be overrun. Our resources are now nearly depleted. We have refugees from the north, as you saw, crowding our plaza, and when they fled they brought little by way of foodstuffs. And winter is fast approaching.

'Our fishers and hunters roam the lands to the south of here, but we have scant hope to hold off starvation for little more than a month at best, and should the demons return . . .' He made a despairing gesture.

Pug took a moment to consider, as they left the conference room and moved deeper into the building, then said, 'If we do not run afoul of your priests, perhaps we can help.'

'You must understand we will not be able to stand apart should you, indeed, run afoul of the priests. We are created in such a way that we must defend all or any of us.'

'I understand,' said Pug, not entirely sure that he did.

They walked down a long hall until they found themselves at a circular staircase cantilevered into the wall of what appeared to be a tower. Pug judged it would rise into that large edifice he had seen behind the city's southernmost wall.

'You are regarded here with some degree of animosity, despite our understanding why you destroyed so many of our brethren. Especially the eggs in the crèches. Some of them most likely would have been more like those who you see here than the priesthood. We mourn their loss above all.'

Pug could only nod.

'As I have said,' continued Tak'ka, as he led them upward, 'we have diverged from our kin.' He led them to a large landing at the top of the stairs, sheltered from the elements by a tall dome, with an open door facing into what appeared to be an immense garden.

Pug took only a single step outside: confronting him was a completely unexpected sight. Six tall pillars of light in a diamond configuration stood in the middle of the garden. From each a faint humming, almost musical, could be heard.

'Sven-ga'ri,' said Pug.

5

FUGITIVE

Three cloaked figures hurried through the dark alley.

For the fourth time in three months, Hal and Ty found themselves being moved from one of Lady Franciezka Sorboz's safe houses to another. The two young men had fallen into the routine of simply picking up their meagre belongings and quickly following whoever came for them without question.

This time there seemed to be more urgency, more need to move quickly and not be seen. Hal wasn't sure why it felt that way, but in the months he had been hiding with Ty he had come to rely more and more on his hunter's skills, adapted to an urban setting. Alleys and streets were no more or less treacherous than trails and paths, and the predators in Roldem made up for their lack of fang and talon with guile and weapons.

It was early in the morning, perhaps an hour before sunrise, so the sight of three men skulking would certainly raise a hue and cry, given that the curfew inflicted on the population weeks before was enforced with severity by the roving gangs of marshals appointed by Lord Worthington.

Little word had reached them from their benefactor: Lady Franciezka had only visited them once in the last three weeks, and then had been tight-lipped. Something was afoot that she felt was best kept from the two young men, but both Hal and Ty could see that she was deeply troubled by whatever it was.

Since then they had been forced to endure isolation. For the frontier-bred Hal, used to wandering at will, it was more torture than he had endured in his life. He had combated it with a regimen of reading anything he could find – the lady had a prodigious library in every house she owned – and vigorous exercise, which he discovered not only enabled him to keep his weight under control, but reduced his worry and helped him sleep. And he spent hours practising his swordplay with Ty.

Ty was easily the most gifted swordsman Hal had ever faced. But in those hours of sparring, he had come to recognize patterns and weaknesses, and eventually he had begun to score his share of touches. Hal doubted he would ever be Ty's equal, but it was likely he'd never face another swordsman better than himself.

Their guide held up his hand and they stopped. He peered around a corner and motioned for them to stay close and together they hugged the storefronts that were deepest in shadow as the dawn light shone into the city. As in most ports, there was a morning mist that would burn off early in the day, but for the moment it served their purposes in shrouding their passage.

They took a circuitous route but at last found themselves at the corner of an alley and a narrow street with high buildings of two and three storeys turning it into a dark canyon.

Hurrying along, they reached a door and were inside before anyone might spy them. Inside, two armed men waited and when the three threw back their hoods, sword points were lowered. 'Good,' said one of the two who waited. 'This way.'

They followed their new guide down a short hall to the house's back stairs – the servants' passage – and ascended. On the third floor they entered a small room, used by the maid to prepare the service of meals.

The guide and the two armed men were unknown to Hal and Ty. All the two young men knew was they were working for Lady Franciezka Sorboz. All three looked dangerous. If nothing else had convinced them that the lady was important to the crown of Roldem, the seemingly endless number of these capable men at her beck and call confirmed it.

One, tall and heavily muscled, wearing the short-sleeved, close-fitting shirt and bell-bottomed trousers of a sailor said, 'A pledge, gentlemen. Lady Franciezka asks you to swear that what you are about to see remains with you and no matter what may occur in the future, you will hold your silence. Agreed?'

Hal and Ty exchanged quick glances. Then both said, 'Agreed.'

Their escort pushed open the door to the large master suite and the two young men entered. Three women sat quietly waiting inside a finely appointed parlour.

Lady Franciezka rose and waved with her hand for Hal and Ty to enter. They hesitated for a moment, for the second woman in the room – girl really – was Princess Stephané, the King's daughter. The third woman was unknown to either of them, but she was as striking a beauty as the other two.

'Your Highness, Lord Harold of Crydee and Tyrone Hawkins.'

Stephané smiled and both young men felt their stomachs

tighten, as they had the first time they had been presented to the royal family after their duel at the Masters' Court. Ty had won the Championship after Hal had been forced to withdraw due to a muscle pull during the final match.

The Princess was clad in a travelling dress, dark blue cut straight across the bodice and three-quarter-length sleeves, with a hem at mid-thigh and matching leggings. Her boots were plain and serviceable, suitable for hiking or walking. She wore no jewellery and her hair had been gathered back and pinned high.

'This is Lady Gabriella, the Princess's companion.'

Both young men bowed to the Princess and nodded acknowledgement of Lady Gabriella. Both Hal and Ty thought they must have caught a glimpse of Gabriella at the gala; but each wondered how he might have missed her if so. She was easily six feet tall in her stockinged feet, and like the Princess was dressed in travel garb: tight trousers and tunic, high boots, and a hooded cape.

Ty glanced at his companion and tried not to grin. If Franciezka noticed the byplay she chose to ignore it. 'We have a problem,' she said plainly.

Without hesitation Hal said, 'How can we help?'

'Can you sail a boat?'

They both nodded. Hal said, 'I grew up in a coastal town. I've sailed small craft since I was a child.'

'Me too,' chimed in Ty.

'Good,' said Franciezka. 'We haven't much time, so attend closely. While you two have been doing a fine job of staying out of sight, there have been events unfolding both in the palace and here in the city that were not visible to the populace. The short of it is that a coup d'état is under way.'

Both young men were stunned. At last Hal said, 'The King?'

It was Stephané who replied. 'Father and Mother are safe, for the time being.' Obviously under stress, she still managed to remain admirably calm about the danger to those she loved. 'Lord John Worthington wouldn't harm either if he can convince them to sanction my marriage to his son. Once that happens, then he can do what he needs to do to make his son king.'

'But your brothers—' began Ty.

'Safe, for the moment,' said Franciezka. 'None of them are where Worthington assumes them to be. For the time being, Lord John is content to think he has the three princes confined.'

The two young men glanced at one another, both instantly realizing that it would be futile to ask where they were.

Franciezka said, 'What I need to do is take care of two problems at once.' She looked at Hal. 'Kesh has agents looking for you. I seem to have blunted their search, but there is another player, whom I do not know, and that has me concerned. Those agents are doubly dangerous because some of them used to be mine.'

Hal and Ty said nothing, but their expressions revealed surprise.

'I was certain by now you had some sense of my role in the affairs of Roldem.'

Hal said, 'I assumed your role was important, but I hadn't thought about spies.'

Ty said, with some chagrin, 'I did, but dismissed the idea. I thought you might be . . . a special friend to one of the princes?'

At that Stephané laughed. 'My brothers? They are sweet, but none of them could keep up with our good lady here.' Her tone revealed a mix of admiration and no little distrust. If Franciezka was the spy-mistress of Roldem, that distrust was likely well earned.

'With former agents of mine in play, my identity is no longer a matter of state secret. Once this is over, and should we all survive, I will be of little use to the Crown in my current role.'

'Are these turned agents working for Lord Worthington?' asked Ty.

'Almost certainly. I'm the only one who knows where the

Princess is hiding. Otherwise Lord John would have sent squads of soldiers to my door to fetch the Princess back. The princes are currently surrounded by men of unquestioning loyalty, but those are few in number. The rest of the army and navy take their orders from the Crown, which at this point means they take orders from Lord John Worthington. But should he attempt to force them to return to the palace, it could start a civil war he's not certain to win.' She took a deep breath, crossing her arms. Her right index finger tapped idly against her left arm while she considered. 'No, we're dealing with a handful of my former men who know me well enough to pick their moment, once they discover exactly where I've hidden Her Highness. They don't have enough swords to do otherwise, and even if they could overwhelm those loyal to me, they would expose themselves as traitors.'

Ty said, 'What must we do?'

'For about two hours, nothing; but then we must move and do so at great speed. Kesh's flotilla is anchored less than a half-mile outside the harbour mouth. They are content to let ships bound for the Empire pass without trouble. Their position appears to be one of keeping a wedge between the two Kingdoms, and to keep Roldem's war fleet from venturing out. We've managed to move a few smaller ships – refitted to look like trading vessels – out of the harbour, heading south, as if heading for Pointer's Head. Any ship headed towards the Eastern Kingdoms is stopped at the Straits of Ilthros, boarded and searched, and if no contraband is found, it is given safe passage.' She paused to see if the two young men were following. 'Do you understand what you must do?'

Hal nodded. 'I'm vague on the details, which I'm sure you've already anticipated, but we are to get the Princess and her companion off this island, to somewhere beyond Worthington's reach.'

Ty said, 'You want her in Rillanon.'

Franciezka smiled. 'Aren't you the bright one?'

'Rillanon?' said Hal. 'I would have thought somewhere in the east, like Olasko.'

Ty shook his head. 'Worthington might be able to pry her from the gentle protection of the Duke of Olasko, if he's ignorant of what's occurring here. But if Her Highness is safely visiting King Gregory's court, with the Kingdom and Keshian fleets between Worthington and the Princess . . . ?' He smiled and looked at the Princess. 'It seemed a bit obvious to me.'

Hal's brow furrowed. 'Well enough, but exactly how are the two of us going to sail from here to there? That's almost the entire length of the Sea of Kingdoms.'

'That would be foolish. No, we'll hide you in a ship bound for Watcher's Point in Miskalon, but at the right time you'll be put over the side in a specially-provisioned boat, and with the gods' grace, you'll land in Ran.' She turned and picked up some folded parchments. 'With these documents, you'll have safe passage should you encounter any Roldemish ships.'

Hal inspected them then handed them over to Ty. 'The King agrees?'

'The King wishes to be ignorant of the details. I've forged his signature enough times no one can tell the difference, not even the King.'

'The seals look perfect,' said Ty as he inspected the documents.

'They should be,' said Lady Franciezka. 'I have the royal seals safely hidden away.'

Ty grinned as Hal's mouth dropped open.

Lady Franciezka smiled. 'The King might be persuaded to sign decrees against his better judgment by Worthington, but without the seals . . .' She shrugged, then handed a purse heavy with coin to Ty. 'Now, you should be able to arrange for a fast Kingdom ship from there to Rillanon. You'll be behind the Keshian blockade. If that turns out not to be the safe choice, then hire a coach to Bas-Tyra.'

'When do we leave?' asked Hal.

'In two hours. My cargo ship has already been inspected prior to departure. We'll slip you aboard moments before she weighs anchor. My only concern will be getting you past the Keshians at the blockade line, but I think everything is ready.'

Hal and Ty exchanged a look that silently communicated they hoped all was ready as well.

The quarters were cramped aboard the ship, *Meklin's Lady*: one small cabin for the four of them. Hal and Ty tried to ignore each other when they slept side by side on the narrow floor but in vain since each swell the ship breasted caused them to roll up against each other. The two young women, however, seemed able to abide sharing a narrow bunk designed for one person, despite Lady Gabriella's height.

They had come aboard two mornings previously, an hour before dawn, while most of the crew still slept. Only the captain, first officer, and a few of the crew knew about the passengers. The rest were kept ignorant, and by design the second officer's cabin had been left unfilled this voyage. Designed for one person, and that barely, it proved very cramped for four. One berth against the bulkhead, a single large window, a tiny chest under a small table with a water basin barely gave anyone room to move. A single curtain opposite the bunk opened on a small door through which they found the officer's garderobe, called 'the captain's jakes.'

It had taken remarkable self-restraint to keep calm and relaxed in those quarters, but the four had discovered that telling humorous stories passed the time. As it was rare for any common seaman to venture into the stern-castle, they did not fear being overheard, but still tried to keep their voices low. Food had been provided in the form of a large sack of dried fruit, jerked meat, fresh bread, and two large water skins. Their confinement was only for two days and nights, but they could not leave their quarters, save for a quick dash to the captain's jakes, which proved to be nothing more than a seat with a hole that hung over the open water. Ty found himself wondering how the officers employed it during rough weather.

In the two days the young men found the two young women to be excellent company. The Princess was well educated, which was to be expected, but she was also a young woman of strong opinions, which was not. Rather than some prized flower to be sheltered and shielded, she seemed to have a point of view on everything, not least of which was the rise and ambition of Sir John Worthington. Hal could not keep from grinning when she described how she wanted him treated when her father regained control of the state. To call some of the images grisly was to understate. Hal realized that in its own way, court politics was warfare and a princess of Roldem had to be a different sort of warrior. His initial infatuation was soon replaced by a strong attraction coupled with newfound respect. Whoever married the Princess would be a lucky man; one with his hands full, but lucky nevertheless.

Lady Gabriella was less chatty than the Princess, but she was pleasant. Hal noticed that Ty seemed very taken with the tall lady-in-waiting, which wasn't difficult to understand. She was stunning once you accepted that she was not the usual, dainty lady of the court. From the way she looked, Hal reckoned she was a trained fighter, and her role was more than that of a simple companion. Franciezka had most certainly hand-selected her to act as Stephané's bodyguard. She was a woman of few words, content to let the other three banter as much as they wished, apparently comfortable with silence. Hal watched how she moved with economy, her eyes always glancing around, even in these closed quarters, in case a threat should suddenly appear.

Now they waited. Within the hour they should be sighting Kesh's picket ships, on blockade against any ship bound for the Kingdom of Isles ports. The captain had taken a deliberately slow tack so they would reach the point of inspection after dark. He wanted bored, tired Keshian sailors inspecting his cargo.

Hal smiled nervously. 'I've never liked waiting,' he admitted.

Stephané grinned. 'And I've never had to wait for anything.'

Ty laughed. 'The baby daughter with three older brothers? And a princess, to boot? Of course you never did!'

All eyes turned to Gabriella who shrugged as if waiting was no issue for her. 'It will take the same amount of time however we feel about it. We might as well rest while we can.' She sat up slightly and glanced out at the falling light through the rear windows of the cabin. 'I suspect soon things will get exciting enough.'

There came a knock at the cabin door and the captain opened it gently – last time, he had banged it into the back of Hal's head. 'It's time,' he said. 'Stand aside, please.' He moved to the small chest under the tiny table, opened it and put a sack inside. 'If they find nothing to confiscate, they get suspicious. Something slightly illicit, such as a sack of Dream . . . ?' He smiled as he closed the chest.

Ty grinned. 'Illegal in Roldem—'

'And the Isles,' interrupted Hal.

'—but not in Kesh,' finished the captain. The mildly hallucinogenic drug was made from the oil of a common plant in both Kingdoms.

'And the next ship by might benefit from a less alert crew,' offered the captain. Then, losing his smile, he said, 'Come with me.'

They gathered up the sack of food and the water skins and followed him. They had been expecting to go deep into the hold of the ship and be secreted somewhere among the cargo, but instead they were taken mere steps, into the captain's cabin. It was easily three times the size of the second officer's quarters, and Hal glanced around feeling a little envious.

'Help me,' said the captain, indicating that the two young men should grab the other end of the large bed set hard against the starboard bulkhead. It was a standard looking affair with a six foot long bunk set above two rows of double drawers, in which the captain's personal belongings would be placed. They lifted the mattress and bed board easily, so they carried it away a few feet, and placed it on the deck. 'Now the tricky part,' said the captain. 'The drawers have to come out in a certain order. That one, first,' he said, pointing to the upper left one.

As Hal pulled it out and lifted it, he heard a tiny click.

'Now that one,' said the captain, pointing at the lower right. Ty pulled it out and a second click was heard. Then came the upper right, and lower left, and when all four drawers were sitting on the deck, the captain reached down into the now empty space where his bed had rested and pulled up on a well concealed removable section of floor. The board was hinged, six feet wide and three feet deep. 'You've got a tight fit, but if you wiggle down in there, you can lie side by side with your heads under the bed. Be careful not to knock the supports for the drawers out of kilter – have to get them back in place.' He glanced and said, 'I think you lads on either side, in case we get to rolling a bit – it'll make it easier on the ladies.' He motioned to the Princess and Lady Gabriella. 'You first, ladies.'

Both women in turn stepped over the front of the empty drawer front and wiggled to get down in the empty smuggler's hold.

'Now you lads,' said the captain.

Hal and Ty clambered over the low barrier, avoiding the supports for the drawers as they moved between the girls and the walls. Hal was embarrassed to discover he had no room to move and was pressed hard against the Princess. He muttered an apology as the captain lowered the flooring over their heads, only to find a slender finger pressed against his lips. 'I don't mind, really,' she whispered. The drawers were replaced and they found themselves in darkness.

A few moments passed by with Hal being painfully aware of the contact between them. As well as being the most beautiful young woman he had ever encountered, she was wonderful company. He had got to the point where at least once an hour he had to remind himself that she was unobtainable, and his only reasonable course of action was to be a gentleman and her friend. But now, with the scent of her hair in his nostrils somehow blanking out the wretched aroma of bilge water below them, he was finding that very difficult.

He wondered how much of this was due to being confined and not wanting to be overwhelmed with a sense of vulnerability. Damn it, he thought to himself, it was Martin who was the introspective one who let this sort of business slow him down. Thinking of Martin, he let his thoughts wander to his father and brother, to his mother and Lady Bethany and all those back home. He wondered how they were and prayed silently that they were safe and well.

Everyone lay silently, listening to any sounds from above. At last faint voices could be heard, though the words were unintelligible. In the dark Hal could only sense Lady Gabriella and Ty, though he knew they were only a hand's span away. The only reason the situation didn't become embarrassing was the sense of risk and danger. The part of his mind not achingly aware of the Princess pressed hard against him was attempting to picture what was taking place on deck, the conversation between the captain and whoever the Keshians sent aboard to inspect the ship. Would it be a quick, cursory inspection, or would they be crawling over the ship from topmast to bilge, eventually pulling out the drawers above them?

And for how long? He was feeling slight cramps from the awkward position in which he found himself and the air was growing close. He knew that should they be discovered he would be unable to leap to his feet to defend the Princess.

In short Harold conDoin, unknown to himself the new Duke of Crydee, was feeling something he had never experienced before in his life: helplessness. And he didn't care for it one bit. Time had become meaningless and it felt as if he had been motionless for hours, not minutes.

Suddenly the sound of the drawers being removed intruded upon his thoughts. Then up came the floor and for a second the light was blinding.

'Out you come,' said the captain and Hal reached up and took the extended hand. He almost groaned from the stiffness in his shoulders, back, and legs as he was glad for the help up. He pulled Ty out and in turn they helped the Princess and Lady Gabriella out of the cramped hiding hole. 'No troubles, then?' asked Hal.

'No,' said the captain. 'This one took to haggling a bit longer than usual on the price of the "fine" for the bag of Dream, and I didn't want to make him suspicious by agreeing too quickly to the "fee" for safe passage. It may be Lady Franciezka's gold I'm bribing him with, but I had to act as if it was my own.'

'You bribed him?'

'Not a ship leaving Roldem gets past that Keshian picket without a hefty bribe, sir.' The captain grinned. 'It's why I think the Kingdom wins the war at sea. Less corruption, you see, almost as hide-bound as Roldem's fleet; comes from being island kingdoms, I expect. If I tried to bribe a Kingdom picket captain, well, I'd be clapped in irons and my ship impounded straight away.' He glanced at the ladies as they adjusted crumpled clothing and said, 'I'd wait a bit, but soon you'll be free to come up on deck and get some air.'

Ty said, 'We need it.'

'It was a bit close in there,' said the Princess. She glanced at Hal and gave him a small smile.

Lady Gabriella shot Ty an appraising look. 'You didn't seem to mind.'

Ty had the good grace to flush. 'Lady, I assure you.'

'No insult, sir,' she said with a slightly mocking tone. 'You were as much a gentleman as the circumstances allowed.' Then she added, *sotto voce*, 'Which wasn't much.'

Hal laughed. 'She's onto you, Ty.'

Shaking his head Ty said, 'Apparently so. Anyone thirsty besides me?'

When affirmative replies were voiced, he said, 'I'll see about getting something to drink, wine perhaps if they have it?'

'On this ship?' said Hal. 'Spirits most likely, or ale, but I'll settle for fresh water.' He indicated the almost depleted water skins.

'As will I,' said Stephané.

Ty stepped out of the cabin and was back inside moments later. 'Sailor says he'll fetch us something.'

An awkward silence followed as the four waited. The two young men had various encounters with young women in their day, but neither had been forced into such familiarity with ladies of rank. Now that the immediate danger was past, Hal was profoundly aware of just how close he had been to the Princess. Silently he cursed to himself; did her skin have to be that soft? He forced himself to take a breath and studied the object of his affection. She seemed lost in her own thoughts; or perhaps she was avoiding eye contact.

Something similar seemed to be going on with Lady Gabriella and Ty, though Hal thought she seemed amused by Ty's awkwardness rather than embarrassed.

It was hard to judge. Even after all this time in close quarters, Hal knew next to nothing about her. She was a big woman, but there was nothing about her plump or soft. Her face was classically beautiful, with her brown eyes and a nose that was straight and delicate, her mouth occasionally revealing a stunning smile. In her leather travel togs, she looked as if she'd fit right in at Crydee, and Hal could imagine her riding next to Bethany on the hunt.

Thinking of Bethany he realized he had barely spared her a thought, or at least no more than he had his brothers and parents, since coming east. He missed Crydee, and worried how his family fared now that war had come, but he felt no more for Bethany than before he had left the West. She was nothing like the Princess, who was everything he expected in a court lady: more, she was his perfect image of a princess.

What Hal found remarkable about Stephané was she was tough; not strong in an overt fashion, in the way Bethany or Gabriella were, but she had a subtle toughness, a resilience, an ability to face threat quietly and with dignity, rather than crumbling before what must certainly be the most terrifying experience of her life. The most eligible woman in the Sea of Kingdoms, the most sought-after bride in recent history, she had been spirited from her home in the middle of the night, away from her family for the first time in her life, hidden from men determined to capture her and use her for their own political ends, risking dangers undreamed of in her life, yet here she sat, quietly chatting, composed and showing glimpses of humour, and calm.

Hal realized he was falling desperately in love with her.

He buried such emotions deep inside. His father had always expected him to marry Bethany, but had often talked of political marriages for Martin and Brendan. This much Hal knew: his wife, if it wasn't Bethany, would be a woman who gained some political advantage for Crydee, and the marriage would be a benefit to the Kingdom as a whole, or at least the Western Realm. And in this time of war, who knew what that might mean? But if it was Bethany, it would be a woman he loved already, even if it was as a sister, and one who would prove to be worthy of all the devotion he could provide. He closed his eyes a second and tried to will his mind away from his true feelings.

Moments later, the door to the cabin opened and the captain stuck his head in. 'It's time.'

They rose and followed him up to the main deck.

The departure went quickly and quietly. A dinghy rigged with a sail was already halfway over the side by the time they had reached the deck and a rope ladder was thrown down. Ty and Hal were first over the side, followed by the Princess and Lady Gabriella. The captain had pointed the heading and Hal and Ty fixed their position by the early morning stars and shoved off.

The sail had proven problematic as the boat tended to drift to port, but as they were aiming for a long stretch of Kingdom coastline, a slight deviation from their course shouldn't be a problem. Either side of the Kingdom city of Ran would be acceptable, and should they spy the harbour, all the better.

There was little conversation as the women huddled under a great cloak provided by the captain against the night's chill. The two young men were intent upon keeping their course as the sun rose and when it did they thought they could see land.

Hal pointed to a brown smudge to the northwest and said, 'Head for that!'

Ty nodded. If Hal was correct that smudge would be cooking fires from a coastal town or even the port of Ran. The wind rose with the morning sun, a spanking breeze but from the north-west, forcing them to tack on some very long reaches. Hal sat at the tiller with Lady Gabriella and the Princess sitting on the windward side of the boat, while Ty waited in the bow ready to haul on the sheet to trim the single sail. Each time they shifted course, Hal had to duck his head under the wide swinging boom while the girls ducked down and waited, then shifted to the opposite side of the dinghy.

The coast grew progressively closer each time they swung to the north, but as they were almost sailing into the teeth of the wind it made for slow going. Two hours after sunrise, Ty shouted, 'Sails, off to port!'

Ty risked standing for a moment, then sat down again and said, 'That can't be the Keshian picket. We haven't sailed that far.'

Ty shielded his face from the low sun. Finally he said, 'I see red sails!'

'Oh, bloody hell,' said Hal. 'Pirates.'

Ty said, 'That's a Ceresian raiding fleet or I'm a duck. Turn about and make a run for the coast!'

'Ready about!' Hal cried warning he was turning the boat hard, and to be wary of the swinging boom. It would be very inconvenient if someone fell over the side at that moment. The girls ducked as he pulled on the tiller, saying, 'Hard a'lee!'

The two women moved swiftly to the windward side of the boat and Hal lost any concern for a cautious approach to the coast. He shouted to Ty, 'Are we seen?'

As low as their boat was to the water and as far as they were from the sails, it was possible that they would go unnoticed by any lookouts aloft on the pirate ships.

'I can't tell!' Ty called back. Then he pointed. 'Look!'

The brown smudge they had first spied was resolving itself into a column of smoke rising from fires along the coast. As they were heading straight to it, it quickly became apparent this was a coastal raid.

'Where are we?' shouted Hal.

'I don't know,' answered Ty. 'That's too small to be Ran. Lister perhaps? Or maybe Michaelsberg?'

The air now had the acrid tang of smoke and was turning hazy as they were sailing directly into the wind as best as Hal could manage. Their eyes teared from the sting and Gabriella sneezed.

'We've got to get out of here,' said Ty.

Hal pulled gently against the tiller until the sails started to luff. He was gauging when best to turn back towards the coast on a long tack away from the fight.

Ty said, 'That ship we're following is slowing!'

Hal stood slightly to look over the girls' heads. 'They're trimming sails.'

Suddenly they were running straight at the stern of the ship and Hal shouted, 'Ready about!'

The girls ducked as Hal turned the boat and the wind blew away a particularly hazy patch of smoke so that the sterncastle of the ship they had been trailing could now be clearly seen.

The three-masted ship heeled over slightly as the crew adjusted the sails and Ty shouted, 'It's a Ceresian dromon!' This one was painted black with red trim around the rails, and the sails were dark red tanbark. The ship was common to Kesh, but many such had found their ways north to the shores of the Eastern Kingdoms. Usually crewed by forty to sixty men, plus a bank of rowers, they were not as fast as Kingdom ships but their shallow draft and lateen sails allowed them to sail much closer into shore than the deepwater square-masted Kingdom frigates. And in close, with the rowers providing the power, they were good for short bursts of speed that could bring them into contact with their prey before a ship with only sails could manoeuvre away.

A lookout on the stern chanced to turn; he saw the small dinghy, pointed and shouted.

Ty cried, 'We're seen!'

Hal hauled over on the tiller without warning and the two women ducked under the boom just in time. Ty almost lost his balance.

'Sorry!' shouted Hal.

The dromon was a shallow draught ship, but it couldn't ride into the beach as the dinghy could. If they beached the dromon the crew would have to dig sand trenches beneath the hull at low tide, unload every piece of cargo and provisions, then wait for high tide to lift her and try to tow her back to sea with longboats.

Hal glanced back a moment and saw that the pirate vessel was now reefing sails and that men on deck were scrambling to lower boats. 'They're coming after us!'

Ty said, 'There!' pointing at the shoreline.

Hal stared at the open beach on the other side of the white foam breakers. Ty waited until they could feel the shore current and the boat lifting on a swell and he leapt to unfasten the sheets and lower the sail. Hall let go of the tiller and lashed down the boom so it wouldn't swing.

Lady Gabriella was already pulling up one oar as Ty reached to grab the other. Unceremoniously, Ty shouted, 'Move!' to Stephané, then belatedly added, 'Er, Highness.'

Stephané ignored the lack of formality. 'Their boats are in the water.'

Hal looked over his shoulder and saw a boat pushing away from the ship, now anchored, and another with crew climbing down ropes ready to follow. He looked ahead and shouted, 'Pull!'

Ty and Gabriella both hauled on their oars and the boat moved up and away, rising on another swell as they edged closer to the beach. Hal looked back again and saw the pirates' longboats each had six oarsmen and he knew they'd be a lot closer by the time the dinghy reached the beach.

Hal looked beyond the approaching shore and saw a fairly uniform rise beyond the sand. Tableland overlooked the beaches, but no more than ten or twelve feet above. With careful slow climbing they could probably reach the grass if they had time to find a suitable gully. Then he spied a sand mound that rose up to the tableland. He turned the bow of the dinghy towards it.

'Ready!' shouted the Princess as they were picked up by a comber that turned into a wave and accelerated them into the shore. The dinghy rode it into the sand then ground to a sudden halt.

'Over there!' Hal shouted, pointing to the mound he had spied. They climbed quickly out of the dinghy. Ty grabbed one bundle of provisions and Hal the other as he leapt out. The pirate longboats were bearing down. Hal judged they might be lucky to have a five-minute head start.

They turned and ran.

6

CONSPIRACIES

Jim ran.

The vaguely important, always elusive minor noble from the west forced his way past startled courtiers and annoyed servants as he raced through the halls of the King's palace in Rillanon. Dishevelled and dirty from miles of fast travel, he was nearly exhausted yet found the strength to single-handedly disrupt the business of the palace for the day. His violent haste was understandable and those who recognized him quickly nodded in sympathy: his grandfather was dying.

Jim cursed the gods, the fates, whim, bad

luck, any other agency he could imagine who might have conspired to have him away from the Kingdom's home island when word reached him of his grandfather's illness. His last Tsurani transport orb had been destroyed by a Keshian agent, and he had to rely on Pug's son Magnus to return to Rillanon from Sorcerer's Isle after his last meeting with Pug. He had agents, if he could trust them, attempting to secure more orbs from a LaMutian artificer of Tsurani descent who claimed he could make them, but as yet none of the promised devices had been forthcoming.

As a result of this, when word of his grandfather's situation had reached him on the mainland he had been halfway to the city of Ran to observe Keshian activities in that region. He had ridden like a madman to the royal docks in the city of Rodez, only to discover the entire royal fleet had been dispatched to picket duty in support of the fleet out of Ran. So he had purchased outright the fastest ship he could find, a dilapidated fishing boat in need of a complete overhaul, and made straight for Rillanon.

Jim had encountered no Keshian ships this far inside Kingdom waters but had been challenged on the outskirts of Sadara, the Kingdom's second-largest city outside the mainland. He presented his documents, then ordered the crew to sink the schooner rather than bother towing it, and commandeered their frigate.

Riding horses into the ground, sailing on a filthy fishing boat, and having no means to improve his appearance on the frigate lent him an entirely woeful and disreputable appearance when he finally reached the royal docks in Rillanon City. But if the naval guards at the quay wondered who this dirty traveller might be, the fact that he was rowed ashore by a very deferential crew of sailors from a royal frigate caused them to stand aside as he hurried past and up the long incline to the main street above.

Jim had dodged indifferent workers, curious merchants, and concerned guards. Rillanon was on a full wartime footing and the appearance of anyone out of the ordinary was cause for alarm. He had been challenged by the officer at the gate, but in less than a minute he was riding on that officer's horse, racing up the long road from the harbour to the palace.

Nearing his grandfather's private chambers now, he saw two guards posted outside. He spoke forcefully, 'Open the bloody doors!'

'No one is admitted without—'

That was as far as he got before Jim shoved past the guard and started to push open the door. The other guard reached over and found himself on the floor before he could put hands on Jim.

The doors swung wide into the antechamber of his grandfather's apartment, and Jim was confronted by another pair of sentries, but with the addition of a sergeant of the royal household guard. Rather than try to physically attack Jim, the old soldier merely stood before the door with his hands up, palms out saying, 'Hold up a minute, Jimmy.'

Recognizing the sergeant, Jim said, 'I want to see grandfather, Jacky.'

Sergeant Jack Mallory nodded. 'He's sleeping, and you're a fright.'

Jim began to calm down as the guards he had knocked over hurried up behind him. The sergeant made a shooing motion towards the outer door.

'How is he?' asked Jim.

Motioning for Jim to follow him, the sergeant moved away and keeping his voice low, said, 'Well, your grandfather's old, Jimmy. But there's something else . . .'

'What?' asked Jim, his eyes narrowing.

'You know I've been with the old man for . . . well, since you were a baby,' whispered the sergeant.

Jim nodded.

'I think I know him pretty well, his moods, his good days, his bad days, you know what I mean.'

'Yes,' said Jim. 'What is it?'

'Something's not quite right here. I can't put my finger on it, but your grandfather started complaining about his stomach a month ago. You know him. He doesn't complain.'

Jim nodded again. After a moment he said, 'You suspect poison?'

'After the way things have been around here, I suspect everything.'

Jim felt exasperated. He had raced without rest from halfway to the eastern border of the Kingdom only to return to this. 'What do the healers say? The priests?'

'No one says anything, and whatever you hear comes from the office of Sir William Alcorn. That's why those lads outside were so anxious to stop you. Orders are no one sees your grandfather without Sir William's writ.'

Jim reached into his tunic and pulled out a small purse hanging from a cord around his neck and opened it. A folded piece of parchment was all it contained and Jim took it out, unfolded it and handed it to the sergeant.

Sergeant Mallory read it. Then he said, 'You play Follow-the-Queen Poker, Jimmy?'

'Terrible game. What's the point?'

'Well, as we'd say in that game, a command from the Duke of Rillanon trumps any orders given by Sir William, despite him having the title of King's Magistrate.' He grinned. 'Or at least that's how I see it and even if the King should think otherwise, I'll stand before him and say that's how I see it right now.'

'Thank you, Jacky.'

'Now, you get to your quarters and get cleaned up, and as soon as he stirs, I'll send for you. You look like you could use a bath, meal, and nap, Jimmy.'

Jim smiled. Sergeant Mallory was one of the few around who called him 'Jimmy.' It came from when he had been a little boy and used to play being 'Jimmyhand' his legendary great-grandfather, Lord James, the first Jamison.

Without another word, Jim nodded, turned and left the

antechamber to his grandfather's private apartment and walked slowly towards his own quarters. He saw a page hurrying down the hall and stopped him.

'Sir?' the boy asked.

'Do you know me?'

The boy almost squinted as he looked at the dishevelled, dirty man before him, then recognition dawned. 'Sir James?'

'Close enough. I'm going to my quarters. I wish to be undisturbed for two hours. After which I want a hot bath, and while it's being prepared I need half a roasted chicken, a bowl of rice, roasted potatoes, or turnips. A flagon of wine, and whatever fruit and vegetables they have ready to serve. Do you understand?'

'Yes, m'lord.'

Jim walked to his own quarters and was almost staggering by the time he reached them. He fell onto his bed and was asleep before his head struck the pillow.

Jim was vaguely aware of a warm body snuggled in close behind him as he woke up. It took him only moments to be aware of his surroundings, but he still felt groggy as he asked, 'You awake?'

'Of course,' said the female voice behind him.

He rolled over and found himself looking into a pair of dark eyes set in a lovely face of dusky skin – Keshian ancestry that had served her well over the years. James lifted himself on one arm and saw a maid's dress draped over the chair at his writing desk. He glanced down at the naked young woman. 'You're a maid again?'

'I thought it best to be in a believable role should someone interrupt your sleep. It also explains why I might have lingered after bringing in all that food you ordered.' She indicated the large tray placed on a table opposite the bed, an ornate silver affair with a matching flagon.

'The young lord and the willing maid, it is then?'

With a mocking smile she said, 'Young lord?'

'I said to be awoken, then brought food while I bathed.'

'I tried to wake you,' she returned. With lowered lashes and a half-smile, she added, 'In several ways. It was obvious you needed sleep. You were exhausted. You slept through the night. I'm afraid the wine is no longer chilled and the chicken is cold.'

'Better than I've had for a while.'

'No doubt. I can send for fresh.'

'Don't bother. Now, what do you know?' said James as he rolled off bed and realized he was also naked. 'Did you undress me?'

'Yes,' she said standing up. 'It wasn't very convincing me being naked under the covers and you being full dressed on top.' She grinned. 'It's not the first time I've removed your clothing.'

He returned the smile. 'Well, you certainly didn't bathe me,' he said, wrinkling his nose.

'Your bath's been ready for almost an hour. I ordered it when I thought you likely to wake.'

'So what's your name?' he asked as he followed her, admiring her nearly-flawless body as she proceeded into the bathing chamber. Her soft curves belied a toughness he had personally honed over the years. Of all his agents, she was not only one of the best at getting information, she was as hard to kill as a cockroach. A childhood with the Mockers of Krondor had trained her in ways few not born on the street could begin to imagine. He had never asked her to play the role of assassin, but he suspected she would do so without question and very effectively.

She opened the door and moved aside so he could step into a warm tub of water in the middle of a room. 'I'm called Anne right now.'

He settled into the still-warm tub and gave a satisfied sigh. Many times in his life his chosen role had required him to go days, weeks even, without being properly clean. He sat back as Anne poured a jug of warm water over his head and began shampooing vigorously. 'Weren't you Anne in . . . ?'

'Salador,' she supplied.

'So, what do we know?' he asked.

Leaning over the edge of the tub, Anne said, 'I've been here about a month, since I got your message in Krondor. I've found nothing substantial, but this palace is awash with rumours.'

'It's the palace. There are always rumours.'

'Yes, but as you taught me,' she said scrubbing his back, 'there are rumours and there are rumours.'

'I don't have time to sift through rumours. If you can't tell me what you know, tell me what you think.'

Leaning over to scrub his chest from behind, her face near his ear, she whispered, 'Sir William Alcorn is putting those loyal to him, or at least in his debt, into key positions and the King seems to have no objection. Your grandfather most certainly did.'

'And you think this has something to do with my grandfather's health?'

'Hard to say, Jim,' she said as she draped her arms around his neck. 'I've nosed around as much as I can and the healing priests and chirurgeons all seem above suspicion. Maybe one of them might be working for someone trying to get your grandfather out of the way, but the others would have likely found some hint of magic or poison.

'He is an old man, Jim.'

'He's the only family I have left, or at least the only family left that still speaks to me.'

She shrugged. As an orphan she had even less family, but over the years she had come to appreciate that the topic of Jim's family was only under discussion when he brought it up. She knew there had been many difficulties between Jim and his father, his Uncle Dasher, and his cousin Richard. Some of it was political, for reasons Jim never mentioned, and some of it was family history, for reasons even more obscure. But she had been around Lord James long enough to read his moods. 'You're really worried, aren't you?'

'I am.'

'I have a theory should you wish to hear it.'

'Go on.'

'I believe your grandfather may have been poisoned, but not to the extent of trying to kill him.'

Jim was silent for a moment, then said, 'Keep him out of the way, but not raise suspicion by a death?'

'He's been too ill to be an effective counter to Sir William Alcorn's shenanigans for over two weeks.' She paused, then said, 'He's very clever, our Sir William, and very deft. It's as if he has everything slowly moving until he's poised, then suddenly—,' she clapped her hands together, '—he's moved two or three people around before anyone can mount an objection. Moreover, even before your grandfather took ill, his influence had grown. His relationship with the King, going back to when they were young soldiers together . . .' She let the thought run out, and shrugged. Both knew that the 'simple' court knight had become the most powerful man in the Kingdom, usurping the position held by Jim's grandfather. 'What do you think?' she asked.

Before he could answer, the door in the other room opened and someone came in. Anne leapt into the tub with Jim with a squeal of laughter, splashing water over the floor.

Jim looked up to see a soldier standing inside his quarters looking embarrassed. 'Sorry sir, but I knocked and you didn't answer.'

Feigning annoyance, Jim said, 'Can't you see I'm occupied?'

'It's your grandfather, sir. He's awake and asking for you.'

Jim made a show of forcing Anne off him, grabbed a towel and saw the guard trying very hard not to watch Anne as she climbed out of the tub. Whoever he might report to would hear only a sordid narration of a bored noble and a maid of easy virtue, nothing out of the ordinary in the palace.

Jim dressed quickly, tossing a look over his shoulder to Anne. 'Be on your way, girl. Perhaps I'll have time for you tonight.'

'Sir,' she said as if annoyed yet hopeful. She knew that

meant she was to find him tonight so they could compare notes on what he had learned.

He dressed quickly and followed the guard to his grandfather's apartment where Sergeant Mallory was back at his post. 'Sir,' he said with a quick salute as two guards opened the doors into his grandfather's apartment.

Propped up in his large bed, James Jamison, second of that name to hold the title of Duke of Rillanon, beckoned for his grandson to come closer. No one needed to say anything; Jim took one look at the old man and knew he was near death. He walked to the bedside and leaned over, kissing his grandfather's forehead.

'Good to see you, lad,' whispered the old man.

'Good to see you, Grandfather.'

'Now,' he said patting the bed beside him, 'sit down and shut up. There's a lot I need to tell you and not much time.'

Jim sat down and waited for his grandfather to tell him something vital.

It was a shaken James Jamison who left his grandfather's quarters an hour later. Even those who knew him well might not see any outward sign, but inside Jim was as near to a state of panic as he had been in his entire life. His world was coming apart at the seams.

Jim was the eyes and ears of the Kingdom, the trader in secrets and hidden truths, but his grandfather had command of the Congress of Lords and knew the temper of the nobility of the two realms, from the Duchy of Ran to the Far Coast. Between the two of them they had pieced together a puzzle that had been baffling them both for more than a year prior to the outbreak of war between Kesh and the Kingdom.

Politics was more the province of his grandfather. His late uncle, Dasher, likewise had been a political animal. Jim's father had been much more like his great-grandfather, Arutha, son of the first James, a gifted administrator, bright and likable, but otherwise not especially remarkable. And his cousin Richard was a soldier with all the noble and annoying traits that required. One thing about Richard, Jim knew, was that he might currently be one of the few soldiers he could rely on, and that he commanded the Prince's Army in Krondor, which might prove vital before all was said and done.

Not all Jamisons were suited to governance; most were gifted in whatever role life provided, but only Jim had developed the same lethal set of skills and the cold nerve to use them in service to the Crown that his namesake, the original James, Jimmy the Hand, had enjoyed. And now it looked as if he was going to need every shred of talent he possessed as well as every bitter experience, harsh lesson, and the famous Jameson luck to thwart what was now clearly shaping up to be a bid to seize the crown of the Kingdom of the Isles.

While he had been busy trying to uncover who had been subverting or killing off his operatives and why Kesh was moving towards the Kingdom, someone else had been busy plotting a coup d'état and from what his grandfather had said, they were close to ready.

James stopped as he reached the major hallway bisecting the palace. Ahead were his own quarters and those of other royal retainers and functionaries, while to the right were offices and the guards' quarters to either side of the entrance to the royal wing, containing the great hall, the King's apartments and the living quarters of the household staff. To the left was the grand entrance and steps down to the palace's marshalling yard.

In as many years as he could remember, this was the first time Jim Dasher, Lord Jamison, had no idea where to go next. He knew that he must be in the palace for at least another night and day, but after that?

His network of agents was compromised; yet he had been almost arrogant in his certainty of his own cleverness in taking what his grandfather had begun, grafting onto it his great uncle's Mockers. He had spent years successfully infiltrating every stratum of Kingdom society and not a little of Kesh, Queg, and the Free Cities in the west with spies and provocateurs. No activity from affairs of state down to smuggling along the coast escaped his notice, and he had been supreme in the Bitter Sea.

Or so he had thought until Amed Dabu Asam had tried to kill him. His most trusted agent in Kesh, one of his most trusted anywhere, and now he was a man Jim would take great delight in seeing dead.

With Amed compromised, Jim assumed his entire ring of spies west of Land's End must be untrustworthy. Even if he was to survive all this . . . if the Kingdom was to survive all this, not one man in Kesh could be trusted.

From what he had been able to discover on his own coupled with what his grandfather had told him, Jim could assume only about a third of his agents were still in place and trustworthy.

He realized palace servants and minor Kingdom officials passing by were taking notice of him. If he was going to dither, he might as well do it while going somewhere. He knew a place near the merchants' quarters where he could both dine and arrange for certain agents to find him. He turned towards the grand entrance and the outer gates of the palace.

It had been nearly a year since he had been in Rillanon, and while his grandfather's loyal agents had most of the city under observation, it was clear there was what, as Kaseem Abu Hazara-Khan – his opposite number in Kesh – had observed, 'another player' in the game. If Lady Franciezka Sorboz's spy ring in Roldem had been compromised, and Jim's in the Kingdom crippled, Kaseem's had been utterly destroyed. When last Jim had seen him he had been a hunted man. No doubt he was secreted away somewhere until he could safely resurface or give up any hope of continuing in service to the Empire. If the latter and he could safely reach his people in the Jal-Pur desert, he might live to old age as a nameless tribesman. Jim considered that last option very problematical given how far Kaseem had to travel to reach the safety of his family's camp.

Jim reached the steps leading down into the palace courtyard and made straight for the small personal entrance, the
size of an ordinary door set into the large, ornate iron gate
that guarded the entrance to the palace grounds. The large
gates, opened to admit detachments of horse and large carriages, was closed as a rule, but now he was surprised to find
the small gate also barred and two guards posted before it.

'Sir?' one challenged him as he approached.

'I'm James Jamison, the Duke's grandson. I thought I'd
get out in the city and stretch my legs a bit.'

The guard nodded. 'Well enough, sir. If you can show us
your pass.'

'Pass?' Jim's face darkened. 'Since when does a member
of the royal court need a pass to enter and leave the palace
grounds?'

'Since the order was posted this morning, sir. You need a
pass signed by the Viceroy's office.'

'Viceroy?'

'You've not heard, sir?' said the guard in affable tones.
'Why, this very morning the King named his friend Sir William Alcorn Viceroy, to help him run things until the old
duke, I mean your grandfather, is back on his feet. Orders
came down with the changing of the guard; no one in or out
without the Viceroy's approval.'

Pushing aside his sense of outrage, Jim forced a smile.
'That must be it, then. I came in late last night, exhausted,
and slept in until meeting with my grandfather. I'll go at
once to Sir William's office and see to the matter. Carry on.'
Jim turned and marched back towards the palace steps.

There was only one possible reason for the new requirement for a pass: Sir William had decided to limit the com-
ings and goings of those in the royal household, including
the Duke's staff. Had his grandfather been fit, Jim had no
doubt that pass requirement would not have lasted more
than a half-day, but his grandfather was soundly sleeping
after being forced to imbibe a sleeping draught by the royal
chirurgeon.

Jim knew it would be suspicious if he didn't put in an appearance at Sir William's office, but he didn't feel the need to go straight away. He had a half-dozen ways to leave the palace whenever he wished, and no doubt Sir William knew about two or three of them.

First he needed to find Anne and send her on a little errand – and then make a quick check on his grandfather. And he desperately needed to get something to eat. He was starving, having not eaten for nearly three days. If they hadn't cleared the tray out of his room, he'd eat whatever was there, no matter how cold, dried out, or stale it might be.

His frustration gave way to a rare flight of fancy. His tasks would have been so much easier if he'd had a magician on his staff, someone like Magnus who could just transport him to one place or another. That returned Jim to thinking about his last visit to Sorcerer's Isle and he wondered how Pug was getting on with uncovering his own personal nest of traitors.

As he climbed the wide steps into the palace that thought sent a new chill down Jim's back: should Pug's problems turn out to be as grave as his own, the consequences of what he faced was probably far more dire than the situation here. For if Jim failed in his tasks, his King and the conDoin dynasty might fall, perhaps even the Kingdom of the Isles in its entirety, but should Pug fail . . .

Jim shoved aside the thought. He didn't want to contemplate what might happen to this entire world if Pug should fail.

Pug sat quietly, his face an unreadable mask as he listened to the debate taking place on the floor of the Academy Council. A strange sense of déjà vu struck him for a brief moment: the Academy was becoming more like the Assembly of Magicians on Kelewan where he had trained.

Currently there appeared to be four groups represented among the members, groups that had formed around the teachings of three men, each reflecting a different philosophy, and a fourth, uncommitted, faction. Pug realized that of those in attendance, he was the only person who had actually known those three men. Two of them had been his students, Korsh and Watoom, two very talented magicians of Keshian ancestry. The third faction had been influenced by his close friend for years, Nakor. He wondered what his old friend might think of what had become of the Academy were he alive to see it.

A tall, slender magician named Natiba stood and addressed the twenty members of the council. 'The Wand of Watoom has met in caucus and we have weighed the warning carried to us by Pug.' He bowed slightly in Pug's direction.

As founder of the Academy on Stardock Island, land once ceded him by the Crown of the Kingdom of the Isles, Pug was viewed with veneration but since he had renounced his loyalty to the Kingdom and given Stardock and the Academy autonomy, he was also viewed with some suspicion, an unspoken concern he might some day choose to attempt to reclaim the school of magicians and the town of Stardock.

Pug appeared ageless, looking much as he had for the last century and more, with his dark hair and beard. He was slender and short, but had a wiry strength, an aura of toughness and resilience. He might be the single most powerful magician on this world – though he considered his son Magnus might soon surpass him, if he had not already – but he had begun life as an orphan kitchen-boy in far-off Crydee Keep and had endured four years as a slave on the Tsurani home world of Kelewan. He was no lifelong academic.

Pug had seen death and destruction on a scale unimaginable to nearly every other magic-user in attendance and considered this current debate trivial, pointless, and a waste of time. Yet he endured it, because he honoured his pledge and would let events take their natural course.

The Wand of Watoom was one of the two Keshian-dominated factions in the Academy, the other being the Hands of Korsh. Watoom had been a Keshian, but not a Trueblood, like Korsh had been. The difference between those friends had evolved two groups, who were both conservative by nature. The Wand was by far the more cautious and reactive of the two, keeping themselves focused on internal matters almost to the exclusion of the outside world. The Hands of Korsh was still conservative in its outlook, but was more inclined to take active part in events beyond the Island of Stardock.

The third faction called themselves the Blue Riders in honour of one of Nakor's more colourful affectations: a grand blue robe that had been a gift to him from the Empress of Kesh. That and a beautiful black stallion he had ridden like a madman until it died. The Blue Riders believed there was no magic, and that anyone could learn 'tricks,' so they were constantly at odds with the other two factions. They were far more progressive and believed in an active, ongoing engagement with the outside world.

As usual the Hands were the swing faction, standing between the Riders and the Wand, with the uncommitted members likely to bring matters to a resolution. The topic being debated was the warning Pug had just delivered to the Council regarding the demon incursion into Midkemia and the possible threat posed from them and the forces behind the demons, the Dread.

The debate had been taking the better part of a day, and for Pug it had been tedium piled upon pointlessness. He had arrived the night before and conferred with the senior members of the Council, called the Administration: five members, one from each of the three named factions and a further two selected from the undecided members. Pug did not like the idea of any faction having automatic placement on such a body, it reeked too much of the party politics that had plagued much of the Empire of Tsuranuanni for centuries, but he forced himself to remain silent on all matters of governance over the Academy. For it to be truly independent, he must merely be seen as another magician.

Natiba finished his remarks, like many of those before merely a rehash of positions already argued, as if some members felt the need to speak even if only to reiterate what had already been said, in case they somehow might lose position or prestige in this council by staying silent.

Another magician rose and was given the floor. Pug was pleased to see this one was dressed in a plain brown robe, making him look like a mendicant friar of one of the temple orders rather than a magician. Too many of the magicians here, especially those in the conservative orders, affected the black robes similar to those worn by the Tsurani Great Ones. Pug absently wondered how much of that was due to his own choice to wear those garments, to constantly remind him of how he had come to be 'the Black Sorcerer.'

The magician in brown said, 'I am distressed that so many of our brothers and sisters are determined to continually revisit the same points without any apparent progress in reaching a conclusion we can, at least, debate. So, I will make this proposal and ask the Administration to put it before the membership and call for a vote.

'I ask that we agree that Pug would not have come to us save in the face of the most dire threat and that time must be counted as a critical issue. Moreover, without a clear purpose as to where we can best lend our talents to protect our world from the demon threat and the Dread—,' as he said that, the young magician glanced at Pug with an expression that suggested he wasn't willing quite yet to believe that such a horror could exist, let alone threaten this world, '— we should consider making a plan to answer any call Pug might make and how best to do that.'

The room erupted in comments and chatter. Several members voiced the opinion that it was too soon to be coming to any sort of vote on any issue, while others suggested the young magician overstepped his bounds. The Chairman stood and held up his hands for silence. He was a portly magician from one of the Eastern Kingdoms, by the name of Eslon Makov; he possessed a sense of gravitas well suited to moments like these. He said, 'A question has been put to the vote of the members. To restate the question—'

Pug let the restatement fade into the background as he saw the young, brown-robed magician move in his direction, climbing the steps of the circular hall to where he sat. 'A moment, if you don't mind,' he said.

Pug nodded and rose to follow the young magician up a few steps to the top tier of the Academy's main hall, then out of the door to the antechamber.

The young magician said, 'I am called Ruffio, Pug. I've not had the honour of meeting you before.'

Pug smiled. 'I appreciate your support in there.'

The young man shrugged and smiled hesitantly and Pug was suddenly struck by Ruffio's resemblance to himself at a much younger age. He had a thick shock of dark hair and a similar build and carriage. 'It was an obvious point to make, I thought. And if dire events do transpire as you fear, it might make it easier for this august body to reach a conclusion and act before we all die of old age.'

Pug laughed as they walked past a pair of older magicians who cast them a quick glance and continued on their own way.

Pug and Ruffio exited the antechamber and walked down a wide set of steps to a walled garden. When they were alone, Ruffio said, 'I think if there are members of some unknown agency embedded here, they've blended in successfully. For a week now I've reviewed every discussion I've been involved in, overheard, heard of, and I'm forced to admit . . . nothing.' He looked Pug in the eye. 'It may be that the very nature of this society of magicians is exactly what our opponents desire: a tendency to wish to do nothing.'

Pug nodded. 'We have traitors in the Conclave, Ruffio. Otherwise how could so many things have gone so dreadfully wrong in the last few years?'

The younger magician nodded, remembering the assaults on Sorcerer's Isle that should never have succeeded, the worst of which had cost Pug the lives of many, including his wife and son. 'Still, that doesn't mean they've infiltrated here.' He looked unhappy. 'We should return. The vote on the motion should begin soon.'

'Thank you for putting it forward.'

'A necessary step.' The young magician was thoughtful as they reached the entrance to the meeting hall. 'The Academy lacks the exceptional talents of the Conclave, but we have many powerful men and women in our ranks. If the need arises there are enough of us in the uncommitted faction to force through a vote to help.' He smiled. 'Even the most conservative member of the Hands won't oppose preventing the world from ending.' His smile broadened. 'At least I don't think they would.'

Pug stood alone for a moment and said quietly, 'I hope you're right, but sometimes I wonder.'

Considering what Ruffio had said about the talent in the Academy, Pug wondered if he had been too strict in keeping those in the Academy ignorant of the Conclave's existence, save his own agents of course. He stood hesitant. He needed to return to Amirantha and Sandreena soon, but thought before he returned he would do well to spend a few days informing a few key members of the Academy of some of what might be a threat in the days to come. He turned and began moving towards his old quarters, always kept ready for him, and decided he'd send word to Magnus to work with Amirantha and Sandreena on what they found on the Isle of the Snake Men, and then join them later. He once more felt he had too much to do and not enough time to do it in.

7

ALARM

The warning bells sounded.

Martin was already out of his bed and dressed and on his way to the kitchen for breakfast. Buckling his sword belt around his waist, he met his brother coming out of the kitchen.

'Damn,' said the commander of the city. 'I'm famished.'

Brendan smiled. 'Just ate! If you don't get yourself killed, have them fetch you something.' Playfully smacking his brother's stomach with the back of his left hand, he added, 'Besides, the last week's quiet is making you fat.' Before Martin could respond, Brendan was off at a run towards the wall.

Martin indulged in a momentary expression of exasperation that went unnoticed by anyone, then set off after his brother. Brendan was at the top of the wall by the time Martin got there. He pointed out into the harbour.

'What is it?' asked Martin.

'I have no idea.'

In the centre of the harbour the water was roiling, bubbling and capped with foam, as if the water below was beginning to boil.

Martin shouted up to the northern tower, 'What do you see?'

From above the reply came, 'Just a lot of dirty water bubbling, sir. It's been that way for a good five or more minutes.'

'What could it be?' asked Martin quietly, turning back to watch.

After another few minutes Lady Bethany and Lily appeared, both sporting what Martin had come to think of as their 'fighting togs': leather breeches, woollen shirts, and leather vests and boots. Both carried bows, though Bethany was the only true archer. She had been giving Lily lessons with the bow and the girl was now able to draw and loose a shaft, though Brendan – who'd watched closely since he'd taken an interest in the girl – didn't think she stood much chance of hitting anything save by chance, as he had confided in his brother. And since Brendan was probably the only archer who exceeded Bethany's skills in the city, Martin took his judgment at face value.

Brendan's close attention of Bethany had caused a great deal of agitation in young Captain George Bolton, now third-in-command of the city, who obviously had a deep infatuation with the mayor's daughter. Brendan's interest was more passing, given the lack of attractive young women in the city to compete with Lily; almost all the rest had been sent north to Zün for safety. She had refused to travel north and stayed in the city with her father, as he felt obliged to stay and defend his city.

Bethany looked excited as she asked, 'What is it, Martin?'

'I'll tell you when I know,' he snapped.

Her eyes widened; then she realized the strain was finally taking its toll on him.

Martin called up to the lookout above, 'What do you see?'

'The same, sir. Just bubbles and silt.'

'Should we send someone out to investigate?' asked Brendan.

Martin was silent for a moment, then said, 'No, we wait.'

'Wait for what?' asked his brother.

'Your guess is as good as mine,' Martin replied.

The four figures at the corner table were quiet, and while the room had cycled from an almost-sullen silence to a near riot of noise and back again over the previous day, these four were unnaturally silent.

Arkan had found little to divert his attention since reaching Ylith, so he spent his time studying the customers in the inn, jammed cheek-to-jowl as they were before him. It was a little like hunting, thought the moredhel chieftain, sitting in a hide observing the game through the swaying trees.

There were no rooms for rent, and every available floor space from the basement to the attic was occupied by exhausted workers and stranded travellers. So Miranda, Nakor, Calis, and Arkan had been content to stay at their table, occasionally leaving to use the public jakes out back.

Arkan and Calis were of elf stock, so silence was not difficult for either. The two demons in human form reflected the nature of their human identities, Miranda's moods being manifold. Nakor was by nature ebullient, but he could also embrace solitude and quietude, so idle conversation had withered hours before.

Now all four of them sat and covertly studied the other four men. They were rather ordinary looking, apart from the unnatural silence they observed. Had they been monks of some contemplative order, they couldn't have been less talkative. Still, that wasn't the only thing about them that caught the attention of Calis and the others.

The Prince of Elvandar had lived among humans more than the other three, even though the two demons possessed Miranda and Nakor's memories. All questions about how the two supposedly dead friends had reappeared in Ylith had been deflected, and Calis had dropped his inquiry, assuming he would learn the truth in good time. Like his mother's people, he had greater patience than humans.

It had been Arkan who had first noticed the four quiet men. He had simply said, 'There's something off about those four.' He indicated the four men at the table in the corner on the other side of the rear door.

'Off odd, or off dangerous?' asked Calis, taking an interest.

'I'm not sure, which probably means dangerous,' said the moredhel chieftain. 'They are trying to appear to be strangers, sitting at the same table by happenstance, yet despite the differences in their attire, each sports the same fashion of hair, as if they are members of the same clan.'

Nakor grinned. 'Monks, perhaps?'

'Not likely,' said Miranda.

'No visible weapons, so they are either harmless or have other means to protect themselves,' continued Arkan. 'Magic would be my best guess, as there are no obvious guards nearby.'

'Agree,' said Calis, glancing at Miranda. 'Anything?'

Miranda knew what the elf prince was asking, but she hadn't told him yet that she wasn't who he remembered and lacked the original Miranda's ability to detect magic. She glanced over at the men and said only, 'Nothing useful.' She felt a familiar, distant sensation being near these four men, like almost remembering a name, or trying to place a faint aroma, maddeningly familiar but just beyond recall.

Nakor grinned. 'I could go and poke at them.'

'I don't think that is wise,' said Miranda.

'Why?' asked the little man.

'I think they're waiting for something. It might prove futile to do anything until that moment arrives.' Her tone and expression communicated to Nakor that she was on the verge of recognition. He turned his head slowly and studied the four men, then his eyes widened slightly. He turned back and nodded almost imperceptibly. He now felt it too.

'It might be too late,' suggested Arkan. 'I have spent little time among humans, save when trading in Raglam or Caern, but I have fought them and dealt with human prisoners.' He lowered his voice. 'These have the look of prisoners condemned to the mines.'

'Not hopeless,' said Nakor. 'Resigned to their fate.'

'They expect to die,' said Calis. 'Here, in this inn?'

'I don't think so,' offered Miranda. 'How much mischief can they start here?'

'A nice brawl?' asked Nakor with an evil glint in his eye.

'As amusing as that might prove to be,' said Calis, 'Miranda is right. If those four are up to something, it's not here. At some point I expect one or more to leave the inn.'

'So we wait until they leave?' asked Nakor.

'And follow them,' said Arkan.

'What's your interest?' Nakor ask the moredhel.

'Anything that gets me out of this reeking inn is my interest.'

Nakor raised his eyebrows in amusement and inclined his head as if he understood.

'So we wait a bit longer,' said Miranda with her first hint of impatience.

An hour wore on as the bubbling in the harbour continued. Martin finally grew bored with watching it and said to his brother, 'If it's a threat, it's not immediate.'

Brendan nodded. 'Though I wouldn't discount it being a sudden one if whatever is going on out there is finished.'

'What could cause such a thing?' asked Bethany, standing at Martin's side. She glanced at Brendan and Lily.

Lily said, 'I've lived here my entire life and have seen nothing like it.' Then her expression grew thoughtful. 'But I know someone who might know.'

She vanished from the wall and a few minutes later returned followed by an old man. 'This is Balwin,' she said. 'He's the old harbourmaster.'

'You ever see that before?' asked Martin.

The old man was slender, but not frail. He looked wiry and fit for someone who appeared to be eighty or more. He squinted against the afternoon sun, now gleaming off the water in the distance and said, 'No, but I've heard of its like.'

Suddenly Martin was interested. 'Really? What?'

'Story told me when I was a boy.' Balwin grinned as he remembered, his leathery face wrinkling in amusement. 'If I remember this right, it was the old imperial governor in LiMeth was behind it.'

LiMeth was the westernmost coastal city, little more than a convenient port for pirates and smugglers, in the Empire along the coast of the Bitter Sea.

'Somebody or 'nother was foolish enough to go looking for gold up in the Trollhome Mountains.

'Now, anyone who knows anything about the Trollhome knows there's a reason they call it that. Mountain trolls everywhere, so it doesn't matter how much gold is up there; you're not going to get it unless you've got more guards than miners.' He tapped the side of his nose. 'So the governor decides he's going to tunnel up from beneath the water, starting off shore and moving up through the bluffs to the west of LiMeth, right up into the guts of the Trollhome.'

'What happened?'

The old man laughed. 'Lot of miners drown is what I heard. But for a while it worked. Got some sort of magic-user to make some sort of air bubble and the men worked in that until they got up into the ground where they could drive an air shaft to the surface.' He rubbed his chin as he remembered. 'Thing was, water goes where it wants to go and seeks its own level, so as I heard it told, tide collapsed the lower end and the whole thing fell in on itself. Doubt the Governor even got enough gold out to pay for the cost. Anyway, the thing was when the magician had that air bubble in place, it leaked a bit and you could see bubbles rising to the surface. That's what this reminds me of, that story.'

Martin and Brendan looked at one another. 'Crossing the Bitter Sea underwater?' asked Brendan.

'Is it even possible?' wondered Martin. 'I mean, a stationary bubble. Men diving into the bubble then working up the mountain . . .' He sighed. 'I find that story hard enough to believe. Where are they tunnelling from? They'd have to start somewhere over there.' He pointed to the south-west then leaned forward, behind the merlons on the wall, as if to see better. 'We'd have seen anyone on the shore attempting any sort of mining.' He shook his head. 'It's a wonderful tale, my friend, but even this close to the city, tunnelling under the Bitter Sea is more than an army of dwarves could achieve in this short a period of time.'

'Army of dwarves?' said the old harbourmaster. 'Never met a single one myself.'

Martin said, 'I have, but that's beside the point. If I could wish up a tunnel . . .' He snapped his fingers.

Brendan said, 'Magic tunnel?'

Martin looked concerned.

'We really need a magician around, don't we?' asked Brendan.

Martin glanced at his brother then nodded. 'Time was the Dukes of Crydee had one on staff for a reason.' He peered out at the water. 'I don't suppose there's a diver in town we can send down for a look?'

Harbourmaster Balwin said, 'No, not many around here, and the few we had went off with the Duke's army to the south. You're free to try to find someone but most won't dive that close to the city. Waters are too rough: got that tide-race to the south-west, and nothing but rocks to the south-east once you get past the beach over there. No reason to dive, 'cept salvaging. Even then not much visibility. But I may have a way for you to take a look if you're willing to row out there.' He paused, then smiled suddenly. 'I'll be right back.' The old man turned and hurried away.

Less than ten minutes later he returned holding what looked to be a large wooden bucket. 'This might help,' he said, presenting it to Martin.

Martin turned it over and saw that it had a clear bottom. 'What is this?' he said, tapping on what looked to be clear glass but gave back a dull sound when struck.

'Don't rightly know. Some sort of crystal. Much tougher than glass. A salvager named Pevy used it outside the harbour, along the tide-race, when a ship went down. Very handy. Other lads would be diving off the side of their dinghies, searching, while Pevy and his boys would row around, looking down through this thing until they saw something, then the boys would dive right under it.'

Martin and Brendan exchanged glances, and the younger brother said, 'I'll go.'

Martin nodded. All three brothers had been raised on the coast, and by Crydee tradition had been apprenticed for a short while at every trade in the duchy, including fishing. Hal was the best sailor, Martin best at boat repair and gauging the weather, and Brendan was the best fisherman and diver.

Balwin said, 'Get a little boat and launch off that beach down there—,' he pointed to the south-east, towards the old fortification, '—and you won't have to navigate through all those burned-out pilings and rubbish.'

Brendan said, 'I'll need someone to row while I look.'

Balwin said, 'Old Pevy's youngest son's serving in the city muster. His brothers do the diving, while he and his dad row. His boat is still in their shed. I'll go fetch the lad for you. His name is Evard, but everyone calls him Ned.'

'I'll meet you down by the main gate,' said Brendan. He nodded to his brother and Bethany, then impulsively kissed Lily hard on the mouth.

She nearly reeled from this unexpected display of affection and said, 'My!' Her cheeks flushed as she watched the young noble walk swiftly away.

Bethany's eyes were wide and Martin tried very hard not to laugh aloud. After a moment Bethany said, 'Well, I think he just let you know how he feels about things.'

Lily lowered her head slightly and tried to hide a grin as she quickly glanced around. 'I wonder if George saw that?'

Bethany's eyes narrowed. 'Really?'

Lily said, 'I like them both.'

Martin laughed. 'Should we somehow survive all this, Brendan will some day be Baron of Carse.'

'Oh?' said Bethany, looking over her shoulder at Martin, who was standing behind her.

Glancing down at the gate, where Brendan was meeting a young, thick-necked boy in an ill-fitting tunic of the city watch, Martin said, 'Hal will need me in Crydee more than in Carse, most likely to command the Jonril garrison. As you have no brothers, it will be up to Hal with the Prince of Krondor's permission, to install someone in Carse *many many years from now*, when your father's gone.'

Bethany's expression turned anxious. 'I wish I knew how he was.'

Trying to keep the tone light, Martin pressed on. 'So, it's the nephew of a minor functionary in Yabon or a baron.'

Lily said, 'Oh, they are both very sweet.'

Martin laughed. 'Follow your heart, then, Lily my darling. Just be gentle with whoever's heart you break.'

Lily looked concerned.

'Assuming we all survive this coming war and my brother doesn't manage to go out and drown himself,' added Martin.

All eyes turned to follow Brendan and the Pevy boy.

Brendan and Ned Pevy hurried along on the soot-covered stones of the street before the wall, all that was left of the foulborough. The Keshian raiders had been effective in ensuring everything above the tideline from the wall to the end of the longest dock had been burned to cinders. What few frames and beams had been left upright after the fire had crumbled in the first thunder storm to hit the city after the raid, leaving the entire area reeking of wet charcoal.

Ned led Brendan down to the north-east corner of the stone wharf and then up a small street lined by charred houses. These were still relatively intact: as they were not directly before the city gates, the Keshian raiders had ignored them. Only the spreading fire had been a threat.

'Pa kept our boat up here,' said Ned, pointing to a shed behind one of the buildings. 'Ma'll have a fit when she sees what those Keshians did to her house.'

Trudging up the small gravel path that ran between the Pevy home and the next one, Ned glanced at the back yard. 'Don't know how the garden's going to go with all this smoke and ash.' He shrugged as if it was of no importance.

He stopped at the entrance to the shed and pulled aside the bar, opening a single wooden door. On two saw-horses rested an overturned rowing boat. Ned moved to the rear and Brendan followed. Brendan knew what to do without being told. He lowered the bucket he carried and turned around and picked up the small boat by the gunwale and when Ned said 'up' he lifted with his right hand and put it on his shoulder, then put his left hand on it and when Ned again said 'up' again he lifted, grabbed the other gunwale with his right and hoisted the boat overhead. The two oars rattled under the seats as the two young men lifted.

'Ready?' he asked.

'Ya,' came the answer.

'Walk,' said Brendan leading the way.

The boat was small enough, about twelve feet long. It was a fair hike to the water's edge, past the burned-out piers, and Brendan was thankful they didn't have a bigger boat to carry. A small rowing boat would get around the mess in the harbour, but even something as shallow draught as a longboat or captain's gig would need to be hauled all the way down the sandy beach a half-mile farther along. The two young men moved to the water's edge. Brendan swung around to present the boat sideways onto the water and they lowered the boat into the bay.

'Done this before, have ya?' said Ned with a grin.

'Once or twice,' said Brendan.

'I'll run and fetch that bucket, if you don't mind,' said Ned.

Brendan nodded. 'I want to take a quick look around to make sure we're not totally mad doing this.'

'Sir,' said Ned as he turned and scurried off back up the street to his house. Brendan found a piling that still rose above the street by two feet and stepped on it. He could see the frothing bubbles about three hundred yards from his current position. He couldn't be sure but it looked as if the affected area was bigger and more agitated than before.

Ned returned with the viewing bucket and they got into the small boat, Brendan in the bow and the salvager's son rowing. 'Right to the bubbles,' said Brendan.

Soon they were squarely in the middle of the bubbling water and Brendan put the bucket into the water, pressing it down hard to stop it flipping over, and looked down.

At first he couldn't make out anything except the bubbles striking the crystal in the bottom of the bucket. 'Stick your face in a bit,' said Ned. 'It'll help get your eyes adjusted.'

Taking the experienced salvager's advice, Brendan found that it was just big enough to accommodate his face and leaning in actually helped him keep the bucket in place. For a few moments the darkness below and the froth of bubbles confused his vision, but soon he began to see shapes and movement.

As his eyes adjusted he began to make out creatures busily scurrying across the bottom of the sea floor, perhaps a hundred feet below the boat. They were frog-like, man-sized, with large shoulders and narrow lower bodies, long legs and arms. The light was too dim and the distance too great for more detail, but just the sight of them made Brendan's hair stand up on his neck and arms.

The creatures were churning up the sea bed. There was no tunnel of magic or bubble leaking air, but there was something buried under the mud of the ocean floor and they were clearing it away. Like ants swarming, they were constantly moving across an increasingly larger opening. The churning of the sea bed was releasing bubbles adhering to the surface of whatever was under the mud they were moving, and the rising bubbles further confused Brendan's view.

He caught glimpses of a shape beneath the tireless creatures and wondered what it was. He thought for a moment it might be an ancient statue of heroic proportion or a monument of some kind, for it was massive and only part of it had been uncovered.

Brendan lifted his head from the bucket and scanned the distant shore to the west, but there was nothing out of the ordinary to be seen. Where had these creatures come from? Was this part of some Keshian plan to take the city? He looked back into the bucket. Far below, for a moment, he thought he could make out a contour then it was obscured by a swirling cloud of silt. It diminished as more of the creatures hauled away mud, gripping it in large ridged fins at the end of their arms, like elongated fingers with webbing between. Brendan calculated how long they had been aware of these bubbles in the city, and decided these creatures had been working for several hours, possibly from late afternoon or early evening the day before. He peered deeper into the gloom.

The shape *was* a giant statue, he decided, for the contour of it appeared to be a face of some sort. Not human, but Brendan had been told about statues in Kesh with animal heads, ancient gods of the desert people.

Then he saw something move, not among the workers, but as if the head of the statue had turned slightly. He tried moving the bucket but the bubbles obscured his vision.

Then they cleared and he could now make out the ridge of an eye and a cheekbone, the bridge of a nose and part of the nose itself.

Then the eye opened and a globe of fiery red stared at Brendan.

Suddenly the creatures that were clearing away the bottom mud stopped their activity and looked up at the boat. Brendan jerked his head up and shouted, 'Back to shore! Closest landing place!'

The urgency of the command wasn't lost on the Pevy boy, who immediately put his back into pulling on the oars and the rowing boat nearly leapt forward. Brendan stood up, and the young salvager turned soldier shouted, 'Sit down . . . ah, sir! You'll turn us over.'

Brendan ignored the request and drew his sword. 'Whatever happens, don't go in the water!' He set his feet as best he could in the now wildly bobbing boat, attempting to keep his balance. The first creature reached the surface mere yards behind the boat and stuck its head out of the water.

The frog-like face scanned around, seeing Brendan and Ned a few yards away. It fixed large, bulbous yellow eyes on them. Then, with a gurgling cry, it dived under the water and sped towards the stern of the boat.

Brendan was stunned by how fast the brute could move underwater. He could make out more of their forms undulating just below the surface as they chased after the boat.

The first frog-being reached the boat and two green scaled, webbed hands with long green talons reached up to grab the gunwales. Brendan slashed down and chopped off several fingers as the creature started to pull itself upward. The cry of pain was more a watery gurgle than anything else and the frog-beast released its grip and fell back below the surface.

The next creature didn't bother trying to crawl aboard: rather it leapt up out of the water, like a dolphin dancing on its tail, and fell towards Brendan.

The youngest brother of the new Duke of Crydee was hardly a battle-tested warrior, but he had seen enough in the last few weeks to test a veteran, and he knew that no matter what he faced, his worst choice was to panic.

Brendan measured his target and swung hard, knocking

aside the creature as the blade dug deep into one of its shoulders. He almost lost his balance as the creature was flung to the right and he leaned left.

'What!' exclaimed Ned, almost dropping his oars.

'Row!' commanded Brendan as another creature leapt from the water. Brendan sliced sideways, removing the frog head from the creature's shoulders, while trying to fend off the falling body with his left arm.

The thing's corpse was only half Brendan's size, but it was enough of an impact to knock Brendan backwards. Reaching out with his left arm to break his fall, he slammed into the bottom of the boat, causing it to rock dangerously. Ned attempted to keep it upright and still row furiously.

Another creature appeared over Brendan, who instinctively stuck up his sword, allowing the creature to impale himself on the point. It flopped frantically for a moment, making horrible gurgling, croaking sounds. The thing stank of decaying fish and ocean mud and Brendan could not get his free hand any purchase on the creature's slippery skin as he tried to get it off him.

A brief shadow told Brendan another of the things was leaping into the boat, and he felt the boat wobble and then heard the heavy thud of wood accompanied by a gurgling cry of pain followed by a splash. Brendan brought his knees up and then pushed with his free hand and knees and the now-dead creature atop of him rolled to his left.

Now two more of the sea dwellers were attempting to grip the gunwales. They might not be able to come aboard in sufficient numbers to swarm the two humans, but Brendan had no doubt he and Ned would be dead men within minutes of hitting the water.

Ned had been barking his knuckles with his oar, smashing the frog creatures hard enough that they released the boat. He pulled his oar out of the way as Brendan returned to dealing with their foes, slashing down and removing fingers. The creatures released their hold on the boat. Ned lowered the oar and put it back in the oarlock and again started rowing.

Brendan saw more ripples in the water attempting to overtake them, and got ready for another assault. The creatures came to within striking distance, but as Brendan readied himself, the two frog-like beings just turned and headed off in the opposite direction.

After waiting a moment, Brendan put up his sword. 'I guess they were more interested in chasing us away than catching us.'

'What were those things?' said Ned.

Brendan looked back and saw that the stocky youth was pale and wide eyed, and still rowing as if they were being chased.

'I don't know.' As they approached the shore, Brendan pointed to the bow behind Ned and added, 'We're getting into the ground swell. Slow down a bit.'

With a grin that bordered on the panic-stricken, Ned said, 'Been doing this all my life, sir. Don't even think about it. I'll have us in safely.' The rapidity of his speech and his ashen face testified to just how frightened he was, yet he kept his head and rowed quickly to shore.

Someone at the city gate had been watching closely for as they pulled the boat up on the beach, six riders reined in before Brendan, all Crydee veterans. Brendan motioned to a young soldier near his own age. 'William, help young Ned here take the boat back to its shed.' William jumped down from the saddle and handed his reins to Brendan. To Ned, the youngest conDoin son said, 'Well done.'

'Thank you, sir,' said Ned his face splitting to a smile for a brief second, then his eyes turned to where they had been beset by the water creatures and his expression turned grim again.

'I know,' Brendan said. Then he mounted and without another word signalled for his escort to follow him back to the city gate.

Martin listened to Brendan's report in the privacy of the mayor's office, which he had commandeered as his command centre. The mayor, Captain Bolton, and the two senior sergeants, Ruther and Magwin, all listened, along with Harbourmaster Balwin and Ned Pevy. Martin knew just outside the door Bethany and Lily were fuming at being excluded, but he had decided the room was crowded enough. And, he honestly had no idea how they'd handle this revelation. He had come to that conclusion before he heard the report, based on just seeing how deeply his brother held his own fear in check, and now that he was hearing what Brendan had seen, he was glad he had made that choice.

Martin turned to Balwin. 'Have you ever heard of creatures like this before?'

The old man barked a laugh. 'You're a sea coast man, young lord! Do you think such a thing could be seen of, spoken of by any man, drunk or sober, and not have the tale retold in every sailor's hiring hall, chandlery, or ale house from here to the Sunset Islands?' The old sailor added, 'I've heard of many things, from great serpents that can swallow a ship whole to a whale the size of a mountain, ships caught in a calm devoured by wood-eatin' fish, an island out in the endless sea with a volcano that spews gold . . . I've heard all the tales an old sailor can hear, but unless those things your brother saw were buxom beauties from the waste up with fish tails, mermaids of lore, then no, nothing remotely like it. Certainly no frog-headed fish men, whatever they were.' He lowered his voice. 'And nothing sleeping under the mud with no demon red eye.'

Martin said, 'Whatever it is, we need a magician and a powerful one.'

'Magician?' said Brendan.

'Those are no natural creatures uncovering that thing I'll warrant, some Keshian spell-caster has somehow . . . I don't know, wished the monster up. Or found it asleep and is waking it up . . .' He looked at the mayor and Captain

Bolton. 'You certain there are no magic-users in the city?'

The mayor looked almost apologetic. 'We have had a few mountebanks and tricksters come through, and witch-women with their charms and love potions. We encourage them to move along quickly.'

Brendan said, 'So you're not hospitable?'

The mayor said, 'You must understand. We are as busy a trading port as any on the Bitter Sea. We are the gateway to Yabon, and anything heading up to there or LaMut comes through here, and likewise anything leaving the duchy comes through here. Such traffic means lots of sailors and lots of gold.'

'Which means lots of predators,' said Martin.

'Well, if it's widely known that you have no love for magic-users, perhaps they just don't announce their craft,' suggested Brendan.

Martin nodded. 'Head to that inn where travellers are being housed and start sniffing around for anyone who might help.' He turned to Bolton. 'Get a small patrol and if you hear any rumours about witch-women or sorcerers in huts or caves in the surrounding countryside, go investigate. Check all the outlying villages if any are still occupied, and inquire there.' He glanced away, as if through the walls he might glimpse the still-roiling water in the harbour off in the distance. 'I need to know what it is I'm fighting. If this is some beast the Keshians plan on turning against us . . .' His voice lowered and only his brother could detect his fear. 'I need to know what's out there.'

8

ASSAULT

The inn was packed.

Brendan could barely get through the door as he entered and made his way through the press of bodies. As soon as he returned to Martin he was going to suggest they open another building, perhaps one of the nearby stores, and house some people there. This one was fit for a brawl at a moment's notice given how crowded it was. Moreover, with nothing else to do, most of those in the commons were just drinking, and a room full of unhappy drunks was a recipe for disaster.

How to begin? thought Brendan. He couldn't

just stand up on the table and ask if there was a magician in the room. He moved slowly through the press, trying not to jostle anyone holding a drink while he scanned faces. Almost everyone he spied was obvious in their calling: teamsters from the north, traders from the Free Cities. One fellow caught his eye until he realized he was the storyteller-minstrel who had tried to convince the mayor to let him sing for his supper at the mayor's house until Martin had him escorted down here.

Towards the back of the room were two tables, one occupied by four men and the other by an odd assortment of two elves, a short man who looked Keshian, and a striking-looking woman who was vaguely familiar to Brendan. He wondered what it was about the four men that struck him as odd. They were wearing travelling clothes of good cut and fabric, but not overly fine. None appeared to be armed, but even at his young age Brendan had learned that a wily man could secrete half a dozen blades on his person. Then two things struck him at the same moment: their hair was cut in identical fashion – rather than long over the ears as most poor workers often wore, or cropped short and rudely cut, these men had a well-barbered look that one saw on rich men and in court. The other thing that struck him was the fact that although they were sitting together, the four appeared to be studiously ignoring one another, pretending to be four strangers who found themselves at the same table. When he glanced downward, he saw they wore identical boots.

Brendan veered away from them and approached the other table. By then the two elves and their companions had taken notice of his approach, the woman staring hard at him. As he reached the table, she said, 'Martin?'

He smiled. 'My brother. We are often mistaken for one another.'

She returned the smile. 'You're Brendan, then.'

'Yes,' he said, his smile becoming a quizzical expression. 'Do I know you, lady?'

'You were very young when I last visited Crydee,' she said. 'I spent most of my time with your father and your eldest brother. How are they?'

Brendan's smile faded and he said, 'We lost father in the war, and Hal was last heard from in Roldem, where he was at university.'

'I am Miranda,' she said, rising.

'Wife of Pug?' asked Brendan. 'Then you are exactly who we need. Please come with me.'

She glanced at the others and Nakor said, 'You scoot along. We'll watch . . .' He shrugged and she knew he meant the four men.

Brendan said, 'I scarcely believe my fortune in finding you.'

Heads were turning as those nearby couldn't help but overhear the exchange. 'Let's talk outside, shall we?' suggested Miranda.

Before they could reach the door, a sound split the air unlike anything heard in this city's history. It was a bellow of rage so loud that the buildings shook and plaster dust and fell from the ceiling. It was as if an earthquake rocked the city.

A few of the drunker guests of the inn fell down. Some ducked under tables, while others pushed towards the door.

Brendan acted without hesitation, drawing his sword and slamming the basket hilt into the stomach of a man attempting to push past him towards the door. 'Sit down!' he shouted, as he struck a second man across the jaw. For a brief second the surge halted. He might be young and slender, but Brendan was the one with the sword and the best most of these drunks had was a belt knife.

As the men in the commons pressed toward the door, the four silent men in the rear of the inn stood and as one reached up to unfasten their hooded robes. The robes fell away. Beneath, each man was dressed alike, in a deep red tunic and black trousers ending in black ankle boots. Around each man's neck hung an amulet and in its centre a red jewel glowed.

'Oh, my,' said Nakor. He felt the hair on his arms, neck, and head prickle with gooseflesh, and he was sure he could smell a very familiar magic stench. To Arkan and Calis he said, 'Please, kill those four men. Quickly!'

Calis took a moment to consider, but Arkan acted without hesitation. Whatever else these annoying humans might be, he had been around beings of power enough times in his life to recognize that the little man and the tall woman were far more formidable and dangerous than they appeared to be. Moreover, he had been watching those four men on the other side of the room more closely than the others had and by now possessed a firm sense that they were not only dangerous, but that there was something wrong with them. It was like running across a sick animal in the wild. You might not at first be able to judge what the problem was, but in an instant you knew it wasn't a healthy bear or deer. It didn't matter if the animal was rabid, poisoned, wounded from an earlier struggle, you just knew you had to kill it as quickly as possible before it infected other animals.

Arkan's second arrow was back to his ear by the time the first one struck one of the four men in the neck, killing him instantly. He let it fly as Calis loosed his first and two more men died. The last man began an incantation, uninterrupted by the death of his companions. They must be spell-casters! Arkan's third arrow finished his chant.

Bedlam erupted as those nearby dived for cover and shouts of anger and fear filled the room. Brendan wisely stepped aside as the second surge of the crowd towards the door threatened to overwhelm him.

Miranda grabbed the nearest man, a very drunk teamster by all appearances, and with little apparent effort picked him up by the front of his tunic and threw him into the crowd, causing a general collapse of bodies. 'Outside!' she shouted at Brendan, who took no pause in turning, opening the door, and leaping through.

The two city watchmen posted at the door were turning

to investigate the noise as Brendan made his exit, almost knocking them down.

'Sir?' asked one, a youngster barely big enough to hold the pike he'd been given.

'Let them through,' said Brendan, stepping to one side, followed a moment later by Miranda. Then there was an explosion of bodies out of the door, as those who had been trapped inside for days came flooding outside to scatter in all directions.

The other watchman, an elderly, toothless man, said, 'What are we to do, young sir?'

'Don't get trampled,' said Brendan.

The bellow that had begun the ruckus was repeated, clearly coming from the direction of the harbour. 'And that, young sir?' asked the old watchman.

'We'll see to that,' said Miranda.

Brendan said, 'You know what it is?'

She nodded. 'Only too well.' Her tone left no doubt that Brendan wouldn't care for the revelation.

'What about these blokes, sir?' asked the young watchman as the last of the inhabitants of the inn who didn't wish to remain exited the building.

'Let them scatter as long as they don't cause trouble. We'll round them up later, if we survive what's coming,' said Brendan. 'They've nowhere else to go, so it's either to the wall to fight, or back here to drink. Just make sure no one tries to go out the northern gate.' The young soldier saluted and ran off in that direction.

Nakor and the two elves exited, and Nakor said, 'Keshian Demon Masters.'

Miranda nodded. 'Dead?'

'Yes,' said the little man. 'Our elf friends are very efficient.'

'Well, one problem solved, and another begun,' said Miranda. 'Come, to the wall!'

Nakor said, 'Yes, I can feel it,' as if answering an unasked question.

'Feel what?' asked Arkan.

'Don't worry,' said Nakor. 'You'll get to kill a lot of humans shortly!'

'Just make sure they're on the other side of the wall,' said Calis, as the group broke into a trot.

The wall and main gate hove into view as they rounded a corner. Brendan sprinted the last ten yards and took the steps two at a time. Reaching the wall, he could barely negotiate the press of bodies gathered there and as he moved past Bethany and Lily, who were now stationed with the archers nearest the steps to safety, pushing through a knot of soldiers, towards his brother, he began shouting, 'Back to your posts! There could be more than one—'

He stopped as he saw what everyone on the walls was staring at. A nearby soldier in a Crydee tabard said, 'I pray there's not more than one, m'lord.'

Another soldier in the city militia said, 'One is more than likely enough, m'lord.'

What they saw was a monster, looming twenty feet above the water as it slowly walked towards the gate. The head looked like a cross between a lizard and monkey's, but it was covered in scales and possessed fan-like ears that swept back from the side of its head. Down its back ran a ridged fin, like a sailfish. The body was roughly humanoid in shape, though the shoulders and chest were massive and each hand ended in talons as long as swords. The reek of the thing was nearly overpowering even from this distance, as if every dead thing on the sea floor had been scooped together and somehow fashioned into the creature. As it slowly rose up out of the bay, sheets of water poured off it, the sun glinting off its scales. Reaching the shallowest part of the bay, which was still deep enough for large boats to ferry cargo to the quay, the monster now walked in water barely reaching mid-thigh.

'My gods,' said Martin. 'What is it?'

Far behind the thing, boats were coming into view. Brendan estimated at least fifty. He looked to the western road to

Crydee and saw dust and banners in the distance. 'Looks as if the Keshians have got tired of waiting.'

Martin said, 'They want that thing to knock down the gates, then they plan on hitting us head-on; not a lot of subtlety there.'

'None needed,' said Brendan.

Martin glanced past Brendan and saw the woman moving up to his brother's shoulder. 'Miranda?'

'You remember me?' she said.

'Yes, and your timing is excellent.' He pointed at the massive creature approaching the city. 'Can you do anything?'

'It's a water demon!' shouted Nakor with a tone approaching delight.

'Water demon?' asked Brendan. 'I didn't know they existed.'

'All sorts of demons exist,' said Nakor in an almost jocular tone. 'Water, air, earth, fire, animal, bird. Some are very smart, others very stupid. The demon realm is a very confusing place, even for demons.'

'You sound as if you know a lot,' said Martin, glancing at Miranda.

'Nakor,' she supplied.

'Nakor,' continued Martin. 'What are we to do with this one?'

The creature was starting to rise up near the burned-out docks. It bellowed again and this time those on the walls crouched lower as the stones beneath their feet vibrated. The creature looked first one way, then another, as if seeking something or someone.

'If we had a summoner, he could control it or banish it, but unfortunately we just killed whoever that was,' said Nakor.

'What?' asked Brendan.

'There were four Keshians of some order or cult.'

'I saw them.'

'One of them was a summoner, certainly. The other three were his acolytes or guardians.'

'Archers!' shouted Martin.

Those with bows rose up, nocking arrows and taking a bead on the creature.

'Save your arrows,' said Miranda. 'They'll only annoy it.'

The creature took another step, raised a foot as if contemplating stepping up onto the quay, then slowly lowered it back to the water, hesitating. It bellowed, stopped and looked around, as if confused.

'What's it doing?' asked Martin.

'It's looking for whoever summoned it,' said Nakor. 'Four men, even if only one is a summoner, means very powerful skill is needed to bring it here and control it. It was conjured out there—', he pointed at the harbour, '—because it was the only water deep enough.'

'Under the mud,' said Brendan.

'Even the water wasn't deep enough,' amended Nakor. 'It doesn't like being up in the air, likes land less, and hates fire.'

'Should we use fire arrows?' asked Martin.

'Only if you *really* want to annoy it,' said Miranda.

The summoned demon waited, looking from one side of the harbour mouth to the other.

'What happens next?' asked Martin of Miranda.

'When it gets tired of waiting to be told what to do, it will decide if it's more irritated by being here or hungry. If the first, it may decide to come here and rip up the city out of spite, or it may turn around and start swimming out to sea, looking for food.'

'This one is pretty stupid,' said Nakor. 'If we don't annoy it may just look for food. It will probably eat half the fish in the Bitter Sea and any ship it happens across.' He pointed to the longboats that were hovering just beyond the creature. 'If there's another Demon Master out there in a boat, we'll know soon.'

'Can't it be banished magically, back to wherever it came from?' asked Brendan.

'Only by a Demon Master,' said Nakor.

'Or if you kill it,' added Miranda.

'Can *you* kill it,' asked Martin, 'with magic?'

Miranda looked at Nakor and they both knew the answer. The real Miranda could almost certainly have disposed of this creature, if not quickly and cleanly, eventually, but Child only knew what Miranda knew in the abstract. She knew the spells Miranda would have employed, but she could not use them. But as Child she had learned her own combat magic.

'No,' said Miranda, jumping up into a crenel. 'I'll have to do it the hard way.'

'What?!' Martin reached out as if to stop her, but she was over the wall.

'Is she mad?' exclaimed Brendan.

'Most of the time,' answered Nakor, looking down to where Miranda had landed without injury.

'Amazing,' said Martin. 'She should be dead.'

'Almost certainly,' agreed Nakor.

Miranda reached down, grabbing the back hem of her dress, pulling it up and hiking the hem of her dress up to the top of her thighs. She tucked the extra fabric into the leather belt she wore, in the fashion of fisherwomen along the coasts in any country.

'Not fighting togs,' said Nakor, 'but they'll do.' Then with a grin he added, 'I always thought she had wonderful legs.'

Both brothers looked at the short gambler with expressions that indicated they both now regarded him as completely mad.

Miranda stood upright and held her hands aloft, incanting a spell. Then she stepped forward. As she strode towards the demon she began to draw energies around her. The hair on the arms and necks of all on the wall stood up at the charged feel of it, as if lightning had been discharged nearby. Miranda held up her hands, palms outward, flexing her fingers, as her nails started lengthening, apparently growing into claws.

'What is she . . . ?' asked Martin.

'It's a good trick. Watch,' suggested Nakor.

The water demon ceased scanning the horizon for its summoner, and fixed its eyes on Miranda, as she strode towards him. Here was something he definitely recognized. The shape was alien, but the scent and the power exuding from it were familiar. Another demon approached and not of the water kind.

'He's big, but his kind are stupid,' said Nakor from the wall. 'He doesn't know where he is or why he's here, but he's forgotten anything else now that he has someone to fight.'

'He's still five times bigger than she is!' said Brendan.

'Watch,' said Nakor. 'She's smaller, but she's a lot smarter, and she has lots of tricks.'

As he said that, Miranda leapt upward and in an impossible arc sped through the air straight at the water demon's throat. She landed and seemed to dig in with both hands and feet, ripping and tearing and even bringing her teeth to bear.

The blow shocked the demon, who staggered backward a few steps, almost losing his balance. He bellowed as he began pummelling his smaller opponent.

'Once she digs in, she's like a bulldog,' said Nakor.

At last the dim-witted monster got one hand completely around one of Miranda's arms and yanked hard. He dislodged her claws and sent a fountain of blood spurting across the water and the quay beyond. Then he used his other hand to pull her away, and before she could grab his hand, he flung her into the stones of the street where she slid all the way to the gate, striking it hard enough to be felt by those above it.

'Gods!' exclaimed Martin. 'He's killed her!'

'I don't think so,' said Nakor with a grin. 'She is very tough, and has some tricks, remember?'

The water creature hesitated, bringing his hand up to the wound Miranda had caused in his neck. He touched it, winced in pain, and brought away blood-covered fingers. He sniffed at them, looked at them, then bellowed again in rage.

Astonishingly to those watching from above, Miranda stood up, took two steps, then started a run at the water demon. With a sudden jump, she flew through the air at the monster for the second time.

Nakor said, 'This may take a while.'

Martin replied, 'I don't know if we have a while. Look.'

The Keshians on the ridge of the western road were now moving forward in orderly fashion, while the longboats were moving in a long arc which would land them on the south-east shore, next to the road.

'How are they doing that?' asked Martin, indicating the boats. Each was unmanned by rowers, somehow moving without apparent means.

Brendan pointed to the rear of the lead boat and said, 'Those frog-things I told you about!'

Martin couldn't make out specific features as they were splashing wildly, but took his brother's word for it. All he could see was a splashing at the rear of every boat as if someone was in the water pushing it along.

'Archers!' shouted Martin. 'One man in three over to the south-east wall!' He motioned for George Bolton. 'Take charge of the other wall. Do not fire until the Keshians get into range, then give them everything you've got!'

Bolton saluted, turned and headed after the archers making their way to the far wall. He knew as well as Martin that if the Keshians got a foothold on the south-eastern road and could attack the eastern gate, Martin would be unable to defend both that and the main gate.

Nakor rubbed his chin and his expression was thoughtful as he watched Miranda tearing at the now-enraged water demon. She was far more powerful than her present state suggested, Nakor knew, and could take a lot of punishment before her demon-magic defences gave way. Yet there was always the chance something could go wrong, leaving her helpless before the behemoth. Moreover, in less than two minutes the first Keshians would be ashore and there was no telling what might happen after that. They obviously had more than one magic-user with them, probably more than the four who were killed in the inn. Someone had to remain on the distant shore, or in one of the boats in the rear, directing those water creatures in the pushing of the boats. Moreover, Nakor was now convinced the boats had departed just down the coast and had remained undetected due to a shrouding magic of some sort, a spell of blending or invisibility that allowed the boats to appear suddenly.

Then his face split into a grin. 'I have a wonderful idea!'

'I would welcome that,' said Martin.

Nakor turned to a boy holding a flaming brand next to a bucket of oil. 'Give me that torch,' he said, grinning maniacally. If the defenders reached the gate, they were going to be met with flaming death from the wall above.

The boy handed over the torch.

Before Martin could frame any sort of question, Nakor leapt up into the crenel and dropped over the wall. Martin, Brendan and the others who could leaned out to see the small man land on his feet with ease.

'How do they do that?' asked Martin of his brother.

'I have no idea,' replied Brendan.

Nakor ran to where Miranda and the water demon battled. Shouting at the water demon, Nakor managed to get close enough to burn his legs with the torch.

The monster howled in rage and pain. Throwing Miranda hard against the city wall for a second time, he turned his full attention on the pesky little man with the torch. Nakor leapt aside deftly as the water demon raised a massive foot out of the harbour, water cascading off it in streams. To Miranda Nakor shouted, 'Stay where you are! I have an idea! Find the last magic-user!'

The water demon lifted the other leg out of the water. Now he was fully on the land.

Miranda slowly stood up, holding up her hand to indicate she understood.

Nakor darted in and thrust the burning brand hard against the creature's leg. It howled, lifting a massive foot to crush him, but he leapt nimbly to one side, darted in, burned the creature a second time, then turned and ran.

Nakor wove a course up the hill, diving to his left, then his right, occasionally stopping long enough to dart back and smack the water demon with his torch. The demon was surprisingly quick for its size, but Nakor was always just out of reach.

Suddenly the air was filled with arrows as the Keshian commander on the hill realized what Nakor was attempting. Whoever was supposed to be controlling this monster obviously was not doing so, and it posed a threat to his own forces.

Nakor seemed able to dance between falling feathered shafts, and when one did strike, it bounced off, as if striking an invisible shield. His shrieks of delight seemed only to further infuriate the water demon who redoubled his efforts to get his claws on the maddening little man.

With a whoop of naked glee, Nakor turned and ran straight towards the waiting Keshian army.

'He's insane!' said Martin.

Calis, who had known Nakor for years said, 'That's hardly a unique opinion, yet I've seen him do madder things.'

Brendan looked at the elf prince and said, 'Madder than this?'

'He once annoyed an invading group of magicians so much they nearly burned down half a city trying to blast him with fire bolts.' He shook his head and said, 'There is so much more to that little man than any of us will ever know.'

Brendan glanced down and saw Miranda had returned to her feet. At the same time, she looked up and pointed towards the far south-east corner of the harbour-side, the point where Brendan and Ned Pevy had launched their boat. Brendan waved back to show he understood. He turned to his brother. 'The Keshians are turning to come ashore, over there.' He pointed to the narrow stretch of burned-out quay before the rocks that separated the quay from the distant beach. 'It's a bottleneck!'

Martin took only a moment, then said, 'We don't wait at the wall! I want you to take every man who can ride, especially bowmen, and set up a welcome for our Keshian guests. If a boot touches the stones, I want the man dead before he takes a second step!'

Brendan was off as fast as he could, calling for horsemen to join him. A good thirty men left the wall with him, and Martin did a quick reassessment of his position. So far he'd lost no one and the Keshian battle plan was completely confounded. Now it was clear that the monster was supposed to have battered the door down at the south-west corner of the city, opening the way for the Keshians to charge downhill from the west, while another force would assault the eastern gate after they had gained the shore by boat.

Martin saw Bethany and Lily standing nearby and pushed aside a sudden urge to order them off the wall. He knew it would be a waste of time and energy arguing with the headstrong daughter of the Earl of Carse, and while he might succeed with Lily, as long as Bethany refused to yield ground, he assumed Lily would hold as well. He said, 'You two, make yourself useful and go over there.' He pointed to the south-eastern corner of the main wall. 'If Brendan and his troops are forced to withdraw, provide cover fire for them.'

Bethany studied his face for a moment as if weighing whether he was placing her out of harm's way or giving her an important task. She nodded once then led Lily to the far corner of the wall.

Martin turned his attention back to the struggle outside.

Miranda shook off the last vestiges of shock. She could use much of her magic skill to create some mystic armour, but that still didn't prevent such a massive impact from affecting her. She glanced to her right and saw Nakor's mad dash into the Keshian line and for a brief moment, both aspects of her being, Child and Miranda, marvelled at the seemingly incomprehensible behaviour of that little gambler. Yet the part of her that was Miranda knew that if there was ever a being for whom the phrase 'Method to his madness' was justified, it was Nakor.

She looked to where the Keshian boats were making ready to come ashore. Then she turned her attention farther to her left and almost out of sight from her vantage point, she glimpsed a company of riders approaching. She took a few steps away from the wall and saw young Brendan forming up his horse archers, ready to greet the Keshian marines as they came ashore.

A strange but familiar tugging at the corner of her mind made itself felt and for an instant she experienced an odd confusion, unsure if it was Child or Miranda who recognized this call. At last the part of her that was Child realized what it was.

The lesser water demons, the little frog-headed creatures that had been summoned to dig out their massive brother, were now pushing the boats towards shore, and calling out, asking for guidance.

Miranda considered the simplicity of it all. At first she had wondered why those Keshian demon summoners had taken up residence in the tavern. Not the how of it, because what passed for security in the city was a joke; the boys from Crydee might be earnest and brave, but they were hardly experienced, and there was no one in the city to look after details. So the four Keshian spell-casters had simply come in with the refugees from the west, no doubt. No, how they got in wasn't the question, but rather why.

Now she understood. It was so very simple. The demon summoner or summoners would have placed themselves at risk trying to observe and control the huge water demon, let alone this herd of small ones. It was much easier to sit in the tavern, waiting until some mystic signal indicated the demons were ready, then only one simple command was needed: come to me! With an additional instruction to de- stroy anything that got between the demon and the summoners. Had the summoners lived, the massive demon would have certainly had the gate down by now and in the confusion that would have ensued the Keshian Demon Master would have found a place inside the city to orchestrate the landing. With the summoners' deaths, the demons had stopped with the last command given. The massive water demon had tried to answer its last summoning, but the battle with Miranda and Nakor's had distracted it from that command and now its rage had brought it full into the Keshian army to the north.

With an evil grin matching Nakor's most malicious expression, Miranda decided what to do. As Child she had commanded demons much more powerful than these frog-creatures. While they might be dangerous as a group, alone each was pitifully weak, both physically and mentally. She merely sent out her own command and suddenly chaos erupted near the shore.

Rather than pushing the boats into the shore, now the small demons were swarming them, leaping out of the water to attack the unprepared Keshian soldiers. Many were knocked out of their boats to be pulled down below the surface by the weight of their armour.

Brendan saw his opportunity and shouted, 'Wait! Pick out your targets, then kill any Keshian who sets foot on Kingdom soil. Do not waste arrows on those in the boats!'

A few Keshians in the nearest boats managed to leap into the shallows, only to be met by a fusillade of arrows. Several were missed entirely but were pulled down from behind by the little water demons. Immediately sensing he was wasting arrows, Brendan shouted, 'Cease!'

A few of the less experienced youngsters fired again until Brendan's commands registered. Then the defenders stood silently and watched as horror unfolded.

Some of the Keshians in the boats were being torn apart by claws and fangs, some of the demons pausing to eat human flesh. Around every boat was a slick of blood and the water that lapped against the quayside was a frothy pink.

Bubbles were still rising where men were gasping in vain for their last breath while bodies floated everywhere.

Brendan looked over to where Miranda stood and saw her indicate with one curt motion of her head that he should return within the city walls and safety. Feeling no inclination to argue with her, he shouted, 'Back inside!'

Without one defender sustaining an injury, half the assault on the Kingdom city of Ylith had been utterly obliterated.

Miranda turned to see how Nakor was doing with the other half. Something in the distance was causing her sense of danger to increase and she reached out mentally and sought out the source. Suddenly recognition hit her like a blast of icy water and she was off and running after Nakor and the demon, praying she might reach them in time to save the little man's life. Again.

Nakor howled with glee as he rolled across the ground, ducking under the demon's clawed hands by inches. The Keshian cavalry was providing additional amusement for him as their horses were bucking, running in circles and generally ignoring their riders as they attempted to get as far away from the demon as they could. It didn't help the situation that the frustrated demon had managed to crush two animals who had shrieked in panic; that, along with the smell of horse blood, had pushed most of the mounts far beyond their otherwise solid battle training.

The Keshian field commander was trying to restore order, but at least a hundred of his footmen had followed the horses' example and were turning west and fleeing back over the rise towards Crydee. His officers were riding around as best they could trying to maintain order, despite their own mounts' increasingly balky behaviour.

Nakor was starting to think this time he might have over-extended himself, for while he was still finding the current situation hilarious, he could feel a strange and dangerous sensation beginning to manifest itself close at hand. Sparing what little attention he could from the general mayhem on all sides, he saw what looked to be a clutch of officers standing atop a nearby hill, before a proud array of Keshian battle standards and signal flags. In their midst was what obviously appeared to be a magician.

Nakor desperately hoped he was not another demon summoner, for if he was he might quickly see through Nakor's guise and discover the essence of Belog beneath the human exterior; should that occur, Nakor would be in for a terrible battle. He had no doubt that with what he had learned from Nakor's memories and the power he had gained travelling with Child he could resist all but the most powerful Demon Masters, but while he might best the man face to face, the attention such a confrontation would require would certainly leave him vulnerable to attack from other quarters.

And with a massive water demon and half the Keshian army attempting to kill him, that would prove a problem that even Nakor's legendary luck and cunning couldn't overcome.

Still, always trying to find a way out of seemingly impossible situations, he decided to see how well Keshian officers did in confronting a massive water demon. He dodged as he felt more than saw a blow coming from his left, and rolled on the grass, holding what was left of the burning torch high. He knew he'd stand a better chance of surviving if he threw it away but the fire seemed to be the only thing that kept the demon from chasing after him rather than stopping to randomly kill and eat horses and riders.

Nakor saw the officers draw their weapons when he started running toward them, and the magician began an incantation. Nakor wasn't particular eager to find out what sort of magic the man was attempting; a protective shell or something along those lines would only be annoying to the demon, but might put Nakor at a disadvantage, while any sort of seriously destructive spell could end his existence in seconds. Nakor had a limited supply of magical tricks at his disposal – right now all his demonic energies were directed to speed, extended senses to anticipate any blows headed his way, and a slight armour magic that made his skin and clothing as tough as plate armour – but he knew that a well-placed blast of magic energy could light him up like a holiday bonfire.

Moreover, it appeared that the magician had taken note of Nakor's antics and had judged correctly that as long as he was around, the water demon would follow him, and if he ended Nakor's existence first, then the demon might prove more tractable.

A sizzling bolt of energy, blindingly bright, shot over Nakor's head as he tried to burrow into the dirt, singeing his hair and leaving the stench of lightning in the air. A monstrous howl of pain and rage cut through the air and shook the ground where he lay.

As much as Nakor would have loved to have rolled over and observed what had just happened, his instincts forced him to leap to his right, then suddenly to his left, tuck and roll across the ground, then turn and leap back in the opposite direction.

He caught a quick glimpse of the water demon charging up the hill, one leg half-dragged behind him as he lunged towards the knot of warriors and the lone magician on top of the hill. Nakor had judged rightly: the energy blast meant to end his existence had struck the demon instead. If he wasn't trying too hard to stay alive, he would have found the situation hilarious. But not for long, as a Keshian soldier charged at him, chopping his blade through the air.

Without thought, Nakor dropped the torch and reached up to seize the man's sword arm. The soldier cried out in pain as Nakor squeezed his wrist, shattering it. With a single push he sent the man flying five feet back, despite his heavy armoured breastplate and helm.

Nakor paused for a second to catch his breath and shook his head ruefully. He had been thinking so much like Nakor, he had almost forgotten he wasn't the little bandy-legged gambler, but was really a demon with all the strength and toughness a demon possessed. And as it was obvious that the magician not too far away was not a demon-summoner, Nakor decided it was time for more direct action.

Another solider ran towards him as the water demon began to wreak havoc on the officers and those soldiers desperately trying to defend them. Nakor waited until the Keshian swordsman swung and with cat-like reflexes grabbed his arm and broke it as a child would a twig. The man fell to the ground shrieking as Nakor turned away. He had spent his entire existence as the demon Belog using all his energy for intellect. And yet as he had travelled with Child through the demon realm he had gained prodigious physical strength, even if he wasn't used to employing it. He decided now was the time to use that raw strength.

A third warrior started moving towards him when suddenly another figure raced in from Nakor's right, blowing over the swordsman completely. Miranda turned and said, 'Are you all right?'

Nakor laughed. 'I'm strong!'

'Yes,' said Miranda. 'But you're also foolish. You had no idea what type of magic you were about to face.'

'Let's go find out.'

'I want him alive if we can manage it.'

Nakor jumped in a majestic arc over the cluster of warriors attempting to stop the water demon.

That massive creature was starting to show the effects of being away from the nurturing water and dealing with huge expenditures of energy and multiple wounds. Miranda wasn't concerned with that, for she knew that the creature would die, returning to the demon realm from where it had come before it could threaten the city again.

She had found what she had sought, the magician who had tried to blast Nakor. He was holding his robes up so as not to trip on them, running down the hill away from the fight. He would have been comic save for two things: first, he had just tried to help kill a great number of people and while Child found nothing remotely distasteful in that, Miranda did. With each passing day, she was becoming more Miranda and less Child. Secondly, Miranda recognized the magician and that discovery filled her with both disappointment and anger.

She could run like a gazelle, and she had discovered she could leap nearly a hundred yards, so in one jump and a sprint, she was behind the man. She reached out and grabbed him by the back of his robe then stopped, letting him almost break his own neck when he came to an unexpected and sudden stop.

Turning, he drew back his right hand and Miranda could feel the magic form. Knowing instantly what he was doing, she slapped him hard across the face before he could finish his conjuration, breaking his concentration and causing his eyes to brim with tears.

'Hello, Akesh,' she said in tones venomous. 'It's been a while.'

The Keshian-born magician was stunned and shocked. 'Miranda!' he blurted. 'But—'

'I know,' she interrupted. 'Dead. Apparently, not as dead as people thought.'

'But—'

'Silence,' she said, 'or I will happily knock you unconscious. We have much to discuss.'

She didn't release her grip on his robe, but turned to see the water demon faltering as it was now surrounded by archers. In its weakened state its already meagre intelligence was pushed to the limit, and it stood uncertain of which way to attack.

Nakor had found a clear path down the hill and he trotted to where Miranda stood holding the magician. When he got near he grinned and said delightedly, 'Akesh! So you were the one trying to kill me!'

'I could scarcely believe my eyes when I saw you out there,' said the Keshian magician. 'I thought it had to be another madman. Besides—'

'I know,' interrupted Nakor. 'You thought we were both dead.'

'Let's go somewhere we can talk,' said Miranda.

Nakor turned to take in the scene. 'The demon is almost done, and if I were the Keshian commander, I'd be withdrawing.' He pointed to the north. 'We can go that way until we find the entrance to the keep on that high bluff over there.' He waved in the general direction of the old castle overlooking the city. 'And then we can go up, and back down to the city.'

'That's a long walk,' said Miranda.

'Or we can go sit over there in that copse of trees and wait for the Keshians to leave, then walk back down to the city, that way,' said the grinning little man, pointing over his shoulder to the city.

'Better idea,' said Miranda. Looking at the magician she had captured she said, 'I can rip your head from your shoulders before you can conjure, and that is no idle boast. So, behave yourself and you may survive to apologize to Pug for taking sides in this war and betraying the Conclave. He may let you live.'

The magician said nothing, but his expression reassured Miranda and Nakor he was unlikely to try to escape or otherwise cause grief, and the three started walking over to a stand of trees where they could rest until the Keshian army had withdrawn. Even by the time they reached the trees, the sounds of battle and the roars of the water demon were diminishing.

Miranda said to Nakor, 'Keep an eye on things until we have a clear path back to the city. And please resist the temptation to do something amusing.'

Nakor nodded, attempting to look serious but failing. 'I'll try.'

To the magician named Akesh, she said, 'Sit and rest. We will likely be here for a while, and while we're here, you can begin by telling me how you came to be serving as a Keshian lap-dog when you took an oath at the Academy to stay apart from conflicts between nations as well as your oath to the Conclave.'

The magician looked at Miranda sullenly. He might not know what she was capable of in this form, but he knew her from her human incarnation; and after Pug and their son, Magnus, she might very well be the most powerful magician in the world. And Nakor, despite his reputation as something of a joker and card cheat, was also counted a very dangerous opponent.

Akesh took a deep breath, then began to speak.

9

EVASION

Jim leapt over the wall.

Crouching down he waited until he heard the patrolling sentry reach the far end of the wall and begin his trudge back to where the Baron of the Prince's Court, Envoy Extraordinaire of the Crown, and any other number of titles bestowed on him by the King at his grandfather's behest, waited like the common thief he was in his other life. He held a dagger close to his chest and prayed he didn't have to use it. Right now he had more than enough troubles without adding gratuitous bloodshed to his list of malefactions.

Jim tried to make himself as small as possible as he hunkered down behind a bush. He had picked this spot to escape the confines of the palace for three reasons: first, it was one of the two exits that wasn't being watched by agents of Sir William Alcorn; second, the other escape route was through the harbour and involved a fair bit of swimming and he wasn't in the mood to get wet; last of all, this was the most direct route into the city. All he had to do was time things so that he could be over the wall as the guard was one step away from turning at the end of his patrol, then dash for the darkness of sheltering doorways.

The problem was when the guard was walking right towards him: Jim's only cover was two shrubs and a dull grey cloak which he had gathered around him like a tiny tent. If the guard didn't glance down as he passed the shrubbery, and James didn't draw attention to himself, he thought he had a fair chance of making it into the city undetected.

If not, a loyal member of the King's palace guard would be dead for no good reason and Jim's escape from the palace would be noticed earlier than planned. He really didn't care much about the latter issue, as he was bound to be missed before noon in any event. He just hated the idea of murdering a career soldier merely because he happened to be given this duty this night by his company sergeant.

The guard passed, and Jim let out his breath slowly in relief, for no needless blood would be shed tonight. He waited, listening as the footfalls moved away, then quietly he stood up, glanced at the retreating back of the sentry, and was away.

A silent sprint took him to a deep doorway in a storefront across the street, and he watched as the bored guardsman turned and started back on his rounds.

When the guard was at the far end of his patrol, Jim darted off in the opposite direction and a moment later, he turned the corner and was off into the darkened streets of Rillanon.

There was the sound of a dull thud of a cleaver slamming into a butcher's block as a stocky man in a bloodstained apron cut through a haunch of pork. He was heavily muscled under the fat and sported a large gut that belied a turn of speed when it was needed. He had a pair of crystal spectacles pushed up on top of his head, for his eyesight wasn't what it used to be, and he needed keen vision for his accounting. He had paid dearly for them, but they served him well in balancing his ledger.

He nursed a pipe of tabac, the pungent aroma competing with the stench of old blood and ageing meat, and he hummed a nameless tune as he worked. When he had cut a nice dozen chops from the carcass, he picked up the remains and hung it on an iron hook in the corner. 'Why don't you come out now? I'm done with the morning's work.'

Jim stepped out of the shadows and the two men confronted one another. 'Bill,' Jim said in neutral tones, as meagre a greeting as he could manage.

'Saw you slip in and was quite able to split your skull with my cleaver, but when you didn't move out of the corner, I thought I'd wait a bit to see what you were up to.' William Cutter, known as Bill the Butcher smiled with a mix of amusement and menace. 'Lord James, or is it Jim Dasher of Krondor today?' He paused. 'QuickJim? Jimmyhand? Jim the Fixer? Or perhaps another monicker with which I'm unfamiliar?'

'Neither or both, depending on what I leave knowing.'

'*If* you leave,' said Bill. 'Come, I'm being inhospitable.' He turned his back and walked through a curtained door towards the front of his shop. The sun was rising and the day's business would begin soon.

The store front was modest, and the butcher's counter was low and broad, each section with a small hole to facilitate the draining of blood. The stone floor also had a channel for drainage when it was washed each night, the run-off emptying out into the rear alley, above a sewer culvert. In the corner sat a small table and chair, incongruously bearing some delicate china cups and saucers. 'I take a minute before the business of the day starts to enjoy a quiet cup. Join me?' Bill waved a meaty hand in the direction of the table and Jim nodded. A brass pot sat over a small brazier, the water just shy of a rolling boil. With deft fingers, Bill the Butcher prepared tea.

They sat down and Bill poured two cups. 'I take my tea black, so I'm sorry I have no lemon or milk. I've some sugar in the back.'

'Black is fine,' said Jim.

'Now, whoever you are at this moment, what brings you to my humble shop and why should I let you leave alive?'

Jim weighed his words. The man opposite him was the head of the biggest underground crime gang in Rillanon. Less organized than the Mockers of Krondor, the Sewer Rats were the largest gang in the city, the centre of a loose association of many gangs: the Dock Stalkers, the North Street Rangers, the Jiggle Purse Bunch, the Greenhill Boys, the Starving Dogs, and a dozen others. To keep mayhem between gangs under control, the Council had been formed and today it was controlled by one man, William 'Bill the Butcher' Cutter. More men were subject to him for their lives than any single noble in the east.

'I need your help,' Jim said at last.

A harsh barking laugh was followed by silence, then a sip of tea. Putting down his cup, Bill said, 'You have rocks on you, I'll give you that. Stones the size of boulders, Jim. I've planted brothers and paid widows because of you more than any man in Rillanon, and you're hardly here for more than one day in twenty. So why should I let you leave here alive, let alone help you?'

'Imagine the Kingdom ruled by Sir William Alcorn.'

Bill slung his arm across the back of his chair as he leaned into the wall. His eyes turned away from Jim and he looked out the window as he thought. Finally he said, 'That's a compelling argument. A strange coincidence of events, Jim, has conspired to keep you alive. For the time being, at least. Tell me more.'

'Coincidence?'

'After you tell me what brought you here.'

Jim outlined the general deterioration of his network and the betrayal of key agents, without providing information that might prove useful to Bill in his role as ruler of the Council. When he was finished, Bill said nothing for a minute. Then he asked, 'Both Mockers and royal agents?'

Jim sat back and considered. Then he said, 'The only Mockers who were turned were also royal agents.'

Again Bill was silent for a while. 'So, your trouble is all within the straight world, not on your dodgy path.'

'Apparently.'

'So you have few, if any, here in Rillanon you can trust?'

'Also apparently.'

Bill Cutter shifted his weight, leaned forward, and whispered in mock confidentiality, 'So you're forced to come begging for favours from ol' Bill the Butcher?'

'Something like that, though not really favours, but rather coming to an understanding.'

'Ah,' responded Bill slowly. 'Understanding.' He almost massaged the word as he spoke it. 'I do enjoy a good one. What do you have in mind?'

Jim considered how best to make his point. 'Your buried brothers and grieving widows, we can cut down on that a great deal.'

'You'll call off the Crushers?'

'To a point. You limit your happy gang of cutthroats to stealing, larceny, and selling stolen property, and cut back on the violence and bodies floating in the bay, we may be able to look the other way from time to time and not be so swift to pursue.'

'Tempting,' said Bill with a nod. 'And in exchange for reaching this understanding?'

'As you've observed, there are people within my straight organization who have betrayed me. You are the eyes and ears of the criminal underground in Rillanon. You have contacts in Kesh and Roldem I lack. My contacts in Kesh are compromised, and my—,' he thought about Franciezka and felt an unexpected pang, wondering for a brief second how she fared, '—associates in Roldem are also at risk. From what small intelligence I have gained, the crime associations in both Kesh and Rillanon have so far been ignored by whoever is raising hob with each nation.'

Bill sighed and leaned back against his chair once more. 'Ah, then, there's the heart of it. I want more.'

'What?'

'I want the Mockers.'

Jim was speechless for a moment, his mind racing. The original Upright Man had been an evil bastard named Don the Chandler, a dockside merchant in Krondor who had used brutality and guile to create the illusion of the powerful, mythic and shadowy personage who controlled all crime in Krondor. He also was Jim's three times great-grandfather: the legendary Jimmy the Hand had been one of his bastard sons. So in a way, the Mockers had been in Jim's family for five generations in one form or another. 'Who will you send to run it?' asked Jim at last.

Bill gave out with a barking laugh. 'And I should share that with you because . . . ?'

'Because it's a condition of the negotiation.'

'I have a son, one among many, but one who is especially gifted and bright and he's a little too anxious for me to visit Lims-Kragma's Hall so he can take over the Council. If I send him to Krondor . . .' He shrugged.

'You double your criminal empire and remove your most dangerous threat in a single moment.'

'It's a difficult situation,' said Bill. 'One of the reasons he's such a threat is I'm fond of the lad and he knows it. Moreover, he also knows his mother would be beside herself if I cut his throat—,' he shook his head ruefully, '—and she can be a force to be reckoned with.'

Jim laughed, then said, 'Done.'

Bill looked surprised. After a moment, he said, 'Done?'

'If we survive this coming war, I am retired, Bill. I'm done with murder and intrigue and betrayal. I would need to install another as Upright Man, so why not your boy?' He almost laughed. 'Though I will put conditions on him; how the Mockers survive in on a high level of trust within those who call Mother's home. I will not have that betrayed.'

'Well, and done!' said Bill slapping his hand on the table. He extended it, and Jim shook it in one sharp gesture. 'Now,' said the butcher, 'on the subject of betrayal . . .'

'Yes?'

'I have heard things from both Kesh and Roldem. The Ragged Brotherhood in Kesh is keeping watch on all that occurs within the Upper City and are closely following the ins and outs of Trueblood politics. Likewise, the Shadows in Roldem are painfully aware of the changes there, as the embargo from Kesh has dried up a great deal of their business, though we do manage to keep a certain level of commerce active: Kesh's fleet is not incorruptible and smugglers are not a priority for them.'

'So what do you know?'

'Know? Not much, but I suspect a great deal. To the point, this war makes no sense on any level I can imagine. I am no historian or scholar, nor am I a true master of commerce. But in our line of work you do learn a thing or two along the way. War is about two things,' said Bill, extending two fingers and tapping the first. 'It's about miserable failure in diplomacy, admitting you couldn't get what you wanted by arguing or persuasion, pleading or threatening.' He tapped the second finger. 'And it's about profit. New land, booty, creating vassal states or any number of things that look like a profit to the winner. Even if conquest is not the reason, beating up your neighbour, winning, demanding ridiculous reparation, then going home, is profitable.'

'But there's a third reason?'

Bill grinned. 'You're anticipating me. Yes, the one reason no one cares to consider is madness. Some insane ruler or mad prophet or high priest hears a voice in his head and off march the armies.'

'So, which is this?'

'There's the thing,' said Bill, almost too delighted to speak.

Just then the door opened and a small man carrying a sack began to step over the threshold.

'Get the hell out!' bellowed Bill Cutter in a voice to tear the bricks off the wall. 'We're not open yet!'

The man leapt back, slamming the shop door so that the windows rattled.

Turning back to Jim, Bill said, 'Best hurry. I'm late to open. Now, where was I? Oh, yes, the thing is, this war meets none of the three reasons we enumerated. There was no failed diplomacy. Correct?'

'Kesh made no claims in the west beyond their usual rants about the Vale of Dreams,' agreed Jim.

'And from what we can see, they appear to be hurtling towards bankrupting the imperial treasury to claim lands in the west that will not provide enough revenue to recoup in the next decade. More, the excuse they need to relocate recalcitrant vassal tribes from the Confederacy to take pressure off the Empire is patently false.' He held up an index finger for emphasis. 'For centuries Kesh has kept the Confederacy bottled up below the Girdle and watched with cold amusement as the nations of the Confederacy slaughtered one another for whatever reasons they dreamed up, enduring the occasional rebellion as a consequence, but that is merely the cost of doing business.

'At times I am convinced that had the Empire had the resources, they would have built a big bleeding gate between the Belt and the Clasp, and thrown away the key. Now suddenly they start a war with their most powerful opponent in the world, to seize almost worthless lands in Crydee and Yabon just so they can move some rebellious tribesmen halfway around the world . . . for what? To make the Truebloods in the Upper City of Kesh feel good about their humanitarian impulses and their love of less fortunate subjects? Hardly.'

Jim nodded, uncertain where all this was going.

'So, let us for a moment consider the two northern kingdoms. Roldem buttons up their little island and tucks in their fleet. First they try to play honest broker, but quickly they're scolding both sides, threatening to go one way then another, ally with the Kingdom should Kesh initiate hostilities, yet give no assurances to the Kingdom they will aide them, even though Kesh could overmatch either fleet, but not both. Should Roldem declare for the Kingdom and sail, the Keshians in the Sea of Kingdoms would be quickly driven back to their ports and then the Kingdom has leverage to convince Kesh to withdraw from the west. So, why doesn't Roldem declare?' Leaning forward, Bill said, 'Because—'

The door opened and before Jim could see anyone through it, Bill bellowed, 'We're closed!' and it snapped quickly shut.

'Where was I? Ah, yes. Because Roldem seems intent on using the war as a massive distraction for the benefit of its citizenry while a gentleman named Lord John Worthington attempts a rather neat little coup d'état. From what I hear, princes and princesses are in hiding, there's secret police everywhere, and the King and Queen are comfortably at rest in a wing of their palace where all their servants wear weapons and ignore royal commands. Word is Lord John means to marry off his eldest to the Princess Stephané, which would give him a very real presence in the royal household. Which brings us to the Kingdom.'

Jim nodded. 'The war is being conducted not to lose, as opposed to trying to win.'

'And even there it's being waged badly. So badly we have reports of Ceresian corsairs sailing from whatever misbegotten pest hole they call home to raid along the coastal waters from Ran to Watcher's Point. Word is they sacked Prandur's Gate with impunity while the Lords of the Border sat and did nothing. They sail right past Kesh's pickets and are ignored.'

Jim sat back. 'That I did not know. That could bring the Eastern Kingdoms into the fray. If they think Kesh is allowing the Ceresians to raid their ports . . .'

'Well, you just got back to town and from what my people tell me you had a long ride halfway to Rodez for no good reason.'

'What do you know of Rodez?'

'The command there is intact as of two weeks ago. They sortie against any ships that come too close, pirate or Keshian, and prevent further encroachment into Kingdom waters. But there's a line in the water, apparently, from Ran to the northernmost peak of the Quor, through the Straits of Ilthros, beyond which no Kingdom authority exists. Makes it ripe for the Eastern Kingdoms to settle old grudges, so expect that soon.'

Jim said, 'What's your conclusion?'

'That no one is fighting to win. They're just fighting.'

'To what end?'

'That, my new ally, is the heart of the matter. Who wins a war that no one wants to win?'

Jim was silent then said, 'Someone who wants the war to continue.'

'Very good. Now, who might that be?'

Jim's mind was racing and already a pattern was beginning to emerge. 'I think I might know, but I'm not yet certain.'

'Then you best hop on that question.'

Jim looked at Bill and saw that he was grinning. 'Tell me of Kesh. Who is truly in command?'

Bill's expression became more considered. 'A minor nephew to the Emperor. The Truebloods breed like rabbits so there's no shortage of opportunities for nepotism in the Upper City. This magistrate is called Prince Harfum, but he has cleverly managed to install his own people in every key position. So while the Gallery of Lords and Masters thunders in debate, the bureaucracy quietly goes about the business of running everything in Kesh.'

Jim held up his hand, showing three fingers. 'Prince Harfum, Lord John Worthington, and Sir William Alcorn.'

Bill nodded. 'Three men with little history or power who've insinuated themselves in positions of critical influence and who, amongst the three of them, have managed to plunge half the world into a war no one wants to win.' He pointed a finger at Jim. 'Find out what they have in common, or who they work for, and there's your unknown player.'

Jim took a slow deep breath. 'There's little I can do now.'

'Oh, you're a resourceful lad,' scoffed Bill. 'You have assets you haven't deployed yet, I'm certain. But the Council will be alert and should anything of value come to our notice, we shall inform you as quickly as we can.'

Jim was silent.

'Now, to the business of my son.'

'I'll pen a missive to my senior man in the Mockers. Your son will have to present himself as an apprentice or the rest of the Mockers will grow suspicious. There are only ten people in the world who know the true identity of the Upright Man, and you are only the second who knows who isn't my employee or an ally.'

'And the other?'

Jim just smiled, choosing not to reveal the name Lady Franciezka Sorboz.

Bill said, 'Very well then, be discreet. And I will instruct my son to do the same.'

'What is your son's name?'

Again a barking laugh, and Bill said, 'There's the black irony of it. His mother named him James.'

Jim laughed. 'There is a bit of irony, isn't there?'

'Be off. I have a business to run and should I need to reach you, my lads will find you quickly enough if you're on the island. If you go to the mainland, seek out a tavern in either Bas-Tyra or Euper, by the name of the Black Ram in both cities. Just hand a silver real to any barman and say, "To settle a bad debt," and within minutes someone will take you aside and start the chain of getting a message back to me or delivering one I've left for you.'

Jim stood. 'Thank you, Bill.'

Bill slapped the table as he rose and said, 'Well and done, Lord James. I never thought I'd say this, but being with you today has been a pleasure.'

Jim found himself smiling. 'Oddly enough, I'm forced to agree.'

He quickly left the shop and slipped into the morning's traffic. He was about to employ one of those unused assets Bill had mentioned and he had much ahead of him. The mysteries he had begun to unravel were hinting at dangers he dreaded discovering were true. Still, he felt somehow relieved and his burden lightened, and he realized that giving up control of the Mockers was the most welcome thing he had encountered in a very long time.

Within another minute, Jim was lost in the crowd of the city.

Hal signalled for quiet and everyone stopped speaking and listened. For the better part of two days they had been eluding bands of pirates, bandits, and local gangs. The entire region was in chaos and whatever law that had existed before the war was now gone.

The four of them sat huddled under an overhang while a torrential summer storm slammed the coast of the Kingdom. Ty was the most familiar with this region and guessed it would blow through in less than a day, perhaps in a few hours. But it was punishingly wet, like standing in a waterfall at times as water cascaded from branch to branch, finally to unleash sheets of water at random moments. Moreover, the wind brought a quick chill. As there was no dry place to attempt to build a fire, they crowded together for warmth.

The rain brought one blessing: it muddied their trail and conspired to keep them hidden from searchers.

They had come ashore just minutes before the pirates and had climbed a narrow pathway up the twenty-foot escarpment. While not too high, the bluffs were difficult to climb and the pirates almost overtook them as a result. A few well-pitched rocks by Hal and Ty slowed them down for a few moments while the two young women reached the tree line and then the two noble sons sprinted after them.

Once in the woods, Ty showed an almost supernatural ability to pick a course through the thick trees, enough to impress Hal who had grown up running through forests all his life. Ty had learned a great deal of Orosini lore from his father, one of the last of his mountain tribal people. Talwin Hawkins, once called Talon of the Silver Hawk, had spent a year and many resources helping those few survivors rebuild their traditions. A single Orosini village now lived once more in the mountains to the north-east of where Ty and the others waited, and perhaps some day the Orosini would reclaim their ancient lands.

The pirates were uncompromising in their determination to overtake the fugitives. For reasons Hal and the others could only guess at, they had not given up the chase after the first few hours, as had been hoped, but simply kept at it. Hal didn't know if it was by some magic or intelligence, or simply on a whim that they had decided the four in the boat were worth the effort of apprehending. Stephané was highly recognizable to anyone familiar with Roldem, so perhaps a sailor had spied her white-blonde hair and striking beauty from a distance. Perhaps they had simply assumed these were fugitives from Roldem who might bring a handsome ransom if caught. But for whatever reason, they just kept coming.

The previous night, the four of them had found a naturally-formed rock outcropping around which Ty had fashioned a rough shelter. It had proven adequate enough they had managed to sleep a while, the two young men splitting the watch. Early in the morning they had found the King's Highway, but following it had almost ended in disaster.

A band of mercenaries or bandits had ridden unexpectedly over a rise, and they had managed to get off into the undergrowth before being discovered. For the rest of the morning they had moved parallel to the road, but keeping off the road for fear of sudden discovery.

Every so often Hal would fall back to see if they were still being followed, only to discover that the same band that had come off the beach was still doggedly in pursuit.

When the rains came they sought out shelter and found the overhang and waited for the misery to abate. They said little, whispering to avoid being overheard, taking what comfort they could salvage from their closeness and the hope of eventual arrival at a haven. From what little they could see, the coast seemed subject to all manner of predation, and ravagers seemed to roam free. Hal had decided their best course was westward, for though they might have to circle and skirt raiders along the coast, inland they could forage and hunt, and eventually as they moved deeper into the Kingdom, they were certain to find royal forces to protect them.

Ty said, 'I think I'm going to take a quick look around and see if those pirates are still after us.'

'Be careful,' said Stephané as she huddled between Hal and Gabriella.

He waved casually and vanished into the darkening forest.

'What time do you think it is?' asked the Princess a moment later.

Hal said, 'Difficult to tell, but I think it's almost midday.'

Gabriella nodded. 'My best guess as well.'

'What's Crydee like?' asked the Princess.

Hal considered for a moment, then said, 'Not too unlike here. A little cooler I would expect. We're a bit farther north than this coast, and you've got all that warm current coming up from Kesh here. It's why all the islands in the Sea of Kingdoms are so lush. Where I'm from it's a bit more rugged.

'But it's home.' He got a faraway look and said, 'The sunsets are magnificent, as you look out straight to the west from the top of the keep. It's best in the summer when the days are long and you can sip wine or drink beer as you watch after supper. The evenings are soft and gentle.' Then he laughed. 'Unless you get one of these,' he said, indicating the rain. 'We have a fair share of summer squalls there, too.'

'I'd like to see Crydee,' she said. 'Other places, too.'

'Maybe some day you will, Highness,' said Hal, instinctively moving just a bit closer.

Rather than pull away, she snuggled against him. 'I doubt it. Princesses don't travel, except if they're meeting kings or princes, if possible marriages are being arranged, and I don't think any member of the Royal Family in Roldem has ever seen Krondor, let alone the Far Coast. Oh, we've read about it, because, well it's your history in the Isles, and Roldem and the Isles are brother nations, I've been taught since I was a baby.'

'I believe we've had a war or two along the way,' said Hal lightly, 'but otherwise, yes, we are close.' He looked down at her in the grey light and with her hair matted against her head and her nose slightly red from the cold weather, she still looked beautiful to him.

He stopped staring when he felt Gabriella's eyes on him. Pushing away the feelings that were starting to form in his chest, he let out a long, silent sigh.

'I wish it would stop raining,' said the Princess softly.

'It will soon,' he promised.

A few minutes later, Ty came hurrying back and ducked under the overhanging rocks to kneel next to Gabriella. 'They're still following us. They're hunkered down less than a mile back. I almost walked into them, as they're under an overhang like this one. They're not being very quiet about their complaints, so I heard them before blundering in.'

Hal said, 'Then we should get moving. We're hardly any drier for staying here, the wind is lowering, and if we put more distance between us, perhaps the rain will wash away our tracks.'

Ty glanced at the young women. Gabriella just nodded once with emphasis and the Princess said, 'I'm ready.'

They moved off and headed west.

Princess Stephané stumbled and Hal barely got his hand out in time to keep her from falling into the soggy, muddy mess of leaves, twigs, and water they struggled through. Ty had been reading the land as they went, trying to find the best course that would also have the best chance of throwing off their pursuers. The rain had fallen off to a constant mist, enough to keep everything wet, but not so much that they could count on the pirates staying put.

They travelled uphill from the King's Highway but out of sight of any casual passer-by. The footing was treacherous and they moved slower than any of them liked, trying to avoid a nasty tumble down the hillside.

Mud was tricky, for it could either quickly be washed away, hiding tracks, or it could hold as small pools for a long time providing easy to read tracks. Moreover, it could yank a boot off a foot covered in wet stockings. The sandy soil on the hillside was better while it was raining as it quickly eroded any signs of passage, but now that the rain was slackening, that was less likely. So rocks were best of all, for any mud they tracked on them was quickly washed away in the still sheeting run-off.

So against every instinct they followed difficult terrain rather than keeping to the easy, more open passages in the woods. Hal kept looking back while Ty picked out the trail, Gabriella and Stephané between them.

Ty said, 'Quiet! I hear something.'

Everyone stopped moving and listened, and a moment later the others could hear movement behind and downhill from them. 'Behind the trees!' whispered Hal, pointing to a thick stand of beech trees a few yards ahead. Their branches were hanging low, with water still dripping off them, and it was the best cover they could manage.

They ducked behind the slender boles and crouched, gathering their dark cloaks around them, hoping that the shadow and mist would hide them. Within a minute they could see men moving on a parallel course to their own, but perhaps ten or fifteen yards farther downhill. Through the trees they could make out a man in a russet long-sleeved shirt and black vest, and see the exasperation on his face as he shouted at another man, 'You said they were coming this way!'

There were eight pirates, and they were wet, miserable, obviously cold from the wind, and no doubt as hungry as the fugitives, but they were bearing up with considerably less grace. The leader stopped and looked around, glancing directly at their hiding position, but their mud-spattered travel cloaks and the gloom conspired to keep them almost invisible.

'Damn it!' the man in the black vest shouted. 'If we come back without her, it'll be our necks in a noose, and that's if we're lucky!' He turned and jabbed a finger into the chest of another man. 'You're supposed to be our best tracker. Why can't we find them?'

Frustration was fraying tempers and the other man yelled back, 'Because whoever's with her knows his way about these woods, Marstan. He's clambered over every bloody boulder, walked up sand washes, waded down pebble bed creeks, used every trick there is.' His bald head sheeted water as he hunched his broad shoulders. 'But I'll wager my share of the booty that they're close enough to hit with a rock.'

The man named Marstan turned full circle. 'But which way?'

'This rain, I'm saying back downhill,' said the tracker. 'More mess washing down these hills and the ground's full on as wet as can be; leeches the sand out in place, leaving cracks in the soil; big hunks of it can come crashing down without warning.' He glanced around and moved his hand in a circle. 'Lots of years the King spends his taxes clearing all the road below 'cause half these bloody hills come washing down every third or fourth rainy season.' He pointed directly up at the four crouching hiders. 'Wouldn't want to be up there on top of all that ground if it suddenly comes sliding down. Besides, they've been staying close enough to the road to see where they're going.' He turned and pointed downhill slightly. 'They're probably heading that way. Only five more miles to the garrison at Farborough, so they may feel safe enough even to be back on the road.'

The man called Marstan nodded once and moved in the indicated direction and the others quickly followed.

Ty waited until they were gone then said, 'Glad I picked up and not downhill.'

'Where do we go?'

Ty smiled. 'We follow them. The one place they won't be looking for us is behind them.'

'Is that wise?' asked the Princess.

'Not very, but it's less risky if we know where they are. Less chance we'll blunder into them or give ourselves away by accident. Just be as quiet as you can and ready to run if I tell you.'

Lady Gabriella and Hal nodded.

'Good,' said Ty. 'Let's go.'

Into the now-driving rain they moved, following the pirates who were seeking them.

The afternoon wore on. Ty stayed as close as he could to the pirates, keeping the back of the last pair trudging through the mud in sight, and the others lingered far behind the young noble from Opardum. He felt confident of being able to avoid detection should the pirates double back to check if they were followed or otherwise proved problematic for the fugitives from Roldem. He held up his hand and turned behind a bole, and Hal moved in the same direction, the two young women a moment behind.

One of the pirates had glanced over his shoulder and now stood motionless as if he had seen something. He was on the verge of speaking when a shout from ahead caused him to turn. Hal could barely make him out but had no doubt he was pulling his sword and running forward. Turning to the women he said, 'Stay here and don't move.' He nodded to Gabriella to emphasize she was responsible now for the Princess's safety, then hurried to where Ty waited. By the time he reached him the sounds of combat were unmistakable. The two young men moved as quickly as the terrain allowed, and came to a small rise where they both fell to the ground, ignoring the mud, and crawled forward to observe the conflict.

A dozen horsemen in the royal tabard of the Kingdom, wearing badges familiar to Hal, were cutting through the pirates like a scythe through wheat. The pirate leader, Marstan, was face down in the mud, his blood pooling around him, while five others also were dead or dying on the ground. The last two pirates were attempting to run downhill, never a good idea with horses in pursuit, and died before they got out of sight.

Ty grinned and was about to say something when Hal put his hand over his mouth. He pulled himself close so that Ty's ear was less than an inch from his lips and whispered, 'Boots.'

Ty looked and his eyes widened in understanding. The riders were dressed as Kingdom light cavalry, but sported a wide variety of boots, some not even proper riding boots. The riders who had cut down the last pirates returned and as they reined in, the entire unit showed no sign of military discipline. One man said, 'Well, you know the orders. If that idiot Marstan didn't have her, she's somewhere up in those woods.'

'You sure, Gravan? Maybe they headed back towards the Eastern Kingdoms.'

'You get paid to kill, not think, Colver. If what I was told is right, she's with two pups from the Kingdom – one's some duke's kid – and a bodyguard. Don't take that one lightly. She's a woman, but she's a killer.' He stood up in his stirrups and looked around into the trees. 'If we're going to search, we need better weather.' He pointed to the bodies on the road. 'Let's clear away the trash and pull back a way. If they think it's clear ahead to Farborough, they may just come wandering in without any help.' He sat back down and said, 'I'm going back to report. Finish up here and take a quick look, but I'll be surprised if you find anything. Get back and I'll start organizing a proper search.'

The lead rider put his heels to his horse and set off down the road while the other eleven men dismounted, three taking reins, and leading the horses away, while the others began gathering the dead. As they started carrying the first two downhill, it was clear the closest thing to a proper pyre they'd come across was a sailor's burial at sea, or being tossed off a cliff into the surf.

Ty signalled and led Hal back to where the two women waited. 'Someone's taken Farborough,' said Hal.

'What do you mean?' asked the Princess.

'The pirates are dead, killed by horsemen wearing Kingdom garb, but it's all a sham. They talked, they're all in it together; maybe the riders were pirates, too. They killed Marstan and his men for failing to find you.'

'They have different boots on,' said Ty.

'Boots? I don't understand,' said Stephané.

'They got the uniforms off of dead Kingdom soldiers, no doubt,' said Ty.

'No,' said Hal. 'If they were stripping corpses those tabards would be bloody. And they would have taken boots.'

'Fair point,' conceded Ty.

'No, someone supplied them those uniforms, but couldn't supply boots.'

'If we can't go to the town of Farborough,' asked the Princess, 'where do we go?'

Hal looked at Ty who said, 'I have no idea.'

10

WILDERNESS

Ty threw a rock.

He gathered in the makeshift sling as the rock struck the rabbit on the head, killing it instantly. The still-wet ground sucked at his boots as he made his way to the kill. It was the third coney he had felled, using slinging skills he had learned as a boy. He was well pleased that he had retained the knack of it and knew the others would be more so for the soon-to-be-cooked rabbits. He glanced at the sky as he turned to head back. It looked as if the rain was finally over. The air had a heavy feeling to it, hot and swampy, but it wasn't as sultry as it had been as the sun set, and his mountain-bred weather sense told him it was getting dryer.

As he trod the game trail, he hoped Hal had managed to get a fire started so that they could quickly dress and cook the rabbits. It had been three days since they'd left the ship and escaped the pirates and what little food they had carried in their belt pouches was long gone. What had started off as a quick hike to a safe village had now turned into a rigorous overland trip into dangerous territory.

Ty reached the clearing they had elected to use for a camp for the evening. While hunting he had looked for signs that anyone was on their trail again, but it appeared as if the false Kingdom soldiers who had been searching for them were far enough away that they could risk smoke from the cook-fire. Hal helped Ty dress out the rabbits and while they were cooking, he went to bury the hides and offal. 'No sense in having carrion eaters circling overhead and calling attention to us,' he said.

As the rabbits cooked, Princess Stephané asked, 'What do we do now?'

Ty said, 'I've been thinking. It's probably more dangerous to double back to the east and head for the border states. Moreover, we can't be sure any of the Eastern Kingdoms haven't allied with one side or the other. We blunder into Prandur's Gate or Maladon, you could be held for ransom or turned over to Lord John Worthington's agents for your "protection" as soon as we surface. No, we strike for Ran. Unless it's fallen, we'll be safe there.'

Hal said, 'If Ran's fallen, we'll have more to worry about than ransom, Princess. It would mean a Keshian presence on the Kingdom mainland in the Eastern Realm, for the first time in history.'

Ty nodded. 'Those false soldiers were almost certainly Kingdom men, from their speech, not Keshian, and they were in league with those Ceresian pirates, so we have no idea whom they serve.' He sighed. 'I know my father is taking care of my mother, and as a minor Kingdom noble he's probably being watched, but it's unlikely more than that.' He glanced at Stephané. 'I know you worry about your parents.'

She nodded. 'And my brothers.' She looked from one to the other. 'My parents have loyal followers. I know Lady Franciezka is important in all this intrigue, but she would die to protect my family. She'll ensure they're safe and it's not in Lord John's interest to harm them. He just wants me married to his son.'

'Which means you're worried about your brothers.'

She smiled a tight smile. 'My brothers are men of character and tougher than one might think.'

Hal smiled. 'So is their sister.'

She glanced at him and saw open admiration in his expression. 'Thank you,' she said. 'That was gallant.'

'Well meant,' he returned. 'You've held up like a soldier.'

Ty turned the rabbits. 'I suggest we eat and move on. Bury the remnants of the fire, just enough to be discovered if someone chances by, then lay in a false trail to the south.'

'We go north-west?' asked Hal.

'If I can read these hills,' he said, looking in that direction, 'there should be water sources up there in that low gap. That means rivers for ample water and caves most likely. We can shelter for a day or two, rest up, fish, hunt, and then strike south-west to Ran.'

'Rest would be good,' said the Princess.

Hal reached out and gently touched her shoulder. 'We'll get you to safety, I swear.'

Stephané smiled and they gazed at one another for a moment, then the Princess looked away to watch the rabbits cooking.

Ty watched this. Then, with a slight incline of his head to Gabriella he added, 'I'm going to scout a bit for shelter.'

Gabriella at once got to her feet. 'I'll go with you. I want to stretch my legs.'

Both Stephané and Hal frowned slightly at the remark, but said nothing.

When they were out of earshot of the others, Ty said, 'Stretch my legs? After three days of hiking these mountains?'

'It was the best I could think of impromptu. Now, what did you want to talk about?'

'What just happened? Back there I mean, with Hal and the Princess?'

Gabriella's eyes narrowed slightly. 'You feeling a pang of jealousy then, young rooster?'

Ty didn't know whether to be amused or annoyed. He chose the first. 'Hardly. Our young lord there may be dreaming of your charge, but I've spent enough time in court to know the Princess will not be married off to some rustic lord, even if he is to be Duke of Crydee some day, let alone a down-in-the-heels, title-poor, back-door-noble son such as myself.'

He grew thoughtful. 'Men who think they need to protect their women get ferociously brave and stupid. If he's being courtly, fair enough, but if he's becoming a love-struck puppy, it would be wise to know.'

She shrugged. 'I can't tell. Some of your Kingdom of the Isles nobles are as untrustworthy and conniving as Roldem's best, but this one?' She fell silent for a moment as they moved towards the sound of water. 'I think he'll do the right thing, no matter what. He's a very . . . well-brought-up young man.'

He smiled. 'And me?'

'You are the sort my mother warned me about.'

He laughed. 'And you?'

She looked off into the distance and said at last, 'I am not usually comfortable speaking about myself.'

'Fair enough. Comfort has been a quality sorely lacking lately. But if you prefer to remain a mystery, I'm fine with that. I just need to know that if it gets bloody, you're there.' He saw her jaw firm and said, 'I assume it's safe to conclude you're not a lady-in-waiting.'

'I am the Princess's personal bodyguard.'

'Damn,' he said lightly. 'I knew you were dangerous.'

Caught halfway between confusion and humour, she frowned. 'Dangerous?'

'I don't usually encounter six-foot-tall beauties, and none before have been as adept at woodcraft as you are. You remind me of my mother.'

'Your mother?'

They found themselves on a slight rise looking down at a large, fast-running creek and half-walked, half-slid down the incline to the bank. Ty looked in both directions then pointed upstream. 'There I think.'

As they moved against the flow of the water, Gabriella asked, 'What is your mother like?'

'Strong, like you,' he answered without hesitation. 'But in a different fashion.'

'Different?'

'Like a slender tree; she bends with the wind, but endures.'

'I think I understand,' said Gabriella. She pointed. 'Look.'

He saw the cave she indicated and as they walked towards it, continued, 'Before I was born, the summer my father was undergoing the naming rite of his . . . our people, the Orosini, a man named Kaspar of Olasko ordered the obliteration of our people, because we would not allow his army to pass through our lands so that he could attack the Duchy of Farinda. Our homes in the High Fastness were destroyed and the few survivors were sold into captivity. My mother was one of those.'

'And your father?'

'My father, my real father, was some unknown soldier of Olasko.'

'But I thought . . . ?'

'Talwin Hawkins married my mother. He had loved her since they were children, and he gave me his name.'

'But I saw you together. You look so much alike.'

Ty grinned. 'An interesting coincidence, isn't it? My father must have been a handsome devil, I always say.' His grin faded. 'Talwin Hawkins is the only father I have ever known and I love him as such. He has cared for me as if I were his own. It's reasonable I'd mimic him as I grew. My mother has not been able to have more children, so he's stuck with me,' he added on a lighter note.

She was silent for a moment then asked, 'Have you a wife?'

'Ha!' he laughed so loudly it echoed through the dell.

He covered his mouth and she looked at him wide-eyed in surprise and covered her own mouth a moment, before saying with a smile, 'I assume that means no.'

'I . . . haven't had the time,' he said quickly. 'My family is . . . the demands . . .' He let the thought go unfinished.

'I was wondering,' she said as they reached the entrance to the cave. 'Rare is the noble that can catch rabbits like a poacher, or fish with mere twine and a tree branch. You know your way in the wild.'

'As do you.' He paused, looking at her. She really was a beauty, though her manner disguised that, and being next to Stephané could render a goddess invisible. He quickly tore his gaze away as he realized he was staring and glanced around. 'I don't like the idea of going in there without a torch.'

'Not much dry wood to make a torch,' she observed.

'We might not have to,' he said, hurrying down to the edge of the river. The heavy rain had washed a large amount of detritus into the creek, depositing it here and there on the shore. He found a likely-looking branch and hurried back. 'Wait here a moment,' he said, and ducked into the cave. A short time later he emerged with a massive clump of moss. 'This will burn slowly and give a weak light, but it's light.' He wrapped the moss around the branch in as tight a knot as he could, then took out flint from his belt pouch and used his hunting knife to strike sparks. He blew into it and got it smouldering and picked up the torch and blew hard on one sport until a flame flared. 'It won't last more than a few minutes, but I'll get a look around.'

'Be careful of the bears,' she asked.

He smiled, knowing the old joke that was coming. 'How can I tell if there's one in there?'

'Usually from the bleeding.'

He shook his head and as he turned to enter he said, 'How many brothers?'

'Four.'

'All older?'

'Yes.'

Shaking his head he only said, 'No wonder,' and entered the cave. She followed him, smiling to herself.

In the gloom they found a widening path that led downward, into a very large cave. Once fashioned by flowing water, the underground hideaway was now above the water table, providing a dry floor upon which to rest. Ty poked the torch around in every corner making sure they were alone, then said, 'Something made a lair here, but two, three years ago.'

'Bear, I think,' said Gabriella.

He made one quick circle around and then said, 'Let's head back. If we wait too much longer, there'll be no rabbit left for either of us.'

'Yes, I've been away too long as it is. The Princess is my charge and I've already violated it by leaving her alone.'

'Then why did you?' Ty asked as they exited the cave.

'It seemed like the right thing to do at the time. Besides, she instructed me that at some point I should go off with you for a short while, as she had something she needed to discuss with Lord Henry in person.'

'Lord Henry?'

'That's how she named him. I assume it must be something she considered a matter of state.'

Now Ty looked completely confused.

'Despite what one might think, Stephané is a very serious-minded woman when she chooses to be. She knows she will be highly placed in marriage, a duchess or even a queen, and that she will play a role vital in keeping peace between Roldem and their neighbours.'

'Now my curiosity is piqued,' admitted Ty. 'Affairs of state, out here of all places.'

'No more improbable than affairs of the heart, surely.'

Not entirely sure what to say to this, Ty merely nodded.

Stephané watched as Gabriella and Ty vanished from sight and turned to Hal who was turning the rabbits. 'How much longer until they are cooked?' she asked.

He said, 'Another half hour. If we had a hotter fire, sooner, but too hot and it dries and is tough. Too slow and it's chewy and tough. Just right and it's savoury . . . and tough.'

She laughed. 'You do manage to keep your spirits up.'

Hal let out a small sigh. 'Truth, Highness? I'd as soon be riding through a thousand Keshian Dog Soldiers with a wooden spoon as my only weapon than having to drag you through this wilderness.'

'You're not dragging me,' she said, smiling. 'I'm escaping.'

He laughed. 'Speaking of keeping one's spirits up.' He turned the rabbits again. The spits were twigs and they rested on rocks, and seemed constantly to want to turn back one way. Vigilance was needed to ensure the rabbits weren't burned through on one side and raw on the other.

She was silent for a moment, her expression turning pensive, and at last she said, 'I wanted to have a chance to speak to you alone.'

He turned to give her his undivided attention. 'Yes?'

'My position is at best difficult,' she began, hesitantly. 'Lady Franciezka holds you and Ty in high regard, or she never would have entrusted me to your care. Yet I fear that your king may not be . . .'

'You worry King Gregory might see you as a bargaining chip, much as your Lord John does.'

'I don't know what to think, Hal,' she said plainly. 'All my life I have been trained to rule, but in the Roldemish fashion of a queen, to offer quiet counsel to my husband when alone, and to smile and remain silent in public.'

Hal thought of Bethany and laughed. 'It's a bit different in the west, especially along the Far Coast. Our mothers, and wives, are hardly shy in letting their feelings be known.'

'What I'm saying is that if it comes to a conflict, I'm not certain I can stand my ground. If Gregory threatens . . .' She fell silent. 'Roldem's fleet combined with that of the Isles would drive Kesh back to their own ports.'

Hal shook his head. 'I know that's conventional thinking, but with those pirates in league with . . . someone, raiding free along this coast the balance of power may not be what we thought.' Seeing her troubled expression, he decided to change the subject. 'But you didn't ask to be alone with me to speak of warfare. I pledge to you that as a son of the House of conDoin, I will give my life if need be to keep you from any harm. When this madness is over you shall be safely returned to Roldem. And you'll have a Kingdom-born husband in tow only if that is your pleasure.'

She smiled. 'Thank you.' Impulsively she leaned forward and gave him a quick kiss on the cheek. 'I am in need of a good friend.'

For reasons Hal didn't fully understand, hearing that phrase caused his stomach to sink a bit. Pushing aside his feelings, he said, 'It is the burden of your office that you marry at your father's pleasure. Not the pleasure of Lord John Worthington or Sir William Alcorn—' His eyes widened.

'What?' asked Princess Stephané.

'When did Lord John rise to such great influence in your father's court?'

'I'm not sure. He's been around for quite some time. He was very nice to me when I was little.'

'But when did he gain control, er, start to manifest enough influence to get your father to begin making policy changes in Roldem?'

She thought for a moment, then said, 'Five years ago, maybe six.'

'Immediately after the Three Moon Banapis?'

She thought, then said, 'I think so.' Six years earlier, one of the rarest of events had taken place when all three moons rose full, as one, on the eve of Banapis, Midsummer's Day. It happened once every century, more or less.

'That's when Sir William began asserting his influence.'

'What does that mean?' asked the Princess.

'I'm not entirely sure,' said Hal, taking the rabbits off the fire. 'All I do know is that we must somehow get you safely to Rillanon, and to enter the city without drawing attention to ourselves, I think we need to find Lord James Dasher Jamison.'

'Why him?'

'For many reasons, least of which is that he is by a strange twist of history a very distant cousin of mine but, most importantly, he's the one man in Rillanon I am certain is not under the control of Sir William Alcorn.'

Ty and Gabriella appeared and Ty said, 'We found a cave.'

'Good,' said Hal. 'Rabbit?'

Neither bothered to answer as Ty tore one in half and handed it to Gabriella while Hal did the same for the Princess. Around a mouthful of hot coney, Ty said, 'We should stay dry in that cave and we can rest up for a day or two.'

Hal shook his head. 'No, we need to leave at first light tomorrow and start for Ran.'

'Ran, you certain?'

Hal nodded. 'Yes. From there I can use my father's rank to convince someone to sail us to Rillanon. We must get there as quickly and secretly as possible.'

'Isn't that going to be a little difficult if you're bullying naval captains with your father's rank?'

'Not if I'm accompanied by my . . .' he waved his hand, 'companions. We'll contrive a story, but this young beauty is no princess,' he nodded at Stephané. 'She is someone or other's daughter whom I'm using badly as she hopes against hope to marry above her station.'

Stephané actually laughed. 'Now you play the role of a young noble of my nation.' She sighed. 'Even my brothers.' She leaned forward and touched him on the arm. 'I will say, Lord Henry, if other men of the west are like you, the ladies of my nation would do well to visit the Far Coast.'

Hal actually blushed and Ty laughed. Gabriella contented herself with a knowing smile, and they began to fashion a story that would pass muster once they reached Rillanon.

Assuming they reached Ran, which meant getting through these mountains without running into bandits, false Kingdom soldiers, or wild animals. Two swords, three belt knives, and a sling might gain them a meal, but against what lived in these mountains they were little defence.

Still, Hal turned his mind away from the dangers and considered what needed to be done to get the Princess to his king. He was determined to ensure she arrived safely and departed as she willed, or he would give his life in the attempt.

Hal awoke suddenly, and saw in the half-gloom of the cave both Gabriella and Ty on their feet with weapons in hand. Ty motioned for Hal to stay silent. He realized his arms were around the Princess, and that she was looking at him with questioning eyes. Untangling himself, he put a finger to his lips and drew his sword. The last he remembered was standing his watch at the cave mouth and returning to wake Ty, then snuggling in behind Stephané for warmth. Summer it might be, but in that cave in the mountains it was anything but warm. At sometime during the night she had either backed into him or he had reached out, but waking up in that intimate proximity was troubling.

He moved quietly until he stood on the other side of Lady Gabriella, who crouched with a wicked-looking dirk in her right hand, a shorter belt knife in her left. He remembered the belt knife, but couldn't help but wonder where she had been hiding the dirk.

Voices from outside were now intelligible. 'Bloody nuisance, checking every cave from here to Ran. They're miles east of here, I'll wager.'

'You're not paid to wager or think,' said another voice. 'If the captain wants you to dive into every stream, climb trees, and look under rocks, that's what you'll do.'

'And who made you king of the day?'

A meaty smack followed, and the first voice cried, 'No need for that, Neely! I was just saying . . .'

'Say any more and you'll be crawling back to the camp. Now, get in and check that cave!'

Hal glanced around. The cave was larger in the rear than at the mouth, with an 'S' curve coming in, so they might be able to hide. Hal indicated to the Princess that she should move into the farthest corner and she nodded and hurried over on silent feet.

He then motioned for Lady Gabriella to stand opposite the second curve of the entrance, where she would be seen as soon as the man stepped inside. She indicated she understood and moved to the indicated position. Hal tapped Ty on the shoulder and they moved until their backs were flat against the wall, just beyond the curve that hid them from anyone coming into the cave.

Hal put up his sword and pulled out his belt knife just as a man came into the cave, squinting as his eyes adjusted to the gloom. Gabriella moved and the man's eyes widened. 'You!' he began.

Hal stepped up behind him and clamped his hand over his mouth, quickly cutting his throat and with a yank, tossing him to one side. Ty was already moving to protect the entrance, sword at the ready.

After a moment, a shout from outside was heard. 'Booker! You taking a piss in there or what?'

Ty glanced at Hal who shook his head, indicating that they both should stay silent.

'Booker?' came the inquiry as footsteps could be heard entering the cave.

'Neely!' shouted Hal, trying to disguise his voice.

'What?' came the reply. A beefy man stepped into view.

This time it was Lady Gabriella who stepped out of the shadows and had a blade across the man's throat before he could react. Even before he had hit the ground, Ty was moving towards the cave mouth to see if any others waited outside.

A moment later he was back. 'Just the two of them!'

Hal said, 'We move now. If they're out in pairs, it means their camp is close by.'

The four of them came out of the cave and saw two horses tied to low-hanging tree limbs. Ty kept his gaze moving and seeing nothing, he clambered up a pile of rocks until he was standing on top of the overhang above the cave entrance. Finally he pointed to the south. 'Smoke. Campfire. Maybe a mile away, no more.'

He scrambled back down and jumped the last five feet to land beside the Princess. Looking at Hal he said, 'We ride?'

'Double,' said Hal.

'We won't be moving fast that way,' said Ty.

'If they have patrols out in spokes of a wheel, we travel straight away from this cave and that campfire smoke, and no one will come back here for hours, after those two fail to report back. We may get until tomorrow morning.' Hal looked around. 'I know nothing of these mountains. Which way?'

Ty pointed. 'We follow the water course. There will be a cut in the mountains, or we turn west when we run out of trail. Either way, we'd best be miles from here when they find those two inside the cave.'

Hal nodded agreement and the two women hurried towards the horses. Ty and Hal grabbed some loose brush and moved it around, masking the horse prints back to a patch of rocks, then hurried back up the slope. Hal mounted then extended an arm and the Princess swung up behind him, Ty doing the same with Gabriella.

Without further discussion, Ty took the lead, and they began the slow climb up into the mountains, farther away from civilization every step.

11

TREACHERY

J im kept close to the wall.

The city watch moved down the street in noisy fashion, six men, two abreast, marching as if on parade. It would have looked comical, except that it was the dead of night, hours before dawn, and the city was now officially under martial law. That martial law had been declared mere hours after Jim had slipped out of the palace seemed more than a coincidence.

Jim waited. As he expected, a few minutes after the passing of the watch, a pair of keen-eyed men came peering into every shadow, doorway, and window, moving as quietly as cats. Sir William Alcorn was sparing no effort in locating the ailing Duke's grandson, apparently.

After leaving Bill the Butcher's establishment, James had intended to check on one of his safe houses, a small rented room over a dry goods store where he had secreted a fair amount of gold, several different documents and disguises, and a sufficient number of weapons to ensure his ability to defend himself.

He had almost walked into a trap.

His 'bump of trouble' had tripped when he started down the street where the shop lay, when he noticed a man lingering at the far corner. Had he approached from that direction he would certainly have been sighted. Depending on how many agents Sir William had nearby he might have been able to escape. Or he might have ended up in chains. Or dead.

He walked into a tavern at the corner, convinced he hadn't been seen, and sat there nursing a pint of ale, spilling most of it on the floor when no one was looking. The straw covering the stones was changed almost every day, and this early it was relatively fresh. It could soak up a lot of ale.

He waited until to make sure he hadn't been seen, then ducked out the back. He had wandered the docks, moving in a random fashion, until he was completely certain no one was following him, then headed for what he considered to be his safest safe house on the island. He was especially cautious approaching this one and was relieved to see no hint of anyone watching it.

It was a shack at the end of a long beach just to the east of the southernmost wharf in the city. It was called Old Wharf, for it was the oldest one left standing, and had the benefit of having been neglected to the point of being useless. Jim had seen a couple of recommendations it be torn down for one civil improvement or another, but had managed to misdirect those memoranda so that no one in authority could ever act on them.

There was no reason for keeping the wharf in place, save

one: it provided a safe exit out of the city for Jim. There was an ancient culvert, used by fishermen in ages past, where refuse from catches had been dumped before being taken into market. Flotsam, kelp, thrown-away fish, and the occasional corpse had been dumped into the culvert for decades. The high tide would come in and wash it clean twice a day. As the small town became a big city, the wharf proved less and less effective until it had been entirely abandoned more than a century before.

But that culvert still was washed clean of debris every time the high tide went out, and Jim had more than once used it as a way out of the walled city of Rillanon. He reached the shack after sundown, while there was enough twilight to see anyone within a half-mile, and he knew no one had followed him.

The shack was one of a half-dozen or so abandoned buildings from times long past when net mending and other fishing-related activities had taken place on the beach. Fishermen had graduated from the shallow-draught, two- or three-man craft used still on other parts of the island, to larger, deeper-draught boats that now required anchorage in the harbour. So the shacks went unused.

Except by Jim.

The third one from the end, unguarded even by a door, presented a gaping maw of an opening and one empty window. Jim stepped inside and fell to his knees, scooping sand up and throwing it to the side. It took ten minutes of digging but at the end he had a mound of sand in one corner of the shack and a trap door revealed in the other.

He opened it and dropped in. Feeling around in the darkness he found a small table upon which was placed a torch dipped in dried resin and a flint-and-steel igniter. He tripped the igniter and soon the torch illuminated the room.

All was as he had left it and he placed the torch in a iron holder on the wall, went to a rack of clothing and began picking out what he needed.

An hour later a scruffy-looking sailor with a large dufflebag emerged from the shack and hurried towards the old wharf, knowing that he would get through it only minutes before the tide filled it. He didn't mind swimming through the channel surge, but did not wish to explain how he was drenched when he reached his next meeting place.

He got back into the city proper with only soaking trousers below the calf and they would quickly dry out as he walked. He resisted the urge to scratch at the false beard he now sported and the theatre paint that had been applied to his face to make him look swarthier than usual. The accent he adopted was that of a Kingdom sailor from Pointer's Head, most of whom had ancient Keshian ancestry and thus a tendency to be darker than most in the Kingdom. Unless Sir William's agents could anticipate his disguise, they would still be searching for a man younger, fairer of skin, and without facial hair.

Jim entered a dock side tavern and glanced around the room. In the corner sat a young man, waiting patiently. Jim sat and if the young man was surprised at his appearance, he masked it well.

'Karrick,' said Jim.

The young man nodded and didn't use his name. 'Quite the . . . look you have there.'

'I'm outbound on a ship in an hour.'

'I won't ask where.'

'Good,' said Jim. They both knew that Karrick couldn't be forced to reveal what he didn't know.

Karrick was young, no more than twenty-one years of age, but he was perhaps Jim's most trusted agent in Rillanon. He was also the man Jim had got closest to Bill the Butcher. The organization of the thieves in Rillanon was different to that in Krondor, but there was still a need for communication between Bill's Council and various gang leaders throughout the island.

Karrick had been working for Bill since he was a boy of ten. But he had been working for Jim since he was a boy of nine.

He looked enough like Jim to have been his son, and to be honest Jim had a little trouble remembering exactly where he had been nine months before Karrick's birth, yet he doubted it. As Jim Dasher he had bedded his share of whores in Krondor, but James Jamison rarely frequented the ale-houses and brothels in Rillanon. Still rarely was not never and there was a resemblance. Karrick wore his hair down to his shoulders, but he was clean shaven, and had blue eyes rather than Jim's brown. Yet there was a smile and tilt of head that looked very familiar, so occasionally Jim wondered.

Most of those in the thieves' trade had little memory of their childhood. Either they had been orphans or they chose not to remember fathers who beat them, mothers who were drinking or taking drugs to endure being touched by loathsome men. Urchin gangs roamed the streets here as they did in every other big city, for despite being the Jewelled City of the Kingdom, at heart it was grimy, dark, and dangerous, including all the unpleasant realities of a city: sewers, slaughterhouses, rendering shacks, fish wharfs, and as assorted a collection of seedy taverns and filthy brothels as you'd find north of Kesh. So despite the magnificent splendour of the palace and every other building on the hills being faced with brilliant stonework, it was still just a city. And whatever Karrick remembered from his childhood he never shared with Jim.

All Jim knew is that while Karrick had lived his entire life within sight of those magnificent edifices atop the hill, he barely noticed them. He was too concerned with staying alive. He said, 'It's been, what? Five years?'

'Six.'

'I was surprised when Anne from the palace contacted me and told me to be here.' Karrick leaned back, one wellmuscled arm draped over the back of his chair. A serving man came over and took an order for two jacks of ale.

When he was gone, Jim said, 'I have always tried to give

you what I could, to supplement what you've had to learn on your own, but contact between us was never a good idea.'

'It was a good year,' said Karrick, and Jim knew exactly what he was talking about. In their first year together, Karrick had been a promising nine-year-old with a toughness, resiliency, and deep rooted sense of survival far beyond his years. He had been running a gang near the docks, and boys four, five, even six years older than him had taken his orders.

Unbeknownst to the boy, two men had taken notice of the enterprising boy: Jim Dasher of Krondor and Bill Cutter of Rillanon. Jim had got to him first.

For that first year, Jim had spent time with Karrick ensuring that he was better trained in hand-to-hand fighting than the other boys, teaching him the sword, when no other lad had that skill. Locks, how to set up a lookout, a thousand subtle but critical knacks that set apart a thief like Jim or his great-grandfather Jimmy the Hand from any common street thug.

From Jim's point of view, Karrick was as close to Jimmy the Hand as any man living. He was faster than Jim was, even if only by a little. He was better at climbing the walls and roofs of the city, though Jim reserved the thought that had he been Karrick's age, he would have kept pace with him. He knew everything Jim could teach him about locks and traps, and to pick one and avoid the other. And also he had taught him to read and write, skills sorely lacking in the other urchins of Rillanon.

In the end, that year had cemented a bond that Jim had continued even after Bill the Butcher took Karrick in. Jim never came to Rillanon without spending time with him, and always ensured Karrick had gold beyond what he could steal for himself, and the means to hide from Bill and flee the island safely should the need arise.

Then, six years before, Karrick had been promoted to a position with the Council itself. Their last meeting had been the night Karrick told Jim of that elevation. Jim had said, with some true sadness, that there could be no further contact between them unless the situation was dire. As Bill's chosen agent, Karrick would be under close scrutiny and it was too risky for them to remain in touch. So, a code word and a venue was selected for any future meeting, and each went their separate way.

Karrick said, 'So, I imagine this means that grave crisis you always spoke about has arrived?'

Jim smiled. 'You mean beyond the war with Kesh and the attempt to incapacitate the Duke of Rillanon, and Sir William Alcorn's apparent attempt to seize control of the Kingdom?'

Karrick smiled, and again to Jim it was like looking in a mirror. 'Well, there is that.'

Jim nodded. 'It's time for you to take over the Council.'

Karrick said nothing for a while. Then he said, 'That will be difficult.'

'If it was easy, I wouldn't need you.'

Karrick's eyebrow lifted slightly, and he smiled again. 'Need me?' He leaned forward. 'All these years . . . since we met, I've wondered at what point you would finally decide that I was ready to serve.'

'You've been ready to serve for at least six years, Karrick.' Jim fell silent as the ale appeared and the server walked away. 'I just didn't need your particular gifts until now. More to the point, the Kingdom didn't need them.'

Karrick nodded, and there was a strange hint of sadness in his expression. 'Have you ever lived a lie so long that it became true?'

Jim looked around the room, not liking where this conversation might lead. Seeing no one but the barman and one other customer, a elderly drunk, he felt his anxiety lessen.

Karrick chuckled. 'No, Jim, I'm not betraying you to Bill.' He looked at the disguised noble. 'You're the closest thing to a father I ever had, even though I barely saw you for more than a week for the first five years after we met. As I said, that first year, that was a good year.'

Jim said nothing.

Karrick said, 'Have you ever wondered . . .'

Jim knew exactly what was being asked. 'Yes, I have. Now, speaking of sons, I've arranged for Bill to think his boy James is taking over the Mockers in exchange for helping me with a few things during the war.'

Karrick could barely contain himself. 'He believes you?'

'He believes because he wants to believe, and frankly, I was convincing.' Jim looked around the inn and said, 'I'm honestly going to be done with all this when this war is over. I am not exactly sure where I'll end up, assuming it's not at the end of a rope, but when this is all over, I am letting go.'

'The Mockers?'

'Everything.' He leaned forward and lowered his voice. 'I've already dispatched messages to Krondor. Bill's boy is to apprentice with the Nightmaster. He is supposed to assume control of the Mockers, become the next Upright Man, when I step down.'

'I know James well,' said Karrick. 'He's as cunning as a sewer rat and ambitious: which is why his father wants him on the other side of the Kingdom. But he lacks the skill to manage things. And he has a temper.'

'That's useful.'

'It should keep him from forming quick alliances in the Mockers,' said Karrick.

'It's immaterial,' said Jim. 'He'll be dead sooner or later. Bill will get a message of condolence saying his boy died during a job gone terribly wrong, slain by the Crushers. That's assuming, of course, that Bill's still alive.'

Karrick said, 'I gather that means I'm supposed to decide when it's time to remove Bill?'

'How many know that Bill is the Council?'

'His three sons, myself, two others. After that it's much the same as the Mockers. A message comes through the local gang chief from the Council, delivered by a street boy.'

'And you control the street boys, still?'

Karrick nodded.

'One son to Krondor. Arrange with an army sergeant you trust to have one other son arrested and sympathize with Bill when he dies trying to escape. The last son, leave until after Bill's death and keep close to him, make yourself indispensable until it's time for you to take his place. The two others you decide if they will serve you or need replacing.'

'They'll serve,' said Karrick. 'And I know which son to arrest and which to commiserate with . . . for a while.'

'When Bill's son James is on his way to Krondor and after I'm gone begin these tasks. Ensure that Anne always knows how to reach you.'

Jim was ready to leave and said, 'Our relationship cuts both ways, Karrick. Not in issues of blood, no matter what they may or may not be, but of this: as close as I may be to being a father to you, so you are to being a son to me. It is not ideal; I have no such illusions, but you've been loyal and reliable, as much as any father would wish a son to be. When all is said and done, if it is within my means, I shall deliver you to higher standing than a king among thieves.'

Karrick laughed. 'You see me standing in the palace with starched shirt and brocade coat? Dancing with the ladies?'

Jim shared the laugh. 'What's the matter? You can't dance?'

Karrick kept chuckling and said, 'All will be done as you've instructed. I will wait to hear from you.'

Jim thought for a moment. Then he said, 'If you don't hear from me within the month, send word after this thing is done to the Black Ram in Ran. I believe that is Bill's usual place to exchange messages. We might as well continue to use his couriers.'

'Bill alive or dead, that's the easiest way,' agreed Karrick. 'So that means you're bound to Ran?'

'Sooner or later,' said Jim as he rose.

'I'll finish my drink,' said the young thief.

'Fare well.'

'Fare well all of us,' replied Karrick.

Then Jim was out of the door.

Jim made his way to the docks where a ship was ready to depart for Ran. He had already had his name added to the roster of sailors. Now he purchased a small bottle of evil-smelling distilled spirits and poured it over his head before reaching the royal docks.

He feigned being intoxicated as he hurried along the long pier jutting out into the harbour. He knew that Sir William would have agents watching every ship leaving the harbour, but assumed he might be less vigilant on the Navy Pier, given that it was already crawling with military, any of whom would be quick to seize a suspicious-looking character like Jim in time of war.

But there was one ship on the pier which was not a warship but a transport vessel, and it had a civilian crew. And when he reached the gangway, two bored-looking Royal Marines were flanking the plank up to the ship.

'Papers,' one demanded as he got there.

Then from above, the bosun's voice cut through the air like a knife. 'Jax! You drunken whore's son! I should leave you there and make you swim after the ship! Get your lazy arse up here!'

Jim successfully looked unfocused and unsure. He fumbled in his shirt as if he was trying to find his papers, and the bosun roared, 'Now, damn your eyes!'

The marine shook his head slightly and said, 'Go on, then.'

Jim went up the gangway and received an ungentle slap to the back of the head as he passed the bosun, another of the few agents left in the military he could trust. Jim would no doubt get punishment, and the rest of the crew knew better than to question the presence of a newcomer if the bosun knew him: they'd assumed he'd sailed with that man before and was getting a second chance, a story that Jim would relay if asked.

He hurried below, stowed his gear, then headed back on deck. He might reek of spirits, but he was not drunk, so he quickly made his way to the topgallants and made ready to lower sail.

Jim felt an unusual sinking in his stomach and realized that never before in his life had he felt this sense of foreboding. And he felt an unfamiliar pang; he was betraying Bill the Butcher. Usually such treachery would hardly give him a moment's pause, but for some reason this time he felt bad about condemning the man to death. He realized that despite what he had said to Bill, he really did want to get out of this business and what he had said to Karrick was the truth. He would quit and find a suitable replacement for both Jim Dasher of Krondor and James Jamison, agent of the King.

For a brief moment, Jim could hang in the yards, his feet supported only by footropes, as he waited for the command to lower sail. He reflected on his decision and knew it was the right one; he was spent. He would die for the Crown, but he would not waste away for it.

He wondered how his counterparts, Kaseem and especially Franciezka, were doing and hoped they were experiencing better fortune than he was at the moment.

Lady Franciezka Sorboz crouched low behind a decorative hedge, one hand resting on a lethal dagger. The blade was coated with a venom that would paralyse whoever was cut within seconds, preventing an alarm being raised. For an instant she was struck by the incongruity of sneaking into the very palace in which she often resided, the defences for which she had helped to fashion. She particularly loved this garden, behind the guest quarters now occupied by Lord John Worthington. She remembered lovely summer nights like this with the air spiced by the scent of jasmine and gardenia.

Franciezka wore tight-fitting travel togs and boots designed to permit quick movement, and minimize snagging on branches or the iron spikes embedded into the wall she had just climbed.

She was desperate to break the stalemate within the palace.

The King and Queen were locked up in their apartments, sumptuous surroundings for certain, but no less a prison. All communication with the household staff and the government were being conducted through Lord John Worthington's most trusted lackeys.

Franciezka was reduced to a handful of agents she could trust, but none were placed close enough to the royal family to help. Her entire organization had been designed to look outward, at Kesh and the Isles and the Eastern Kingdoms, not inward. Kesh might have their secret police, but it was not under Kaseem Hazara-Khan's purview. Jim used his Mockers in Krondor and his contacts with other criminal elements to gather information, but given the politics and history of the Kingdom of the Isles, a revolt by the nobility was more likely than any popular uprising, and the last one they had endured was over three hundred years ago.

Roldem's population was far more homogeneous than either rival nation. The Isles and Kesh were like conquered city-states and regions forged into a single empire or kingdom by centuries of occupation and absorption. But Yabon was different to Rillanon, and the Isalani people were nothing like the Truebloods of the Overn Deep. Roldem had always been one people.

Given Roldem's history, a coup d'état was unthinkable. And even under Lord John's offices, it didn't feel like a coup, at least not yet.

But something was under way that was creating disastrous consequences for the Kingdom of Roldem. Trade was at a standstill and the only goods produced on the island were still in abundance, but they were quickly being consumed or bought up by speculators. She reckoned they were less than three months from a scarcity that would have the population demanding an end to the Keshian blockade. A month after that would come food riots in the streets of the capital.

She moved along the wall, alert to any passing patrols or guards, but found this portion of the palace unguarded. She wasn't entirely sure why, as the rest of the complex was ringed with guards.

A loyal servant had mentioned that something was planned for Lord John's private quarters, as instructions had been given that two hours after sunset his quarters were to be sealed off and he was not to be disturbed until he personally opened the doors. No visitors were scheduled but he had requested that food and wine be provided. Even his son and most trusted aides were being ordered out of his quarters.

His determination for privacy played to her advantage, because he had ordered the guards who might patrol outside his quarters out of this garden. They were now patrolling on the street beyond the wall she had clambered over, their usual routine disrupted and their vigilance compromised. Not that they were ever that vigilant, thought Franciezka as she moved through shadows; the palace guards not detailed to protect the royal family were soldiers of little value used mostly for ceremony. She crossed an open expanse of lawn to reach the wall of the palace, ducking into the shadow of an elm tree that would cut the afternoon's glare through the terrace windows of Lord John Worthington's quarters.

She was determined to discover what it was Lord John was up to. Inching her way to the balcony outside Lord John's private quarters, she listened.

She could hear men's voices inside, though the words were indistinct. She peered up over the edge of the balcony, between stone risers and then ducked back down. Lord John's quarters had large glass doors opening on to a broad low balcony, and in the heat of summer he had left them open. But getting up over the railing would prove difficult without being seen.

Glancing up again, she saw that the two men in the room with Lord John had their backs to her, so she moved to the closest point to the wall where the balcony began, just out of Lord John's line of vision, and nimbly leapt up to the rail, then down, landing silently. Her knees hurt slightly and she realized she was starting to feel her age.

She crouched down, back against the wall, knowing that on either side of the doors were matching framed floor-to-ceiling windows with sashed curtains. Pulling a small folded hood out of her belt, she quickly donned it. Black knit with two eye holes, it would not reflect the light coming though the glass. She inched her way along the wall until she was just next to the edge of the glass surrounding the doors and peered in. Her eyes widened and only the most rigorous training over the years kept her from exclaiming.

There were three John Worthingtons in the room!

They looked identical: could they be triplets? One was clearly Lord John, unmistakable in the forest-green jacket he preferred to wear most days. The other Lord John was dressed like a Keshian noble of the Trueblood, bare-chested and shaven headed, with a circlet of gold ending with Keshian royal falcons upon his brow, arm bands of gold, and cross-gartered sandals. He wore a heavy linen skirt, girdled with a wide crocodile hide belt fastened with a gold clasp.

The third Lord John was dressed like a noble of the Kingdom of the Isles, and it was he who was speaking.

'This is unwise. We should not be gathered together in one place.'

'Brothers,' answered the Lord John she knew. 'There is no risk. Roldem is at peace, albeit a fragile one, so this is the safest place to meet. Kesh is crawling with guards, legionaries, nobles armed to the teeth ready to kill one another, and that palace has few places to be unobserved. The Kingdom is still infected with those damned agents of Lord James's grandson.'

The Isles version of Lord John said, 'I've had most of them out, those that I couldn't turn. His skill in picking agents with strong minds . . . our magic was not as effective as we thought it might be. Good resources were wasted when we had to start cutting throats.'

The one Franciezka thought of as the 'real' Lord John said, 'I had the same experience here, but the Lady Franciezka's agents were not as numerous. Roldem has grown complacent over the centuries.'

Franciezka bristled, but kept listening.

'Still, the two elder princes are out to sea somewhere, Grandprey is in the mountains with a large part of the army still loyal to the Crown, and the Princess is missing, almost certainly off the island by now. So, our plans for Roldem must be placed in abeyance for the time being. How fare things in Kesh?'

The Keshian answered. 'Their intelligence is crushed and Hazara-Khan hides in the northern desert among his kin. The desert people have always been loyal but they are far from the capital. There is nothing to keep us from moving forward with our plans in the City of Kesh.'

'Good,' said the real Lord John. 'Let us inaugurate the second stage of our plan when you return. What of the Isles?'

'It is most well suited for our next phase. There is no announced heir, but many potential claimants. We have displaced their armies, so the King's Armies of the West cannot respond to any calls for aid from our valley.'

Franciezka frowned. Our valley? she wondered.

'Good, then see King Gregory on his way as soon as you return.'

Franciezka's heart pounded. These three men, brothers, whatever they were, planned on murdering the King of the Isles!

The Keshian asked, 'What of the elves? I can order our forces outside of Ylith to E'bar if needs be.'

'Those damned elves are impossible,' said the 'real' Lord John.

The Isles John said, 'Every agent we've dispatched, from either Isles or Kesh has failed to report back. We assume them dead at the hands of those Star Elves.'

The real John said, 'All we can do is what we've done before; throw what's left of the demon legion at them and keep them busy until it's too late for them to take a hand.'

'We'd best depart,' said the Keshian. 'I hold no belief we shall be able to dispatch the Emperor: too many attempts over the years makes it problematic; but we can certainly keep Kesh so occupied with this war that they will be ineffective in challenging us.'

'Then to you, brother,' said the real John, 'comes the task of beginning our great work.'

'I lack certain advantages,' said the Isles John. 'If I had killed Duke James, there would be too much scrutiny. I've isolated his grandson and rendered him impotent, but he's still out there somewhere and not to be underestimated. I lack the convenience of a son to marry to a princess so my motives are somewhat questioned. Still, they are Kingdom simpletons and think merely of personal gain; they see me positioning myself as the next Duke of Rillanon, and that answers all their questions as to my actions.'

'Raw ambition is so easy for these humans to understand,' said the real John. 'The boy I charmed into thinking I was his father fits the role admirably. And those I control will rally to support his marriage to the Princess, if we can find her. I almost regret the need to kill him when the time comes.'

'Regret?' asked the Keshian.

'I said almost,' replied Lord John. 'Now, let us be about our tasks. Our master grows impatient and his wrath is not to be courted. Let us serve and serve quickly.'

Suddenly the two visiting versions of Lord John vanished from sight leaving only a faint grey smoke hanging in the air. Franciezka pulled her head away from the window and without hesitation leapt from the balcony and sprinted for the outside wall. She had no idea how she was going to find Jim and get word to him, but someone was about to try to kill his king and he might be the only man in the Isles who could save him.

With almost effortless ease, as the stress of the moment made her heart pound and her limbs feel light, she leapt onto a trellis and from there to the branch of a tree near the wall, then on top of the wall, avoiding the iron spikes, and over the wall to the cobbles on the other side.

Within seconds the Lady Franciezka Sorboz was lost in the darkness.

12

ONSLAUGHT

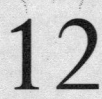

Martin shouted.

'Damn!' He slammed his fist against the table.

Brendan shook his head at his brother's frustration as they sat alone in the kitchen of the mayor's house.

Martin's vexation was self-directed, but he managed to get the attention of everyone in the room. Brendan signalled to the two cooks and their three helpers that he needed time alone with his brother. They exchanged glances; then the head cook nodded and they left through the back door.

'What is it?' asked Brendan.

After the water demon assault, Martin had been reorganizing the city's meagre defences, while Miranda and Nakor had been interrogating the rogue magician, Akesh. Brendan had spent that time inventorying the city's remaining resources and had given Martin the list to read a half-hour ago.

Martin appeared lost in thought and didn't answer his brother's question.

In the three days since that assault, the Keshian commander had been obviously content to take his time and return to a more mundane approach to siegecraft. He was constructing massive trebuchets on the crest of the western road, and it was obvious he would soon begin pounding at the gates of the city.

Bolton had made a thorough investigation of the old keep above the city and the escape tunnel that led to a short distance behind the Keshians' position. Martin was desperately trying to concoct a plan to send men through that tunnel and assault the trebuchets, set them ablaze and then escape, but he was convinced there was no way to do that without losing every man on the raid, as well as having no guarantee that the siege engines would be destroyed.

'What I'd give for one company of heavy horse right now,' he said. In his mind he could see them cutting through the Keshian defences, enabling the raid against the trebuchets to work. Then the absurdity of his position struck him and he said, 'If I'm wasting wishes, I should wish for the bulk of the King's Armies of the West to be marching up from the south.'

Brendan pushed away a now-empty lunch plate. Stores were beginning to be a problem, so Martin had ordered rationing. Bethany had successfully argued for full rations for those fighting and half-rations for the rest. When Miranda and Nakor told him about the wagon caravan parked outside the city, he had sent out a detail to bring them in only to discover they had turned back toward Zün when the last attack had begun. He now was questioning his own ability to protect this city.

He had nearly had a stroke from anger when he learned how easily the Keshian demon-summoners had infiltrated the city, and had put Bolton in charge of interrogating every traveller still incarcerated in the inn at the city gate and a nearby store converted to housing. He wasn't certain how effective the young captain might be in ferreting out more Keshian agents, but it was better than just waiting for one to reveal himself to the detriment of the city.

Martin felt overwhelmed, and was doing his best to hide that, but both Brendan and Bethany knew he was approaching his limit. It was one thing to study tactics, strategy, siegecraft, and the other military subjects, and to command a garrison for a short time as field experience, but it was quite another to bear responsibility for a city at war. Granted, most of the inhabitants had fled, but there were still women and children within these walls and while everything he had studied said the same thing – focus on the military aspects and let the civilians fend for themselves – still he could not bring himself to pretend they were not here, not a responsibility, not *his* responsibility.

Brendan waited for his brother to relax slightly before he said, 'We have what we have.'

Martin nodded, pushing aside the list. Food was not critical yet, but it would be. Water was not a problem due to the numerous wells inside the walls. Arrows were becoming important, mostly because the finely fashioned ones had all been spent and now they were relying on those fashioned by boys pressed into acting as fletchers, using whatever feathers could be found for each flight. Weapons were not yet critical, either, but uninjured men to wield them was his most pressing need.

Earlier in the day he had seen the Keshians moving at the ridge line, the first sign the Keshian commander was getting ready for a conventional attack.

At last he said, 'An attack through the tunnel from the keep to take out those siege engines risks too much. I think we'd lose too many men and might gain nothing tangible from it. Moreover, we'd have to block the tunnel to prevent the Keshians from using it and I'd like it available to us against future need.'

Brendan couldn't find any reason to disagree so he merely nodded.

Glancing around, Martin realized they were alone in the kitchen. 'Where is everybody?'

'Giving us a little privacy.'

Martin grunted. He waved his hand in the general direction of the front gate to the city. 'The Keshians still mount a superior force, despite that fiasco with the demons. Even with their magician neutralized by Miranda and Nakor, they have the strength to beat down the door eventually and walk right in. We're beginning to run low on supplies and in another week, we'll be at less than half-rations.' His voice lowered. 'And then the real panic begins. If we're still here defending. And to defend the city we have an untried boy with delusions of military genius.'

Brendan laughed.

'What?' barked Martin, looking annoyed.

'I'm sorry,' said Brendan, 'really, I am, but for a moment you were again the angry brother who couldn't quite beat Hal at a game. You used to pout like a little girl.'

Martin's eyes widened. 'I did not!'

'You did so,' said Brendan. 'And you were doing it again. Look, be kind to yourself a moment, and stop wading in pity. If the King's Marshall was here, with only what you have to defend with, nothing more, do you think he would have managed any better? What would he do? Gather everyone in the city square and with a rousing speech, get them all fired up so they'd charge out the gate and thrash the Keshians to the last, man and boy?'

Martin started to chuckle. 'All right, a little pity if you must.'

'You're doing as well as any man, I reckon.'

Miranda and Nakor came into the kitchen. Between them was a very obviously beaten Keshian magician. Both of his eyes were swollen, the left completely shut, and he couldn't manage to put his weight on his left foot without wincing. 'We have wrung everything from him we could,' Miranda said to Martin.

Nakor said, 'It's not his fault, really. It seems someone put some ideas in his head.'

'Magic?' inquired Martin.

Miranda nodded, while Nakor said, 'It's a very subtle trick. I think it's been there in his head a very long time, years perhaps, so that he thinks everything he did was his own idea, but really, someone else made him do it.'

Brendan said, 'I'm not sure I understand. You're saying he's some sort of dupe?'

'Hard to say,' replied Nakor. 'He may have been thinking bad things before this trick, or he might have been thinking good things, and the trick turned him bad.' He grinned apologetically.

'Either way he's a traitor,' said Miranda.

'To whom?' said Martin. 'He's Keshian. How is he a traitor?'

Miranda realized that one fault with having dual memories was that she sometimes forgot the context of things, certain nuances. Martin was ignorant of the Conclave so he would have no notion of Akesh's disloyalty to Pug. Improvising, she went on, 'I was speaking of the Assembly of Magicians at Stardock. They are pledged to neutrality, no matter where they are born.'

Before another word was spoken, a loud crashing from the direction of the front gate was followed by alarm bells and horns. 'Damn,' said Martin. 'The attack is starting.'

He stood, grabbed his sword belt from where it hung on the back of a chair, and watched in shock as Miranda reached out and seized Akesh by the throat and with a squeeze effortlessly crushed his windpipe. The magician fell to the stone floor, gasping for breath that would not come and in a moment his face turned blue and he died, eyes open.

'Why?' demanded Martin.

'Because,' said Miranda, 'he was a traitor. And who can you spare to guard him? He may have been beaten within an inch of his life, but you have no one besides Nakor and me who could deal with his magic once he recovered.'

Nakor nodded. 'I knew him; he was not what I would call powerful, but he had tricks that would hurt you if he used them behind your lines.'

'What would you have us do, stand over him so that if you somehow survive this war we can take him back to Stardock so he can be tried and executed there?' asked Miranda.

Her eyes fixed on Martin and suddenly he knew fear. There was something behind those eyes that was powerful and unnatural and he wished no part of it. 'Fine,' he said sharply. He could not be distracted by this now. He turned to Brendan and said, 'Find someone on the staff to dispose of this body. I fear we're going to have many more to add to the pile before this fight is over.'

Brendan nodded, turned and headed to the rear of the kitchen just as the alarmed-looking staff began to return. He pointed to the corpse of the traitor and said, 'See to that, then get ready to care for the wounded!'

Then the two brothers raced toward the coming battle.

Martin ordered the men off the wall and stationed two lookouts on rooftops behind it. The Keshian trebuchets were merciless. At this distance they looked almost like child's toys, but there was nothing remotely amusing about them. Large towers with an asymmetrical swinging arm and a basket full of heavy rocks at the short end, and a sling at the long end, they could hurl a boulder it took four men to lift as a child would throw a pebble.

There were four of them on the crest of the road, and they flung their heavy missiles in order, the farthest to the left first: one, two, three, four; then over again, the first being reloaded by the time the fourth had released a massive stone. To those in the city it felt like an endless barrage. Those stones that struck the wall bounced away, showering the ground before the city with masonry dust, dirt, and shattered builder's blocks. Those that hit the gate caused the metal hinges to protest with a shriek while the wood groaned as ancient grain was parted and splintered.

A few stones topped the wall to bounce into buildings or careen down boulevards and an unwary defender was lucky to be spared a shattered leg or crushed skull as the boulder bounded by. A few were not so lucky and were carried to the mayor's house or the inn across the street, where those detailed to receive the wounded waited to care for them.

Brendan and Martin stood exposed and wary in the main street, ready to duck around the corner should they have to avoid a boulder. Martin had ordered Bethany and Lily to care for the wounded and protect them should the Keshians get that far into the city. Bethany had appeared ready to be defiant, but at the last had merely nodded and left to do as asked. Martin couldn't be sure that would last. He also knew it futile to order her out of the city. She was her father's daughter and she would fight until the last. She also would be disinclined to let the Keshians take her alive; she knew what happened to attractive young women taken in war; if she and Lily survived the rape of the city, they would be bound for a slaver's pen in Durbin. It would be a miracle if anyone informed the commander that she was the daughter of nobility and worth a ransom, and Bethany would certainly not say a word while others around her faced such a fate.

A stone smashed into the gate and the entire front of the wall trembled. 'A few more of those and they'll come charging in,' said Brendan.

Martin shouted up to the closest lookout, high on the rooftop above, 'Do you see horse?'

'Just now, my lord,' he replied. 'They're riding slowly around the siege engines and taking up position. They do not appear to be in any hurry.'

'They can wait,' said Brendan. He glanced at the sun and

said, 'Why wait until noon to begin the assault? Why not attack at dawn?'

'Darkness means confusion and terror, and that benefits the Keshians. Had he begun at dawn, the gates would be down now and we'd have had time to organize defensives throughout the city. Now if we try that, it's in the dark.'

'How long can we hold?'

Martin said, 'I don't know. Every man and boy is willing; this is their home they're defending and the Keshians lost many men with that demon attack. If we can wear them down between here and the city square . . .' He was silent for a minute, then said, 'Get a company. Go find anything, furniture, shelving, storage crates, whatever is at hand and build a barrier in the square.' He knelt and drew a semicircle in the earth. 'Here is that weaver's shop, the one with the green door? Start here and stretch it across to here, the butcher's. I want it twelve feet high with whatever you can stand on behind it, so that it's a breastwork.'

'The miller's!' Brendan exclaimed suddenly. 'There are hundreds of bags of grain spoiled for sitting there and no way to get it out of the city! That'll make a sturdy breastwork, Martin!'

Martin smiled. 'Good. Build steps behind so a man can fire a bow over it. When I give the order here, I want the archers to fall back and be ready there to shoot crossing the square. Do you understand?'

'Yes,' said Brendan.

As he was about to leave, Martin seized him by the arm. 'That odd little ballista from LaMut, where is it?'

'We moved it a couple of times. I'll find Sergeant Ruther, he'll know. Why?'

'Take a wagon and put it in the middle and if you see any heavy horse ride into that square, use it on them. They'll be bunched up and unable to spread out, so that might prove a nasty surprise. Go, and spread the word.'

Brendan nodded once then dashed off.

Boulders thundered into the walls and the air became thicker with stone and mortar dust. Hours dragged on and the sun crawled across the sky.

Martin waited patiently until with an ear-shattering twist of wood, the gate on the right pulled loose from its upper hinges. Martin shouted, 'Return to the walls!'

He saw the two elves and waved them over. There was something he couldn't quite put his finger on about the one called Arkan, but Calis had been a family friend since the time of his great-grandfather and namesake. When they reached him he said, 'I have a favour to ask of you.'

Arkan said nothing, studying the young leader. Calis said, 'Ask.'

'I plan on leaving that wall quickly and retreating to a secondary position within the city square. We have many inexperienced youngsters up on the wall. If you would each take one side of the gate to ensure they do not waste arrows or freeze and do nothing, and then make sure they leave quickly when the order is given, I would be in your debt.'

Calis said, 'Of course.' Arkan looked at Martin and something akin to approval crossed his face briefly, and he nodded.

They hurried off to opposites sides of the main boulevard into the city, while Martin reviewed his strategy. His plan was to bleed the Keshians with two or three volleys of arrows as they charged the gate, confident he'd have enough time to retreat to the barricade Brendan was now finishing. He had dispatched runners with his final plan. He hadn't really had a plan until a short time before, but he told the men he didn't want to confuse the orders until the last minute. Sergeants Magwin and Ruther were both positioned with flying companies at the first intersection of streets behind Martin's position, to encourage the Keshians along the path of least resistance.

Then Martin heard the horns. The Keshian commander was ordering the advance.

'Archers! To the walls!' Martin bellowed and his own

voice sounded strong and confident to his own ears, which surprised him as he felt anything but strong and confident.

He hurried forward through a cloud of dust and saw that the gate on the right was almost off its hinges and realized that the Keshian commander had made his first mistake. It was a natural choke point as no more than two or three men at a time could climb into the city through the gap between the edge of the gate and the wall. The Keshians would try to flood the breach, for to wait for horse and chain to drag away the gate risked losing it to a defenders' rally. As Martin hurried up the steps to the wall, the nearest lookout shouted, 'They're bringing a ram, my lord!'

As he topped the shattered palisade, half crumbled and littered with rubble, he saw a hooded ram being propelled by a company of riders. It was tented, providing the men inside with protection from arrow fire and burning oil.

Calis said, 'I can't see anyone inside it.'

The elf's eyesight was superior to Martin's own, for at this distance he couldn't tell. Soon, the ram picked up enough speed he knew no man could run and push that fast. Instead the riders were pulling it with ropes and were starting to pick up speed. Suddenly Martin had an idea what was happening and shouted, 'Off the walls! Everyone off!'

They didn't need to be told twice. Martin ran down the stairs, crying, 'Archers to the square! Man the barricade! Runners to me!'

Two boys, almost comical in oversized helmets and huge quilted vests appeared, stern expressions on their faces. 'You,' he pointed to one, 'find Sergeant Ruther. You,' he said to the other, 'find Sergeant Magwin. Tell them to pull back out of sight and wait until the Keshians are into the square, then hit them from behind.' He jabbed his two fists together for emphasis. 'Like the horns of a bull! At their discretion they are to pull back, circle around the side streets and get behind the barricade if needs be. Do you understand?'

Both boys nodded and ran off. Men flooded past the city's youthful commander as he watched the now-empty wall. He hated sending boys on errands of war, but he had no one else.

Nakor appeared at his side. 'What are you thinking?'

'Where have you been?'

'Looking around. Trying to think of some tricks.'

'Did you think of any?'

'Not yet but they're not here yet.'

'Where's Miranda?'

'She is making sure there are no more magicians with the Keshians. That would be bad.' Nakor watched the retreating bowmen and asked, 'And, again, what are you thinking with all this running away from the wall?'

'I'm thinking that ram isn't a ram, but a tented wagon with some barrels of Quegan Oil.'

With a grin Nakor said, 'I didn't think of that. That's a very good trick.' Then the grin faded. 'But you know what I am thinking?'

'What?'

'If you're right, we're standing too close to the gate!'

Martin's eyes widened and without another word the two of them turned and ran up the street as the sound of the rumbling wagon became audible. They were halfway down the street to the first intersection when the wagon slammed into the remains of the gate.

The explosion struck with the force of a thousand battering rams. The gust of air knocked both Martin and Nakor flat to the ground as a wave of heat washed over them. Both had their backs to the gate so neither was blinded, but when they turned over both saw a monstrous fireball rising into the sky. Waves of heat rolled over them as the wooden gates were now ablaze and even the stones seemed to burn as the flaming liquid ran down the blackening stones.

Helping Nakor to his feet Martin said, 'How long do you think it will burn?'

Nakor said, 'That's a lot of oil. Hour, maybe longer. That sticky oil takes a while to consume itself.'

Martin glanced at the low sun in the east and said, 'They'll hit us after sundown.'

'That gives you an hour or more to think up a new strategy.'

'Nothing new. We stand and we fight. If Kesh takes this city, the Kingdom will never regain the Far Coast and will lose Yabon into the bargain.'

'Well, I've seen a lot of fights, with worse odds than you're facing.'

Martin's brow furrowed. 'Really?'

Nakor grinned. 'Well, maybe not many. Say, just a few.' He began walking to the barricade and said, 'All right, not a few, but there was this one time . . .'

Martin said, 'What?'

'I'm trying to make you feel more confident.'

'You're not very good at this are you?'

Nakor sighed. 'Out of practice, I think.'

Martin found and fought an urge to laugh. He had a sick feeling in his stomach that if he started laughing, he might not be able to stop.

The defenders readied themselves and after the sun set, they waited through the twilight. Again the two elven archers, the eledhel prince and the moredhel chieftain were given responsibility on either flank to keep the young archers calm.

When full darkness was on the city, the Keshian trumpets sounded. Sergeant Ruther had taken a few moments to speak with Martin after he had changed the city's defensive plans. Now Martin told his brother, 'They'll hit with the heavy horse first, trying to clear out any resistance along the main street. Foot will follow in the traditional Keshian fashion. They'll try to seize this square and establish a defensible position with pikes and shields to defend against counter-attack. Bowmen will be last. Light cavalry will be held in reserve and loosed to pick off anyone on the edge of battle or chase those who are fleeing to prevent a rally. If they leave their light horse out of the city for an hour or more, we have a chance.'

'What do you propose?' asked his brother.

'If we can halt the heavy cavalry between the entrance to the square and this barricade, the heavy foot will pile up behind, and they will get jammed together. Pikes will be useless and shields will gain them no benefit. The archers at the rear will then pile up against the heavy foot. Ruther and Magwin will hit the archers first, and should make short work of them hand-to-hand, and then they'll be carving up the footmen from behind. Swords and knives against pikes in close combat; jammed together, the Keshians number advantage will mean little.'

'You sound as if you think we can survive,' observed Brendan.

Martin said, 'I think we can *win*!'

'As long as the Keshians behave like you expect.'

'They'll behave like Keshians.'

'Where are Miranda and Nakor? Some magic right now would be very useful, I think.'

'Miranda is ensuring no Keshian magic-users are moving against us. Nakor has run off to make merry with the Keshians in his own fashion,' said Martin. 'I wasn't in a position to tell them how best to use their craft.'

'Nor were they likely to listen, anyway,' said Brendan.

Horns sounded and there was a rumble as a company of heavy horse began their advance down the boulevard. Two single columns rode side by side, but closer than was customary for protection from possible attacks from side streets. The litter of rubble on the cobbles forced them to advance slower than they would have liked. Even so, Martin knew they could easily overrun his defences if they were not slowed.

'Archers!' shouted Martin. 'Ready!'

The first horses came into view and Martin reached over the barricade and said, 'Now!'

The two soldiers managing the old ballista from LaMut

fired and the bolt flew true into the first pair of horses, cutting through them to slice into the pair behind, and the third pair, before losing energy and landing with a heavy thud on the ground before the fourth pair of riders. The vanguard was disrupted as horses shrieked and riders were tossed as the first six animals struck went down, thrashing and shrieking in pain.

As Martin had hoped, the assault faltered before it was begun and riders cursed as those still alive before them fought to free themselves from thrashing or dead mounts.

The two men in the wagon quickly reloaded the ballista and fired a second shot which took down another pair of riders. 'I don't think you can do more!' shouted Martin. 'Break that thing and get back over the wall.' One man leaped onto the barricade and was hauled over by those waiting to help, while the other soldier took a heavy blacksmith's mallet to the ballista, breaking the firing mechanism so that it could not be used against the defenders. He leapt and was also hauled over the barricade.

Martin shouted, 'Archers! Volley fire! Fire!'

A flight of arrows arched up from the barricade, and descended against the horsemen. Screaming men and animals signalled its effectiveness, and the battle for Ylith was fully joined.

Martin's plan worked for the first two hours of the night. Three flights of arrows broke the Keshian heavy cavalry before they could deploy properly and the two sergeants' companies obliterated the Keshian archers. Calis and Arkan especially were lethal, taking two officers and four sergeants out of the fight.

The heavy foot proved to be more difficult than Martin had anticipated, for while they were in no position to inflict significant damage on the Kingdom forces, they were also heavily armoured and able to crouch behind shields, thus protecting themselves from damage.

Martin felt a tug on his sleeve and turned to find a blood-spattered boy waiting to report. 'What?'

'Sergeant Ruther says them Keshians have reserve companies and they're bringing in their other horse.' He paused for a second with a quizzical expression as if trying to remember if he had got it right. Nodding to himself, he continued, 'He says the foot is getting itself organized, so he's pulling back so as not to get sucked in behind them into the square here, but he can keep those horses from the side streets 'cause it's narrow and they'll pick them off one by one.'

At this point Martin wasn't entirely sure which they were going to pick off, but he thought he had the gist of it. He didn't want to interrupt the boy as he was doing the best he could.

'So you should expect all them Keshians to be coming straight at you soon. He'll do what he can.' The lad paused, then said, 'That's all, my lord.'

'You did well. Go to the mayor's house and help with the wounded.'

'Sergeant Ruther's waiting for me to go back and fight, sir.'

'Ruther will know what to do. Do as you're told, boy, and help with the wounded. It's important work.'

Not hiding his disappointment, the boy turned and scampered off.

Brendan said, 'Ten?'

'Nine, more likely. Got a lot of fight in him.'

Martin returned his attention to the far side of the square where footmen were dragging away dead horses, clearing the way for the remaining riders and the heavy infantry behind them.

Brendan said, 'How do you think they'll hit us?'

'They'll fan out along either side of the square, then all at once.'

'They'll lose some to the archers that way.'

'They have them to lose,' said Martin as the Keshian heavy foot started running in exactly the formation he anticipated, fanning out on either side until they had two men deep opposite the barricade.

A trumpet sounded and the footmen advanced at a run. Martin ordered the archers to fire. As he had expected, the bowmen were not as effective as Brendan had anticipated for the Keshians were heavily armoured with quilted jack vests designed to protect from arrows and large shields they could easily crouch behind. When they were halfway to the barricade they sprinted. Every other Keshian solder dropped his shield and grabbed the end of the shield held by the man on his right. The soldiers behind dropped their pikes and shields, drew their swords, leapt atop the held shields and were lifted up; and suddenly Martin and the other defenders had enemies mere inches away.

Martin swung his sword at the first face he saw in front of him and the man screamed in pain as he fell back. Others were cut down before they could gain access to the barricade, but the few who did found themselves confronted by a mix of seasoned soldiers from Crydee and many inexperienced militia from Ylith. No matter how willing the militia, they did not have the necessary skill to deal with this assault and suddenly defenders began to die.

Martin hewed at another Keshian as a second wave of attackers was lifted up and he cursed himself for not anticipating how the Keshians would get over this breastwork. He had thought the Keshian commander would simply hurl his heavy horse against this position, but instead he was trying to get a foothold on the barricade so that his infantry could knock down the defences and clear away enough bags of grain to make a path. Once the horses were through, the battle was effectively over.

Martin swung and parried until his arms felt numb. He could hear shouts behind him, so he assumed the attackers had already gained a foothold somewhere nearby, but he was too pressed to look around and apprehend exactly what was going on. On and on he fought, his mind blank.

A momentary pause allowed Martin to scan the defences.

They were holding, but barely. He looked to his left and saw the odd elf, Arkan, bow cast aside, wielding a short-sword with what looked to be glee. He was actually grinning as he beheaded a Keshian mounting the barricade with a single blow.

Then a shriek of impossible volume split the air and several combatants hesitated or were distracted, and died for it. Martin killed the man trying to come over the breastwork in front of him and when another didn't immediately appear, cast his glance towards the source of the sound.

Miranda was standing on a rooftop pointing her finger at the Keshians and suddenly a ball of fire shot forth, striking the next advancing wave of soldiers in the middle of their formation. It struck the ground and rolled like a wheel, spewing flames in all directions. Men shrieked in terror and pain as they flailed about, their skin and clothing ablaze.

The fire seemed almost a thing alive and everywhere it spread it leapt and twisted, tiny gyres of flame that moved oddly, ignoring the direction of wind. Where men slapped at them they suddenly vanished, and eventually the flames suddenly went out, all in a second.

Martin didn't know what he had expected, but the fireball had been effective in blunting the attack, for a few minutes at least. The Keshians withdrew a short distance and the defenders gained a short respite.

Martin looked up again, but Miranda had vanished from the rooftop.

Too exhausted to consider whether this would be the only contribution the magician from Sorcerer's Isle was making, he returned to await the next wave of attackers.

It took the Keshians nearly half an hour to regroup from Miranda's attack, then once again they came on. In that time Martin had drunk water, poured some over his face, listened to reports he wasn't sure he understood, and discovered that at some point he had been struck a glancing blow on the head. He was covered in blood, most of it his own. He remembered what his father had taught him; scalp wounds looked ghastly, but were rarely fatal.

Miranda had cleared the square in front of the barricade, and Arkan, reclaiming his bow, had killed enough retreating Keshians that the survivors had retreated half a block up the main boulevard. But Martin knew they would be back soon.

Horns sounded and once more the Keshians came, and Martin and the defenders braced themselves for another assault. Through the next hour Martin lost the ability to organize his thoughts. His entire being was consumed by the need to raise his sword to ward off attacks, or to kill attackers. He heard things and saw things, but his mind did not retain those sounds and images, his only concern was staying on this wall.

Then somehow a Keshian atop a shield leapt at him, knocking him off the grain bags to the hard packed earth of the city square. Martin lost his grip on his sword, but had his belt knife out and rolled to his feet, only to be bowled over again by the Keshian soldier. They grappled, each man with his hand locked around the wrist of the other, each seeking to drive home the blade he held.

Martin rolled with the man atop him. He drew up his right leg, trying to get his knee under the man so he could lever him off. It proved a vain attempt, for the Keshian was relatively fresh to the fight and Martin was close to exhaustion. He could feel his left arm giving out as the Keshian tried to position his blade above him, and in a blinding moment of panic he thrashed to the right. The blade struck the ground next to Martin's face, and the Keshian drew back. Instead of keeping his grip, Martin let go and the man pulled back with too much force. Martin struck with his now-free left hand, jamming his fingers into the man's windpipe. The blow was not fatal, but it startled his opponent enough that he hesitated and reflexively reached for his throat, loosening his grip on Martin's knife hand. Martin slid his hand free, along the ground and hit the man in the ribs.

It was another non-lethal blow, but it gained Martin a moment, and he reached across his own chest and struck a backhanded blow, his blade slicing through the man's throat. Martin rolled and tried to get to his feet, but his legs wobbled.

Steadying hands gripped him from behind and Sergeant Ruther said, 'Time to go, sir!'

Martin shook his head to clear it. 'The light horse?'

'We held them up as long as we could, and the Keshians are now in the square. We need to fall back to the mayor's house—' The sergeant's eyes widened and he went limp. A Keshian soldier pulled out the blade he had just stuck in Ruther's back and began to strike at Martin.

Martin leapt back, looking around for a weapon, and saw his sword a few feet away. He jumped for it as the Keshian's blade parted the air where he had been, hit the ground and rolled. He came to his feet, barely able to stand, but in a defensive crouch. He was ready to die where he stood rather than retreat another step.

The Keshian soldier was fresh and he grinned as he approached, ready to quickly dispose of the obviously exhausted young defender. He raised his sword for a killing blow.

Martin was determined he would not merely give in. He grimaced at the Keshian, working out in his head how he would parry and riposte.

As he did so a horn sounded, a call Martin had not yet heard.

The Keshian hesitated, then when the call was repeated, he stepped back, his expression a mixture of confusion, anger, and resignation. He held his sword tightly, ready to defend himself, then raised his free hand palm outward and stepped back. He slowly moved his sword so the point was up and away, mimicking his free hand, almost a sign of submission, or at least a show he was no longer a threat. He continued to step back until he reached the grain bags, where he was forced to glance around to find a way back through the now-crumbled defence.

Martin glanced one way then the other and saw that every Keshian not locked in close combat was doing likewise. Those still fighting were trying to disengage themselves and a few managed, though a few died trying.

Martin looked to his left and saw a blood-covered Brendan standing with a confused expression to match his brother's as the Keshians slowly backed way. The sounds of struggle fell away, to be replaced by the huffing of tired men, the moans and cries of the wounded, and the sounds of crackling flames from a fire that had broken out somewhere nearby.

The Keshians continued to back away, at a slow, steady pace, until they were back on the other side of the square. Martin staggered over to one of the breaches in the grain bags and Brendan came to his side.

'Why?' asked Brendan. 'They won. Why are they withdrawing?'

'I don't know,' said Martin and his voice sounded raw and hoarse in his own ears.

'Are you injured?' asked Brendan.

'A small scalp cut.'

'Looks worse than it is,' finished Brendan, looking dazed. 'Father was right. It looks a fright.'

A horseman rode into view from the main street bearing a white banner. He reined in.

Martin shouted, 'Hold!' as bowmen began to draw a bead on him. 'Truce is called!'

The herald slowly rode forward. Behind him came the Keshian commander. They halted just the other side of the barricade. 'We meet again, young lord!'

Martin could barely speak. He lifted his sword in an awkward salute. At last he said, 'Did you come to surrender, my lord?'

The Keshian laughed. 'You have fine spirit, my worthy opponent. Orders have reached me. The war is over.'

'Over?' said Brendan. Whispering to Martin he said, 'It's a trick.'

'Why? They were minutes away from victory.' Martin kept his eyes on the Keshian commander.

Hearing the exchange the Keshian commander said, 'No duplicity, young sirs. Orders reached me by ship and rider no more than a half-hour ago. My only delay was in sending orders to my field commander to sound the call for disengagement. What you heard was the call for parlay. My orders are to hold what we've taken, but to advance no more. Armistice is granted. We will, however, respond with vigour if attacked, but we will no longer attack until this matter is resolved.'

'What does that mean?' asked Martin.

'It means what I said.' He motioned with his hand. 'The city up to that barricade is mine, the rest is yours. We will let our masters judge who is victorious this day. Your king and my emperor, blessings be upon him, shall decide how much or little was gained and lost this day.'

Martin looked at the carnage around him and said, 'The gods robbed you of victory today, my lord.'

Nodding, the Keshian commander said, 'Or gave you one as a gift, young lord.' Turning his horse, he rode away and left his deputy commander shouting orders to those men still ready to fight. Slowly the Keshians withdrew, save those positioned as sentries along what might some day be a frontier, but for now was an arbitrary line cutting the city of Ylith in half.

The two brothers, numb from fatigue, terror, and bloodshed stood looking at one another, wondering what had just happened.

13

SEARCH

Jim threw his knife.

It struck the wall next to Jacobo's ear and the stout trader reached up and touched his left lobe. His fingertips came away smeared with blood. 'Why are you doing this, Jim?'

'Because trust is rare these days and while I have no proof you are disloyal, I want to make it clear just how difficult a time I'm having these days.' Still garbed as a common sailor, Jim was visiting an old contact in Rodez. He was on his way to Ran, either by ship or fast horse depending on which was more expedient. To discover his safest course, he had decided to visit Jacobo.

'I need information that is timely and accurate, and honest, or that will not be the last drop of your blood you see this day.'

Jim regarded the portly man. He affected simple garb, though he was one of the wealthiest traders in the region: a short-sleeved linen shirt and stout woollen trousers. His only indulgence in vanity appeared to be a single ring of silver worn in his right ear. Perspiration beaded on his brow and the top of his head, now bald and fringed with long, greying hair. Jim had always thought his eyes beady, but now they were wide, showing them to be a vivid cornflower blue.

'I have never been anything but loyal and honest, Jim!'

Jacobo the merchant was a dealer in general stores, selling to ships outward bound, buying from merchants across the Sea of Kingdoms and, up to this late unpleasantness, one of Jim's most valuable assets. He was neither part of Jim's criminal organization nor his royal operatives, but was a source of intelligence with little regard for who was paying him gold. Jim had never attempted to recruit him as an asset for either of his organizations, rather letting him remain apart. Now that seemed like brilliant planning, even though at the time it had just been a whim. Jacobo's deal with Jim was simple; Jim got anything of value first, then Jacobo was free to sell the same information to anyone who came looking so long as Jim's advantage was not compromised. How long Jacobo remained silent was a function of how much Jim paid. The more gold, the more time. Rarely Jim had bought his complete silence. The arrangement seemed suitable for both parties.

'I need a few facts cleared up,' said Jim, walking over to the wall and pulling the dagger out. They were in the back room of Jacobo's shop. Jim's ship had sailed in on the morning tide and been escorted to a dockside berth. He had been part of the crew rowing the towing boat, and after that he had come ashore and tied off, then merely walked away. Captains were always looking out to prevent sailors from jumping ship, but never at their destination when the only task left was to pay them off.

'Whatever you wish, Jim! Please, I've never broken a trust with you. Never!'

At this point Jim had no option but to hope this was true; his own network of agents was so shredded he had no way of knowing upon whom he could rely. When this bloody business was over he would have to begin to slowly rebuild, and those very few agents he still trusted would be overburdened until he could repair the damage done to an espionage network over three generations old.

'Let's start simply,' said Jim, gesturing for Jacobo to sit in a chair in the back room. Jim had already drawn the curtains and placed the closed sign in the front window. They would remain undisturbed. 'What news you consider valuable?'

Jacobo sat down. 'Rumours and stories I hesitate to share with you, lest you count me unreliable.'

'Just tell me what you've heard and I'll decide what's useful and what's not,' said Jim as he sat opposite the fat merchant. He thumbed his dagger for emphasis and glanced around the cluttered storage area of this store. 'You ever going to organize this mess?'

The fat merchant said, 'It is organized. I know where everything housed here and in three separate warehouses is, Jim.' He tapped the side of his head. 'The reason I'm so valuable to you is I remember everything.'

Jim conceded to himself that everything Jacobo had reported over the years had been accurate and useful. 'Well, then, to it.'

'Late last night a royal cutter hove to and a longboat rowed in. As soon as the boat touched the docks a courier dashed to a waiting horse and off he went to the city commander. The Duke of Rodez is in Rillanon, with most of the Congress of Lords, to discuss the conduct of the war, I'd imagine, so the orders to the garrison should have come from him. But instead it appears they came from one Sir William—'

'Alcorn,' interrupted Jim, a look of disgust passing over his face. 'Go on.'

'No official announcement has been made, but the rumour is Kesh and the Kingdom have agreed to some sort of truce.'

Jim sat back. He was silent while he weighed up what he had just been told. This was as unexpected as the outbreak of the war had been. Kesh had gained little of importance anywhere except possibly in the west; reports from the Far Coast and Yabon had not yet reached the capital. Certainly in the east they had achieved nothing except spending a great deal of gold and alienating both their neighbouring states.

'Go on.'

Jacobo seemed at a loss as to what to say next, then his eyes widened and he said, 'A trader reports that Kesh holds to their line with ships on sentry, but are allowing Ceresian pirates to enter Kingdom waters to pillage. Prandur's Gate is said to have been sacked, and pirates are reportedly raiding the smaller towns and villages along the coast between here and Ran.'

Jim considered this rumour. The Kingdom was on a war footing and every inch of coastline would be garrisoned with both regular soldiers and levies against any Keshian landing, or ventures by one of the more opportunistic Eastern Kingdoms. So the pirates were either incredibly bold, incredibly stupid, or had some reason not to expect Kingdom intervention. Under normal conditions, a town of any size should hold a garrison large enough to repulse pirates with punishing results. A village, perhaps, could be sacked, but the booty would not amount to enough to pay for the food needed to feed a good-sized pirate crew. Moreover, the Ceresians were rarely organized enough to mount a major raid, usually being content to plunder shipping and fight amongst themselves.

His mind raced as he let his imagination run rampant for a full minute, before reining it back in. There was something coalescing in his thinking, but it was not near enough to fruition for him to fully grasp it. There was something about Sir William Alcorn, a pointless war with Kesh, and pirates making free in the waters of the Sea of Kingdoms; under normal circumstances, even should the Kingdom be idle, Kesh would sink every Ceresian dromon and begala they sighted, no questions asked, and any surviving pirate would be hanged at sea or sold into slavery depending on the Keshian captain's ability to keep prisoners or not. Letting them pass signalled an understanding of some sort.

Jim said, 'Tell me more of these pirates?'

'I know only what I already told you: they come ashore, burn towns, take booty and captives, and the local garrisons hunker down within the walls of their fortresses.' Then a quizzical look passed over Jacobo's face. 'There is this one other thing, Jim: the pirates seem to be seeking something or someone.'

'What?'

'No one knows, but a trader by name of Gersh, a man of uncommon honesty, told me he had left Ran when the pirates were making a landing near a town called Farborough. Some pirates caught sight of his wagon as he was turning around and began to give chase. But while Gersh looked on in wonder, their leader ordered them back and up into the hills north of the town. Gersh swears they were spreading out as if on a manhunt. Gersh has given votive offerings to Ruthia twice since coming back to Rodez.' Thanks to the Goddess of Luck there was more proof the story was true than not.

'How long ago did this happen?'

'Four days, perhaps five, I'm not certain. Gersh came to me seeking a ship for Ran I might have cargo upon, with which he might bundle his trade goods, for a small fee, of course. I was happy to accommodate him, and as there appears to be a truce verging, it may be that ship will actually get to Ran. First trade goods in after peace is declared will fetch a good price.'

Jim had a hunch, but he would not share it with Jacobo. 'Anything else?'

'Nothing at the moment, unless you wish to hear about trade speculation and hedges against the coming drop in prices of goods if the war ends soon. One man's opportunity is another man's disaster.'

'No,' said Jim standing. He pointed to Jacobo's ear. 'Sorry about that, but trust has been hard to come by lately. I'll see you're taken care of for your troubles. Just remember I was never here and we never spoke.'

With a slight smile Jacobo said, 'Is someone there? I can't see anyone or hear anything.'

A second later Jim was through the curtains at the front of the store and gone. Jacobo waited for a moment, then stood and slowly made his way to the front of his establishment where he was delighted to find the curtains drawn back and the closed for business sign taken down.

Two blocks away, a bored-looking seaman leaned against a piling on the pier, absently whittling at a stick of wood as he glanced around from time to time. Jim had found this location years before and it enabled him to see anyone coming or going from Jacobo's shop, as the only exit from the alley onto which Jacobo's back door opened was just three buildings away from the street upon which his shop sat.

After half an hour, Jim was satisfied that Jacobo had been telling him the truth, or at least the truth as he knew it, and was not seeking to announce to the world that Jim Dasher was in the city. And so Jacobo survived another day to increase his prosperity.

Jim looked around one last time, ensuring he was not being observed, and took a deep breath. He had one safe house close by, and he would thoroughly examine every approach to make sure it was clear, then he would go to ground. He would need to spend at least a week to discover the truth behind Jacobo's rumour of peace. In general, he welcomed such news, but behind it he sensed a great mystery. Who was the shadowy player who had meddled so effectively in the affairs of three great nations, and to what end?

Much work lay ahead and there were few if any in the region Jim could safely trust. Still, he was not without his own resources and had others like Jacobo who were not part of the loose criminal brotherhood to whom his role as Upright Man of the Mockers of Krondor gained him access, nor part of his network of royal agents.

Knowing that caution overrode urgency, Jim vanished into the crowd in the bustling city of Rodez.

Lady Franciezka sat quietly in her study, before the window, knowing she was under observation. She had identified Worthington's agents weeks before and knew exactly where they were. She had turned it into a bit of a game, having come up with names for each, though she did not yet know their true identities. Right now, she was being observed by 'Pierre,' who was situated in a window in a rented room across the square opposite a tiny garden behind her townhouse. 'André' was drinking numerous cups of tea at a small table in the café at the corner, which allowed him an unobstructed view of her townhouse's entrance. At sundown they would be replaced by 'Anton' in the room, and 'Serge' at the café, who would retire to the corner and a miserable doorway in which to huddle after the café closed.

She had turned this into a game, slipping in and out of her home unobserved, or making a grand show of leaving to go shopping or the rare trip to the palace to look the part of an unneeded lady-in-waiting to the Queen. The rest of the time she conducted her own business. She had grown so bored with the game she had taken to leaving her window shutters open at night when she bathed so that her silhouette could be seen on the gauze privacy curtain, hoping it teased or annoyed Anton. For a moment her thoughts turned to James Jamison, and she wondered if Jim would be annoyed or amused to discover her teasing. She would be certain to ask him when next they met, if they again met.

She tried to be the professional about this, but found her mind often turning to Jim and she realized that a man she already had tried to have killed twice was the only man she'd ever encountered who truly understood her. She felt herself torn between loving him for that and wanting him dead even more. She confessed to herself, not for the first time, that affairs of the heart were not good for her: she was bad at them. It was when she didn't care that she was her most effective, when she could use her acting skills and her body to convince a man to do whatever she wanted. When she started to care, then she got into difficulties.

A serving girl knocked lightly on the door and she bade the girl enter. The maid presented a parchment bearing the royal seal, and said, 'From the palace.'

Turning away from the girl, she broke the seal on the parchment. Quickly reading the message, she read it again to ensure she hadn't misunderstood anything. She assumed her observers were likely to know what was in this message. Turning back to her maid, she said, 'The royal blue dress, I think, the one with the white-trimmed hem, not the silver. It is after all, court, not a palace gala. Tell Gregor to have the coach ready in an hour. We are going back to the palace.'

'Yes, madam,' said the maid.

Waiting for her maid to go about her business, Franciezka sat back as if calmly considering what was happening, but inward she was seething with conflict. By nature, she hated anything happening in which she had no control, and even though life had taught her control was most often an illusion, she found she was happiest when influencing events and people. She had learned every weapon there was from fear to love, seduction to bribery, gratitude and taking advantage of other people's better nature. Her only saving grace was that it was all for the Crown, and if she'd willingly give her own life for King and country, she had no problem giving others', let alone causing a little annoyance, anger, fear, or an occasional broken heart.

What was troubling her most of all at the moment, was the idea that Lord John Worthington was making an unexpected move. Not even a simple case of him doing something recognizable at an unexpected time, but rather doing something totally unexpected, irrespective of the timing.

He was hosting a gala for the King.

Reading court language as well as anyone, the tone of the invitation told her that nothing short of being on her death bed could permit her declining. Moreover, something of significance, even something momentous, was being celebrated.

She was doubly suspicious because it was so sudden. Even modest parties by the Crown's standards took days to prepare. But then it occurred to her that perhaps it wasn't so sudden. Perhaps preparations had been under way for days because Lord John knew exactly what was coming.

They couldn't be celebrating the death of King Gregory: even with magic it might take some time to dispatch the King. No, this was something else. And it couldn't be Lord John's announcement of his son's betrothal to Stephané, since she couldn't be betrothed in absentia. Her curiosity was piqued, and that outweighed her caution. She picked up a small bell and rang it. A moment later the maid reappeared and Franciezka said, 'I've changed my mind. The red, with the silver trim, and the ruby earrings. Now, send for Millicent and tell her I need my hair up within the hour.'

'Yes, my lady!' The maid ran off.

Then she remembered something Jim had said to her. 'Whatever happens, at least it's interesting.' That had been in another context, but it certainly applied here.

Then she wondered where he was. For the first time in her life, she worried for his safety.

'Damn that man,' she whispered to no one.

Carriages rolled into the palace as the sun set in the west. Footmen were turned out in formal palace livery, pale green jackets with white silk collars, pale yellow hose, and their heads topped with small yellow caps to match the hose. Idly, Franciezka considered there must be someone locked deep within the palace, unknown to any but a few key people – the King alone perhaps – whose only task in life was to devise odd uniforms for the servants in Roldem, a uniform that changed each year.

Fashions for the nobles changed as well, of course. She knew a handful of designers and their seamstresses competed each year to set the tone for the following year's 'look' – how low the neckline should be or how many petticoats were to be worn under the skirt, what colours were current and which adornments were now passé. Once a look had been achieved, others slavishly followed, and a year later those styles were being imitated in the Isles and the Eastern Kingdoms.

At least the Keshians, tradition bound as they were, avoided such petty concerns about fashion. More to the point, such gowns and jackets would have been uncomfortably hot to wear near the Overn Deep. As her carriage came to a stop, she decided the Keshians were extremely practical to run around nearly naked. If she had to endure that beastly heat, she'd do the same.

The door opened and a footman extended his hand to allow Franciezka to descend from her carriage with grace, despite the ridiculous skirt fashion dictated she wear this year. At least she liked the colour, a brilliant crimson that suited her colouring and brought out what colour there was in her otherwise pale cheeks. Jim had once observed that if she were any more fair she'd be as white as muslin. Damn, she was thinking of him again . . .

She moved as quickly as decorum permitted from the massive courtyard up the sweeping staircase that led into the palace. Once inside, she hurried towards the royal apartment, half-expecting to be barred by guards under orders from Lord John Worthington. She was relieved that not once was she challenged and by the time she reached the royal family's apartments within the heart of the palace, an illusion of normalcy had almost returned.

As she approached, two pages pulled wide the large doors leading into the royal quarters, a palace within the palace effectively. The entranceway to the family's living area was larger than Lady Franciezka's entire house, a two-storey, vaulted antechamber in which a half-dozen ladies already were gathered to accompany the Queen. She knew that in another part of the apartment a like number of lords of the Kingdom would be waiting to accompany the King. The oddest quality of royal life, Franciezka had always observed, was how the King and Queen shared a bed every night, but on formal occasions dressed in different rooms, departed from the apartment through separate doors, and met in the large hallway before their entrance to the throne room or the grand hall as if arriving from different places. She had once asked the royal historian about it, and he had been at a loss for an answer. The best he could summon up was that this was the way it had always been done.

She nodded greetings to the other ladies who returned polite words, then swept past them into the Queen's private chambers. The Queen was just rising from her vanity table, having endured, no doubt with her usual good grace, the ministrations of her attendants in applying whatever final touches they deemed necessary to achieve fashion perfection.

Franciezka curtseyed before her Queen and then came to kiss her on either cheek.

'You've been gone too long, my girl,' Queen Gertrude scolded with affection. She hugged her and whispered, 'We have no idea what is taking place. Lord John has said nothing.'

Franciezka nodded. 'We must all be ready for anything.'

'My daughter?'

'Safely away,' Franciezka whispered back.

Barely holding back tears, the Queen said, 'Good.'

A page approached and said, 'Majesty, the King is ready.'

So practised were the ladies of the court that it took no more than five minutes to have everyone in place outside the entrance to the Queen's boudoir. A nod from an assistant to the Master of Ceremonies had both the King's and Queen's parties moving at precisely the right moment, so that they both reached the intersection of the grand hall entrance and the hallway marking the boundary of the royal apartment.

Massive doors swung wide as the Master of Ceremonies intoned, 'My lords, ladies, and gentlemen, the King!'

Franciezka was one step behind the Queen, in her place on the right as her senior lady-in-waiting, but something felt amiss. Then she recognized what it was. The four children were missing. Crown Prince Constantine, the Princes Albér and Grandprey and Princess Stephané should be entering behind their parents. The court had a pensive quality to it, as well, for while this was ostensibly a gala, there was obviously nothing to celebrate, at least in the minds of the lords and ladies in attendance.

Franciezka saw Lord Servan, the King's nephew and her most trusted agent, the man who would take over all of Roldem's intelligence concerns should anything happen to her. He barely nodded greeting and she inclined her head slightly.

Nearby stood three young lords about whom Franciezka had mixed feelings. Foreign born all, they had risen in Roldem's service and been knighted by the King, and all had some sort of relationship with Jim that annoyed her all the more. Yet she had been reassured more than once by Servan that she could count on their loyalty to the end. Lords Jonathan, known as 'Jommy' to his close friends, Tad, and Zane stood quietly alert, much as they had looked when last she had seen them, at the previous Masters' Court. Zane was re-

cently married and a little distance away his wife was showing with their first child, talking to the wives of the other
two young lords.

Had it only been months ago? she silently wondered. It felt
like years since the last gathering.

Waiting to greet the King and Queen at the throne dais
was Lord John Worthington, his son Serge at his right hand.
Now titled Prime Minister of Roldem, Lord John bowed and
waited until the King and Queen were seated. Then, turning
to the assembled gathering, he announced, 'My lords, ladies
and gentlemen, I have the great honour of announcing—,'
Franciezka half-expected that he was going to announce the
betrothal of his son to Stephané despite her absence, '—the
cessation of hostilities between the Empire of Great Kesh
and the Kingdom of the Isles.'

This was completely unexpected, but welcome news, and
the applause that greeted his words was heartfelt as a wave
of relief swept through the room. Perhaps, more than one
lord thought, things will now begin to return to normal.

The applause grew in volume until suddenly there was
cheering and foot stamping. Finally, Lord John held up his
hand and a moment later quiet returned.

'I am pleased to announce that our most gracious King
has offered to broker a final treaty between our neighbour-
ing nations, and that within a month Gregory, King of the
Isles, and Sezioti, Emperor of Great Kesh, will arrive in
Roldem for a supreme conference to bring final peace to the
Sea of Kingdoms and beyond.'

This brought applause but no small chatter, for in the history of the Empire of Great Kesh, the Emperor had never
left his home above the Overn Deep. And no sitting King of
the Isles had ever visited Roldem – princes later to be kings,
yes, but never once the crown was set upon his head. This
was unprecedented.

Franciezka cursed silently. She had mistaken Lord John's
words to his Kingdom double. He didn't mean to dispatch

the King as a euphemism for killing him, he meant dispatch him to Roldem.

Franciezka Sorboz, Queen's lady-in-waiting and head of the nation's intelligence network, glanced over at her deputy, Lord Servan, whose dark features reflected exactly the same thought as her own. What exactly was going on here?

14

ESCAPE

Ty held up his hand.

Instantly the others fell silent. He motioned to Gabriella to move with the Princess into a depression below the road and hide out of sight. To Hal he pointed behind and then held up his hand to his ear, and then again pointed to the rear.

Hal paused, cocking his head to one side, and then he heard it: distant footfalls, slowly coming their way. He motioned back to Ty to take up a position on either side of the game trail they had been following.

For two days they had circled up into the high

foothills heading mostly west by north, then straight west, roughly parallel to the King's Highway, hoping to reach the road close to the city of Ran. They had subsisted on stream water and summer berries found along the way, but otherwise had nothing. They might be young and fit, but hunger was robbing them of strength daily, and Hal and Ty knew they would be less able to fight as time wore on; it was time to make a stand.

Hal motioned again and Ty nodded, understanding he wanted their pursuers to come past them before they attacked. Both young swordsmen hunkered down behind concealing undergrowth.

Soon the sound of footsteps grew louder and four men in the tabards of the Kingdom came into view. Hal didn't have to look at their boots to know they were counterfeit soldiers, as they were as ragged and unkempt a lot as he had ever seen. Pirates in stolen tabards was his best guess, and they looked ill-humoured and angry. For them to still be on the trail of the fugitives indicated the lesson of those slain on the King's Road hadn't been lost on the rest of them. Hal could hear them speaking in a language foreign to him, and guessed they were Ceresians.

They were not being especially quiet, but they were being cautious, and the man in front appeared to have some tracking skills as he pointed to the prints Hal and the others had just made. He knelt for a moment, placed his hand into the depression of a boot heel and pressed with his fingers. He raised them up, rubbing with his thumb and Hal knew exactly what he was doing.

The leader tracker said something as he drew his sword and pointed down the trail to where the ladies lay in hiding. Hal waited until the last of the four was past, then leapt at him from behind, cutting him down as Ty went past to take out the next man.

The fourth man turned to intercept Hal, but the tracker hung back, shouting, 'They're here!' at the top of his lungs. He managed to get three shouts out before he suddenly stiffened and then collapsed, revealing Lady Gabriella standing behind him with a bloodied belt knife.

The two best swordsmen at the previous Masters' Court finished off the two remaining pirates in quick fashion, but shouting from the distance told them the damage had been done. Ty cast around, determining where the noise was coming from. 'They're above us!'

He started down the hillside as fast as trees and brush would allow, assuming, correctly, that the others would follow without question. As they reached a clearing he paused to seek the next path down and said, 'We got below all of them but that one that stumbled on us. Had we been a little quicker maybe . . .' He looked back. 'We need to strike for the King's Highway and hope we can outrun them to Ran.'

'How far?' asked Gabriella and with a slight incline of her head showed she was asking on behalf of Stephané, not herself.

'If I'm correct, three, maybe four miles.'

'We'll never outrun them,' said the exhausted Princess. 'Leave me. You go and get help and come after me.'

Almost simultaneously Hal and Ty cried, 'No!'

Hal put his arm around her waist, half-lifting her, and started toward the downhill slope.

'No!' shouted Ty.

Hal turned to look, and Ty pointed off in another direction. 'That way.'

Hal took off and Gabriella and Ty followed. Without communication it was understood. Hal would keep going with Stephané no matter what happened, while Ty and the Lady Gabriella would turn and hold off the pursuers as long as possible should they be overtaken.

After a moment, Stephané said crossly, 'This is impossible!' She pushed herself away from Hal, shouting, 'I can run!' and took off at a staggering run down the game trail.

'Don't!' shouted Ty, but it was too late.

Four staggering steps sent her tumbling and she cried in pain as she rolled down the trail.

'Oh, gods!' Hal leapt after her, almost losing control as he raced down the trail after her, Ty and Gabriella a step or two behind him.

Stephané continued her out-of-control tumble, crying as she struck rocks and branches tore at her clothing and flesh, until she hit hard against an outcropping of rocks at the lower end of a small clearing. Hal was at her side a moment later. Kneeling beside her, he said, 'Don't move.'

She looked up at him. 'I'm an idiot,' she said weakly.

He pressed quickly where he could, seeing if anything was broken, and found a spectacular collection of abrasions, bumps, and small cuts, but at last said, 'I don't think you've broken any bones.'

'I feel dizzy,' she said weakly as Ty appeared.

'She must have bumped her head.'

'Can we move her?' asked Gabriella.

'Yes,' said Hal. He picked up the Princess and tossed her over his shoulder as he would a sack of grain, ignoring her moans. He set off down the trail, hearing the voices of their pursuers.

'There they are!' cried Ty.

Hal turned and as gently as possible put the Princess down, drawing his sword. 'I can see the road below,' he said, 'but we might as well stand here.'

Ty had his sword out and Lady Gabriella her long belt knife when the first two pirates hove into view. One almost ran up on to the tip of Ty's sword, barely backing away in time. The other jumped towards Hal and for his trouble had Hal run him through the stomach as Gabriella slashed his throat.

The first pirate's heel caught a rock and he fell backwards, just as three others approached slightly more cautiously. They spread out and one spoke. 'Give us that girl and the rest of you can go.'

'Found your friends, did you?' asked Ty, with a grin.

Hal said, 'Four to three. Shouldn't be much of a bother.'

Another half a dozen men came up behind the first pirates. 'Well, ten to three,' said Ty. 'That might pose a problem.'

'Your last chance,' said the leader. 'Walk down the hill and you live. You'll be in Ran inside two hours. Stand another minute, and you'll die, and we get the girl either way.'

'Ah, where's the sport in just walking away?' asked Ty with a grin.

'You take the five on your side,' said Hal loudly. 'You're the Masters' Champion, after all.'

'Well, you almost beat me,' he replied.

Several of the pirates laughed, but the leader looked at Hal and said, 'You're Duke Henry's boy?'

'I have that honour.'

'Lot of ransom.' He motioned to his men. 'Take him alive too. Kill the other two and if the girl is alive, have your way with her, but first to touch the Princess dies at my hand, understood?'

As he turned to look to see if his men were following orders, he heard a dull thud a moment before he reached up to his throat. His eyes widened, then started to go blank. Gabriella's throwing blade was lodged firmly in his throat and he died trying to pull it out with weak fingers. 'Now, who wants to be the first to try to have his way with me?' she hissed as she held her dripping dirk and another knife she had drawn out of her boot.

The pirates hesitated. Hal, Gabriella, and Ty formed a semi-circle between Stephané and the would-be abductors. The attackers approached cautiously and Hal said, 'If the lady doesn't carve up too many of them, perhaps we can settle once and for all who's the best blade. Most kills?'

'Loser buys dinner when we get to Ran.'

The pirates shouted and charged and Hal was almost bowled over by a burly man who received a wicked slice along his arm for his pains. Blood spattered over Hal, and over Stephané where she lay on the ground behind him, and he howled in pain.

Ty let the first man on his right extend and overbalance, then grabbed him in a headlock, slicing the back of his sword hand with his blade, then wheeling him around so that his rump faced the other four men, just as one struck a blow, taking his companion in the backside. The man howled in pain. Ty released him, then drove his left elbow down into the man's neck, stunning him.

The half-dazed man served as a momentary human barrier, and Ty reached across it to cut the sword hand off another of the remaining three men. His stump fountained blood and he cried out as his sword hand fell to the ground, and backed away.

Both Hal and Ty were trained in swordcraft far beyond most young men. Moreover, they were not merely competitive swordsmen, but sons of fathers who understood the skills of brawling as well as soldiering.

Men who had not trained to fight alongside one another were often more of a liability than an asset, and Ty and Hall moved instinctively away from one another, while Gabriella stayed close to Stephané, her own blades ready to protect the princess.

Hal ducked and sliced at a man's hamstring as he stepped by, Hal's finely-honed blade cutting through a heavy leather boot to topple the man. Now there were six.

Realizing almost simultaneously that their biggest risk was being swarmed by the rest, Ty and Hal began furiously to hack and lunge, inflicting half a dozen minor injuries before the men fell back.

One man bumped against the man next to him, moved the wrong way and Ty skewered him in the lower abdomen, causing him to collapse in a groaning heap. Now there were five.

Seeing so many comrades fall, the remaining pirates pulled back, stealing glances at one another as if attempting to coordinate their attack. Their expressions showed each was waiting for another man to take the lead.

One muttered, 'It's our necks if we come back without her.'

Another said, 'And it looks like it's our throats if we keep trying.'

What the remaining pirates saw was Hal and Ty hiding their exhaustion, and a strong-looking young woman crouched low with two weapons she had already shown she knew how to use. Even Stephané sat up, back to a rock, holding a dagger, determined to make any man who touched her pay a heavy price. The remaining Pirates appeared uncertain of which way to move.

There was a moment of silence, then as one the five pirates launched their attack, followed an instant later by three others, the fourth turning his attention to the girls. Ty parried the man on his left but took a nasty cut along the ribs from the one on his right before slamming the man in the face with his right elbow, the blow catching him under the chin and driving his jaw upward, stunning him. Ty turned full-circle and cut the other man across the back of the neck and he fell like a rag doll.

Hal spun to his left, taking him beyond the two pirates who had launched themselves at him, causing the man who had moments before been about to take Hal on the left, to discover Hal now far to his right. As he attempted to turn, to open up, he died from a deep thrust through his right side. Ty was quickly dispensing with the other two men, as they conveniently got in one another's way, allowing the young master swordsman the opening he needed to quickly impale both with sharp thrusts.

Hal shouted, 'Gabriella, guard the Princess!' He realized his warning was gratuitous, as Gabriella made short work of the pirate who had foolishly picked her as an easy target. He had come in expecting the longer reach he had with his sword to give him an advantage, and made the mistake of making a cutlass slash rather than a killing thrust. She had ducked under the cut, come up inside his reach and used her two blades to carve him up before he could recover.

The last man tripped over that corpse as he backed away from Hal, falling on his back at her feet. Gabriella knelt and without emotion drove her dagger into his throat.

Two wounded men groaned, while a third was unconscious and bleeding. Hal nodded once with a grim expression to Ty, and soon the three men were dead.

Hal turned to confront an ashen-faced Stephané. 'Are you hurt?'

Quietly she said, 'Did you have to kill them all?'

Hal looked into her eyes and without emotion said, 'Yes. If others come by they won't be alive to raise alarm or tell which direction we've fled.' She nodded. Again he asked, 'Are you hurt?'

She said, 'Just my ankle. No one got near me.'

'Good,' said Hal. He put up his sword, grabbed her by her left arm and drew her over his shoulder, as he would a sack of grain.

When they reached the road and stepped out, they were greeted by a waiting squad of men on horseback, swords out and two bows trained on them. 'Halt in the King's name,' said the ranking sergeant.

Hal put Stephané down and drew his sword. Ty said, 'Boots.'

Hal saw these men were uniformly equipped and let out a slow breath of relief. The sergeant pointed uphill and indicated two of his men should head up and see what all the noise had been. 'Now, who are you and what are you doing on the King's Highway?'

Ty glanced at Hal as if silently asking how much they should say. Hal answered, 'No disrespect, Sergeant, but I really need to speak to someone of higher rank in the city.'

The sergeant, his face looking like a sack of sunburned leather, large pouches under his eyes from too much drinking and too little sleep over the years, rubbed his chin with a heavily-gloved hand. 'Higher rank, is it?'

The two riders returned, 'Lots of bodies, Sergeant. Wearing the King's tabard.'

Swords started coming out of scabbards but Hal said, 'Pirates, wearing Kingdom tabards. Have your men go back and look closer. You'll see clothes, weapons—'

'Boots,' interjected Ty.

'—from no garrison stores in the Kingdom.'

The old sergeant sat back, his expression revealing he had little use for complications in what should be an otherwise ordinary patrol. 'We've had word of such to the east.' He motioned and the two returned up hill, only to come back a few minutes later. 'It's as he said, Sergeant,' said one rider. 'Cutlasses and the like. One of the dead has Keshian sandals on.'

'Well, then,' said the sergeant. 'So far you're telling the truth. Now, about this need to speak with someone of higher rank . . .'

Hal stripped off his left gauntlet and moved to the other side of the sergeant's horse, which blocked him from the sight of the others. He pulled off his signet ring and handed it to the sergeant. The seagull crest of Crydee with the cadency mark of three points over the gull, indicating the eldest son, was clearly carved into the fine gold alloy.

'Where did you get this?' asked the soldier.

Quietly Hal said, 'My father gave it to me.'

'And where did *he* get it from?' asked the sergeant, his tone softening.

'From his father, who got it from his before he became Duke of Crydee.'

For a moment the old soldier's expression showed that truth or lie, this was a problem for someone of superior rank, so he turned and shouted, 'Tanner, Williams, your horses!'

Two soldiers dismounted and came over. To Hal he said, 'For the ladies, so they may ride if they are able. You lads can walk with my boys. I've got a patrol to continue.' To the two soldiers he said, 'Take them to the captain,' and without another word, raised his hand, signalling that the patrol was to continue.

Hal looked to Stephané who said, 'I can ride,' before he could ask, and he smiled at her. She returned one, though weak and exhausted.

Gabriella helped Stephané mount and then climbed into the saddle of the other horse and the four fugitives and their two escorts turned west.

Hal asked, 'How far to Ran?'

One of the soldiers said, 'At a walk? We'll be there in two, three hours.'

Hal and Ty looked at one another and both managed a beleaguered smile.

Despite days in the wild, the trek along the highway was the most tedious portion of the journey. The road to Ran led down from a series of escarpments above the shore and so the city came into view miles away. As they trudged along it appeared to be getting no closer, but at last they were suddenly outside the city's eastern gate.

The guards at the gate raised a hand and one said, 'What this then?'

'Captain?' was all the soldier said and the sentry nodded, waving him through.

They moved past a crowded area, part caravanserai, part customs inspection point, ringed by make-shift booths and stalls where hawkers sold a variety of goods. The smells of cooking food caused all four of the travellers to realize they were weak from hunger and Princess Stephané said, 'Oh, whatever that is, I'll eat it here in the saddle.'

'We'll get you fed soon enough,' said Hal, his own stomach reminding him how long it was since he had had a handful of berries.

They reached the office of the city patrol and the soldier who escorted them in saluted before a bored-looking young captain sitting behind a small desk, and said, 'Sergeant says you should talk to these people, sir.'

The captain waved him away and looked at the four of them. Seeing the young women he perked up a little, for despite their road-dirt and fatigue, they were still attractive women. He stood up and motioned for Hal to fetch over another chair. 'Ladies, please, you look exhausted.'

Sitting on the desk, he looked first at Ty, then Hal. 'So the sergeant says I'm supposed to talk to you. About what?'

Hal said, 'Forgive me a question, Captain, before I answer you. Who is in command of the city?'

The captain looked at Hal as if he was joking. 'The Duke of Ran, of course.'

'I mean is he in the city or in the field?'

'Here, in Ran. The army of Ran has been recalled and even as we speak is disembarking from ships in the harbour. The war is over, if you've not heard.'

'Over?' asked Ty.

'What about Roldem?' asked Stephané.

'We've no news from Roldem, lady, so I assume all is well there.'

'I must speak to the Duke,' said Hal.

'First you'll speak with me,' said the captain, not happy at Hal's tone.

'Sorry, but I must speak to the Duke.'

'And who might you be to tell me you must speak to the Duke?'

Hal took off his gauntlet again and held out his ring. 'I'm Henry, son of Henry, Duke of Crydee, and you have the honour to address Her Royal Highness, Princess Stephané of Roldem.'

Stephané gave a wan smile.

The young captain was completely flummoxed for a moment, then looked again at Hal's ring. If it was a forgery or ruse of some sort, let the Duke's personal household guard captain sort it out. He was just a garrison captain ordered to patrol the King's Highway and arrest smugglers. Decision made, he shouted, 'Williams!'

A soldier stuck his head inside the small office. 'Captain?'

'Get a carriage and take these people to the palace.'

'Where am I going to get a carriage at this time of day?' he asked, showing a casual disregard for the formalities of rank.

'I don't care if you steal it! Get a carriage now!'

The soldier vanished, his expression showing shock at the young captain's tone. 'My name is Greyson,' said the captain. 'Can I get you something, anything while you wait?'

'Water,' said Gabriella.

'And something to eat,' said Stephané.

Hal and Ty looked at one another and in unison said, 'Ale!'

Still fatigued but now fed, Ty and Hal stood before Duke Chadwick of Ran. A stern-looking man in his late fifties, he still had the look of a brawler about him. He was thick-shouldered, and deeply tanned from years of soldiering, but his once-red hair was now white, as was the small moustache and pointed beard he sported. The young women were being seen to by the Duchess and her women and were enjoying baths and fresh clothing. The Duke had felt the young men's stories were important enough to demand a hearing straight away, so here they were, still dirty and tattered.

Ty and Hal had been somewhat circumspect in naming particular players in the political game in Roldem, but in the end the Duke had said, 'Odd that the King and Queen should feel the need to smuggle their daughter out of Roldem rather than simply call this Worthington fellow to account.' He was silent then said, 'A coup?'

Ty said, 'After a fashion, I suspect, Your Grace. The rumour prevalent in the capital is that Lord John is ambitious to have his son wed to the Princess.'

'Who wouldn't be?' asked the Duke with a laugh. 'Had I a boy of the right age, I'd be sending him to Roldem. But my sons from my first wife are all grown, and those from my second still toddlers.' He grew thoughtful. 'Still, as the King's Chancellor, Lord John has more power than any man non-royal in Roldem, so what's to be gained from forcing the girl to a marriage no one but Lord John wishes?'

'She's fourth in line for the Crown,' answered Hal.

'Roldem, of all places.' The Duke shook his head. 'I just can't see it.' He glanced around to see if they were overheard. 'Here, the Isles? That's another kettle of fish. You're a royal, young Hal, albeit a minor one, so there are people out there who wish you had never been born. If the King doesn't get on with it and father another son one of these days, we could have a serious mess on our hand in a few years.'

'Few years?' asked Hal.

'Well, Gregory's not a well man by all reports. Oh,' he added quickly holding up his hand, 'not that he's at death's door or any such, just that he's not robust and has had bouts of ague over the last few winters. Certainly, there are healing priests and chirurgeons hovering when he's taken ill. If he passes any time soon, it'll be because Lims-Kragma wants him now!' He barked out a laugh, to show he was making light of the matter. 'You've got a dozen cousins who would happily dance on your corpse rather than see you standing before the Congress of Lords claiming the crown, young Henry. It'll stay that way until the King names his heir.'

'If you remember, Lord Chadwick, my ancestor, Martin, King Lyam's brother, renounced the throne for our line.'

The Duke waved it away. 'Western honour. I forgot. It's very quaint and charming.' He leaned forward. 'Just be ready. If anything happens to the King, your father will have a dozen knives seeking his throat at first chance, and you'll be next. Any other brothers?'

'Two.'

'Well, they would be on that list after you.' Leaning back, Chadwick said, 'You're a conDoin, boy. Since we left that damned island to conquer half the north of Triagia, a conDoin has sat the throne in Rillanon. Some better than others, granted, but always that bloodline. There are some who would see it end with Gregory.'

'That's treason,' said Ty.

'Not if the King doesn't name an heir. Then it's up to the Congress of Lords and that means it goes to the highest bidder.' He paused. 'Or the man with the biggest army. Bah!' He dismissed the conversation as meaningless. 'This is the Isles. We're always looking for a way to gain advantage over our neighbours. My family's been at odds with Rodez for over two centuries, and for the life of me I can't tell you why.' He grinned. 'Still, we pester one another when we can. But Roldem . . .' He shook his head. 'Lore says we of the Isles and Roldem were once a single people. Heaven knows the languages are enough alike that it takes little effort for one to learn the other. I know that our noble families have intermarried so often we might as well just call ourselves cousins. But we're the difficult cousins, and they're the refined ones. We build armies; they build universities.' He pointed to his own back. 'Had the cane myself a few times as a student there. You?' he asked Hal.

Hal nodded.

He looked at Ty, who shook his head. 'You missed a lot then, lad. You don't appreciate learning until you're away from it for a while. That school there, it's a wonderful place. My two elder boys went there and my little ones will go when they're old enough.' He leaned back and again rubbed his chin. 'Roldem,' he said softly.

'What should we do, Your Grace?' asked Hal. 'The King and Queen sent their daughter to safety. We are supposed to see her to Rillanon.'

'Then see her there you shall,' said the Duke. He picked up a little bell and rang it. When no one answered he rang it again, harder. After a moment, he bellowed, 'Makepeace!'

An old servant appeared and said, 'Your grace?'

'Send word to the harbour that my ship is to be ready to sail on the morning tide to Rillanon. And tell my wife to stop fussing over those girls.' He glanced at the two young men and grinned. 'We only had sons, so she aches for a daughter to dress in fine clothing and all that paint women wear.' Turning back to the old servant, he said, 'And ask her to see to supper. We're entertaining royalty tonight!'

He stood up, as did the two young men. 'I don't envy you, either of you,' he said softly after the servant left. 'Fate has set you on a path that will I think have many traps and dangers. I was called to the capital in any event so I'll just leave a few days early. The Congress is gathering as there is much to discuss. Kesh is suing for peace and we must ask about that nonsense.' He thought for a moment, then added, 'Yes, let the King decide what's to be done with the lovely princess and then you two can get back to doing whatever it was you were doing before this fiasco began.'

Hal and Ty looked at one another.

'Come!' the Duke cried. 'Let's go to my favourite balcony where we can watch the sun set and drink brandy, and you can tell me about the Masters' Court.'

Both young men were exhausted, but they knew it was likely to be a while before they could rest. As the Duke led them away, Ty whispered, 'Maybe when we pass out face down at the table and they have to carry us out we'll get some rest.'

'As long as it's on a full stomach, I'll even sleep in this road-dirt.'

'I heard that,' said the Duke. 'Bathe first, then brandy!'

15

EXPLORATION

Light exploded.

The blinding display was accompanied by a thunderous boom that caused both Amirantha and Sandreena to flinch and fall back a step. Magnus stood outlined in the brilliance of an oval of light that had formed before him, his hand in front of his face, shielding his eyes.

'What is that?' asked the Warlock.

The white-haired magician turned and said, 'It's some sort of energy matrix. I attempted to probe the Sven-ga'ri to see if it was in any way different to those I've seen in the Peaks of the Quor.' He squinted into the brilliant light.

'This is unexpected.' Magnus had joined the others when his father's message from the Academy had reached him. He found the entire situation fascinating, both the completely unexpected Pantathians, and the alien and odd energy of this place.

The two members of the ruling council of the Pantathians, Tak'ka and Dak'it, who had observed the magician's examination of the alien beings called Sven-ga'ri, were also partially blinded by the light.

Magnus blinked as his vision struggled to return to normal. He asked the two Pantathians, 'Have you seen anything like that before?'

'Never,' said Tak'ka. 'The Sven-ga'ri use emotions to communicate: we believe they may in part be responsible for the changes in those of us who live here compared to those who do not.'

Magnus nodded. The story of these alien creatures was much the same as he had discovered in the Peaks of the Quor: ordered by their Dragon Lord masters to take care of these beings, the Pantathians, like the Quor, had diligently discharged that duty.

'I think I'll need to examine this for a while. I have an idea what it might be.' He turned to Amirantha and Sandreena. 'I think it might be wise if you two returned to Sorcerer's Isle and spoke with my father, if he has returned from the Academy. He has no love of their politics, so I am sure he will be home as soon as he can.' He took out a Tsurani translocation orb and glanced around. After a moment he nodded to himself and began a spell, holding the device before him. It took a few minutes, but then he held out the orb to Amirantha. 'I've programmed this to return here. Father is very powerful, but there are a few things he can't do, such as reach a location he's never seen before. I don't need this to get home. Will you please tell him I think it's going to take all four of us, or maybe even more of our colleagues, to unravel this mystery?'

Sandreena looked surprised. 'Really?'

Turning back towards the oval, Magnus said, 'I have some suspicions about what we're looking at here. This could take a great deal of time.' Then he said to Tak'ka, 'Might I ask for a few things?'

'What do you require?' asked the elder of the two Pantathians. The subtleties of his race's expressions were becoming known to Magnus and he smiled. 'Tea if you have it, please, water if not. And perhaps a cushion upon which I might sit. I suspect I will be here for a while studying this construction.'

Amirantha, Warlock of the Saltumbria, took the Tsurani transport orb from him. 'Will you share your suspicions? In case your father asks.'

Magnus shrugged. 'These beings are as alien to us as any we have ever encountered. As far as I can see they are composed entirely of energy, albeit in a coherent form. For various reasons, we assume them to be sentient, an assumption we made in haste when we first encountered them in the Peaks of the Quor, but that may prove not to be the case.

'Moreover, they seem to communicate on a profound emotional level, which may be subtle enough to convey the most nuanced concepts, but to us are incomprehensible. Imagine, if you will, hearing a group of singers, a choir. Most of us might be able to hear the entirety as a lovely harmony, perhaps much as we experience our proximity to the Sven-ga'ri as a sensation of calm and well-being. Some of us might be able to listen to one voice or another within the choir, somehow isolating it from the others. But I suspect, to hold to this analogy, the Sven-ga'ri are ten thousand voices and each of them holds the ability to listen to each voice as a choir, yet each alone, simultaneously. Whichever it may be, I think they are intelligent in a manner we have yet to understand, and that they are trying to communicate with us.'

Amirantha said, 'Interesting. But what about the oval of light?'

'I think they are tired of our clumsy attempts to communicate, and are now trying something that may be as alien to them as it is to us. Energy is to us most clearly perceived as light, hence I think they are trying to provide us with a means to communicate. I think they may be trying to teach me to read, since I appear deaf to them.'

Amirantha smiled. 'Well, then, we'll leave you to your studies and convey all we've seen to your father.'

Sandreena moved next to her former lover, putting a hand upon his arm. With a final nod to the Pantathians and Magnus, Amirantha activated the orb and they were gone.

Magnus turned his attention to the bright oval, studying the ripples of light, their intensities and colours. He was so focused that when he was brought a cushion he barely registered it. When his tea arrived he did not acknowledge it and hours later, it remained untouched.

Magnus found his senses challenged by a cascade of images. He discovered subtle patterns beginning to emerge as he felt the presence of the Sven-ga'ri, almost as a tactile music in his mind. He let his senses relax and having become attuned to the interplay of emotion – mental music as he thought of it – and the faint patterns within the white light, he began to bring his magic to bear.

More than any magician in the history of this world, including even his father Pug, Magnus could unleash torrents of destructive energies that could shatter mountain tops, turn back the tides, or call up winds to topple city towers, but he also could manipulate the finest threads of a tapestry, capture one raindrop in a storm, or move a sleeping kitten across the room without waking it, using his mind alone.

As deftly as a seamstress threading the smallest needle with the tiniest thread, he reached out and caressed the energies. Gently, he pushed into the matrix and his mind expanded his exploration carefully.

Magnus was overcome by wonder as a crystal-like, three-dimensional network of forces revealed itself. He knew he was barely below the surface of the shimmering white oval, yet at this scale the energies appeared monstrously large and complex. It was like floating through a city of ice, but without streets, buildings arrayed like massive boxes, and in each of those boxes a million pulses of light per second flickered.

Somewhere in all of this was a pattern that would reveal its purpose, and Magnus was prepared to search for as long as it took.

He pressed on.

Perceptions shifted and scales expanded and contracted and Magnus felt as if he was floating through a vast universe composed of energy. His body sat motionless in the garden created by the Pantathians for the Sven-ga'ri, but he now saw himself as physically in this universe. It was as if he flew by will alone through vast spaces, yet he knew those spaces were in reality as small as the space between the tiniest grains of sand on the beach, as small as the space between drops of rain. He reached out with his mind and felt the coursing of energies as they made their way, in this direction or that, up or down, right or left, in a pattern that was always just beyond the edge of his comprehension.

By Magnus's estimation he had explored only the tiniest portion of the energy field, yet a pattern was slowly beginning to present itself. At first he rejected the idea, believing he was misinterpreting what he was seeing but as time wore on he began to see his theory ratified and before long he became certain that it was borne out. Patterns repeated and relationships emerged and revealed themselves. It was a terribly clever and complex creation.

A deep fatigue overtook him suddenly and he realized he had no sense of how long he had been exploring inside the energy matrix. Knowing he would have to stop and find his way back later, he created the illusion of a market, a place to which he could return and renew his exploration, and then deftly withdrew his consciousness.

Suddenly he was chilled and wet and shivering. He blinked. It was dark. A Pantathian stood above him holding a large canvas cover, protecting him as much as possible from the punishingly cold rain.

Magnus raised his hand to his face, wiped away wetness and felt stubble on his cheek. He looked at the Pantathian and said, 'How long have I been here?'

The creature apparently didn't speak the Keshian tongue, but from behind him another voice said, 'All day, the night, the next day, and this night, without moving.'

Magnus turned, and found his body stiff and unresponsive. He saw Tak'ka standing in the rain. The Senior President of the Pantathian nation said, 'We feared you might have been trapped within by some magic, but were uncertain of how to reach you.'

Groaning a little as he unfolded his legs, Magnus said, 'You did the right thing, in waiting. My sense of time becomes lost in there, apparently. It felt as if I were there for minutes, perhaps an hour.' As he stood up his head began to throb. 'I must be careful when next I venture in.'

'You discovered something?'

'I'm not certain. I see a pattern and I have deduced one possible explanation for its existence, but I cannot yet declare that judgment sound. More exploration is necessary.'

'Come, rest. You're obviously chilled and in need of warmth and food.'

'You are very kind,' said Magnus. 'Given the history between us, your generosity is unexpected.' Like his father, he had been astonished at his reception by these Pantathians. As bellicose as their kin were, the residents of this small city were gentle, kind, and apparently, extremely forgiving.

'We are the caretakers of the Sven-ga'ri, and I fear that whatever is moving out there in the darkness, our charges are at risk. I welcome your strength and knowledge in preserving them.'

Magnus nodded, but already he was beginning to suspect that before this exploration was over, preserving the Sven-ga'ri might be the last thing he and his father would wish. His initial impressions were now overlain by a deep sense of growing certainty that these . . . he wasn't sure how to regard the Sven-ga'ri so he continued to think of them as sentient beings, were far different in nature than he had first presumed.

He followed his host inside to warmth and food.

Magnus enjoyed a hot meal and his clothing dried over a small brazier while he bathed. By the time he had donned his now-warm robe, he was already half-asleep. He lay on the pallet provided and within moments fell into an exhausted sleep.

After resting through most of the night, in the hours before dawn he began to dream.

He floated through the matrix again, only this time rather than energy he saw solid objects in bright and muted colours, some flickering between the two states, alight from within one moment, dimmed the next. Lines of silver-white like endless cords stretched down the broad expanses that intersected the structures. 'A city,' he whispered.

'An illusion,' said a voice from behind him.

He turned to see a figure both strange and familiar, a black-bearded man in a black robe, holding a wooden staff. His feet were clad in sandals and around his waist was a simple whipcord rope.

'Macros,' he whispered.

'In a manner of speaking,' said the phantasm.

Magnus had never met his grandfather, for he had died before Magnus was born, but he had encountered a Dasati upon whom the memories of the dead sorcerer had been bestowed. There was as much resemblance between the two as there could be between dissimilar species, but there was more than that. The Dasati-Macros had been ill, in advanced years, and dying.

Before Magnus now stood Macros in his prime, looking no more than perhaps forty years of age, his manner calm and relaxed, yet Magnus could sense hidden power just below the surface.

'I'm dreaming,' said Magnus.

'Yes,' answered Macros, 'but like all dreams, there are open to you avenues into thoughts as yet unexplored. It's the perfect state in which you are receptive to contact you might otherwise not recognize. Besides, you are impervious to spying now.'

'Spying?'

The shade of Macros smiled. 'You have some inkling of those who oppose you, at least in one sense, while in another you have no idea whatsoever what forces are arrayed to destroy you and your father. Time is essential, yet here time is as much an illusion as sight and sound, for we are in the dream.'

He stepped forward then reached out, gripped Magnus by the elbow and gently but firmly turned him around. 'Walk with me and we shall discover much, but you will only know what you already know.'

Magnus allowed himself to be compelled in this fashion, but said, 'I do not understand.'

'I am not Macros, as I'm sure you've already assumed. I am his image, a memory of him made solid and able to converse.'

'Whose memory?'

'Kalkin's, whom you also call Ban-ath.'

'A memory?'

'A god's memory is a powerful thing, as is a god's dream. You are sharing a god's dream and are speaking with a god's memory. Let's move on.' Macros pointed and suddenly they were rising to one of the lines of energy. Letting go of Magnus's arm he said, 'Grip the line and do not fall too far behind. Even a god has limited control on how lucid a dream may become.'

Magnus reached up when Macros, or his illusion, reached up and suddenly he was being propelled along at incalculable speed, yet felt no sensation of movement, just a blurring of all they passed.

Then Macros said, 'In a moment, I will tell you to let go. Do not hesitate.'

A moment passed; then Macros said, 'Let go,' and Magnus complied at once.

They floated before what appeared to be a monstrous fortress, but one created by a demented mind. It sat upon no ground, so a vast wall stretched out before them in all directions. 'Let us gain some perspective,' said Macros, and suddenly the wall shrank to the size of a mere room. 'In dream, all things are possible; within the matrix, what you saw before approaches the truth.'

Magnus examined the wall. It was apparently made of some sort of red stone, with four doors set in the middle, a single square of stone separating them. Two large windows with red iron bars were placed at forty-five degree angles to the upper corner on either side, so that each section gave the vague impression of a face: two eyes and a mouth. Continuing along the line from the door through each window, the top of the wall featured a turret, with crenels and merlons.

'It looks like four castles smashed together,' said Magnus.

'It does, doesn't it?' Macros chuckled. 'It is an image created for your mind to understand. There is no real-world analogue that would do justice to what this really is.'

'What is it called?'

'Many things. The blazing barrier. The fire wall. The terminus. The final barrier.'

'What function does it serve?'

'I cannot tell you, for you do not know, and I know only what you know.'

'So I was aware of this barrier, yet . . .'

'Your mind in dream is apprehending what it is you've

come to understand by inference and deduction. You have not seen the barrier so you have created an image of it, but it may bear no true resemblance to the reality of the barrier. In the end, you will only know when you have reached the barrier.'

'There are so many questions,' said Magnus. 'And yet . . .'

'You cannot frame them, because they are the questions your mind has no answers for. You understood when we first met that I was not your grandfather, and that Kalkin dreamed, and the rest. For more answers within your own mind, you will have to seek out answers in the real world. For more answers from Kalkin, well, you will have to seek him out, and as you know from your father's tales of the Trickster God, even then you may never get answers you can trust.'

Suddenly the image of Macros was gone.

Magnus's eyes opened and it was dawn.

He sat up and stretched, yawning, knowing that after he had braced himself with food and drink he would again confront the mystery of the energy matrix. Perhaps this time he could go deep enough to reach this final barrier and then, perhaps, beyond it.

Sandreena and Amirantha were breaking fast when a student approached. 'Pug has returned and asked that you join him when you're finished.'

Amirantha looked at Sandreena. 'You finished?'

She was on her feet before he could finish the question and he rose to follow her. 'I guess you've finished!'

They hurried through the now almost completely rebuilt Villa Beata, passing through large gardens which had been freshly replanted. In the matter of a few minutes they were outside Pug's office and Sandreena knocked once, then opened the wooden door.

They had both marvelled at how Pug had refashioned his office since the destruction of the original villa. His last office had been small and dark, with only one window, while this one had a large wall made up entirely of panes of the finest clear glass he could find, further refined with some very subtle magic. When sunlight blazed in, it was cool thanks to the combination of clever design – a duct in the ceiling carried the hot air away – and a little more magic.

Pug said, 'Good morning. I wish I had good news from the Academy, but at best it's mixed. What did you and Magnus discover on the island?'

Amirantha had taken to wearing less flamboyant clothing since coming to live at Sorcerer's Isle, and today was comfortable in a loose-fitting white tunic and dark-grey trousers. Sandreena always looked surprisingly delicate for a large, strong woman when not wearing armour. She wore a plain but well-made pair of trousers, a loose-fitting blue linen blouse, and a pair of sandals. They took the chairs Pug indicated with a wave of his hand, and Amirantha looked at Sandreena, who nodded, indicating that he should go first.

'We are not sure,' said Amirantha. 'The barrier we call the matrix is something . . . otherworldly?' He shrugged. 'It exists within this world, but at the same time, somewhere else. Magnus thinks it's as likely to be a trap as a means to communication with the Sven-ga'ri.' He then explained Magnus's surmise on the nature of their communications.

'Really?' said Pug leaning back in his chair. 'At this point nothing should surprise me, but say on.'

'I'm not sure I can add much more,' said the Warlock, 'but there is something . . . odd about all this.'

Pug turned to the Knight-Adamant and said, 'What can you add?'

Sandreena said, 'On matters of magic, I am a novice. What Amirantha said is as Magnus observed while you were away. I spent my time watching them poke at that . . . matrix, and getting to know our hosts.'

'What can you tell me about these Pantathians?'

'They were hospitable and welcoming,' Sandreena continued, 'despite knowing that you and Magnus had destroyed many of their kin. They seem too, well, gentle is the only way to describe them, though their warriors were valorous when fighting demons.'

'Even the meekest of creatures will give all protecting their young and home,' agreed Pug. 'Did you see any Serpent Priests after I left?'

'No,' said Sandreena. 'They were mentioned, and I left with the impression they visit their kin from time to time, but as to where they base their operations since you and Magnus destroyed their previous headquarters is a mystery; I didn't feel it politic at this time to ask the one they call Tak'ka for more details.'

Pug sighed. 'Well, the good news is that we've identified the threat. The Serpent Priests are back again.' He was silent for a moment, then added, 'But we don't know where they are.' He rose. 'At least we know they aren't on that island, which is something.' He motioned toward the door.

They followed him out of his office, through a hallway, and into a large meeting hall. 'Join me as I bring the rest up to date with events in the world.'

'The rest?' asked Amirantha.

'I called a meeting of the Conclave before I left the Academy.'

They entered the newly-finished meeting room, which turned out to be a large covered patio, otherwise open to the daily breezes of the island. A square table had been placed in the middle, one that could be enlarged in any number of clever ways depending on how many people needed to attend a given meeting.

Seven people were already seated when the three entered. The only familiar face to either of the demon experts was Grand Master Creegan of the Order of the Shield of the Weak, Sandreena's mentor in the Order. They had no idea who the other four men and two women were.

Pug motioned for Amirantha and Sandreena to take the two empty seats and he remained standing. 'Those of you who know one another need no introductions. If you do not recognize others, it is best it remain that way, given our current plight. You cannot be made to reveal what you do not need to know.' He took a deep breath. 'So far we have identified five well-placed agents of the Conclave who are traitors. I am certain there will be more. Continue to conduct your investigations: trust is scarce right now; use it wisely.' He motioned to the man closest to him on his right and said, 'What have you discovered in Roldem?'

The man quickly recounted the efforts that were under way in Roldem to prevent further leaking of information, and to discover who might be behind the actions taken against the Conclave. He finished by saying, 'At this time we have no more likely suspect than Lord John Worthington. He is either at the top of all actions taken against the interest of both the Crown and the Conclave, or he reports to the ultimate authority.'

Before Pug could move to the next in line, a man sitting farthest from him interjected, 'I know I speak out of turn, Pug, but that is almost the identical report that I have put together concerning Great Kesh. The man who stands out as the most likely suspect is a nephew of the Emperor, Lord Harfum.'

Instantly, Grand Master Creegan said, 'Sir William Alcorn.' He looked around the table. 'It is the same in Rillanon.'

Pug nodded. 'So, our first priority must be to discover what links these three men.' He indicated that the first two men should depart, but added, 'Grand Master Creegan, remain if you would.'

The remaining agents quickly provided Pug with more information on issues pertaining to the attempts to identify possible spies within the Academy as well as in various less-critical positions of influence and authority. As each finished delivering their report, Pug nodded and the agent rose and left the table. When the last had departed, Pug turned and looked at the three remaining members of the Conclave.

'Creegan,' he said, 'you're our eyes and ears in the temples. Anything?'

Sandreena's former mentor sighed. 'In truth, not much. If anything the temples are more difficult to infiltrate than even the Conclave, for the gods are very jealous of their domains. Several of the martial orders, however, seem to have been slightly compromised: no ordained member is suspected, but a few key servants, or lay administrators, have been weeded out as being undependable. Those identified are being questioned.'

'Which orders?' Sandreena asked.

'The more active groups: the Warders, the Hunters, the Arm, and the Hammer.'

Pug seemed to wilt visibly at the list, and Sandreena said, 'If they infiltrated any significant level of those orders, they are dangerous indeed.'

'Exceedingly dangerous,' said Creegan. Seeing that Amirantha didn't quite follow, he added, 'Of course, you'd know the gods and perhaps those orders by different names in your homeland.' He held up a hand and began ticking them off on each finger. 'The Warders of Law serve Astalon the god of law, the Hunters are followers of Guis-wa the god of forbidden knowledge, the Arm of Vengeance serve Ka-hooli the Vengeful, and the Hammer serves Tith-Onanka, the war god. Many of these, especially the Arm and the Hunters are overt enemies, and would never knowingly work together.'

'I see, and the Shield?' Amirantha looked pointedly at Creegan.

'Our order is one that takes great pains in examining those we employ within the temples; magic is used to determine if those who come to serve have duplicity in their hearts. And unlike some of the other orders, we require our own members to conduct the daily business of the Order, the cooking, cleaning, and maintaining the temples, shrines, and our places of residence. Some of the other orders do not. The Hammer and the Hunters feel that every member must be a warrior-priest, and to concentrate solely on those duties they hire many to serve who are not of the Order. Therein lies their vulnerability. We have been working through the

Ishapians, as much as we can, but it got the leadership's attention and so far no new infiltrators have been found. The other orders listen to the Ishapians, but they do not like it.'

'They'll like seeing their world in ruins at the feet of the Dread even less.'

Creegan glanced at Amirantha, nodded to Sandreena, then turned and departed.

Pug said, 'Now, if you have that orb Magnus gave you, I'd like to return and see what he is doing.' With a wry grin, he added, 'I think I could return there from what I remember, but why chance it?'

'Shall we go back with you?' asked Sandreena.

'No, rest for a few days. You've been travelling a great deal. I'll return with Magnus when it's time.'

Amirantha retrieved the orb from his tunic pocket and gave it to Pug. Pug said, 'See you soon,' depressed the switch on the side and vanished.

Amirantha yawned. 'After that meal, I'm in the mood for a nap. Care to join me?' he asked Sandreena with a smile.

'Those days are long over, you fraud,' she said. Then she smiled. 'Rest, and I'll see you for dinner if you'd like.'

'I would like that a great deal,' he said, and was surprised to find he meant it. 'Dinner, then.'

Sandreena turned and walked away and he watched her go and thought to himself that of all the women he had met and bedded, she was the one he could never get out of his head. With a sign of resignation, he turned and headed to his own quarters.

Pug appeared next to his son. Magnus was obviously in some sort of trance, as he sat ignoring the drizzling rain that had soaked him to the skin despite the best efforts of a Pantathian holding what appeared to be a makeshift umbrella over him. Which meant he had been there for a long time. Knowing his son, Pug judged it had probably been since early this morning. While it was summer in the north, it was winter here and this far south the rain was turning bitterly cold.

At the sight of Pug the Pantathian almost dropped the umbrella and said in clearly-understandable Keshian, 'Oh, you startled me!'

Pug waved his hand. 'Apologies. Here, let me take that from you.'

The reptilian creature seemed relieved. 'He awoke before dawn and has been here since breaking his fast; this is his second day and we are unwilling to disturb him.'

Pug reached out gently with his magic and then withdrew. 'You could probably hit him on the head with a rock and it wouldn't disturb him,' he said, taking the umbrella. As soon as he had hold of it he realized that despite the good intentions of the Pantathian, the gusting wind almost entirely defeated the effectiveness of the thing. Even so, he held it over his son.

'I am La'th,' said the Pantathian. 'I will inform Tak'ka that you are here. I am sure he will wish to welcome you himself.'

As the creature departed, Pug reflected on how ironic it should be to be welcomed by any sort of Pantathian. For his entire adult life all the ones he had ever encountered had been trying their best to obliterate humanity.

While he waited, Pug inspected the tableau. Magnus sat on a soggy cushion facing an oval of energy floating about three feet above the ground. Seeing it and the Sven-ga'ri beyond, he understood why Magnus had forgone the relatively easy task of erecting a shield of magic against the elements. It would have had to be large enough to encompass what appeared to be a massive terraced park atop the largest building in this city, which would have made deploying his other spells more problematic; or if small enough to encompass just himself, it certainly would have distorted any readings or insights gained from that examination.

Gently he sent his mind into the matrix of light before him, seeking out his son's presence. Finding Magnus was like finding his own hand: as father and son they were attached in a way as Pug had never been to any other in his life. His lifelong friend Tomas and his departed wife, Miranda, were family of his heart, and he could find them almost as easily, but Magnus was his blood, his last remaining child.

For a brief moment that awareness struck Pug as he remembered those children he had lost, William, his first boy, dying heroically in the defence of Krondor, and Gaminia, his adopted daughter in that same struggle. Caleb, his youngest, dying with his wife Marie, at the same time Miranda had been lost. Caleb, so strong and willing to serve, yet always the one without magic.

Pug pushed aside that pang, for he knew it led inexorably to his fear of the curse laid upon him by the Goddess of Death: that he would watch everyone he loved die before him. He had foster-grandsons, Tad, Zane, and Jommy, whom he had kept at an emotional distance, fearing that to come to love them as his own would doom them. He could not honestly say if he had succeeded in keeping his affections in check.

Turning his mind away from such morbid turns, he followed his instincts to his son's metaphorical location within the matrix and intruded slightly to let Magnus know he was there.

Father, came Magnus's thought. *I felt your presence when you arrived.*

Pug marvelled at the man and sorcerer his son was becoming. Pug had known other workers of magic: Kulgan, his mentor; Shimon, Hochopepa and other Tsurani Great Ones in the Assembly of Magicians on that now-lost world. Macros and his daughter Miranda. Each had special abilities and in one thing or another surpassed the others. Kulgan was a practitioner of what was known now as the Path of Lesser Magic, a distinction made by the Tsurani. The Great Ones were known to walk the Path of Greater Magic. The Greater and Lesser Paths were pointless labels from Pug's point of view when it came to Magnus. He was a true master of any magic he sought to learn. Even the most arcane of the arts, such as Amirantha's demon lore, Magnus had undertaken to understand, and now he could exercise some small control over demons. And then there was his son's ability for mind-speech, a skill shared with Pug's adopted daughter, a skill Pug had never successfully mastered.

He said, 'Amirantha and Sandreena have told me of your work.' Pug felt another presence nearby and said, 'I think our host is here. I'll return shortly.'

He pulled his consciousness out of the matrix and turned to see an elderly Pantathian in a finely-made red robe with black trim now being thoroughly soaked by the intensifying rain. 'Welcome back, Pug,' the Pantathian said.

'Thank you, Tak'ka,' returned the sorcerer.

'It would be false should I say that you are any more welcome here, but we understand that you and your friends are fated to be here. Too much of our blood on your hands prevents me from offering more than tolerance and a modicum of comfort.' He glanced skyward. 'Though from your son's willingness to soak in this soon-to-be-freezing rain indicates to me that creature comforts are not very important.'

Pug could not hide his amusement. If the Pantathian was unaware of a human sense of humour, he was naturally wry. 'Oh, we appreciate comforts and I welcome tolerance. Perhaps at some time in the future we may discuss our past differences, or at least mine with your more murderous kin, but for the moment Magnus's actions communicate a sense of urgency on his part and I defer to his judgment. As for the wet and cold, we've endured worse, and I expect we shall come through this, though a dry towel when we are done would be most welcome.'

Pug couldn't tell if the creature was amused or not, as he did not understand Pantathian facial expressions. But Tak'ka answered, 'That much can be done. La'th here will remain to provide for your needs should any arise.' Without further words, the elder Pantathian turned and left the roof garden.

Pug actually looked forward to having the opportunity to sit and speak with the apparently gentle leader of the Pantathians. He had understood so little of these created beings, these playthings of an ancient dead Dragon Lord, Alma-Lodaka, who had become a goddess to this race.

But for now, he returned his attention to his son and re-entered the matrix.

Time inside the matrix became meaningless. Pug knew they stood a real risk of passing out from exhaustion if they didn't occasionally monitor their real-world existence. Then he wondered how he would know what constituted 'occasionally,' given the circumstances.

He watched as Magnus probed. He had remained an observer since his son had begun this exploration, for Magnus seemed more deft at discovering his way around this analogue of an energy field than his father would be.

Pug moved within the matrix without conscious thought to where Magnus probed the massive red castle construct. He thought it must be a protective barrier, the red castle representing something that was constructed entirely of energy, and prodigious amounts of energy at that.

They had tried moving around the barrier and learned that the illusion of size and shape was misleading. There was no 'around' nor 'back.' Anywhere they ceased their 'movement' they were still confronted by the red barrier. The more obvious choices had been to 'look' in one of the windows, but that had proved pointless; there was nothing beyond the 'window.' Pug deduced that it might have been some mechanism that allowed observation from within, allowing someone or something inside the matrix to observe what Magnus and Pug were attempting. But who or what that someone or something might be was beyond their understanding.

Now Magnus was probing the 'lock' in the door. Pug struggled to understand the concept. Here was an energy matrix, assembled in such a way as to imply it was a communication of some sort. But it seemed protected in a fashion that whoever placed it here wanted to be sure that only a particular person or group of people might be able to decipher it. That would imply that the information was sensitive.

Pug began an investigation of his own, exploring the limits of the matrix while Magnus continued his probing of the internal barrier. When he was at last convinced he had begun to understand something of the nature of this odd artefact, he gently contacted Magnus, who withdrew.

In a blink they were both conscious of being in the rain, drenched and chilled. They hurried to the entrance to the garden and found La'th waiting, though the Pantathian seemed on the verge of sleeping. He snapped out of his doze and handed them each a towel. 'Is there anything you require?'

Father and son glanced at one another. 'Something hot to drink would be appreciated,' said Pug. 'Coffee, tea, chocha, whatever else you might have.'

'We have tea,' said the Pantathian and he hurried down the stairs.

'What concerns me,' said Pug, 'is the incalculable energy contained within that thing.'

Magnus nodded. 'Me too. When I first began I concluded that this matrix, is somehow an extension of the Sven-ga'ri, and I'm convinced it's their attempt to communicate with us. I just don't understand why, after all this time, and why here, rather than up in the Peaks of the Quor?'

'When we unlock that barrier and if we are able to communicate with these beings, then perhaps we will have those answers. As for the first, I speculate that time may be different to them, and perhaps it's taken them this long to appreciate what manner of beings surround them, and how best to reach out to us. As to why here than there, I do not even care to speculate on that question.'

Pug fell silent as the Pantathian returned with two mugs of hot tea. It was bitter and flavourful and warming and were both grateful to have it. 'How are you doing with that barrier?'

Magnus sipped his tea and Pug studied his son for a

moment. Unlike his eldest son, William, who had borne a strong resemblance to Pug, or like his youngest son Caleb, who had resembled his mother, Magnus barely resembled either of his parents, though Pug could see hints of Miranda around the eyes. His face was currently set in a very familiar expression of thoughtfulness as he answered, 'It's complex, obviously. It's constantly changing but I'm beginning to discern a pattern, a repeating sequences of pulses that prevent a casual probe beyond that wall into whatever is hiding behind there. And then, there's my dream.'

'What dream?'

Magnus told him of his dream about Kalkin and the matrix.

Pug was silent for a moment, then said, 'As frustrating as it has been to deal with the Trickster, we do arrive at the same purpose: preventing the obliteration of our world. But experience tells me to consider what filtered into your dream from . . . his dream, if that indeed was what it was.'

'I think it's true that this is a barrier, and the matrix . . .' Magnus fell silent for a moment, then added, 'Think of it as a lock, but one that has teeth and grooves within that are moving, and out there somewhere is a key that moves in synchronization with that lock, but any other key or lock pick will merely jam the lock, rendering it useless.'

'Or destroy utterly whoever tried to pick it.'

Magnus merely shrugged.

Pug was thoughtful as he sipped his tea. After a moment, he said, 'Still, the matrix did not manifest in such a fashion until you appeared, what, a day after you arrived?'

'Less I think. I may not have taken notice of that aspect immediately,' said Magnus.

'So we might conclude that there's a reasonable expectation that you are either supposed to be in possession of that key or able to pick that lock, correct?'

Magnus smiled. 'Were our positions reversed in this conversation, Father, what would you say in answer to that?'

'I'd say you were making rash assumptions. It could be that the arrival of any magic-user triggers that response.'

'Or any non-Pantathian,' offered Magnus.

'Or demons on the island, or a flock of seagulls flying overhead . . .'

'We should get back,' said Magnus. 'We have a few hours of daylight left, and while it's cold now, it's going to be brutal after the sun goes down. And I feel as if I'm almost ready to try to "pick the lock" as you say.'

Pug nodded. He followed his son out to where the now-totally-soaked and useless cushion lay and watched as Magnus sat on it anyway, and observed him enter his trance state.

A sudden concern struck Pug in the pit of his stomach as he recognized that his last living child was about to embark on what was perhaps a very dangerous exploration of magic. He quickly inventoried his own established spells of protection and realized he'd got sloppy lately.

Pug had almost died because of his own arrogance when confronting the demon Jakan when he was in the guise of the Emerald Queen. That near-death experience had delivered a harsh lesson, but it had proved instructive in preparing for potentially lethal outcomes.

Pug decided not to join his son in the matrix exploration but began to construct a spell of protection for the two of them. Of all spell-craft at Pug's disposal, the most difficult was this, a spell to protect without warning. The difficulty arose that in the time between an attack manifesting itself and the target becoming aware, the target could already be dead before the defence could be deployed. Against arrows and sword, fire and stone, there was no way to protect without advance warning. But against magic there was always a momentary gathering of energies, sometimes less than a few seconds, but always there before the magic was unleashed. It was that fact that gave Pug the idea for this construction of magic.

The shield would engulf him and anyone close, Magnus in this case, and protect them from any magical damage Pug could anticipate. As a master of his craft unequalled on this world, save perhaps for his son, that covered any form of energy, fire, or other discharge that would instantly kill the unprotected. The trick, as Nakor would have called it, was to have it deployed the instant before the attack was unleashed, and that was where Pug concentrated. The instant a malevolent magic was detected, the shield would deploy, and in that instant was the difference between salvation and obliteration. The difficulty was he could only deploy such a defence in a single position, such as on top of this roof in this garden.

Pug fashioned his spell and put the magical 'trip-wire' as he thought of it in place, then let out a long sigh. As long as he stood there and didn't move, he and Magnus stood a fair chance of surviving any trap that could be anticipated.

It was the ones he couldn't anticipate that had him worried.

16

JOURNEYS

Nakor swore.

'We can run faster than these horses,' he complained to Miranda.

'Yes, but after a few hours we'd need to eat them. And there are enough Kingdom patrols between here and Sarth I don't wish to have to explain myself to.'

'Well, Martin gave us a pass,' responded Nakor.

Arkan and Calis said nothing, content to let Nakor and Miranda do all the talking. Arkan was fascinated by the human landscape as they rode past farms and villages down the coast road from Ylith to Sarth. His only remark had been to comment on the richness of this coast compared to the Northlands.

Nakor was riding a bay gelding that seemed to slow down every time he stopped applying heel to barrel, determined to browse anything he could crop irrespective of Nakor's wishes. Miranda had a speckled roan mare that seemed on the verge of breaking down due to an old spavin on her left hind leg. The elves had found a pair of bay geldings, one with a white blaze, both old enough they could not outride the other pair of mounts. So the best they could manage was a posting trot most of the time, with an occasional canter tossed in to break the monotony.

Nakor continued with his complaining. 'I just wish we could have found better horses.'

Miranda smirked. 'The good horses went south with the army, and the five-gaiters went with their rich owners anywhere the Keshians weren't. Be glad we're not riding mules.'

Life along the shore of the Bitter Sea was picking up slowly. Martin had tried to find them a boat to sail directly to Sorcerer's Isle, but it had been impossible. The only boat available was the dinghy used to spot the water demons and even with a demon's strength they couldn't row that many miles.

So they found two horses not worth much and paid too dearly for them, and headed south. Neither Miranda nor Nakor worried about provisions, as they could hunt and forage. Neither was averse to eating raw meat and their taste was diverse. If it could be eaten, they'd eat it. And both elves were expert hunters so if provisions couldn't be purchased, game could be killed.

As for other travellers, few were encountered. A few dispatch riders heading from Sarth to Ylith. Miranda had Martin's report to take to the garrison at Sarth, as she would reach that city before anyone else. There just weren't horses to spare and besides, Martin had to keep his entire force intact to face the Keshians in the middle of the city. The gods only knew how long that armistice would endure.

They had been on the road three days since the truce had been declared, and were determined to reach Sarth as quickly as possible. There they would find whatever craft they could to sail to Sorcerer's Isle. Miranda was constantly battling her frustration at all those things she had once known how to do, as Miranda, rather than Child.

And that was another thing: she and Belog were thinking of themselves more and more as Miranda and Nakor, not as their true demon identities. The emotional wear of wanting to see Pug and Magnus, the mourning over the loss of Caleb and Marie, all of it was as real to her as if she had always been Miranda, and it was taking its toll. The original Miranda, despite years of life experience, had always been impatient and impetuous, perhaps a product of her childhood where she had to scramble to survive. Her mother had been a powerful magic-user, last known as the Emerald Queen, but called Jorma when she was married to Nakor in her youth. The real Nakor and Miranda had never really decided if that in some strange way made them kin, but it had never been an issue, for they were good friends. Her father was Macros the Black, but she had only met him a half-dozen times growing up. If there was ever a man less suited to be a parent, Miranda hadn't encountered him, but in the end he had died heroically, and Pug had survived because of that, and for that she had always been grateful to her father.

She had never truly loved a man until she met Pug, or at least not in the way she had come to understand while with him. Before him there had been lovers, the last being Calis, which was why it was odd for Child to confront the elf prince and feel Miranda's emotions at seeing his face. He had been a partner in many ways, in the first resistance to the demons and Pantathians when the Emerald Queen's army had overrun Novindus. Before that she had been a vagabond, taking and leaving men as she found them. Some she grew fond of, but never enough to give up travel and discovery. A few she thought of from time to time, drifting for a moment on memories centuries old, but one thing she shared with people like Nakor, Amirantha and Pug was that most of the people she had loved.

And apparently, she thought dryly, even dying didn't mean you escaped that fate, it seemed.

The sun was setting as they came upon a village and for the first time encountered problems. Six men, mercenaries from the look of them, deserters most like, were standing near the communal well when Miranda and Nakor rode into view.

Their leader was a disreputable-looking fellow with yellowing teeth, a wall eye, and a large floppy hat underneath which stringy light brown hair flowed to his shoulder. He wore what once had been a fine officer's riding jacket with an array of brass buttons, most of which were now missing. His grey riding trousers and black knee high boots had seen better days. But his weapons appeared well cared for and the six men with him all looked capable enough.

'Well, what have we here?' he asked as Miranda pulled up.

'Travellers,' she answered, 'bound for Sarth. Seeking a night's respite.'

'Well, that's a problem,' said the man as his companions spread out. 'We're Sarth militia, you see, and we've been sent here to keep the road clear of Keshian spies.'

'Deserters, you mean,' said Nakor, jumping down from the horse. He walked up to stand before the leader and said, 'You're bandits plaguing these good people. Now, why don't you leave?'

The man laughed and turned to his companions. 'Do you believe this little fellow?'

Two of the bandits had crossbows, which were instantly brought to bear on the two elves before they could unlimber their bows. The leader made a 'tsk, tsk,' sound. He turned back suddenly with his sword coming out of his scabbard, but before he could draw it fully free, Nakor reached out and shattered his wrist with a single squeeze. The man's howl was turned into a gurgling gasp as Nakor reached up and tore out his throat.

Onlooking villagers retreated into their homes, several pulling the heavy cloth doors closed, while others peered out of the windows. The two men with crossbows let fly, but Arkan and Calis were already out of their saddles, half-falling, half-leaping as the bolts sped through empty air.

'That tears it,' said Miranda leaping from her horse. With two steps she stood next to a bandit attempting to string his bow. She ripped it from his hands and broke it over his head, his eyes rolling up into his skull as he fell to the ground.

Within a minute the other bandits were dead and Miranda called, 'You can come out now! They won't bother you.'

The doors remained closed for a full minute, until a man came out, his face a mask of fear. He held out food. 'It's all we have. Take it. Please, take it and go.'

Miranda glanced at Nakor. They didn't need a place to sleep, but comfort was always preferable to the ground. Yet these people were so terrified of what they had just witnessed, they would do anything to see Miranda, Nakor and the elves depart, despite having just been saved from the bandits.

Miranda said, 'Keep your food. You need it more than we do.' She turned away. They mounted the horses and moved off down the road as the sun turned the sea to the west of them emerald green tipped with amber.

After a few moments, Arkan said, 'That was odd. You saved them, yet they were more frightened of you than the bandits.'

'Normal humans don't break wrists with a single squeeze of the hand, nor crush skulls with a blow to the head with a bow.' She took a deep breath, and then let a long sigh escape. 'We move too quickly, we're too strong. We may look like other people, but we're not.'

Calis shrugged. He knew Miranda wasn't the woman he once knew and loved, but he also didn't know exactly what she was. He didn't press for answers. By nature, he was patient and he knew that the truth would present itself eventually.

Nakor said, 'No matter how vivid our memories, we will never be one with them and they will never accept us.'

Miranda spoke quietly. 'Pug might.'

Nakor didn't know if that was an opinion or a hope. He said nothing.

Sarth had proven an unexpected trial. The city was garrisoning levies of soldiers detailed to Krondor, but Krondor was already over-burdened by those forces already housed there. The entirety of the Armies of the West that had answered the Prince's call to muster had arrived. Garrisons from Yabon in the north, Land's End to the south-west, and everything between Krondor and Malac's Cross to the east.

Had they had somewhere else to go, things might have been fine, but they didn't. They were hunkered down waiting for a Keshian offensive that never came. So the Prince's Knight Marshal of the Principality detailed as many men to Port Vykor and Sarth as he could.

Now there were thousands of bored, uncomfortable, and soon-to-be hungry troops milling around. The armistice was too new for the Prince to send anyone home, though after Martin's report reached him he might choose to return the Yabon garrison north, or at least send enough veteran troops to relieve Martin.

Miranda found the local commander and introduced herself. He was somewhat sceptical of the odd-looking quartet, until he read Martin's report and saw it embossed with the ducal signet bearing the upward-facing crescent, the mark of the second son.

The captain, an old soldier from Krondor, asked, 'So Duke Henry is dead, then?'

'Yes,' said Miranda. 'He was returning to Crydee from the road to Ylith when goblins attacked. One got lucky, or he was unlucky.'

The old soldier got up from behind the table he was using as a desk. He had occupied a chandler's home so the furniture was well-made. It probably had the most comfortable bed in the town. 'I'll pass along the boy's report to the Knight Marshal. Word should reach the King within a fortnight.'

Miranda said, 'Not to make too fine a point of it, Captain, but that "boy" held Crydee for a week, then retreated and held Ylith again against a full legion of Keshian Dog Soldiers, twice that number of auxiliaries, and a full company of Leopard cavalry. With two hundred men-at-arms from Crydee and the rest of the local muster, those left over after the Earl of Ylith marched south. I'd say he's shown that he's more than a boy.'

'Fair point,' said the captain. 'Is there anything I can do for you, lady?'

'If there's a boat for sale or hire, I need to travel to Sorcerer's Isle.'

'The Isle? Even in peace time you'd have trouble finding anyone mad enough to make that journey. It's right off to the west of Krondor you know, and every ship in and out gives it a wide berth.'

'I know where it is, captain. It's my home.'

The captain looked as if he was uncertain what to say. Finally he said, 'Tell you what. Go to the docks and look for an old mad man named Sully. He has a little sloop he's been boasting is the fastest thing in these waters. If Kesh or Queg gets a notion, you might find out if it's true. I've held him here in case I needed a fast boat to Krondor or Ylith, but so far I've had no need of him.' The captain crossed back to his desk and quickly wrote out a note, signed it, and affixed his seal of office to it. He handed the folded document to Miranda and said, 'Tell him he's already being paid if the subject comes up. It's a returned favour from the Prince for bringing us this report.'

'You're more than fair, Captain.'

As they turned to leave, the captain said, 'I've fought Keshians before. If the boy faced Dog Soldiers and Leopard cavalry, he's got sand.'

'Yes, he does,' said Nakor.

They left and went searching for the man named Sully.

The *Seafoam Lady*, a converted freighter turned into the gaudy personal transport of the Duke of Ran and his guests, hove to in the harbour in Rillanon waiting for the proper conduct from the harbourmaster to a berth at the royal docks. Normally a personage of the Duke's rank would be given clear access to the quayside, but as every duke with a ship was either already at anchorage or just arriving, things were getting very crowded and the harbourmaster was down to his last iota of patience.

Eventually, the Duke's party was given clearance and a nicely-appointed longboat was sent from the quayside to the ship. A cleverly-designed if somewhat cumbersome platform on pulleys had been devised as a means to get the Duke's portly wife to the longboat without demanding that she sacrifice her dignity by trying to climb down netting or being carried by sailors in a sling. The device was torturously slow, but eventually the Duke, Duchess, two small sons, and their four guests were in the longboat.

Reaching the quayside, they found a carriage waiting to conduct them to guest quarters in the palace. The carriage barely held the Duke and his family and the two ladies. Ty and Hal were content to borrow horses from the escorts for the ride to the palace.

Both young men had been to Rillanon before, Hal once and Ty on several occasions, but each experienced the same sense of wonder riding from the docks up the King's Highway to the palace. The city was breathtaking from this vantage.

King Rodrick IV, known to some as the Mad King, had undertaken a city renovation project in his first year, insisting that every inch of the palace be faced with the finest rose-and-gold quartz interspersed with brilliant white and pale blue tilework. Then he fancied the idea that the entire city be likewise finished, his ambition being to turn the city into the most beautiful in the world. His vision had been carried through by his successors, Kings Lyam and Borric II.

Now as the carriage rolled along cobbles chosen for their rosy colour, the noon sun turned the entire royal hillside into a stunning display of reflected glory. Light played off one surface then another, as brilliant white façades glimmered with hints of aqua and lavender, rose and gold. Not only the palace and the homes of the powerful and rich were finished in the brilliant stone, but the public face of every house in every sector save the warehouses near the docks. Even those drab precincts were elevated from the mundane by the light that washed over them.

But of course otherwise this was a city like any other: in dark corners evil was plotted and behind those brilliant faces, dark alleys lay wherein murder was done. A brothel or drug house might be dazzling to behold, but the trade within was the same as in the seediest corner of Durbin. As Hal's father had warned him about Rillanon before he set off on his journey to Roldem, 'A whore may be the most beautiful woman you've seen, my son, but she's still a whore.' And as they entered the palace marshalling yard, Hal dismounted and thought to himself, *But she is indeed a beautiful whore.*

Grooms wearing powder blue livery trimmed with golden braid hurried to take the horses and help the guests dismount from the carriage, while a line of royal household guards stood at attention, their black trousers and large, red-plumed black hats, and tabards with a golden lion on a red field making them the smartest-looking soldiers Hal had ever seen. Then his father's voice came to him: 'But can they fight?'

Several officials came forward to greet them, and with what appeared to a genuine love of the theatricality of the moment Duke Chadwick informed the palace's major domo, 'I have the honour of presenting Her Highness, Princess Stephané of Roldem, who seeks audience with His Majesty at his earliest convenience.'

The manager of the King's palace had the good grace to

look nonplussed for the briefest second. Then he turned to his second and said, 'Make sure that the royal guest quarters are readied at once!'

The speed with which that official took off convinced Hal that in the time it took Stephané and Gabriella to walk to the guest accommodations set aside for visiting royalty, windows would be opened, fruit and chilled wine placed upon the table, candles lit, and bedding freshened, as if they had been expecting her all along.

Ty whispered to Hal, 'I think if Sung the White showed up—,' he meant the Goddess of Purity, '—he'd have her room ready.'

The entire party was ushered into a receiving area where a party of government officials were waiting. Standing in the middle of the group was a gentleman of middle years wearing a well-tailored dark green coat of simple cut. He bowed to Stephané and said, 'Highness, allow me to present myself. I am Sir William Alcorn, the King's Chancellor. I can only say this is a most welcome and wonderful surprise. His Majesty will of course expect you to dine with him tonight.' He turned to the Duke and said, 'Your Grace,' then he greeted the Duchess, and returning to the Duke said, 'Many of the Congress have gathered to discuss the coming peace with Kesh. An informal dinner has been arranged for that purpose, if you'd care to attend.'

'Yes, of course,' answered Duke Chadwick.

Turning to the two young men, Sir William said, 'Young Lord Henry, we anticipate your father's arrival with the other western lords in the company of Prince Edward soon. Until then please be our guest.' To Ty he added, 'And you, Master Hawkins, are welcome as well.'

Stephané turned to Hal, her expression fixed in a smile, but her face almost devoid of colour. 'Would you be so kind as to call upon me once you've settled into your quarters, Lord Henry? You as well, Master Hawkins?'

For the briefest moment, Sir William's expression flickered as if he was thinking of a reason to object, but finding none he merely smiled and said, 'Ask any servant and you will be shown the way. Now, if you'll excuse me, I must attend to the business of the day.' He bowed and moved away, whispering to a subordinate, and various servants immediately began escorting guests to different parts of the palace.

The King's palace was set atop the highest hill overlooking the harbour at the northern end of the Island of Rillanon, birthplace of the Kingdom of the Isles. Buried below the foundations of this city were the ruins of earlier settlements and villages. History began where lore ended, and tales of great heroes sung by bards were transcribed and gathered and thus was the history of nations fashioned.

Hal walked past a garden, remembering that Dannis, the first island monarch to set his standard on the mainland, had made a conquest not from this calm sanctuary but rather from a torch-lit stone tor a hundred feet below this palace, covered by centuries of detritus, a single tower that had been raised over a thatch-roofed village of daub-and-waddle huts protected by a log palisade. The mighty Kingdom fleet had comprised a dozen long barques with single masts with less than thirty warriors per boat, and Bas-Tyra had been a rival village on the mainland with its own single tor overlooking log walls.

Still, thought Hal as they reached the apartment he'd be sharing with Ty, thinking of the past with more glory and beauty than it deserved was a common failing of conquerors, and it provided goals for dealing with the dark and murderous reality of today.

Rillanon might be the most beautiful city on the planet, but conquest and murder, betrayal and mayhem had made it that way.

Ty and Hal followed a servant to the Princess's quarters where they were quickly admitted by Gabriella. Both young men were wearing clothing that had been provided by the palace: to their amazement it fitted well, right down to highly polished boots.

The Princess rose and said, 'Please, come into the garden.'

Ty and Hal exchanged glances: in the late afternoon the garden would be quite hot.

Gabriella moved quickly around the perimeter of the garden, obviously looking for eavesdroppers. The garden presented one open side to the city and harbour below, perfect for watching the sunrise should one be up that early, and two low walls, behind which no one lurked.

Softly the Princess said to both Hal and Ty, 'That man who greeted us?'

'Yes?'

'That's Lord John Worthington.'

Both Hal and Ty looked at one another then back at the Princess.

'I know you'll think me mad, but you did meet Lord John at the reception after the Masters' Championship. Don't you remember?'

Ty and Hal again exchanged glances, but neither could conjure up a good memory of Lord John Worthington. Finally, colour rising in his cheeks, Hal said, 'If I'm to be honest, Stephané, I remember little except being in a bit of pain; and seeing you for the first time.'

Stephané's eyes widened slightly and a slight smile passed over her lips, but then her expression became serious once more. 'I'm not jesting with you. If that's not Lord John Worthington who greeted us, it's his twin.'

Ty said, 'I vaguely remember Lord John, but truth to tell, I was in much the same position as Hal . . .. without the pain, of course.' He smiled.

Stephané didn't. She looked at Gabriella.

Lady Gabriella said, 'They are like twins, gentlemen. I've been the Princess's companion for five years now, and I've encountered Lord John on dozens of occasions over the last three. They could be the same man.'

'If they are twins,' said Hal, 'that begs many questions.'

'Worthington is an Isles name,' said Ty. 'Cousins perhaps?'

'More than that, I am certain of it,' said Stephané. With

a slight inclination of her head she instructed Gabriella to take Ty to the far side of the garden so that she could have a moment alone with Hal. When they were as far removed from the other couple as possible, she said, 'I wanted to thank you for everything.'

Hal found himself suddenly speechless, as flummoxed as he had been the first time he had met her. Now, as then, she was dressed in court finery, and although her hair was not set in some grand fashion, it was freshly washed and framed her face in natural waves. Her wide blue eyes stared at him in a way that made him feel amazed and disconcerted at one and the same time. 'Ah,' he began, 'no need. I was only . . .' He couldn't speak.

She looked up into his dark brown eyes and stepped close. Putting her cheek against his, she said, 'I know. I see how you look at me. I treasure that love.'

Hal's mouth was dry.

Stephané whispered, 'Until I return home safely, please do not leave my side.'

Trying to still his pounding heart, Hal spoke quietly. 'I am your obedient servant, Your Highness. I will be but a call away from now until you are with your father.'

'Thank you.' Standing on her toes, she kissed him on the cheek. With her lips next to his ear she whispered, 'I have never met your like, and I will hold you in my heart until death.' Then she turned away, saving Hal further awkwardness.

So many things had happened since that first night Hal had seen her. His feelings were a jumble, and he was desperate to say more to her, but he knew that he never would. She would marry someone important to the Kingdom and he was, at best, years away from becoming a rural duke in the far west. Title and land he would possess, along with responsibility and obligation, but the sort of political influences needed to make him a suitor for the hand of the Princess of Roldem would be but an idle dream. The possibility that she might look upon him as something more than a loyal friend at one and the same time buoyed and sank his heart. He pushed down the ache that was growing and reminded himself that he had been raised to do his duty to king and country.

His reverie was interrupted by the arrival of a page who said, 'Lord Henry of Crydee?'

Hal turned. 'Yes?'

'The King is asking for you now, sir.'

Hal glanced at the Princess, and she indicated with a tilt of her chin that he should go at once; she'd be fine in the company of Ty and Gabriella.

Hal hurried after the page who led him through a series of corridors so that they approached the King's royal apartment through a side door, out of sight of the throng of courtiers waiting in the main hall of the palace for their chance to speak with the King.

Hal stepped through the door held open by the page and was surprised by how sparsely decorated the room was. There was a desk by a window that offered a lovely view of the harbour, a single ancient tapestry hanging on one wall, a small table with a pitcher and goblets on it, and a single chair at the desk. In the chair sat the King.

Hal bowed and the King rose, extending his hand. Hal gripped it and looked into King Gregory's face. He was shocked.

In the few months since he had been presented at court, the King's health had obviously declined. He was thinner, his complexion gone sallow, and his hair hanging lifelessly to his shoulders.

'My boy,' said the King. 'We fear we bear grave tidings and wished to be the one to tell you.'

Fearing the worst, Hal said, 'What is it, sire?'

'Word has reached us from Krondor that your father was taken in battle. You are now Duke of Crydee, Henry.'

Hal was too stunned to speak.

The Princess, Ty, and Gabriella comforted Hal as best they could. While they waited for the summons to the royal dinner Hal recounted his boyhood in Crydee and the good times he remembered with his father, mother, and two younger brothers.

At one point he looked at the ring on his finger and said, 'This will go to my eldest son one day.'

'Your father's signet?' asked the Princess. 'You will take that?'

'It will be buried with him as is traditional, and a new one will be forged for me. My brothers will then give me theirs and will receive rings for whatever offices the Crown sees fit for them.' He sighed and sat back. They were in the little garden next to the Princess's chamber sipping iced drinks of fruit juice and white wine as the afternoon heat was falling away. 'I knew this day would come, eventually, but to come so soon and . . . unexpected.'

Stephané took his hand and gripped it for a moment.

Trying to lighten the mood, Hal said, 'Ty, why don't you come to Crydee? You'd be the greatest swordmaster in history.'

'You're drunk,' said the young man from Olasko. 'Or you should be.'

'Maybe later,' said Hal. 'I do not want to embarrass myself before the King in my first official act as Duke of Crydee. What about it? Care to train farm boys how to be soldiers?'

Ty laughed. 'I don't think I'm cut out for that life, Your Grace.'

Hal held up his hand. 'Not yet, please.'

'I'm an eastern lad, Hal. I love the cities and the dining, the gambling and . . .' he looked at Gabriella, 'the ladies too much.'

She fixed him with a slightly disapproving eye.

Hal went on, 'Assuming there's a Crydee to return to. The reports forwarded to me are not good. A great deal hinges on what sort of peace the King can arrange with the Emperor. I may be a duke without a duchy.'

'I'm sure something good will come out of all this,' said the Princess.

Gabriella smiled. 'Her Highness has always had a far more cheery outlook on how life works than most.'

'Not a bad way to be,' conceded Ty. 'Many get worn down by worry and fretting over things we cannot control.'

'But you have to be prepared for all eventualities,' said Hal, 'including the most dire.'

'Which is why you'll make a wonderful duke and I will not,' said Ty, lifting his glass.

A page arrived and announced the reception would be under way soon. Hal and Ty excused themselves to retire to their quarters and when they reached them, found that sumptuous court raiment had been laid out for them.

Hal was given a russet tunic with the ducal crest of Crydee over the heart, a golden seagull in flight, black leggings and boots adorned with what appeared to be real gold buckles. A finely-made chain sword-belt with a scabbard covered in matching russet velvet set with a line of black opal surrounded in gold completed the outfit. 'Gods, what this must have cost!' he said examining the clothing.

Ty was equally impressed with a powder blue tunic with a small insignia denoting the earldom where his father was reputedly a squire; a fiction created by the Conclave of Shadows for his father when he served them, but as far as the Kingdom's heraldic office was concerned, young Ty was entitled to the rank of squire, even if they had no idea where he was from, or to whose service he was pledged. White hose and black boots and a silver chain sword-belt with a gold-topped scabbard in dark blue velvet studded with three diamonds completed his regalia.

Hal looked at it and said, 'I see your title of Champion of the Masters' Court won you the better scabbard.'

Dryly, Ty said, 'Yes, Your Grace,' as he began to change.

That earned him a pillow thrown at his head. 'Better get used to it, Hal. You'll hear it a lot tonight.'

Hal was silent for a moment, thinking of his family, then he began to dress.

They entered the vast hall and a squire showed Ty to his place at a lower table, as befitted his rank, and then escorted Hal to his place at the King's table. He found himself standing next to Lord Chadwick who quietly said, 'Sorry to hear about your father, lad. He was a very good man.'

Between Chadwick and the empty chair next to the throne where the King would dine stood two other men who nodded politely. Hal recognized them as Lawrence of Salador and Geoffrey of Bas-Tyra. He returned their greetings and they waited until at last the Master of Ceremonies announced the King.

The King entered with his queen on his arm, and Hal was struck by the contrast. The Queen was a beauty to rival Princess Stephané, yet there was something about her that was . . . empty. She smiled and nodded to various members of the court, her behaviour bordering on the flirtatious, and Hal wondered if some of the rumours about her that had reached Crydee before he left were true. However, the rumours were immaterial as she had still not given the King a son, so questions of paternity were moot. And from what he had seen of the King's deteriorating condition, it appeared unlikely there would be one.

Behind them came James, Duke of Rillanon, perhaps the single most powerful noble in the Kingdom. Behind him walked two other men, one whom Hal recognized instantly as Sir William Alcorn, and the other he reckoned must be Montgomery, Earl of Rillanon, the Duke's second-in-command. Suddenly Hal began to understand what a dog-fight would erupt over power if this king died without naming an heir. The only other player who would matter was Prince Oliver of Simrick, who was absent. Hal felt his stomach tighten as he realized he would be concerned with none of this had his father lived.

Once the King was in his place, he waved for the assembled guests to sit. 'My lords, ladies, and gentlemen, our first duty tonight is a sad one.' He motioned for Hal to come and stand on the other side of the table, which the young lord from Crydee did at once. 'I present to you Henry of Crydee, now Duke, upon the death of his father also named Henry, our most loyal servant in the west, and our beloved cousin.' He motioned and a page brought over a cushion upon which sat a golden signet ring. 'As is custom, the late duke will be buried with his signet and I have taken it upon myself to present the young duke with this new one, as a token of affection for my beloved cousin. Kneel.'

Feeling a little awkward, Hal did as ordered. The King stood up then declared, 'Rise Harold, Duke of Crydee.'

There was a smattering of polite applause in the room and Hal received the new signet from the page. He felt the weight and realized it wasn't gold over bronze as his father's ring had been, but rather made of solid gold. He put his old signet in his belt purse, against the day he had a son to whom to give it, slipped on the new ring and found it a good fit.

As he came back to his chair and sat, Duke Chadwick leaned over and said, 'That was a bit of an odd play, don't you think?'

'The table certainly made it awkward.'

'No, not that. He could have waited until court tomorrow to invest you, but he chose to do it here, before all the members of Congress. He might as well have gone out to the archery range and fetched back a target to affix to your back, boy.'

Hal was still coping with the gravity of his new title and missed the point. 'What? I'm sorry, I don't . . .'

'He named you cousin, before every lord in the palace. He's tossed you in with me, Oliver, and Montgomery.' Quickly the Duke added, 'I pray to any god who'll listen not to give me the job of king. Montgomery is not a man for the job, any more than Prince Edward in Krondor is. That leaves Oliver, but now there's you.' With a humourless chuckle, Chadwick said, 'Be cautious, boy. You're about to make a great many new friends, and enemies as well.'

Hal sat back, trying not to feel overwhelmed.

A few minutes later the squire announced Princess Stephané, who made her entrance as the entire company of nobles rose and bowed. Hal could barely breathe at the sight of her. It was the gala for the Masters' Court Championship all over again. The Queen's seamstresses had worked magic in creating a stunning lilac gown edged with embroidered golden pears. She wore a matching set of jewellery, as well as a gold embroidered shoulder wrap. Gabriella entered behind her in a shimmering gown of dark green that set her colouring off to good effect, as did as fine a set of emeralds as Hal had ever seen. He suspected the jewellery were on loan from the Queen's collection.

Stephané moved gracefully until she stood before the King's table and bowed. 'Welcome,' said Gregory. He indicated she should come around and sit to the left of his wife, and when she was in place, everyone again sat down.

Hal hardly noticed when the first course of dinner was placed before him. He looked around the hall and saw it with different eyes, as if he was in the most improbable wilderness one could imagine. Some of these nobles were harmless, while others were as dangerous as any predators in the wild.

He felt eyes on him, and turned to see Sir William Alcorn watching him for a brief second from a seat at the far end of the table, before turning away as if in conversation.

Hal had never felt more out of his depth in his life.

17

REUNION

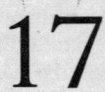

Miranda jumped into the water.

Nakor was a step behind, as both leapt into the waist-deep surf. The two elves followed.

It had taken a little bribery beyond the normal bullying from the garrison captain in Sarth to get Captain Sully to sail to Sorcerer's Isle. Even then, he had refused to come ashore, insisting they wade in from as close as he was willing to get and Miranda had grudgingly agreed, too pleased to have finally reached Sorcerer's Isle to be concerned by the discomfort. Arkan and Calis were elven-kind, so their natural reticence masked whatever they might be feeing at this point.

'Now we hike,' Miranda said briskly.

As they trudged up the long pathway from the beach to the rise that marked the end of sand and beginning of meadow, they were not unobserved.

In the distant tower of the Black Castle, a lookout had spied their boat approaching and had already alerted those whose job it was to guard the island from interlopers.

As they approached the crest of the hill, they saw figures waiting for them.

A young magician named Theodor stood flanked by Amirantha and Sandreena, who had volunteered to accompany the youngster as much out of boredom as any fear of assault on the island. All three now stood in astonishment and confusion seeing the group, one of whom they were sure was dead, climb the hillside.

Miranda waved a greeting, her face split in as broad a grin as anyone had ever seen, such was her joy to be home. Then suddenly Amirantha cried, 'Demons!'

Sandreena put her shield up and drew back to attack Miranda while Amirantha began a spell of banishment. Theodor stood rooted, uncertain of what was happening.

Calis and Arkan were both caught unprepared. Arkan began to unlimber his bow, but Calis put out a restraining hand before the moredhel chieftain could nock and fire.

Nakor felt the banishment magic gather and knew that within a moment he and Miranda would find themselves back in the Fifth World; in the second circle if they were lucky, and if they were not, in the mad lands or into the void. He reached into his bag and drew back, throwing as hard as he could.

An orange struck Amirantha dead in the centre of his forehead, breaking his concentration and interrupting the spell.

Sandreena had been fighting demons for years, so what she didn't expect was one to step away from her attack instead of attacking back. Miranda deftly stepped to one side and let the heavily armoured Sergeant Knight-Adamant of the Order of the Shield of the Weak overbalance when she met no resistance. Miranda couldn't resist sticking out her foot, so that Sandreena tumbled down the path.

Amirantha shook off his blurry vision to find Nakor holding out his hand, and saying, 'Please don't do that until we've talked.' Unable to think of anything better to do, Amirantha reached up and let the little man help him to his feet.

Sandreena finally stopped rolling, came to her feet in a crouch and was about to attack, but found Miranda patiently waiting at the top of the path, holding out one hand, palm outward. 'Don't!' was all she said.

Sandreena hesitated and Nakor laughed. 'You must be Sandreena and Amirantha. I am Nakor. I died before we met.' The absurdity of that statement made him laugh. 'We have a lot to talk about, but let's wait until we get back to the villa. I'm sure Pug and Magnus will want to hear this as well.'

Arkan and Calis exchanged looks, revealing in subtle elven fashion that they found the entire exchange vaguely amusing.

Sandreena slowly shook her head. 'Why not?' She trudged up the path and said, 'We know you're not who you seem to be. Who are you?'

'Well,' said Nakor in obvious delight. 'I am Nakor. This is Miranda. The dark-haired fellow is Arkan, and the fair-haired one is Calis.' He pointed to the elves. 'They're who they appear to be.' He pointed to Miranda and then himself. 'We sort of are who we seem to be, but that's not the full story, which is better told over wine.'

He turned and started walking down the long path to the villa below. Sandreena gave Miranda a wide berth and followed, obviously very unhappy at being made to look foolish. Amirantha fell in beside Miranda and looked at the dead woman who now reeked of demon-magic, absently tossing the orange in the air. 'I suspect wine will help,' the warlock said to Miranda, 'but I'm not certain it'll help me understand.'

She looked at him and simply said, 'Kalkin,' as if that explained everything.

Amirantha said, 'Oh,' then a moment later said, 'Oh! Yes, we do have much to speak of.'

Sandreena tried hard not to turn to look at what she knew to be two demons calmly walking into the heart of the Conclave of Shadows.

Sitting in the kitchen, Sandreena seemed unable to grasp what she had just heard. 'So, somehow . . . Kalkin, Ban-ath, the god of thieves and liars . . . put your minds into the body of demons? In the demon realm?'

Miranda seemed ready to throttle the holy knight, but she restrained herself. Nakor said, 'No, those aren't 'our minds,' but our memories. I do not know what happened to Nakor's mind when he died on Omadrabar. Maybe mind and soul are the same thing? Maybe he went to Lims-Kragma's Hall and started anew on the Wheel? Maybe he didn't. He was on the Dasati world, so maybe he's now reborn a Dasati? I have no idea. But what I do have is all of Nakor's memories.' He shrugged. 'I have the memories of Belog as well. I was Belog first. But the more I live like Nakor, the more like him I feel. Mostly I think of myself as Nakor now.'

'And you?' Sandreena asked of Miranda.

Looking off into space, she replied, 'The same.' She had been crushed to discover that Pug and Magnus were somewhere on the other side of the world investigating the Pantathians, and not for the first time, but with the most vehemence, she cursed not having Miranda's powers. In her mind she could remember how it worked. The true Miranda would have been able to sense where they were and just go there.

Amirantha repeated an earlier observation. 'And we so far have no idea why Ban-ath would do such a thing.'

Nakor shrugged, his hands held out palms up in perplexity. 'The last time was when he put the memories of Macros the Black into a dying Dasati who became important in rescuing that race from a horrible end. Maybe it's something like that. I'm not sure Macros knew that world had been taken over by a rogue Dreadlord who subverted the entire race.'

Sandreena said, 'I remember hearing the details from Pug, or at least those he was willing to share.' She glanced at Miranda who nodded. 'What I never understood is how one Dreadlord could do that.'

'We may never know,' answered Miranda. 'I don't know how often you talked about that after I . . . well, after Miranda was killed.' She rolled her shoulders then chuckled ruefully. 'I can still feel that demon's jaws tearing into my neck.'

Sandreena stood up. 'If you will excuse me.' She tried to sound apologetic and failed. 'I just need some time to think . . .'

Amirantha waited for a moment, then said, 'I'll go speak to her.'

He followed Sandreena out of the kitchen and down the path that led to the quest quarters. 'Are you unwell?'

She rolled her eyes in a way that told him she considered that as stupid a question as could be. 'This goes against every instinct I have, Amirantha. I'm sitting at a kitchen table chatting with demons. All I want to do is break their skulls with my mace and send them back to the Fifth Hell!'

'It's an unusual situation for you, I know,' he said. 'My experiences are different—'

She interrupted him. 'Of course they're different! You summoned them to play your confidence game on gullible villagers and nobles alike. You kept them around for pets. You had one as a lover!'

'I thought we agreed never to discuss Dalthea again?'

'You agreed,' she nearly spat. Amirantha had summoned a succubus as a lover when he grew tired of watching those he cared for die, and unfortunately Sandreena and he had become intimate at a time when he was still under the impression it was a passing thing. It was only after she found him in bed with the demon and tried to murder them both that he understood she had been a great deal more serious about the affair than he. It had taken them years to get past that, and from her current attitude, it appeared she wasn't as far past it as he had thought.

'Look, can we just put that aside until we are in a place less fraught with danger? I don't think you fully grasp the scope of this. Yes, it's startling to see Nakor and Miranda in front of us, and her looking as we last saw her moments before she died.' Neither had met Nakor before, but hearing his story combined with Miranda had given weight to both stories. 'But think of this: a god has manipulated things beyond recognition, towards an end only he knows, but it must be vital, otherwise why bother?'

'The Trickster?' she asked. 'Because he's bored?'

'Maybe, but unlikely. No, this is something critical.' He looked out into the distance. 'Things are moving out there,' he said. 'We've seen too many terrors and wonders in our days not to understand that this is no longer a simple matter of an errant demon blundering into our world to be banished again; these two are here for a reason and we must discover it.' Then he added, 'And I feel we must discover it soon.'

'I don't believe I've ever seen you this serious about anything.'

Amirantha looked away into the distance. 'There are many things I would change if I could, Sandreena. How I treated you is one. But since encountering Kaspar and having him bring Brandos and me here . . . my perspective on many things has changed. I've never spoken of this to anyone, not even Brandos, and you know he's like a son to me.' She nodded, saying nothing. 'As a boy I watched my people destroyed in a mad ruler's war against another petty tyrant. What was left of the Saltumbria was my mother, myself and two crazy brothers, both of whom seemed to spend a large part of their creative energies trying to kill me. We were spared only because we had been driven away by our people because they thought our mother was a witch and mad. Both were true, but that's beside the point. Had we been welcomed within that community we would have perished with the rest of our tribe. Here I found something larger than myself to believe in.' He looked at her. 'You understand that. You would give your life for your order and your goddess.'

She said, 'If need be, yes, but it wouldn't be my first choice.'

'Nor mine, and I'm not even sure if it came to that I could be that self-sacrificing, but I know I never cared about doing the right thing before I came here. Oh, I think I did the right thing in caring for Brandos.' He smiled in remembrance. 'You should have seen him as a boy. He was tough and defiant and could fight like a cornered sewer rat, but there was something in him I liked.'

'So you took him in,' Sandreena said. 'Is he coming back?'

'He and Samantha are keeping to themselves in the tor I built outside Maharta. I think he's worried that if I find out he's ill I'll worry too much.'

'He's ill?'

'Just an old man's cough, but that's the thing, isn't it? I raised him from a boy, and now he looks old enough to be my father.' He held out his hands and turned them over, as if trying to see something. 'They don't look any different than a hundred years ago, Sandreena. I have no grey hair. No wrinkles, and until I met Pug, Marcus, and Miranda, I'd never met another human being who didn't age. There is something here to fight for, even if I'm not quite willing to die for it.'

She nodded, not sure where he was going.

'The point,' he said as if reading her mind, 'is that those two came back from the dead for a reason, and it's that reason we should be thinking about, not that they are here.'

'I think I understand. It's just . . . I've been fighting demons since I took up the shield, and to sit and chat with two of them . . . it takes getting used to.'

'Let's go back and see if we can begin to uncover the reason for this strange turn of events and, please, try not to kill either one before we're done?'

She gave him a tiny smile. 'I'll try. No promises, but I'll try.'

He chuckled.

'What about those elves?' she asked as they walked back toward the house.

'What about them?'

'Calis I like, but that other one, Arkan . . .'

Amirantha nodded. 'There's something different about him, true, but I can't put my finger on it. But then, before I came here the only elves I had met were in Novindus, and down there they are not all that different from you and me.'

Sandreena said, 'I've seen a few up here, and, well . . . he's just different.'

Amirantha remained silent and they returned to the kitchen.

Nakor and Miranda looked as the two of them entered. Behind them, students and magicians who worked for the Conclave began preparing the evening meal.

'It's changed, the Villa,' said Miranda.

Amirantha nodded. 'It was utterly destroyed when you—'

'Died,' supplied Miranda. 'I remember. The dying I mean.'

'Pug abandoned the Villa,' said Sandreena. 'He took your death, and Caleb's, and Marie's very hard.'

Amirantha said, 'He just . . . left, for a while. Travelled I guess. We few who remained lingered at the black castle. The rest scattered.'

'For a while I think he feared another such attack,' said Sandreena. 'It was a dreary few years, but then one day, Pug seemed to have come to some sort of closure and he decided it was time to revive the Villa and bring back the students and teachers. He decided to change things as he went, making some improvements.'

Miranda looked thoughtful. At last she said, 'I don't know

how long we'll be here. Perhaps it's best we not dwell on such things as the past.'

Sandreena looked at her quizzically.

Miranda said, 'We know we were . . . resurrected for a purpose.'

Nakor said, 'And it is most certainly a critical one.'

'But we do not know what that purpose is.' She opened her hands. 'I was hoping once I reached the island, met Pug . . . something would be revealed, our purpose made clear.' She was silent for a moment, then said, 'So we wait until Pug returns. I wish I could go to him.'

'Why not?' asked Amirantha, rubbing his forehead absently.

'I have Miranda's memories, but not her abilities. I have demon "tricks" as Nakor calls them.'

'How did you throw that fireball in Ylith?' he asked. 'I've been meaning to ask you.'

'It wasn't a fireball,' she said with a wry smile. 'I summoned a lesser fire demon – basically an elemental – and threw it at the Keshians. He roamed around randomly until enough of him dissipated that he couldn't maintain cohesion and he returned to the demon realm.'

Nakor laughed aloud. 'That's a wonderful trick.'

Sandreena looked at Amirantha rubbing his forehead and said, 'What is wrong with you?'

Amirantha realized what he was doing and said, 'Sorry, it's just a little tender where he smacked me with that orange.'

Miranda's eyes narrowed. 'Where did you get that orange, anyway?'

Nakor shrugged. 'I just reached into the bag and there it was.'

'But that "there" is a minor rift into that warehouse.'

'Yes,' he agreed. 'And?'

'You can't do that trick.'

His face was alight with realization. 'I just did it! I didn't think about it, or try to do it, I just did it!'

He held up his right hand, his short sleeve falling to his

elbow and moved his hand. Suddenly with a snap, a card appeared in it. He was almost giddy with delight as he made cards appear and started tossing them around the kitchen. Some of the students preparing the evening meal stopped to watch.

'I just did it!' he shouted, jumping up from his chair to do a little dance in a circle. 'I just did it!'

Miranda smiled. She asked, 'Once more? You just did it?'

'I didn't think. I just reached in and grabbed an orange!' His glee was infectious. Sandreena and Amirantha found themselves smiling broadly at his happiness.

Miranda closed her eyes for a second, and then said, 'If you can, I can!'

Without warning she threw out her hand and a column of flames sprang from her palm. With a flick of her wrist and a back and forth motion, she made it vanish. She laughed girlishly. 'Don't think! Just do it!'

She stood up and looked at Nakor with deep appreciation. 'Thank you.' Then, suddenly, she vanished.

'What?' asked Sandreena.

'Where did she go?' asked Amirantha.

Nakor laughed out loud. 'She went to find Pug,' he said. 'She didn't think about it. She just did it!' He continued his dance in a circle, and the two demon experts exchanged glances. They had never seen, nor could they imagine, a demon dancing for sheer joy.

Pug and Magnus were sitting quietly on cushions at a low table, drinking tea. 'One thing that constantly amazes me,' said Magnus. 'There's an illusion of scale that's fluid. At moments I feel as if I'm standing outside a massive barrier, yet at others I feel almost god-like looking down on the most delicate and finely crafted miniatures crafted by a master toymaker.'

Pug nodded. 'Since I returned for Kelewan and assumed the mantle of the Black Sorcerer from your grandfather, I have constantly been astonished at the resilience of the human mind. It interprets what it doesn't understand. What we're studying is a metaphor for some sort of complex energy . . .' He shook his head. 'This is the sort of thing that used to utterly delight Nakor.' He smiled in remembrance. 'I never met a man who so loved mysteries.'

Magnus nodded. 'Have you come to any conclusions about this matrix?'

'I suspect it's a trap of some sort.'

'If so, it's very subtle.'

'Those are the most dangerous,' said his father.

'Why did it suddenly manifest here? Why now? And why not at the other Sven-ga'ri location in the Peaks of the Quor?'

Pug chuckled. 'Impatience?'

'No, just frustration, I guess.' Magnus fixed his father with a pale blue eye and said, 'The hardest part here is not knowing if we're making progress or wasting time.'

'Something in there is familiar,' said Pug. 'Something that echoes . . .' He stopped. 'I find myself when we're in there thinking of Tomas.'

Magnus was silent for a moment, then said, 'Valheru?'

'Perhaps. The Sun Elves told us they were placed to protect the Quor by the Dragon Lords. These Pantathians were created by a Dragon Lord, perhaps to also protect the Sven-ga'ri.'

Pug fell silent, pressing the bridge of his nose with thumb and forefinger.

'Are you all right?' asked his son.

'Just tired. This is exciting work, but I'm not sure how much it bears on all the other troubles we're facing. I'm trying not to let it become a distraction from our other problems.'

'You're doing all you can. Have you identified those who betrayed us in the Conclave?'

'A few of those who are primarily allied with Keshian factions in the Academy,' said Pug. He stretched and suppressed the urge to yawn. 'No one critical appears to have been involved in any acts of betrayal.'

Magnus thought about this, then said, 'Many of our sources have been cut off. Jim Dasher's organization in the Isles is still somewhat effective, though his agents in Kesh are non-existent. Roldem's intelligence is minimal. Kesh's is non-existent.'

'Only magic could have turned that many loyal agents disloyal.'

'It had to be subtle,' agreed Magnus. 'And it had to be practised over a long time.'

Pug chuckled as he stood up. 'The only time we've ever faced this sort of subtle, long term planning, the Pantathians were behind it.'

'The Great Uprising,' said Magnus. 'You've spoken of it many times.'

'Disguising a Serpent Priest as a dark elf . . . that alone is a prodigious feat. Moredhel shamans are like elven spell-weavers; they're in touch with basic elements of magic and can sense disruption. Moreover, the false Murmandamus had a Pantathian Serpent Priest as a servant, which would instantly arouse suspicion, yet he not only withstood scrutiny by the clans of the north, he rallied them and led them against the Kingdom.'

Magnus studied his father. 'What are you thinking?'

'I'm thinking that in all our dealings with the Pantathians directly, little about them is subtle.' He held up the porcelain cup he was drinking from. 'This is subtle, finely made by a craftsman in Kesh. Part of the trade bounty these people have with their neighbours to the north. This is unexpected. These Pantathians might not be capable of fashioning such a fine cup, but they appreciate its beauty beyond utility, because otherwise we'd be drinking out of a stone or metal cup.

'They appreciate beauty,' he said waving his hand around the room, filled with richly embroidered cushions and tapestries. 'Craftsmanship,' he added, putting his hand on the exquisite lacquered table.

'But these fine beings have no magic,' said Magnus.

'Yes, they have no magic,' his father echoed. 'The Shangri, on the other hand are prodigious artificers of magic, yet they are nearly mindless and do only what they are instructed to do. They need constant supervision.'

'And the Serpent Priests are somewhere in the middle,' added Magnus.

'Which leaves us with a final question,' said Pug. 'Who is telling the Shangri what to do and the Serpent Priests when to do it?'

'And you suspect the answer has something to do with that familiar feeling you experience with the matrix, that echo of magic that reminds you of Tomas?'

'Yes, somehow the Valheru are still involved in all this.'

Magnus was also silent for a while. Then he said, 'We need more information.'

'Obviously,' said Pug with a fatherly smile. 'So many times I thought we were passed this or that problem, only to have it reassert itself in a different form. There is some hidden entity behind all of this, perhaps going back as far as the creation of the Lifestone by the Valheru.'

'What?'

Pug laughed. 'If I knew, it wouldn't be a mystery.'

'You're tired,' said Magnus. 'Perhaps we should cease examining the matrix until tomorrow?'

'The sun just set, we can work another—'

Suddenly they both felt a flash of very familiar energy. Magnus rose from his cushions and his eyes widened in amazement. 'Mother . . . ?'

Pug was speechless. Seemingly out of the air his dead wife appeared, now fully restored to life. It was impossible. He had seen her die, her neck torn open by a demon's jaws, her life spilling on the ground before he could react. He had stood silently by, his heart breaking, as Miranda and their son Caleb and his wife Marie, or what had been left of their mortal remains, had been consigned to a funeral pyre. Now she stood before him as he remembered her. He was stunned, unable to move or otherwise react.

As Miranda started to speak, 'I'm not—' Magnus drew back his hand and began a spell.

'That's not Mother!' he shouted, and cast a bolt of purple energy that would stun and imprison her.

Except that Miranda held up both hands and the purple energy seemed to wash around her like wine splashing over a bubble of glass. Globules of energy spun off like spray to dissipate into the air. When the blast finished, Miranda flicked her hands as if shaking water off of them and said, 'I taught you that spell, Magnus! When you were seven, trying to catch that wild kitten you wanted as a pet. Remember what happened? She scratched you until you let her go!'

The voice was his mother's, the memory was hers, but the scent of her magic was wrong. Magnus had an ability both his parents lacked, to sense the author of magic if he or she was known to him, a lingering 'scent' as he thought of it, and while everything else seemed to be his mother returned from death, that scent was not only wrong, it felt inhuman.

'What are you?' Magnus asked hoarsely while Pug stood rooted, motionless, unable apparently to speak.

'I'll tell you everything,' Miranda said, tears welling up and running down her face as she stood before the two people she loved more than life itself. 'Everything,' she repeated. 'But first . . . I have every memory and feeling . . . I . . . I have missed you both so terribly.' Now crying openly, she said, 'And I miss Caleb so very much.'

Pug could barely restrain himself from crying as well. His eyes glistened as he slowly walked over to the demon-turned-human and stood before her. She whispered his name, barely able to speak, and he reached out and touched her cheek, then he slowly reached out and gathered her into his arms.

Magnus watched, his face a mask as he wrestled with equally powerful feelings. He knew in his mind this was not his mother, yet in his chest he felt powerful feelings rising and threatening to overwhelm him.

The being that appeared to be his mother sobbed uncontrollably, saying, 'I'm so sorry,' over and over again.

They stood in silent tableau for a full minute, then Miranda stepped back, still holding Pug's hands. 'It's a . . . difficult story to tell.' She almost added 'my love,' but as much as she longed to express feelings, she knew those feelings were not hers, but those of a dead woman who meant the world to these two men.

She let go of his hands and looked at Magnus, but his expression was unreadable. 'I am not your mother . . . but I am,' she added as she saw his face tighten ever so slightly in a signal that he was growing angry, something few people would notice but a mother did. She held up her hand. 'Keep your temper, Magnus. You were always slow to anger, but when you did you always reacted too harshly. What did I tell you when you hurt those boys bullying Caleb?'

'Stop it!' he shouted, colour rising in his pale cheeks and his eyes narrowing. 'You didn't tell me anything. My mother did, and she is dead! I saw her die! I lifted her body onto a funeral pyre and saw my father light it! My mother was ash before my eyes!'

'Stop. You're right. I'm not your mother. But I do remember everything as if I lived it.' She looked around, wiping tears from her face and said, 'Tea?'

Pug spoke, his voice full of emotion. 'Yes.'

'May I have a cup?'

He motioned for her to sit down, then poured a cup of tea and joined her.

'Where to begin?' she said after she had taken a sip. She glanced around. 'Before I start, where are we?'

Pug explained about the Pantathians and after he finished, she said, 'My story is stranger, but only by a little. Peaceful Pantathians? That's . . . unexpected.'

'As are you,' Magnus said coldly. 'How did you come to be this seemingly perfect duplicate for my mother?'

'A long story. Perhaps you'd care to sit?'

He shook his head and she smiled. 'Stubborn as always.' Before he could object, she turned to Pug and said, 'Remember what you spoke of to me about the seeming resurrection of my father as a Dasati?'

Pug's eyes widened and he said, 'Ban-ath?'

She nodded. 'It is my and Nakor's best guess.'

'Nakor!' said Pug and Magnus simultaneously.

'He's here, too?' asked Pug.

'He's back at home with Sandreena and Amirantha, discussing as much of demon lore as he can.'

Suddenly Magnus's suspicion and anger were replaced by curiosity. 'How did you both come back from the dead? Nakor died on another world, another plane of reality.'

She took a deep breath, then said, 'We come from the Fifth Realm, or Circle, the demon realm of the lower hell, as some call it.'

'You're a demon?' asked Magnus, his suspicion and anger returning two-fold.

She nodded. 'Let me begin by telling you about the Fifth Circle.'

Pug gazed at the perfect image of the woman he had loved and lost, his emotions churning and roiling in ways that confounded and alarmed him. He was torn equally between a desire to take this creature into his arms, to return to the safest place he had ever experienced, the bonding of his own soul's with another, and the desire to push her away, to drive her from his sight.

'The old order in the demon realm is shattered,' Miranda said, glancing at him. 'The first kingdoms are destroyed, consumed by a void that is slowly expanding to devour that entire reality.'

'Void?' asked Pug, shifting his focus to what she was saying instead of who she was.

'I believe it is the Dread, Pug.'

'Why?'

'It bears a strong resemblance to what you two saw with

Nakor in the Te-Karana's sacrificial pit on Omadrabar, that growing monstrosity that devours everything before it.'

Pug sighed. 'It makes sense. There wouldn't be only one Dreadlord trying to enter the higher realms.' He looked at Miranda, but this time his expression was thoughtful rather than wonder-struck. 'Kalkin once told me there had been many attempts in many places by the Dread to cross the void into our realm. He showed me destruction on an unimaginable scale.'

'I don't know what's become of the demon realm after I left,' said Miranda.

'Your story,' said Magnus quietly.

She took a deep breath, composing herself. 'My earliest memories are of my mother, cradling me as she fed me bits of bloody flesh while the world she knew was falling apart around her,' she began.

For nearly an hour Miranda told the story of her evolution as Child and being accompanied on that journey by Belog. When she had finished Pug and Magnus were both silent for a long moment, then Magnus said, 'In all of this, do you have any sense why?'

Miranda looked honestly helpless. 'Pug, you've had more dealings with Ban-ath than any mortal. His games, his mysteries, his misdirection, and lies – but there was always a purpose behind them. I have no idea specifically why he's done this thing to Nakor and me.'

'One can only speculate,' answered Pug, forcing himself to a calmness he didn't feel. 'I suspect that it starts and ends with the survival of our world. That has always been the ultimate goal, apparently. Beyond that I would only be speculating.'

Magnus said, 'There are only two things I can think of that make sense of any of this. Either you are here to provide Father with some intelligence, some useful data he lacks, or you are here because you possess skills he and I together lack.'

Miranda thought about this. 'We can quibble over each other's skills. I think I'm probably still better at locating distant objects and retrieving them, because I doubt you've spent any time practising that while I . . . was away.'

Magnus's expression remained calm, but she could sense his discomfort at that statement.

'And I know I can still transport myself and others better than you,' she said to Pug. 'But you possess a wider range of abilities than either one of us. So, if it's not something overt and obvious, what is it?'

'Perspective,' said Magnus.

Pug nodded. 'You . . . my wife was a remarkable talent. As you observe, she was my superior in several crafts of magic, but you bring all her skills and experiences coupled with a background alien beyond imagining to her.' He looked down for a moment as if what he was saying was difficult. 'I have no doubt should somehow the situation be reversed and she found herself with the growing memories of Child within her, she would have—'

'I'd have walled them off somehow, kept them from asserting control or domination!'

'Yes,' said Pug.

'Kalkin – Ban-ath – picked Child because despite her prodigious strength, she was naïve and unformed. Her personality lacked years of experience and a profound sense of self that would have given her the tools to prevent your personality from dominating.'

Miranda smiled slightly at Magnus's suggestion that 'she' was his mother, somehow.

'Yet,' said Pug, 'there is some component within that is unique to Child, or at least to a demon's view of things, that we need.'

'What about Nakor?' asked Miranda. 'He certainly was no inexperienced babe.'

Magnus let out a slow breath, as if letting go of his anger at this manifestation of his mother as some sort of mockery and now looked on it as something it was critical he understand. 'But you intimated this Belog was some sort of academic, correct?'

'An archivist, yes.'

'A sheltered existence, was my impression of what you described,' said Magnus, 'and not very powerful.'

'Yes, Dahun kept power and knowledge separate.'

'At some future time, perhaps we can take advantage of your unique experience . . .' He looked at the perfect reconstruction of his wife and said, 'What should I call you?'

With a wry expression he had come to know too well, she said, 'No matter how much it distresses Magnus, I think of myself as Miranda. Besides, the last person to call Miranda "Child" was my mother and you know how I felt about that bitch.'

Magnus laughed. 'That was unexpected.' Then he let out a slow breath. 'Then again, perhaps it wasn't. I won't call you "Mother" but I will use Miranda.'

'Fair enough,' she replied. 'And I will refrain from addressing you as "son."'

Now he tried hard not to laugh. 'Mother only called me "son" when she was lecturing me on my shortcomings.' He mimicked her tone and said, '"Son, if I have to talk to your father about this . . ."'

Pug stood up. 'This is going to be difficult for all of us, for some time, I think, but we can all agree that it was not by mere whim that Kalkin undertook such a transformation. In all this there is a constant: Kalkin breaks rules but he breaks them carefully. He could, I suspect, sit down and just tell us all what we're doing here, but there is a reason he doesn't. I suspect he's constrained in certain ways we can hardly understand, but that being said, he has brought the three of us together at this time to contend with something that endangers our world, and if as we all suspect, it is a coming onslaught by the Dread, then we must seek to understand as much as we can of the risk and endeavour to prepare for it as best we can.'

'I suggest we fetch Nakor—' said Magnus and suddenly Miranda was gone.

'She's a lot like your mother,' said Pug quietly.

A moment later Miranda was back with one hand on the arm of Nakor, and Magnus said, 'She's exactly like Mother.'

Nakor grinned and said, 'Pug, Magnus!' He vigorously shook each man's hand. 'It is so wonderful to see you again, for the first time!'

Even Magnus could not help but laugh.

18

MYSTERIES

Jim shouted.

'Land ho!' He had been detailed to the day watch and just happened to be in the forward rigging when the first smudge on the horizon indicated that their destination was in sight. With a sharp wind and a following tide, they would be landing in Roldem within three hours at this rate.

He had been frantically trying to gather as much information as possible before the King's journey to Roldem to meet with the Emperor of Kesh. The meeting was unprecedented and given recent history, Jim had no doubt that magic was involved in the decision. No monarch of Kesh had ever left the Overn Deep, let alone ventured beyond the borders to visit a foreign ruler. From the Keshian perspective they were all social inferiors.

On the other hand, Sezioti was an unusual emperor by Keshian Trueblood standards, being a scholar rather than a hunter. Hunting was the foundation of Trueblood culture, back to the dawn of time when the lion-hunters and crocodile-hunters of the Overn Deep shore roamed, a dream of empire not even within their minds.

If Jim had been unconvinced before about the prevalent use of magic to destroy the various intelligence services, subvert nobles to treason, and otherwise totally ruin his life, this was the ultimate proof. For even if the Emperor was untouched by magic, his advisors and many within the Gallery of Lords and Masters must have been influenced for this massive change in Keshian foreign policy to take place.

He had undertaken to send a message to Pug, though the gods only knew how long it would take to reach him given the current lack of magical transport.

When news had come that the King was entertaining the Princess of Roldem, Jim began using his contacts at the palace to gather intelligence as best he could. He debated returning in his role of Lord Jamison, but decided against it. His grandfather's return to health showed that whatever plan Sir William Alcorn had which required the negation of the Duke's influence, it was tied to this peace negotiation in Roldem.

Anne had proven invaluable in getting what information she could from the palace. Princess Stephané was well, in the company of two young men whom Jim knew would die to protect her. She had said that King Gregory had given Stephané a state welcome, despite the odd circumstances of her arrival, and by some adroit eavesdropping, Anne had pieced together most of what had happened in Roldem which had caused the Princess to flee.

So Jim decided if he couldn't openly travel as part of the

King's entourage, he would travel on the same ship as a common sailor. His only problem was that the King and his guests travelled on a Royal Navy ship, and passing as one of the crew was nearly impossible. He had almost been caught twice, once sneaking into the palace and again as he left, but when he finally was back at the docks he had in his possession a very convincing transfer order signed by an admiral whose signature Jim had forged more than a dozen times.

So, Able Seaman Tuckford Jones had reported to the *Royal Gallant* hours before she set sail. Jim knew enough both about common sailors' duties and military protocol that he managed to fit in, just about.

He had adroitly avoided the rare occasion when he might be recognized by Hal or Ty, and now he was mere hours away from resuming his position as head of the Isles' intelligence apparatus. And that meant finding Lady Franciezka Sorboz. He found himself surprisingly anxious to find her, and was forced to admit to himself that he was probably in love for the first time in his life. He found it ironic that she was probably the one woman he had bedded he couldn't have if he wished. He had always wondered what it was about women that made him attractive; the more of a bastard he was, the more they wanted him. Franciezka was the exception: she was in her own way as big a 'bastard' as he was. Perhaps that was what drew him; she was the only woman who could truly understand him for what he was. Moreover, he was oddly taken by the notion that his most passionate lover was also a woman who could probably murder him with her bare hands should the need arise. With a rueful shake of his head, he considered his life a very odd one, indeed.

He scampered down the ratlines and reached the deck. Moving with purpose always saved him from being put to an unwelcome task by one of the mates. As sailors went, Jim was neither a malingerer nor a volunteer. He stood his watch quietly, competently, and without complaint. He was always affable with the other crew on his watch, but made no close friends or bitter enemies. He worked diligently at being as nondescript as possible and usually succeeded.

Jim made his way to the companionway down to the lower deck and then into the crews quarters. He had little by way of personal belongings, so he threw together his kit quickly. A small bag he could throw over his shoulders, and the only important thing within was a pair of low-cut boots he could don when he reached the shore. Jim's impersonation of a sailor was perfect in all details, save one: he didn't spend enough time out of boots to develop the heavy calluses on his feet that made walking barefoot over cobbles tolerable.

He needed to find Franciezka. He had a good idea where to look, but that was no guarantee he would find her. But unlike the Isles, he had few eyes and ears in Roldem. Still, standing around and doing nothing was not his best choice, so he began to plot.

Hearing footsteps coming down from above, he moved away from his hammock, making sure his kit bag was stowed, then headed for the rope locker in the forecastle. He listened as two sailors came down and did as he had just done, gathered their kits together in anticipation of a swift departure from the ship.

Jim had planned on being among those sailors detailed to carry luggage to the King of Roldem's palace. That changed when he overheard the second mate telling the cargo master that the palace luggage would be handled by garrison soldiers, and the ship's crew would only help offload the commercial cargo.

So he waited until the quarters were again empty then hurried back on deck. As he had expected, no one noticed his coming and going, so he hurried to the ratlines and again climbed to the topgallants. He would linger up there repairing a non-existent crack with a rope brace until it was time to reef sail.

Time passed as Jim scampered about in the rigging, ignoring certain orders and effectively hiding himself from view behind sails when necessary. His one goal was to avoid cargo duty, for that would last for hours and keep him from reaching the palace quickly.

At last the ship sailed into the harbour. Since they were flying the King's flag along with a hastily-fashioned pennant to denote the Princess of the Royal House of Roldem, shipping in the harbour came to a standstill to allow the royal guests a swift passage.

Jim paused for a moment to stare in amazement at the imperial dromon from Kesh that the Emperor's agents had chosen. As no Emperor had ever left Kesh's shores before, no royal transport had ever been required before. Jim recognized it at once as an imperial naval flagship, the vessel of some Trueblood admiral. The Truebloods of the Overn Deep were only freshwater sailors, and although the Overn was a large enough body of water that storms and tides were a problem, at its worst it was nothing compared to the unpredictability of the deep oceans on Midkemia. Three moons ensured that only a veteran captain could navigate uncharted waters.

As a result Kesh tended to be a nation of coast-huggers, comfortable with patrolling the shallows near home, and relying on mostly overland trade, with the Kingdom and Roldemish ships carrying cargo between those two nations. A few brave and resourceful Keshian traders had, of course, mastered the tides of the Sea of Kingdoms and made a handsome profit trading between Kesh and Roldem or Rillanon directly, but they were few and far between.

This ship had been refitted in a hurry, but even so the result was nothing short of miraculous. Every trim was golden or ivory, brilliant in the sun. The shutters on the sterncastle looked to be fashioned of ebony, an impossibly dense wood never used on ships because it had a tendency to sink. Nothing on this ship was base or mean. From his vantage point aloft, it looked as if the decks had been refurbished with teak. He laughed. Knowing the Keshians, this would be the only occasion on which the Emperor of Kesh would undertake an ocean journey, but the ship would never been used again, just in case the Emperor might decide to go fishing one day. All royals were prone to the gaudy and wasteful, Jim knew, but no one did it on as grand a scale as the Keshians. Even the banner, bearing the royal hawks of Kesh, looked to have been sewn with pure gold thread.

The King's ship eased into its berth as Jim furled the sails. When he had finished tying off, he kept out of the view of the bosun's mate and watched as the main hatch was unlatched and moved, and cargo nets were swung into place, while the royal party departed from the rear gangway. The gangway was a lovely device, thought Jim, a canopied covered little landing with stairs and rails that ran right down to the docks. Jim took his time moving to the tip of the yardarm, then dropped a rope and swung down to the docks, everyone on the decks being too focused on the royals departing or on cargo duty to notice him. He wouldn't be missed until that night when he didn't show up to receive his pay.

Moving along the docks he saw a party of nobles waiting to greet King Gregory and his retinue. Jim did a double-take for it appeared that Sir William Alcorn was waiting to meet the King, but upon close inspection it was a different man. The hairstyle was Roldemish, parted in the middle and left to fall on both sides to just below the ears, while Sir William's hair flowed to his shoulders. But the resemblance was uncanny.

'You!' shouted a voice and Jim saw a Roldemish noble pointing at him. 'Come here and carry this!'

Jim knew better than to run so he lowered his gaze and ambled over. He saw bags sitting behind a roped-off area and wondered for a moment why he was being asked to fetch luggage that would be brought along to the palace in quick order. He looked at the noble who had ordered him over and recognized Lord Servan, nephew to the King.

'My lord?' asked Jim in neutral tone. He knew that this man was Franciezka's most highly placed agent within the palace, and wasn't sure if she knew that he knew. So he decided to play the role of common seaman until he knew what was going on.

'Take these at once to the Queen's apartment.' He took off his gloves and pulled out a piece of parchment and a travelling writing case. 'Your back, sailor.'

Jim turned and bent over so that Servan could rest the parchment on his back. He heard the noble spit into the dry ink, then felt as he scribbled something. As he wrote, Servan said, 'My lady bade me find you as soon as this ship landed, Lord Jim. She warns you to be cautious in coming to the palace. Lord John Worthington's men are everywhere.'

'Is that Lord John in the deep blue coat?'

'Yes,' said Servan, affixing his seal to the note. 'This orders you personally to deliver these two bags to the Queen's major domo personally. He's been instructed to take you to my lady.'

'Whose bags are these?'

'I have no idea,' said Servan with a smile. 'Baggage gets lost all the time in the palace. It'll find its owner sooner or later.'

Picking up the bags, Jim said, 'If you can slip word to Duke Hal that I'm in the palace, that would be appreciated.'

'Duke Hal? His father's dead?'

'Unfortunately, and King Gregory has named him "beloved cousin," publicly, twice.'

Servan winced. 'I'll get word to him. You'll find him?'

'I'll find him.'

Jim picked up the bags and hurried after the first carriage that was rolling out of the docks. The pace of the carriage was slow as crowds were pressing to cheer the foreign king and his party. There was a holiday feeling to the scene that lay at odds with what was really under way, which Jim feared was black murder and treason.

Keeping to the side of the carriage away from most of the guards lining the road, the nondescript sailor hauling two bags up the hill garnered scant notice.

Jim barely put the bags down before he was being hustled off by a servant barking orders that he follow her. He did as he was ordered, and was taken around the periphery of the royal apartment to a set of rooms occupied by Lady Franciezka Sorboz.

Franciezka waved away the servant and inspected Jim head to foot. 'I think I've seen you less kempt, but I can't recall when.' Her face was set in a controlled, faint smile, but her eyes shone with moisture.

Jim began to speak, then suddenly was without words. He took two strides across the room and took her in his arms. After a deep and prolonged kiss, he whispered, 'I thought I might never see you again.'

'And I you,' she whispered back. She forced herself back to control and said, 'And you reek. You need a bath.'

'I need a bath, a shave, and a change of clothing.'

'I have a bath drawn in the next room.'

'Are you joining me?'

She spun out of his reach. 'As much as I might like to, Jim, we do not have time if you're going to sneak about and talk to all those people who you need to sneak about and talk to.'

Jim frowned and turned his mind to the business at hand. 'Clothing?'

'I have a complete set.'

'Really?'

'I thought you might need court clothing, and besides,' she added with a slight smile, 'I know your size intimately.'

In the side room he found a tub with warm water waiting. He quickly stripped off his clothing and stepped in. A moment later Franciezka entered with a shaving mug, brush, and razor. He lathered up his hair with a delicate scented shampoo she kept for her own use. The scent of it reminded him he was aching to touch her again.

She poured a bucket of warm water over his head and said, 'Lie back and I'll shave you.'

While she did so she went on, 'I discovered something deeply troubling after you left, Jim.'

'Only one thing?' he said brightly.

'Never make me laugh or get angry when I have a razor next to your throat.'

'Fair point. Sorry I interrupted.'

'After you left I retired to my villa and helped the Princess to escape.'

He laughed and said, 'Now she's back, so one wonders what good all that did.' Feeling the sudden pressure of her razor against his throat he said, 'Sorry,' and fell silent again.

'She was away from Lord John, which was the point.' She deftly scraped his cheek. 'Word reached me of something odd taking place, and the servants being barred from the Lord John's quarters.'

'So you snuck back— Ow!'

She had nicked his neck.

'Stop interrupting! So I snuck back into the palace and watched through a window. I saw the damnedest meeting imaginable. Lord John hosted two other men: Sir William Alcorn and a Keshian prince—'

He grabbed her wrist so that she couldn't nick him again. 'Harfum?'

'Yes,' she said. 'How did you know?'

'A pattern. What did you learn?'

She continued to shave him. 'First, all three of them appear to be the same man, or else some mother somewhere had triplet sons born in three nations to three noble families at the same time.' She finished and handed him a towel. He sat motionless for a long moment, stunned by the news. 'The same . . .' He let the thought trail off. 'The third player.'

'Whoever was behind the war between the Isles and Kesh, certainly,' she added. 'We know the war made no sense, particularly given how it ended, and how this benefits the third player . . .' Again a thought was left unfinished.

He wiped the residue soap off his face. 'How long before I insinuate myself into the royal hullabaloo?'

'All the nobles are resting while their luggage is being un-packed. I expect you'll want to sneak about a bit and speak to someone or another.'

'Hal is now Duke of Crydee. His father perished before the siege of Ylith. I want to speak to him and Ty Hawkins.'

'You have some time. Why?'

He reached over and grabbed her, hauling her into the tub with him. She shrieked for a moment, then her cries turned to laughter.

'Too long I have thought about this reunion, Franciezka, and too long have I thought about what I would say. I'll sneak about later.'

She kissed him. 'Shut up or I'll find that razor.'

He returned the kiss and began unfastening wet laces.

Miranda looked at the matrix and probed it, pulling back instantly. 'There is a demonic element there; subtle, which is why you missed it, but there all the same.'

Pug and Magnus were both silent for a moment, then Pug said, 'Is it a trap?'

'It is hard to judge. As I'm sure you've both come to ap-preciate, it's a complex energy net.' Miranda overlapped her outstretched fingers, as if forming a grid. 'Interwoven spells, and something else, other energy states . . .' She closed her eyes for a moment, then they popped wide open. 'We need Nakor.'

And she was gone. While the three of them had been ex-amining the matrix, Nakor had been in another part of the building exploring the Pantathian archives with a guide.

Magnus said, 'I don't know what unnerves me more, that she is so exactly like mother or how easily I forget she's not mother.'

'I also have to force my mind to that—'

Suddenly she was back with Nakor standing next to her. With a grin he said, 'Pug! Magnus! There are some wonder-ful volumes and scrolls here. A lot of history . . .' He stopped speaking as he saw the energy field behind his three companions and pushed past them. He looked at the large oval of light. 'This is the matrix?' He leaned over until his nose was less than an inch away. 'This is wonderful.' He sat back, his hands just inches away from the surface, but not touching it. 'Demon, yes,' he said. 'But something else, something . . .' He nearly jumped back. 'I recognize it.'

'What is it?' asked Pug, struggling to cope with the appearance of his dead friend as he had his dead wife.

'I felt this in the pit on Omadrabar. There is a touch of the Dread here.' He glanced at Magnus.

'We think it might be Valheru.'

Nakor nodded. 'Yes, I sense it. Elf, Valheru may be what I've missed, Dread, demon . . . But nothing human. This was created a very long time ago, by people who were not human. No hint of dwarf or goblin either! This is from before the Chaos Wars!'

'Tomas said the Sven-ga'ri in the Peaks of the Quor were already there before humans came to Midkemia.'

Grinning, Nakor rubbed his hands together. 'It's a lock, I think, and picking it will take some time.' He closed his eyes, hummed a nameless tune, then said, 'Ah! Dragon! There's dragon essence here, as well.' He laughed aloud. 'All the ancient races! This is quite a lock!' He looked around. 'Don't be shy. Come, see what's inside!' He closed his eyes as if meditating, and the other three sat and joined him in studying the matrix with all the magical skill they possessed.

Later Jim and Franciezka lay in bed, entwined in one another's embrace, her head on his chest. 'You're a very bad man, Jim Jamison,' she said softly.

'Please tell me I have a few good qualities you're fond of?'

'That's just my point.' She pushed herself up on one elbow. 'I am too fond of you. Fool, I've tried to kill you twice.'

He grinned. 'I like to think that's because you didn't know me well at the time.'

'Perhaps it was because I got to know you better?'

He kissed her. 'Seriously, what are we to do?'

She laid her head back on his shoulder and said, 'About us, or about everything else?'

'I fear "us" depends on everything else.'

She sighed. 'Well, then, to business. I have a few agents I can trust inside the palace. Fewer in the city. None beyond our shores.'

'I am in similar circumstances,' he said.

'So let us compare what we know.'

They spent half an hour exchanging information and when they had, Jim said, 'I think our instincts served us well! There is an unknown player in all this and I believe Kesh is as much a victim of this player as is Isles.'

'Explaining that to your King when he contemplates the losses you've taken in the west may prove difficult.'

'Gregory is not a bellicose man. He will consider peace if offered at reasonable terms.'

'What are reasonable terms?' she asked.

'Let's worry about that after we can convince someone in the imperial household that Kesh needs to be reasonable, and not try to dictate out of a presumption of victory. The armistice is unsteady, to my eye.'

'None of this makes sense,' Franciezka observed.

'It does if the reason behind it is not what you would think.'

'What do you mean?'

'You and I have had enough experience with distraction to know its value. What if this war is simply a distraction?'

Her eyes grew wide. 'Then it's a distraction of heroic proportion. What could anyone gain from throwing three nations into turmoil?'

'That is the question, isn't it? I'm of the opinion that there are three people who might be the only ones able to answer.'

'Lord John Worthington, Sir William Alcorn, and Prince Harfum,' said Franciezka.

Playfully smacking her on the backside, he said, 'Time to

get dressed. I'm as curious as anyone what is coming next. And I need some time to talk to our newest duke, find out what he's learned from the Princess you sent him to protect, and then insinuate myself into the King of the Isles' company as if I was there the entire time.'

She pushed hard on his chest, forcing him back down on the pillow. 'We have a little more time, and I'm damned if I'm letting you out of here to get yourself killed before I've had my way with you!'

He laughed and cried, 'Mercy!'

'Never!' Running her hand down his chest to his stomach she said, 'And somewhere in all this there is that one topic we need to return to . . .'

His eyes widened for a moment and he seemed to lose his breath. 'And that would be . . .'

'The subject you and I have been avoiding for more than three years, Jim. Us.'

'I swear by my life, Frannie, if we survive this, somehow, against the wishes of kings and gods, there will be an us.'

'That's all I wanted to hear,' she said, tossing the bed-sheets aside.

Hal sat up suddenly as a curtain in his room moved. He was reaching for his sword when a familiar voice said, 'If you're not safe here, Hal, you're not safe anywhere on this world.'

Lord Jim Jamison came out from behind the curtain and bowed. 'My lord,' he said. Then he took a step forward and gave Hal a hug. 'I'm so sorry to hear about your father.'

'I didn't know you knew him, Jim,' said Hal.

'I made it my business to meet every noble of consequence in my travels. When I was young I ventured to the Far Coast and met your father and mother, back when you were a baby. I encountered the Duke a few times when he visited Krondor. He was . . . old fashioned in a good way. Solid, reliable, with no hint of guile. What the conDoin line was at its pinnacle.'

'Have we fallen that far, for you to phrase it so?' asked Hal.

Jim smiled. 'Not you, nor your brothers if the early reports of Martin's actions against the Keshians is accurate. He and Brendan did your name proud.'

'He lost Crydee.'

'Delong the Great would have lost Crydee given what he had to work with and what he faced,' answered Jim. 'He saved lives and he's held Ylith for now. The Kingdom will negotiate from a stronger position because of his actions.'

'Negotiate,' echoed Hal.

'Leave that for the King and his ministers. I came to speak with you before the festivities begin tonight.' He sat on Hal's bed.

'What do you wish to know?' asked Hal.

'Right now emissaries from the Isles and Kesh are probably arguing about which monarch enters first and who bows to who first. King Carol has an advantage: this is his island, so he gets to sit on his throne. My best guess is both Emperor Sezioti and King Gregory will enter together, bow to King Carol, who will bow back, then the two will bow to each other at the same time. Now, this will probably take an hour or two to decide, so we have time for a chat, because after that they'll argue about who gets to sit to Carol's right and who sits to his left. So, why don't you just start by telling me what happened on your little adventure and don't leave out anything, even if you think it's unimportant. A seemingly insignificant detail might provide some information useful to our king.'

Hal said, 'You're not just some minor noble who happens to be the Duke of Rillanon's grandson, are you?'

'Let's say I occasionally run special errands for my grandfather, and this is one of them.'

Hal smiled. 'Very well,' he said, and he began to narrate his story.

Nearly an hour later, Jim had heard the full tale. He sat back taking it in, then said, 'I don't want you to feel your time with the Princess was an unnecessary risk or waste of your time. I know you endured some uncomfortable days out there along the coast, and killing men, even pirates, is never easy, even if they deserve it. But I think had Stephané remained in Roldem, things today might be different.'

'What do you mean?' asked Hal.

Jim waved away the question. 'I can only speculate at this point, but the rumours about Lord John's son and the Princess were sudden and persistent. I note that even though the Princess is returned for this festival of peace orchestrated by Lord John, her three brothers are still absent.'

Hal fixed Jim with a narrow gaze. 'Lady Franciezka's doing, no doubt.'

Jim laughed. 'You're not quite the rustic you seem, are you Hal?'

'I had the pleasure of the lady's company on a few occasions while we were in hiding. She's very adroit at being a step ahead of Lord John. Which leads me to believe she occupies much the same role here in Roldem as you do in Rillanon. Only she's running the occasional errand for the King of Roldem.'

Jim merely spread his hands and said nothing.

Hal reflected for a moment on how deep and profound his feelings for Stephané had become and said, 'Nothing involving the Princess's safety is a waste of my time, Jim.'

Jim studied the young noble, then changed topics. 'What do you think of our friend Tyrone?'

Hal laughed. 'He's a fine fellow. I'm happy to call him a friend.'

'Good,' said Jim. 'It's just the last time I looked you two were strutting like competing peacocks before Stephané, and I just wanted to make sure there was no rivalry. You may need friends and find few about.'

'I think he's turned his attention more towards the Lady Gabriella.'

'Ha!' laughed Jim. 'That may prove . . . awkward.'

'Why? Is she betrothed to another man?'

Jim chuckled. 'Leave it that her interests lie elsewhere.'

'Oh?' said Hal. His eyes opened wide. 'Oh!' He couldn't help but chuckle. 'Poor Ty.'

'Given our young friend's reputation in Olasko and here in Roldem, there's nothing poor about him when it comes to the ladies. Though he may make a fool of himself over Gabriella if he thinks she's merely playing hard to get. You know how some men can be, wanting what they can't have.'

'All too well,' said Hal, feeling his mood fall.

Jim stood up. 'Should anyone ask, I shared quarters with you and Ty coming over from Rillanon, but was fighting a fever for most of the journey and stayed in my cabin. Understand?'

'Yes, Jim,' said the young duke. 'What now?'

'We enjoy the festivities and see how much bloodshed we can avoid, eat the King's food, drink his wine, perhaps chase a maid or two, who knows? But above all else, listen and observe. There are men and women here who desire nothing more than to plunge this world into chaos.'

'But why?' asked Hal.

'If I knew that,' answered Jim. 'I might have some idea who they were.'

Jim stood to Hal's right, keeping Ty between himself and Sir William Alcorn. If the two twin nobles, Lord John and Sir William, had any issue with people recognizing their resemblance, they masked it well. Granted the fashions and hair styles were different enough it made more of a difference than had they dressed alike, and the Prince Harfum was deep enough in the Emperor's entourage that between that and his Keshian court dress – a linen kilt, sandals, and a great deal of golden jewellery – no one noticed his resemblance to the other two.

Hal had told Ty what Jim had discussed with him, and the young noble from Olasko whispered, 'I might have gone the entire night and not noticed, but you're right. The three of them are as alike as three brothers.'

'And that has me worried,' said Jim.

'Why?' asked Hal.

'Because either they're getting careless – which I doubt – or they don't care, which means they are at a point where they think there's no risk of their plot being thwarted.'

As Jim had predicted the protocol of the event had been tedious, and the two monarchs entered simultaneously. Kesh's Imperial Master of Ceremonies, bedecked in a traditional leopardskin head dress, struck the floor with a massive iron-shod staff topped by a golden hawk, and intoned the thousand titles, ranks, and heroic deeds a ruler of Kesh earned, accompanied by a steady tattoo of drums and clash of cymbals, almost deafening everyone in the hall. Jim had seen the imperial hall in the City of Kesh and it was at least three times the size of Roldem's grand hall. He whispered to Hal and Ty, 'Leave it to the Keshians to have no idea of scale.'

Emperor Sezioti, in his sixties but still a vigorous-looking man, endured it with good grace, displaying a quiet dignity that was in contrast to the pomp and ceremony.

King Gregory suffered it all with restraint, but the three could tell it was a struggle for him and his wife, who half-supported him as they slowly walked from the entrance to the throne. Every ten or so paces, the Kingdom of the Isles' Master of Ceremonies felt obliged to have his trumpeters blow ruffles and flourishes in counter point to the Keshians, the effect of which was musical chaos and seemed to be putting the Roldemish Master of Ceremonies at risk of a stroke. He at least had the good sense to wave off any attempt by the Roldem heralds to blow their trumpets or play their drums. If Jim hadn't been so worried about what was coming next, he would have been highly amused.

What wasn't amusing was the number of armed men in the room. The traditional Royal Guard of Roldem stood eight men deep on either side of the royal dais, but the other two monarchs were conceded their own honour guards. The King of the Isles was accompanied by sixteen white-clad King's Own, wearing the royal red tabard of the Isles. The Emperor had sixteen black-garbed warriors in his personal bodyguard, hand-picked from the best of the Inner Legion.

Hal noticed Jim eyeing the various soldiers bearing arms and said, 'You're worried.' It wasn't a question.

'All it takes is one idiot and there'll be a lot of blood shed in here.' He looked at Hal and Ty, 'How fast could you get up on that dais and protect the three rulers?'

Ty raised an eyebrow. They might arguably be the two best swordsmen in the room, but given the pedigree of those selected for the monarchs' honour guards, probably not by much. Moreover, as Jim well knew, a brawl was a completely different matter.

But Hal was almost instantaneous in his answer, as he looked up at Stephané standing to the left of her father's throne. 'As long as it takes me to draw my sword, Jim.'

Jim clapped him on the shoulder and said, 'Son, I know you'd die for her, but if anything happens try to stay alive for as long as you can. It would be a happier outcome; besides, you're no use to her dead.'

Ty smiled. 'So war is difficult, but peace is more dangerous?'

'Sometimes, my young friend, sometimes.'

Abruptly King Carol stood up and descended the seven steps of his dais and met the other two monarchs on the floor. He came between the two and embraced them both, one in each arm, and said loudly, 'We welcome our brother rulers with love and gratitude for their attendance.' He then allowed both of them to kiss him simultaneously on the cheeks, showing neither the Isles or Kesh favouritism.

'This is well rehearsed,' said Jim.

As if practised countless times, burly servants picked up

the King's throne and carried it down to the floor behind him. Two other identical thrones appeared from two side doors of the room and after they had been placed behind each monarch, Carol spoke loudly. 'No one shall sit above another, for we are all brothers in love and harmony. We seek only peace and understanding, an end to enmity and a future of prosperity for all nations.' He gestured to the others to sit and took the throne placed behind him.

The theatrics were superb; Jim was among the first to begin applause and soon the entire throne room joined in. To Ty and Hal he said, 'Keep an eye on Alcorn, Worthington, and Harfum.' They did, but the three influential nobles seemed content with the arrangements.

Servants appeared with refreshments and started with the monarchs, then moved through the room. All the guards retreated to positions close enough to their monarchs to be on hand should the need arise.

As the nobles from the three nations began to mingle, Jim said to Hal and Ty, 'Be alert but if no one goes berserk and starts carving up the guests, have a little fun.' He paused. 'I fear no matter what we see tonight, fun will be in short supply in the days ahead.'

Hal immediately looked to locate Stephané and saw her looking in his direction while a sallow-faced young man was speaking to her. After a moment, she cut him off with a remark and moved straight towards Hal.

Ty chucked and said, 'I think you are about to become the most hated young noble in three kingdoms.' He glanced around. 'Now, where is that tall wench?' He spied Lady Gabriella and said, 'Ah, there she is. Excuse me, gentlemen.'

As he left, Hal said, 'You didn't tell him?'

Jim said, 'No, some things are best left to learn the hard way. In your case, just remember the fate of three nations is being determined, so don't do anything stupid.' He stepped away, nodding to the Princess as she approached, and left the two youngsters alone.

Stephané ignored Hal's poor attempt at a bow and swept

in to grab his arm. She pulled him close and Hal saw that already others in the room were taking note. 'You look so handsome in those clothes!' she said, almost breathless.

Hal felt colour rising in his cheeks. 'I . . . thank you, Highness. You look . . . nice yourself.' He winced to hear such words coming out of his mouth. She was bedecked in an indigo gown with seed pears sewn into the bodice and an ornate silver brocade strip at the hem. The gown was strapless and she looked far more voluptuous than she had in hunting togs. Hal stared at her and said, 'I'm sorry, but you look more than "nice." You look amazing.'

Her hair had been done up in a fancy gathering of curls behind her head, with ringlets falling behind. A tiara of diamonds and pearls set in white gold was on her head and her hair had been dusted with some sort of powder, rendering it almost white. The effect was stunning.

'Thank you, sir,' she said playfully. She looked around. 'Do you think this will end the war?'

'One can only hope.' He stared about the room.

She reached up and grabbed him by the chin, forcing him to look at her. 'Here. I'm here.'

Hal felt his cheeks turn crimson. 'Are you trying to get me killed?'

'No,' she said with a laugh as she let go of his chin. 'But you seem very distracted.'

He ushered her towards the side of the room lined by Roldem guards. 'If your father doesn't have me hanged, or beheaded, or drawn and quartered, or whatever it is you do to criminals in Roldem—'

'We hang them,' she interjected.

'—then most of the unmarried nobles in this room are likely to challenge me to a duel, a few of the married ones, too, no doubt.'

'I'm not worried.'

'Why?'

'Because you are second only to the Champion of the Masters' Court and no man here can best you with a sword, save Ty, and he would never challenge you; he knows it would be too close.'

'Thank you for your faith in me, but that still doesn't deal with the consequences of my killing a dozen or so nobles. I suspect my king would be less than pleased with me.' He couldn't resist returning her infectious smile. 'You're not taking me seriously, are you?'

'I take you very seriously, Hal. I just don't take your concerns that seriously. My father wants to meet you as soon as this event is over.'

His expression darkened. 'He's . . . ?'

'He wants to thank you personally for saving my life, stupid.' She looked up into his eyes. 'You're not afraid to meet him, are you?'

Hal wondered if he looked as uncomfortable as he felt. 'Stephané, I did what was asked and for that I need no thanks. It was my honour to protect you. But Gabriella and Ty also did a fair share of the protecting, you know?'

'I mentioned that to Father, but mostly I told him how brave you were.'

'Are you trying to get me killed?'

'No,' she whispered, her face darkening. 'I'm trying to get you married.'

Suddenly she turned and walked away, still holding his hand and half-led, half-dragged him across the floor. Several chatting nobles took note of the display, and by the time Hal took a large step to catch up and tried to disengage his hand from hers, she had arrived at her destination.

Queen Gertrude smiled at the couple. 'Welcome, Your Grace.'

Hal couldn't seem to get his fingers untwined from Stephané's no matter how he tried, short of yanking his hand free in a very ungraceful gesture, so he tried as hard as possible to move to a position where it wasn't obvious.

The Queen looked genuinely amused and said, 'Stephané, let go of the poor lad's hand before you cause him to die of embarrassment.'

She looked at her mother, then Hal and said, 'Sorry.' Her tone showed she was anything but.

The Queen said, 'Now, run along and mingle. I have a few things to speak about with the Duke.'

Stephané's face showed she was not happy with the decision, but she obeyed her mother and moved away. Hal glanced around hoping for a goblin raid, a sudden hurricane, or some other calamity to remove him from the Queen's scrutiny.

'Majesty, I'm sorry—' he began, but the Queen raised her hand to cut him off.

Standing, she said, 'Why don't we take a little walk, Your Grace?'

Not knowing what to say, Hal offered his hand as she stepped down from the throne. She indicated with a slight tilt of her head that two guards should accompany them and led Hal down a short corridor to a large, open door leading to a lovely garden.

The sun was setting and the evening breeze off the ocean was refreshing after the close air in the throne room. The two guards stationed themselves outside the door and Queen Gertrude led Hal to the far side. 'Now we can speak in private.'

'Majesty,' said Hal in as noncommittal a tone as he could manage.

'My daughter can't stop singing your praises, Lord Henry.'

Not being entirely certain what he was supposed to say, he offered, 'Please, Majesty, I'm called Hal. My father was Lord Henry and I'm not entirely used to being addressed that way.'

She smiled warmly. 'Very well, Hal. You've made a remarkable impression.'

'We were together in dire circumstances. Many men would have done as I did. Certainly Tyrone Hawkins and the Lady Gabriella also deserve thanks for your daughter's well-being.'

'That's as may be, but she only speaks of you.' Her eyes focused sharply on him. 'Did you manage to put my daughter under some sort of spell, Hal?'

He couldn't be certain if she were joking or not, so he said, 'Majesty, I assure you I only attempted to care for Her Highness, and my attentions were respectful and mindful of the differences in our rank.'

The Queen laughed. 'You Isles folks can be so stuffy, and you westerners are the worst of the lot. Half the nobles in Roldem in your circumstances would have dragged her off to the closest temple for a hasty marriage and arrived here as our son-in-law, a fait accompli.

'Hal, if the King or I thought there had been one moment of impropriety we would be having this conversation in the dungeon, your rank notwithstanding.' She took his hand and patted it. 'And I would be the one holding the red-hot pincers.'

Managing a careful smile, he said, 'I thank Your Majesty for her wisdom.'

Still holding his hand, she asked, 'Hal, are you in love with my daughter?'

Caught completely unawares, he hesitated then said, 'Desperately.'

The Queen said, 'Oh, dear.' She looked out over the city where as night fell lanterns were being lit in windows and on lamp-poles. Finally she said, 'Come. Sit. This is my favourite time of day, though I'm rarely able to enjoy it. I'm usually busy getting ready for some state function or another.' She smiled at him. 'Now, let me tell you a story.'

She paused, gathering her thoughts, then said, 'When I was my daughter's age, I was Grand Duchess of Maladon. My brother was Grand Duke and unmarried. He met a young woman of property from Simrick and with sufficient standing that there would be no raised eyebrows when it was obvious he had married her to bolster our meagre treasury. Maladon and Simrick are merged states, two duchies wed ages ago out of battle.

'My brother wished me wed in the most advantageous way and discovered the then-King of Roldem was looking for a bride for his eldest son. Rather than seeking a wife who would gain him political advantage, say a Princess of the Isles or Kesh, or a highly-placed Roldemish duke's daughter, he sought a girl of rank whose alliance with Roldem would not unbalance a deftly-fashioned relationship between Roldem, the Isles, and Kesh. So, I was the choice. I had rank, not much of a dowry, but my brother's alliance with Roldem would not cause conflict with any of the neighbours. When Carol and I were wed I had never laid eyes on him until the day of our wedding, did you know that?'

'No, Majesty,' said Hal quietly.

'He was shy, though he had enough court experience to hide it.' She looked Hal in the eye and said, 'I'm too old to be coy, young Hal, so all I'll say is our wedding night had its awkward moments. That was thirty-six years ago. I can't imagine being married to anyone else, but once I did, so very long ago. A dashing young captain of my brother's horse guard. He flattered me and paid attention to me, ignoring far prettier girls. I was naive then, and couldn't believe he didn't fancy more than my rank and connections. I think he imagined I would bully my brother into letting me wed him, and be promoted to general or some such.'

Hal was about to protest, but the Queen cut him off. 'Save your empty flattery, Hal. I know I was no beauty. My husband came to love me as I love him, despite our rather plain looks. So let me ask you, why do you love my daughter? Beauty, rank? Be honest. I will know if you are lying.'

Hal weighed his words, then said, 'I've never met a woman besides my mother who was so . . . staunch, save perhaps the Lady Bethany of Carse. In the middle of the wilderness with men trying to capture her, hungry, wet and cold, Stephané did not complain. If anything, she worked to buoy our spirits. Yes, she's the most beautiful woman I've seen, and I know her rank is far above mine, but I'm as certain in my heart as I can be. Her courage is a match for anyone I've met, and she has a generous heart and a level head. She's . . . wonderful.'

The Queen's eyes glistened. 'Oh, you poor boy,' she whispered. 'You know what you must do, don't you?'

Hal hung his head, a pain growing within. 'I know I must not indulge her whims.'

Now a tear ran down the Queen's cheek. 'And you would have made her such a good husband,' she said softly.

'I appreciate the thought. But I know she must marry to protect Roldem's best interests, and I must return to Rillanon and see what duty my king has of me. At present I am a rustic duke without a duchy. Unless the King can negotiate—'

A strange keening filled the air, accompanied by a sensation akin to the moment before a lightning strike. The combination caused the hair on Hal's arms to stand on end; then there was a sudden scream followed by men shouting and the sound of weapons being drawn. It came from the corridor leading to the great hall. Hal turned to the two soldiers and shouted, 'Guard the Queen!' Then he drew his sword and raced into the hall.

19

CONFLICTS

Chaos reigned.

Hal took a moment to comprehend the scene before him. Three rings of guards were standing in protection of their respective monarchs, while everyone who could get out of the great hall was scrambling for the nearest exit. The centre of the hall was a surging mass of movement that took Hal a moment to make sense of, for three alien figures stood in the midst of a litter of bodies.

Lord John Worthington stood motionless, in his hand a bloody knife. His son lay at his feet, his throat obviously cut as blood pooled around him. Lord John appeared transfixed, staring off into the distance, while Roldem's palace guard formed a barrier between him and their King.

Then he saw that Lord John's Isles and Kesh counterparts stood motionless as well, arms down and out before them, hands turned palms up, their eyes closed as if in prayer.

And in the centre of an invisible triangle between those three men raged something dark and murderous.

Hal could not quite make sense of what he was seeing. Whatever was forming there was a blur of motion and a shifting of light. Then Lord John and the other two advisors collapsed as one, and something was released.

The three shimmering silhouettes suddenly threw themselves at the three monarchs. Those not behind the wall of shields and swords screamed in agony as sudden wounds appeared on their bodies, or died silently from instantly killing blows. Blood fountained and spattered everywhere as the apparitions appeared moved around the room in a mad caper of murder, cutting and slashing in all directions.

Hal looked and found the Princess standing behind her father, Lady Gabriella and Ty and a dozen royal guardsmen. Jim and Franciezka were standing between that group and the Isles guardsmen protecting King Gregory, both of them had a pair of impressive-looking blades in each hand.

The Keshians were forming a wall of iron shields and scimitars around Emperor Sezioti who had drawn his ceremonial sword and looked poised to use it if need be. Hal tried to make sense of the mayhem, but had trouble getting the dark figures in focus.

They moved oddly, disjointedly, but even so, their progress was deadly. Blood was splattered on gowns and fine uniforms, giving the entire tableau an otherworld quality. Moreover, the keening sound the creatures made was unnerving. Hal fought down an urge to turn and run and took stock of his next move. His duty lay to his king and he knew he should move to defend Gregory, but his heart was Stephané's and he wanted nothing more than to hurry to her side.

He judged his best choice to join with Jim and Franciezka. He ran past the royal dais and came to Jim's side. 'What are they?'

'I've never seen their like,' said the Kingdom's spymaster. 'But I've read about them. They are called death-dancers, and they are a bastard to kill.'

Looking at the way they flailed about, Hal saw a pattern emerging. 'Then we'd best be about killing them as quickly as we can!' He took three steps forward and as he had anticipated, what appeared as an odd man-shaped hole in the air swung a wide arc of what seemed to be a blade. Hal lunged and impaled it, felt the sword cut deep, felt resistance, then withdrew and knelt as a wildly swinging blade cut through the air where he had stood a moment before. A warbling cry, a sound nothing mortal could make, cut through the air, a sound of raw pain and anger.

'Good!' shouted Jim. 'I think you've really annoyed it!'

The nearest death-dancer turned and seemed to be trying to locate Hal, who backed away ready to move in whatever direction took him away from this thing's attack. He had run it through, somewhere in the lower torso, but it seemed merely agitated, showing no sign of injury.

'How do you kill one of these things?' Hal yelled.

'I don't know, but I do know you can't let it cut you! Its touch is poison!'

'Now you tell me!'

'I'm not the one racing in there, am I?' shouted Jim.

Hal played keep-away with the closest death-dancer and noticed another behind it. There was something dissimilar between the two, but he was too busy dodging to notice. He yelled, 'Jim, what's the difference between this one and the others?'

Jim tore his attention away from the closest as it lunged at Hal who barely leapt away in time. The flickering, featureless creature was difficult to see, and only the young duke's quick reflexes saved him.

'The other one has some sort of lash. Yours a blade, I think.'

'I can't see it well enough to hurt it!' Hal shouted. 'It's like fighting in the dark.'

A noble on the other side of the room, one of the visiting Kingdom lords, screamed and clutched at his cheek as the lash from the other dancer found its mark. He fell to his knees with blood running between his fingers, then his eyes rolled up into his head and he collapsed to the floor. Colour drained from his face, his forehead beaded with perspiration and he seemed to be fighting for breath.

A third death-dancer reached the line of shields protecting the Emperor and was repulsed by the sheer number of blows directed at it. Enough struck that it echoed the warbling cry of the one Hal had wounded and retreated.

Jim watched the frustrating combat, as Hal and Ty and the others defending the monarchs attempted to counter blows from enemies that were at best dancing shadows and at worst nearly invisible. Jim said, 'We need to see them!'

Franciezka said, 'I have an idea!' She turned and for a brief moment thought about dragging the King and Princess Stephané out of the door behind them, until she realized that corridor ended in a terraced garden. The only other way off that terrace was over a low stone wall, then a fifty foot drop to the marshalling yard below.

She ducked behind the throne and made her way through cowering nobles who were trying to stay as far away as possible from the murderous magical beings. A servants' entrance was hidden behind a tapestry and she ducked through it. It was not an effective escape route for those in the great hall, as it immediately wound down in a spiral to the kitchen three storeys below: there would be a stampede on those stairs as people tried to get out.

She reached the kitchen and found the staff oblivious to the mayhem above as the chief cook oversaw a banquet for over five hundred guests scheduled to begin in less than two hours. Servants were already beginning to organize large trays of delicacies and cups were being arranged for wine service. Finally a baker's apprentice noticed Franciezka and his eyes widened at the sight of this woman with her hair dishevelled and a large knife in either hand. Before he could speak, she shouted, 'Flour? Where is the flour?'

The boy pointed as other eyes turned to stare at the intruder. She saw a five pound sack of flour sitting on a large rolling table and another unopened beneath the table. She threw both knives point down into the table and said, 'Don't anyone climb those stairs to the great hall until you've been told it is safe!'

She grabbed both sacks, one under each arm, ignoring the one that was spilling and hurried back up the stairs. A fit woman, she was nevertheless panting by the time she reached the top. How did the servants manage to make that climb dozens of times during a feast, she absently wondered?

She pushed her way past nobles crowding the entrance, and saw a young woman look at her with wide eyes. As that woman took a step towards her, Franciezka said, 'Don't go down there! There are more of them!'

The woman immediately pulled back and screamed. It was hardly noticed in the bedlam. Franciezka reached Jim and said, 'Cut this one!' as she dropped the unopened bag at his feet.

She reached into the open bag and took as large a handful of flour in it as she could, then shouted, 'Hal! Close your eyes!'

Out of breath, perspiration dripping off his brow from dodging and slashing at the invisible creature, Hal shouted back, 'Are you daft?'

'Shield your eyes!' Jim yelled.

Franciezka threw flour in the general direction of the shifting shape and the flour exploded into a white dusty cloud. Suddenly there was an outline Hal could see.

In a fury of blade work, he darted in and started cutting at the creature, retreating when necessary. Then another blade joined his as Ty leapt past Gabriella and stabbed the creature when it turned to confront Hal.

Quickly Hal and Ty forced the closest dancer to retreat,

while some of the more bold guardsmen pressed forward now that they could make out the elusive assassins. Cut, slice, thrust, and the wailing increased until it approached an ear-splitting level.

Hal was puffing as he sought to press the first dancer, his face running with perspiration. Ty shouted, 'Back. Catch your wind! I'll hold him.'

An Isles guardsman attempted to take Hal's place but his move was ill-timed and the dancer wheeled and sliced him across the throat. With a wide-eyed expression the guardsman went to his knees, his neck fountaining blood.

As the death-dancers got more injured they became more frantic, and more soldiers died. Jim moved to a position between the combatants and the now flour-covered Franciezka, shouting, 'Look for an opening, and if you see one, get the King and Princess out of here!'

'I will, but as fast as those things are moving, I doubt one will present itself!'

A bold Keshian legionary leapt forward, attempting a shield bash and was rewarded by the dancer closest to him falling back, its warbling cry tinged with outrage. For his pains, the Keshian soldier felt a cracking blow across his shield that sent a shock up his arm.

That presented the opening needed for Emperor Sezioti to be whisked out of the nearest entrance, into a safer part of the palace. The enraged death-dancer attempted to follow, but the determined legionary again bashed it with his shield and struck out with his scimitar.

Jim saw his grandfather trying to protect King Gregory and the Queen, and motioned toward the doorway through which the Keshians had escaped. Lord James nodded that he understood his grandson's signal, and shouted orders to the guard captain to be ready to move towards that escape should the way open.

Jim saw there was something wrong with King Gregory. His right eye drooped and his right arm was dangling uselessly. Jim prayed the King hadn't been struck by the death-dancer: from what he knew of them from a report Pug had penned years before, few survived such an attack. One who had was Ty's father Tal, but he had the best magic and medicine the Conclave of Shadows could provide, and they had got to him quickly.

Jim looked around and saw that with the Keshians gone, save for the one brave legionary holding the door, two dancers were now attacking the Kingdom defenders. He turned his attention to the one facing Ty and saw Hal leap at it.

To no one in particular he said, 'Damn, those are some brave youngsters.'

'Yes, they are,' said Franciezka at his side.

He glanced at her and would have found her flour-covered visage amusing were it not for the circumstances. Indeed, flour was everywhere, in many places stained with crimson blood, producing an odd pink clump when the two substances combined.

The death-dancers were now frantic to the point of hurling themselves against whatever was before them, people, walls, furniture. Fatigued guardsmen were knocked into one another, and Jim shouted, 'One of the king's is going to die if we don't end this soon!'

Suddenly a humming filled the room and Jim saw a figure standing in red robes on the other side. He held up his hands and the humming grew louder. The instant result was that the three death-dancers ceased moving but rather stood and vibrated as if trying to get into harmony with the note. It grew louder to the point of being painful and men screamed in pain and covered their ears.

Then suddenly the sound was gone.

And so were the death-dancers.

The three advisors were dead. And from preliminary reports from the palace chirurgeon they were never truly alive. Whatever they would turn out to be, they weren't human.

Ruffio sat in the middle of an ad hoc summit of representatives from the three nations. No monarch attended, for reasons of safety. Moreover, word was King Gregory had suffered some sort of seizure and was being attended by priests and chirurgeons.

As the most senior Roldemish noble, Duke Vladislas of Ansevat served as the informal leader of the conference. Next to him at the table sat Lord Jamison, Duke of Rillanon, flanked on one side by his grandson, Jim. Franciezka sat next to Duke Vladislas, and to her left sat the senior Keshian representative, Prince Jantashi, one of the Emperor's many nephews.

Given the dire circumstances of the evening's events, a great deal of wine was sitting on the table and had been partaken of freely. Jim said, 'My lord Jantashi, if I may presume to offer a suggestion?'

'Yes, Lord Jamison?'

'Send word to the Jal-Pur and recall Lord Hazara-Khan. He was wrongly implicated in treason and is innocent of any such thing, but he is a valuable and talented servant of your Emperor, and you will need him in days to come.'

'Odd to consider such a request from an enemy of the state as having any validity.'

'Oh, I am many things, my lord,' admitted Jim, 'but an enemy of Kesh is not one of them.' Glancing around the room, he said, 'Our roles as agents of intrigue are coming to an end, Kaseem and myself.' He neglected to mention Franciezka, assuming she'd prefer to make any such revelation on her own terms. 'He is still too smart and talented a man not to utilize, and I will retire from public life at my king's pleasure. But know I only sought to maintain peace between our nations, as difficult as that proved at times.'

His grandfather barely could contain his own anger, as he said, 'And need I remind you, Prince Jantashi, that we had peace, nearly a century of it, except for those nasty little brawls in the Vale, until your nation launched a full-scale invasion of mine?'

It was the magician who spoke. 'Forgive the interruption,

my lords, from this commoner, but it is clear that magic played a hand. Several of your own parties are repeating that it is as if they have awakened from a dream, some claiming to have been that way for years. The three advisors who perished were not human, but creatures of some alien nature which have been among us for a long time. Sir William was a young soldier with King Gregory nearly thirty years ago, and likewise Prince Harfum and Lord John have been fixtures in the capital for decades, slowly building up their influence. But consider how no one ever questioned the power they so gradually built up.'

Two other magicians had accompanied Ruffio from the Academy and both were, like the red-clad spell-caster, also servants of the Conclave of Shadows. One had been detailed to examine the corpses of the three dead nobles, while the other had been speaking to anyone and everyone who exhibited any signs of having been under those dead nobles' influences.

'We will not know much more for some time to come,' said Ruffio, absently stroking his black beard, 'but I am certain we shall find the recent insanity was the result of this plan, and whoever was behind it.'

'Just who are you?' asked Lord Vladislas.

'A humble servant,' answered Ruffio with a self-deprecating smile. Jim knew better, but kept his mouth shut. 'I teach at the Academy at Stardock. Pug of Stardock asked us to keep an eye on this meeting, for it was obviously a critical one, and his concerns proved justified. I am sorry it took us so long to react, but we thought it wise not to come too close to the meeting.' He glanced around and added, 'We assumed there would be other magic-users, those loyal to the rulers, in attendance as well. This obviously was not the case. Why is that?'

If the idea of a commoner questioning them rankled, the attending nobles kept it under control. It was Prince Jantashi who said, 'The Emperor, blessings be upon him, had a magical adviser, when he was young. It resulted from a horrible attempt on the life of his grandfather. It was before my time, so I am vague on the details. But I know that for many years there was a court magician.' His voice dropped as he said, 'I believe it was Lord Harfum who ended that practice.'

Ruffio nodded. He glanced at Lord Jamison. 'King Borric had a pet magician,' he said gruffly. He looked at Ruffio. 'If you're from Stardock, ask Pug about his last conversation with King Patrick. It's why there's been no court magician in Rillanon since.'

Ruffio nodded. 'I've heard the story, my lord.'

'Roldem has never had any court magic,' said Vladislas.

Ruffio shrugged. 'Had we but known, we might have saved a few more lives.'

Vladislas said, 'Look, this is all well and good and I'm sure Ruffio here will be happy to tell anyone how he did what he did to get rid of those things but our job is to end this damn bloody war.' He glanced at Jantashi, who nodded.

To the Keshian, he said, 'You started it and it was your message to our king that halted it. What do you suggest?'

'To be honest, my lord, I doubt there's a sane man in the Empire who knows why we invaded the Isles. If we were going to attack, the Vale is the only place worth claiming, and the cost of winning it is more than that lush valley is worth. It's clear that the evolution of reasons, the displacement of rebellious tribes from the Confederacy, the "reclaiming" of Bosania, the ultimate subjugation of Queg, and the re-establishment of ancient borders were simply a means to create as much war fever as possible among those members of the Gallery of Lords and Masters who were not directly under Prince Harfum's influence.' He shook his head slowly. 'Until the Emperor, blessings be upon him, is safely back in his palace, I have no idea what is possible.'

'You could pick up your toys and go home,' said Lord James.

'We have colonists scattered from Carse to the Yabon border in the Far Coast region, my lord. We occupy half of the city of Ylith. We have three enclaves along the coast of the Free Cities, and a total blockade of Krondor and Port Vykor. And you want us to "pick up our toys"?'

'Yes,' said James.

Jim watched his grandfather closely and saw a determination in his expression he'd not seen for years. Half of Jim's life had been involved in criminal behaviour, but the other half had been in service to the Crown, and his exemplar for that sat to his right. His grandfather was prepared to die this very moment for what he believed in.

'I have no authority to negotiate a settlement,' said Prince Jantashi.

'Just what authority to you have?' asked Duke Vladislas.

The Prince smiled. 'Not much really. Anything I agree to can obviously be countermanded by the Emperor, blessings be upon him. Just as your kings can overrule you.'

'Understood,' said James, 'but you're not just sitting here taking up space, are you?'

'I can agree to maintain the current armistice until more formal negotiations are undertaken. I think you'll agree that given what we endured earlier today, any hope of a quick resolution is unreasonable.'

'We want concessions,' said James.

'What do you ask?'

'Get your boys out of Yabon. Pull them back to the border with Crydee so we can get some up there. Young Lord Martin's got a starving city and no easy way to bring in food and relief.'

Jim barely could contain himself. His grandfather was lying like a gambler with a pair of loaded dice. Caravans of foodstuff had already been dispatched from Krondor via Sarth and the Quegans were keeping Kesh's fleet south of their island in check. In fact, relations between the Kingdom and Queg had never been better: nothing like a common enemy to get rivals to put aside differences. No, Jim's grandfather was already planning a campaign to retake Crydee from Kesh and wanted Kesh's permission to go ahead. Jim hoped this Keshian prince was as ignorant of geography and politics in the north as most Keshian Truebloods.

Prince Jantashi nodded. 'I'll ask for a withdrawal to the border.' Then he smiled. 'Plot your invasion of Crydee, Lord James. I am certain that within a year or so the Emperor will gladly return it to you. No need for bloodshed if you're patient.'

Jim could barely contain his smile as his grandfather fumed. Apparently this Keshian prince had been selected for more than who he was related to. He turned to Jim and said, 'I will seriously consider your recommendation regarding Lord Hazara-Khan. The men of the Jal-Pur have been among our most loyal subjects for centuries, and he was one of those who obviously was not ensorcelled by Prince Harfum and his minions.' To their host, he said, 'Lord Vladislas, our thanks for your hospitality. Kesh knows that Roldem is entirely blameless for the butchery done this day and our Emperor, blessings be upon him, wishes his beloved brother King Carol to know that he is held in the highest regard. Kesh's fleet in the Sea of Kingdoms will withdraw to our traditional spheres of control.' He rose and the others rose as well, then sat down again after he had left.

'Well, James,' said Vladislas, 'now that the formalities are over, what do you suggest?'

'I don't know about you, Vlad, but I think this would be a very good time to get drunk.' He reached for a flagon of wine as he spoke.

'How is your king?' asked the Duke Vladislas.

James said, 'I fear the worst. Gregory was never a robust man. He . . . looked stricken when they carried him out. We have to wait for what the chirurgeons say.'

'I will pray for him tonight,' said the Duke, and Duke James knew he would, as his old friend was a pious man. Still, he surprised everyone when he reached for a goblet and said, 'But I find your suggestion earlier a very good idea.'

Jim looked at Franciezka, who nodded at him. They

stood up from the table simultaneously and indicated that Ruffio should join them, leaving the two old dukes to spend time alone. When the three were out of the room, Jim said, 'Where is Pug?'

Ruffio glanced at Lady Franciezka.

Jim said, 'Speak freely. I tell her everything.'

If there had been a single moment in her life where the Lady Franciezka Sorboz had to muster up every bit of control she could to keep from laughing, this was that moment. Most of her entire relationship with Jim had revolved around them keeping secrets from one another, secrets the other was desperately seeking to uncover.

Ruffio seemed to understand the jest, and shrugged. 'He and Magnus are off on an errand he judges critical.' Lowering his voice, 'Apparently Miranda and Nakor are back.'

James Dasher Jamison was speechless. Finally he said, 'But they're dead.'

With a rueful smile, Ruffio said, 'Such was the general consensus. Several of my colleagues saw Miranda die, and Nakor never returned from a journey to another realm with Pug and Magnus. But two of my most trusted aides sent word that they had returned to Sorcerer's Isle and were having lunch with Amirantha the Warlock, and Sandreena the Knight-Adamant of the Order of the Shield.'

'Aides?' asked Jim. 'You've been promoted?'

Ruffio nodded. 'Pug anticipates everything. As Magnus will some day replace him, I am to replace Magnus. I am now leader of the Conclave in their absence.'

Franciezka chuckled. 'Well, I'd better update my journals.'

Ruffio said, 'I will leave you now.' He reached into his belt and pulled out a small pouch. 'I understand your last orb failed. Here's another for your convenience. The first setting will take you to the Villa, of course. I've set the second setting to return you to the palace in Rillanon, and the third to the palace in Krondor.'

Jim was delighted. 'Thank you, Ruffio!'

'There is also a small cube. Throw the small switch and

I will be summoned.' He glanced around and said, 'I fear that the damage done by those three . . . homunculi or whatever they were, is far from being undone. We have war and distrust and three nations at a standstill and it may be years before we return to something approaching tranquillity.'

Jim nodded. 'It is my considered opinion that the object of all this madness is nothing more than to lock three nations up in such a fashion that they are unable to respond to any new threat.'

'Such is Pug's thinking,' said Ruffio.

Before anyone could say anything further, a squire in the livery of the Isles hurried by, dashing into the room they had just left. Franciezka glanced at Jim, as the colour drained from his face. She gripped his arm; then he ran into the room.

'I can feel it. King Gregory is dead,' Franciezka said.

Ruffio let out a slow breath. 'May his journey on the wheel bring him more joy.' He looked at her and said, 'I need to return to the Academy and explain that involving Stardock in politics is the height of folly. Then I will away to the Isle and see to the business of the Conclave.' He smiled at her. 'Your reputation does you no justice, in either beauty and acumen, my lady. Know that the Conclave means no harm to any nation or ruler. We serve only to protect the world.'

Then he was gone.

Franciezka turned as Jim came out of the room his grandfather occupied and said, 'Now we have no king, and no heir.'

'What are you going to do?'

'First go to Krondor. I must speak with my cousin Richard and Prince Edward. He ranks highest in office, but his claim is weaker than several others. Speaking of which, would you see to Stephané? Unless I'm tragically mistaken, she means to have young Hal as husband, and if no one has watched closely, she most likely has him between the sheets already; her best ploy may be to announce to her father she is with child and the young Duke of Crydee is the father.'

'She's not that devious,' said Franciezka with a half-smile.

'She's a woman, isn't she?'

'I'll forgive you for that remark if you tell me where you are going after Krondor.'

'To Rillanon, and to see the temper of the Congress of Lords. We have claimants to the throne, including the Princess's object of affection, but no clear favourite. Thrones will be bartered and promises made and broken. Alliance and betrayal are the order of the day, and if someone is foolish enough, we may see civil war.'

'Might it come to that, with Kesh on your borders?'

Jim laughed. 'As my ancestor, the first Lord James is reputed to have said, "Never underestimate the potential for human stupidity when wealth and power are at stake."'

She sighed. 'I fear you're right. Now go, and mourn your king, and see to the business of your nation, but know that I will wait to see you again in happier circumstances.'

'Lady, you have no idea how much it pleases me to hear you say thus. If there is one thing in this bitter experience I would not trade for the Keshian treasury, it is hearing you say that.'

She looked at him for a long moment. 'I do love you, you fool.'

'And I love you more than the breath in my lungs.' He kissed her and held her close, then took out the travel orb and flipped the switch and was gone.

Lady Franciezka Sorboz stood motionless for a moment, having never felt so alone in her life.

Magnus stood alone on the cold beach, ignoring the bitter winter wind from the south. He struggled with dark anger unlike any he had known since boyhood.

Magnus reflected as he stared out at the lapping waves. Fatigue had forced him to take time away from studying the matrix and in his heart he knew part of what was causing it was the conflict he felt at seeing his mother's face every time he pulled away from his study.

Magnus sighed. Staring out at the sea had always been his way to grapple with his internal conflicts. He had been a quiet boy, slow to anger, thoughtful and studious. When his little brother had been born he had been like most other children, torn between loving a companion and resenting an intruder. Caleb had been outgoing and playful, until it became clear he had no magical skills nor would he learn any.

For most children that would have been of no importance, but for Caleb it had been a burden, for he grew up on Sorcerer's Isle, the son of Pug and Miranda, the younger brother of Magnus, and the only child not a servant who was devoid of magical ability.

Magnus had become his protector, his big brother protecting him as much as possible from the cruelties of the other boys and girls, but even then, Magnus couldn't watch over him continuously, and as a result Caleb had still been dealt with harshly.

Pug found his son standing alone and said, 'Are you all right?'

'No,' said Magnus. 'Frankly, I am anything but all right.'

Pug sighed. 'This encounter with those . . . beings . . . I know it's unsettling.'

'Unsettling?' said Magnus, his voice rising. 'I've seen how you look at her. I understand, Father. I have had moments, brief ones, where I forget, and then I remind myself, she is not Mother. She is not your wife!'

Pug saw anger in his son unlike anything he had witnessed before. 'What is it, really?'

Magnus considered his words before speaking, then said at last, 'What is the limit of the price you're willing to pay?'

Pug was unprepared for his son's question. 'I'm not sure what you mean?'

Magnus had always been a self-aware, self-controlled child and adult, but for the first time since his birth, he looked to his father as if it was taking all his self-control to keep from erupting in rage. 'People have died, Father. Not dozens, or hundreds, or thousands, but millions. They have died because of decisions we've made, you and I. When does the price become too high?'

Pug was speechless.

Magnus said, 'I guess it doesn't really matter if you don't know who those people are, or at least if they are not close to you.' Magnus's eyes were wet with barely-contained tears of frustration and anger. 'The stories you told Caleb and me when we were boys. The hundreds that died in the arena on Kelewan? You made your point. The games were evil. And eventually you closed the rift that drew the Dragon Lords, or what was left of them, to Midkemia.'

Pug's stunned shock began to slowly turn to anger of his own. 'Are you suggesting somehow I'm to blame for the Valheru starting the Chaos Wars ages before man came to Midkemia?'

'Of course not!' shouted Magnus. 'Don't insult my intelligence. But have you ever considered that pulling down the arena around the ears of Tsurani citizens whose only crime was to attend a public festival might have been the first time in your life you looked at human life as yours to spend? At whim?'

Pug grabbed Magnus by the front of his robe and cried, 'What is this about, Magnus?'

Pushing his father's hands away, Magnus said, 'You destroyed a world, Father. You did your best to get people free of it, but in the end . . . I don't know how many died because of what you did.'

'I had no choice!' shouted Pug.

'There is always a choice,' said Magnus. 'From the choice to do nothing and let events take their course, to constantly meddling and wreaking havoc on other people's lives. It just seems that your choices bring about the most destruction.' He looked at his father as if seeing him for the first time. 'I don't know you.'

'You know what's at stake.'

'Do I?' said Magnus. 'I know who we face. I will not argue that we have been opposed by forces evil beyond understanding. Madness is their hallmark, and chaos is their chosen mode, but in the end I must ask, have we done our best in opposing them, or do we flail about, breaking whatever gets in our way, because we never ask the question: at what price?'

'We pay whatever price is asked,' Pug answered. 'Otherwise all we know, and more, worlds beyond counting, are lost.'

Magnus turned and looked out over the ocean. 'I stand here and look out and see miles of rolling waves. Under the water life is teeming, oblivious to what we undertake in our struggles. In the sky birds soar, our conflicts meaning nothing to them. And this is but one world. I've seen the stars in the heavens and know the engine of creation is vast beyond my ability to comprehend it, yet in the end I feel as I have said, that there is a limit!' His voice rose and he pointed back towards the Pantathian city. 'In there is an abomination. Two people I loved more than I loved any other, my mother and Nakor, are captured in some evil design and returned to us, and for what reason? Even they confess to not knowing why. But I think it's simply another jest by the gods to convince us that there is no limit to the price. And I want no more of it.'

And with that, Magnus vanished.

Pug stood alone on the cliffs looking at a cold, choppy sea, a chilly early morning wind cutting into him, and never in his life had he felt more alone.

20

MANOEUVRES

Soldiers marched.

The procession that would carry King Gregory back to Rillanon to be interned in the Vault of Kings moved down the long winding street from palace to dockside. Hal watched from a window in the palace, a window in the room belonging to Duke James of Rillanon.

The old duke, his grandson Jim, and the magician Ruffio stood nearby watching the passing funeral parade. Turning away from the window, Hal looked at Lord James who said, 'We don't have much time, my lord.'

Hal was still struggling to accept his rank as

being equal to the man who addressed him. Lord James was arguably the most powerful noble in the Kingdom, especially now that the King had died without naming an heir.

'You must decide and quickly,' said Jim to Hal.

'I honestly don't know what to do,' Hal replied.

Duke Jamison had been a powerfully built soldier in his younger days, but even now as he entered the twilight of his life he was a presence to be reckoned with, and he had been the one to ask for this meeting. He held up a fist and shook it for emphasis. 'Even as we speak, Prince Oliver of Simrick will be almost certain to be on a ship heading for Rillanon and the Congress of Lords. Three days after Gregory is interred in the royal vault, the Congress will meet and those claiming the crown will step forward. You must be there.'

'But my ancestor, the first Martin—'

'Damn it, boy,' said James, 'I know history as well as the next man, and your great-however-many-grandfather did a noble thing for his brother. Yes, it's a bastard line, made legitimate by a death-bed pronouncement, but that doesn't make you any less a conDoin and as strong a claimant as any.'

'Prince Edward—' began Hal.

'Will not stand for the crown,' interrupted James. 'He has publicly and often said he only took the position in Krondor as a favour to his cousin Gregory. He will watch from the gallery like every other member of the Congress, but if the Ishapian priests lay the crown at his feet he'd not stoop to pick it up.'

'Me, King?' said Hal.

Jim said, 'Most likely not. But without you there, we face the danger of someone else declaring for you, in your name, as a means to broker influence. Montgomery will stand as the first alternative to Oliver. He's a court-bred creature and has many friends, but until this moment no influence to speak of.'

'And Lord Chadwick told me he prayed not to have the office fall to him.'

'Ha!' answered James. 'That old fraud would sell his grandmother for the crown. Don't let Chad's affability and easy manner gull you, lad. He's already counting who he can pry away from Montgomery's faction to back his claim, and who among Oliver's followers might be bribed or bullied to switch their votes. You stand as an honest alternative, or at least as honest as we'll ever get in our nation. You're a Westerner, and the last King to come from the Western Realm proved a most able and beloved ruler, Lyam. His brother was a genius and Arutha's son Borric was a fine king. After that . . .' He shrugged.

Jim said, 'No one expects you to be named, but if you are not there . . .' He glanced at Duke James. 'Grandfather is right. You may be able to hold enough votes to prevent the sort of deals that will ultimately harm the Kingdom. Some of the eastern lords will care not a whit that your duchy is occupied by Keshian Dog Soldiers nor that the city of Ylith is split down the middle, one half Empire, the other Kingdom. They will be looking for patents of title and grants of land in the east in exchange for their votes. Some of the eastern lords have friends in Great Kesh who would count it a personal favour if the new king merely grants Kesh her conquests and moves on.' Pointing his finger at Hal, he said, 'You would then be a duke without a duchy. You could move to Krondor, I guess, and become a court noble, but who knows who the new prince in Krondor will be and what sort of role he might see for you?'

'My personal circumstance is of no importance to me,' said Hal. 'The plight of my people is. Crydee must be restored.'

'Only the King can do that,' said Jim. 'You must speak to Oliver and Montgomery and Chadwick and see where they stand regarding the Far Coast and the West.'

'And realize they'll be lying to you every time you see their mouths open,' added James. 'But promises are political capital in Rillanon and if the new king reneges on promises to gain the office, he will have none and his reign will be bumpy. All three know that. Plan your move wisely, and pick the man you think will help you get your duchy back, and pledge your allegiance to him.'

Hal looked at Jim who nodded in agreement. 'Very well,' said Hal. He turned and looked at Ruffio. 'What about you?' Ruffio had told Hal of the Conclave and its role in Kingdom history, and after a long discussion the night before, Hal now considered himself more rural and ignorant than he had on the first day of classes at the University at Roldem. His view of the world had grown so much bigger in the last two days that he wasn't sure he was equal to the task.

Ruffio smiled. 'The Conclave has other concerns than who sits the throne of the Isles, but we will have agents there to ensure the election of a new king goes without magical interference. The political manipulation of the last few years and the war show that our enemies seek to reduce this continent, perhaps the entire world, to a state of chaos.'

'What about your master, Pug?' asked Hal.

'I have prepared a report which is making its way to him even as we speak, and I am sure he will act with appropriate haste to enable us to seek out those behind the atrocities committed in the Great Hall.' When the carnage was over, a duke of Roldem, several nobles of Kesh and the Kingdom, half a dozen retainers and eight guards had been slaughtered by the death-dancers.

As King Carol was in his own apartment surrounded by his personal guards, and Emperor Sezioti was guarded in his apartment preparing for departure, all communication between the three nations had been handled by the Dukes of Roldem and Rillanon, and the Prince of Great Kesh.

Ruffio said, 'I will accompany you, if you have no objection, Lord Henry, and there will be others there as well to protect and serve the Crown.' With a confidence Hal wished he possessed as well, the young magician said, 'No death-dancer or other agent of mayhem will disturb the Congress of Lords.'

'I'll have to find a ship,' said Hal. 'The King's is at capacity, I've been told.'

James laughed. 'Ha, that bastard Chadwick, no doubt.' He put his hand on the younger man's shoulders. 'You're a duke, Hal. From a line of kings. No man in the Kingdom stands above you, but your lord king and his appointed prince in Krondor. Other than that, you can tell the rest of us to go dance if you've a mind to.' Hal smiled. 'No one tells you there's no room on the King's ship. If you have to pitch some vassal baron over the side to make room, that's what you do.'

Hal laughed at that. 'Then I best see to it.'

'No need,' said Ruffio. 'I can get you to Rillanon in a moment.' With a smile and a slightly theatrical bow, he added, 'Whenever it suits you. We can linger here three more days and still arrive in Rillanon before the King's ship.'

James tilted his head as he looked at his grandson. 'Planning?'

'Needed,' answered Jim. 'Let's school this lad and then we'll all go to Rillanon together.'

'You'll all go,' said James, motioning for a page to bring him his cloak. 'As Duke of Rillanon, my place is beside my king, as tedious as this next journey may be. I will sit the death watch with him from here to the family vault.' He kissed his grandson lightly on the cheek. 'You were always a sweet boy, Jimmy, despite being a constant pain in the backside.'

Jim hugged his grandfather in return. 'If Father's stories are to be believed, no more so than you and Great-uncle Dash were to Great-grandfather Arutha.'

'Well,' said the old Duke, 'I was younger then.'

They laughed and the Duke departed. Jim turned and rubbed his hands together, looking out of the window. Then he turned to a servant and said, 'Wine, please, chilled white. Fruit, cheese, hot bread, a roasted chicken and once it's served we are not to be disturbed unless it's by royal order.'

'Yes, my lord.'

'We have a very short time and much to teach you about Kingdom politics, Hal,' Jim said. 'I hope you're a good student.'

Hal sat, shaking his head. 'That would be Martin. I'm the brawler.'

Jim nodded. 'As long as you're not a stupid brawler, and you listen closely to what Ruffio and I will try to teach you, we should have a chance.'

'Chance for what?' asked Hal.

'A chance to save the Kingdom from its own worst impulses.'

Martin looked up as Brendan walked into the room. Life in Ylith was beginning to return to something close to normal, or as normal as it could get with half the city occupied with Keshians. But some townspeople had returned from the forests, and the first ship from Sarth had put in a few hours before.

A Keshian cutter had also arrived, but anchored outside the harbour and sent a longboat ashore to the Keshian side of the docks.

'Orders from the Prince,' said Brendan, dropping the packet on the table before Martin.

'Finally, something to do,' he said. The terror and chaos of the battle had been replaced at first by relief, then boredom as the two sides stared at one another across a thirty-foot wide patch of city market that acted as a no-man's land between the lines.

He opened the packet, breaking the seal of the Prince of Krondor and read. After a minute, he shook his head. 'This is amusing. I am named Acting Commander of the garrison.'

'Congratulations,' said Brendan wryly.

'And I'm relieved of duty.'

'What?'

Martin stood up. 'We are ordered to Krondor to report in person to the Prince.'

Brendan said, 'Is that a good idea?'

'As long as our Keshian friends don't start any trouble, Bolton should be able to handle things.'

Brendan suddenly looked concerned and Martin smiled. 'Give it up. She's been playing the two of you off against each other, but she's got her eyes set on our young captain. Besides, not only are you too young to settle down, you're the younger brother to a Duke and you'll do as you're told.'

Brendan fixed his older brother with a sardonic expression. 'Really, and just who gave you leave to woo Lady Bethany?'

'I'll sort that out with Hal when I see him,' said Martin, fastening his sword belt around his waist. 'Now, you find yourself a girl like her, and I'll fight to the death for your right to wed her.'

Brendan chuckled. 'Fair point.' Then he grinned. 'Still, I don't envy you being the one to tell her you're leaving and she's staying here.'

'She'll understand. Besides, someone has to make certain Bolton doesn't foul things up.'

'How do we travel?'

'Horse,' said Martin. 'Our mounts are growing lazy. We'll each take two and switch as we go. Five days to Sarth, perhaps six, then a fast boat to Krondor to see what Prince Edward wishes of us.'

Bethany was not pleased to be left behind, as Brendan had predicted, but as the brothers were getting ready to ride out early the next day, a guard came running to the stables behind the mayor's house. 'Sir, Captain Bolton needs you at the barricade!'

Both brothers mounted up and rode to the barricade.

'The Keshians appear to be withdrawing, sir,' the captain reported as they arrived.

Martin stared beyond the barricade and indeed, the Keshians were marching in formation towards the city gate. Martin called for two soldiers to make an opening in the barricade and they quickly pulled them away. Even so, Martin rode impatiently over two remaining levels of bags before they could finish. Seeing no opening in the corresponding Keshian barricade he spurred his mount on, shifted his weight forward and urged his horse to jump the barricade.

He trotted up behind the marching Keshians and passed them. Reaching the main gate he found the Keshian commander and his officers gathered nearby watching as troops from his half of the city were exiting. Reining in, he said, 'Leaving?'

The Keshian commander nodded. 'Such are our orders, young lord. It is the pleasure of His Majesty, the Emperor of Great Kesh, blessings be upon him, that we return Yabon to you, and withdraw to the border of Bosania.' He pointed at a hill top. 'Which is over there, if the ancient maps are correct.' With a rueful smile he said, 'Congratulations on your victory, young lord. You have achieved the reclaiming of Yabon without losing a man.'

'If I were in the mood to appreciate the levity, sir, I would laugh. As it is, I've lost too many good men to your emperor's adventure. Now, if I may ask, why is he conceding a hard-won victory?'

The commander held out his hands and shrugged. 'I am not privy to such reasons, Lord Martin. I merely receive orders and obey them. It was never my wish to come to this land, but it was my duty. You do understand duty?'

Martin nodded. 'As such things go.' Turning his horse, he said, 'Let us hope we never again need face one another on the field of battle, sir.'

'If we do, I will count it an honour.'

Martin left the Keshians to their withdrawal and returned to his own lines. To Bolton he said, 'The Keshians have orders to withdraw about three or four miles south-west, to the old border between Bosania and Yabon. As soon as they're out of the city, sweep the area they occupied and make sure they left no spies behind, then rebuild that wall and gate as fast as you can. I'll urge the Prince to send reinforcements back and perhaps even return the Duke here. The worst of this may be over. But it also may just be a lull. Be alert and take care of your city, Captain Bolton.'

'Yes, sir!' replied the eager young officer.

'And take care of Lily,' added Brendan with a wry smile.

'Yes, sir,' said Bolton with the grin of a victor.

The two brothers turned their mounts and started toward the east gates, and their trip to Krondor.

Pug and Miranda sat alone in the quarters put aside for the four humans – at least that's how the Pantathians saw them – as Nakor had decided to explore this alien city. Magnus had not returned since his confrontation with his father.

Miranda felt her heart breaking to see her husband this way, and even though she knew those emotions were not her natural legacy, nevertheless they hurt.

'Magnus was always . . . quiet,' she said. 'He kept things inside. But when he finally showed his feelings, they were always deep and powerful.'

Pug nodded. He struggled to adjust to the knowledge that the woman opposite him wasn't the person in the world he most wanted her to be. Yet with each moment of comfort she brought, he felt another pang of emptiness, of longing for a time before her death. 'I think he learned that from me.'

She smiled. 'Well, he certainly didn't learn it from me – from Miranda. My understanding is that Magnus's mother was not one to hide her feelings on any subject.'

Pug said, 'If it makes things easier, you can continue to refer to yourself as Miranda. I know those memories aren't yours, but they must feel as if they are. I remember talking to your father – Miranda's father—' He laughed. 'Now I'm doing it. I remember Macros not believing he hadn't been reborn as a Dasati with all his memories intact. He was . . . in the end, Macros.'

'Even the ancient Blind God of Chaos doesn't play as fast and loose with people's lives as Kalkin does. Mythar merely unravelled the fabric of existence and let the pieces fall where they might, but Kalkin, he picks his targets and has no concerns over their plight.'

'Magnus is right on one count,' Pug said.

'Which?'

'That I sacrifice others for what I believe is a "higher good."'

She nodded. 'Doing the right thing has always been the heart of who you are. Why do you think I built up my own little network of agents within the Conclave?'

'I've always wondered. At times I questioned your agenda.'

'It was to have a separate source of information, one that didn't pass through that prism in your head, the one that always casts light a certain way, red at one end, violet at the other? Only your prism is always "right" at one end and "wrong" at the other.'

Pug nodded, sipping a cup of tea. 'You always were more pragmatic.'

'I'm older,' she quipped. Both of them had lived over a century, but one of the continuing jests between them was that Miranda would never tell Pug exactly how much older she was. Nakor had married Miranda's mother for a time, while she learned all she could of magic from him, then she had moved on to Macros, the master magician in the world at that time, to glean what she could from him. Miranda had been the offspring of that union, and with both her parents dead, she was the only person who knew the truth.

Pug laughed. 'I have missed you.'

She held up her hand. 'Be cautious, Pug. My feelings are as deep as your own and I would like nothing more than to drag you off to bed and relive some of the happiest moments in my life. But I suspect that would not be a good idea.'

Pug said nothing.

'I ache to have Magnus embrace me as his mother, just one more time, and I hurt whenever I think of Caleb. But Kalkin did not bring my memories back and place them in his body just so you and I could have a joyful reunion. He placed them here so that Nakor and I can help with whatever needs to be done to save this world. For I am certain we are at a crux, and that the outcome of it all is going to determine the measure of life on this planet, and perhaps a larger portion of this universe.'

From behind them, they both heard Magnus. 'I agree.'

They turned to see their son standing in the doorway.

Looking at Miranda, Magnus said, 'You have no more control over who you are than I do. You are as much a victim of this cruel jest as my father and me. Kalkin burdened you with the loves and loss of another and you feel that as strongly as if it were your own, and I do not envy you this.' Then he looked at his father. 'I have not changed my opinion on your choices, but I honour your willingness to give all to protect others. But ultimately, it is my feeling that we are indeed at a crux and that whatever forces have been gathering out there in the universe have picked Midkemia as their battleground. I believe that the final conflict is under way.' He sat between them and added, 'I too must serve in the best fashion I know how.'

Pug reached out and touched his son's shoulder. 'We are free to disagree, but I will never turn my back on you, Magnus.'

Son studied father for a moment, weighing if that was a reproof of his behaviour the night before, or if it was reassurance. He chose to accept the second meaning. 'I know, Father.'

At that moment Nakor hurried in. 'Oh, good, you're all here. Come, I have something to show you. You must see this.'

Without waiting to see if they were following, he hurried out of the room and almost lost them when he entered a busy plaza. Reaching a large building Pug had never seen before, he went inside. They followed him in.

Shelves from floor to ceiling lined the wall and scroll cases were piled in racks across the floor. 'It's a library!' said Nakor with delight. 'These Pantathians have a library.'

'Is there anything in there—' began Magnus.

'About the Sven-ga'ri?' finished Nakor. 'No, not directly, but there were clues in their oldest records. These people have been here a long time. A very long time. I think for many years they were like those Quor, up in the north: primitives, but as they became more civilized, more self-sufficient, they still had this one prime mandate, to care for those . . . whatever the Sven-ga'ri are.'

Having less patience than the others, Miranda said, 'What have you found, you annoying little man? You wouldn't bring us here if you didn't have something to show off!'

Nakor smiled and cocked his head. 'True.' He picked up a scroll and said, 'Look.'

Pug glanced at it and said, 'I've never seen this language before, Nakor.'

'Neither have I,' answered the little gambler, 'but you can read any language if you know the trick.'

Magnus said, 'That's a trick I would like to learn.'

'I'll teach you sometime,' he said.

'What is in there?' asked Pug.

'It's just a clue, but it's a really big clue.' Nakor sat down on the floor and the others took that as a cue that he was about to launch into a long discussion. 'We assumed the Dragon Lords created or found those things on the roof of that building because they ordered the Sun Elves to protect the Quor who are protecting the Sven-ga'ri, right?'

Pug nodded.

'This,' Nakor pointed to the scroll, 'says, "and then where found, they remain, by order of those . . ." I think it means gods-brothers/sisters, or something about Alma-Lodaka and her relatives. Dragon Lords. Don't you see? It's something they found.'

'The Sven-ga'ri pre-date the Dragon Lords?' asked Magnus.

'Or are at least contemporaneous with them,' said Nakor. He looked very pleased with himself. 'They've been around a very long time, back to before the Chaos War, I think.' He waved his hand in an arc over his head. 'Dragon Lords, the gods, the golden bridges, all of that was happening while those singing lumps of light were over there.' He grinned. 'Wonderful, isn't it?'

'Nice to know,' said Miranda, 'but where does it get us?'

'It makes me think the Dragon Lords didn't put guards around the Sven-ga'ri to protect them, but to keep others from accessing them. I think the Quor and these Pantathians have been around them so long they don't even remember why they were put there. The Sun Elves certainly forgot what they were doing there. And the Star Elves don't even remember them, nor do any of the spellweavers in Elvandar. I don't know about the moredhel.' He shrugged. 'I could go ask Arkan, I suppose, but I doubt he knows.'

'Arkan?' asked Pug.

'Oh, didn't I mention?' said Miranda. 'A moredhel chieftain is staying on the Island.'

'You did forget to mention that,' said Pug. 'And who is keeping an eye on him while you're here?'

'Calis.'

'That could prove amusing,' said Magnus.

Pug stood up and said, 'All very interesting, Nakor, but I'm not sure how it's going to serve us.'

'Maybe we should just be more cautious,' said Miranda.

Pug nodded and glanced at Magnus. 'You're the best with protective spells.'

Magnus said, 'I won't argue.'

Miranda laughed. 'It's good . . .' She let the thought go unfinished. It was a life that was not her own.

The portal room was supposed to be unoccupied, by order of the Lord Regent, but two figures approached in the dead of night. Tanderae, Loremaster of the Clan of the Seven Stars moved quietly and quickly along the shadows of the wall. One step behind him was a guard captain of the Sentinels, Egun by name. Tanderae had asked him to accompany him this night because he was certain he was above reproach in his loyalty to the Clan of the Seven Stars and not subject to the politics of the Regent's Meet.

He needed a witness to bear out what he had been uncovering for a year, and it had to be someone unimpeachable. The two brothers, the conjurer Laromendis and the Demon Master Gulamendis, both understood what was taking place, but they were considered questionable witnesses at best: Laromendis was rumoured to have been a member of the Circle of Light, and had been outlawed by the Lord Regent decades before, while his brother trafficked with demons; so no more need be said.

But the young captain of Sentinels was the soul of integrity and if he bore witness to what Tanderae suspected was taking place tonight, the Loremaster would have the proof he needed to save his people from betrayal at the highest level.

Weeks before, Tanderae, Gulamendis, and his human colleague Amirantha, had been summoned to this very building because of an attempt by the demon host, as they thought, to locate them. Instead they had seen something far more terrifying than a Demon King, for a Dreadlord had hovered briefly on the other side of the portal.

Since that night the Lord Regent had ordered the building emptied and the power to the portals deactivated, but several times Tanderae had seen figures entering and leaving late at night when most of the residents of E'bar were asleep.

A few nights earlier, Tanderae had discovered that one of the figures he had seen was the Lord Regent himself. He had followed him into the building unobserved and what he witnessed had frightened him in a way he could never have imagined before, not even having fought demons across the stars.

Now, on stealthy feet, they entered the main hall and moved to the entrance to the main portal chamber. At the far end they saw the Lord Regent place a crystal in the base of the portal and watched as energy gathered between the pillars to form an opalescent surface. The energy swirled and then resolved into a black form of woeful countenance, a thing man-like in shape, but without discernible features. Around its head burned a crown of flames, yet they appeared to give off no light. Eyes like red-hot coals gazed out at the now-prone form of the Lord Regent.

Words were exchanged in a language neither Tanderae or the Sentinel captain could understand, but the very sound of them caused the flesh on his neck and arms to gather prickle, as if a frigid cold swept through the hall.

After some time the vision in the portal vanished. Tanderae and Egun stepped back quickly, and hurried to the entrance. 'Do you understand what you just witnessed?' asked the Loremaster.

'I am not sure,' said the captain. 'What manner of being was that, and why would any Lord Regent prostrate himself before any but our true king?'

Upon rejecting the Queen of Elvandar as not being the true ruler of the Star Elves, the taredhel had decreed that the Lord Regent was the supreme authority in E'bar. The captain was confused and his expression revealed it.

'What you witnessed was something from the Forbidden!' hissed Tanderae.

The Forbidden was lore that pre-dated the flight of the Star Elves from Midkemia to their home among the stars, ages before. Only a few high ranking members of the Regent's Meet, such as the Loremaster and the captain, even knew that the Forbidden existed. Fewer still knew what the hidden lore was.

'You speak of treason,' hissed the captain as they hastened away from the building.

'It is the Regent commits treason. As you say, to whom would he kneel and place his forehead on the stone, as if to worship? That thing within the portal is an enemy more vicious than the Demon Legion. It is a living hate from ancient times.'

'How do we proceed if what you say is true?'

'We must find another who can be trusted.' Tanderae declared. 'Laromendis and Gulamendis both know the truth, but their word would be given scant weight in testimony.'

'Even if another could be found, who would try the Lord Regent? The Meet is chosen by his hand. You stand alone, because of your guild's history, and you would be a voice alone, as would I.'

'Who among the Sentinels can you trust?'

'Now you speak of civil war?'

'I speak of saving the race,' said the Loremaster.

'There is another way, but I fear it will bear consequences as dire as any other.'

'What is that?'

'Call to Tomas of Elvandar. Have him return and then show him what is in the portal.'

Tanderae was silent, standing in the darkness, and after a moment he said, 'That is another part of the Forbidden.'

'But it stands before us in the flesh, and who can deny him? He is an Ancient One and if he says that what we saw is also of the Forbidden, no voice would be raised to defend the Lord Regent. He would be judged guilty by all.'

'I will think about it,' said Tanderae. 'I will send the brothers abroad, so they may make their way to Elvandar. They will not be missed. I thank you for your wisdom, Egun.'

'I will speak carefully with a few I trust, so if it comes to a confrontation we will not stand alone, but this must wait until you have summoned the Valheru.' The captain turned and vanished into the night.

Tanderae had a high opinion of Tomas. He had arrived for his first visit on the back of a golden dragon, but his demeanour had been deferential and respectful of the life the taredhel had found for themselves. He had bid them to visit Elvandar at their pleasure and made no claims of sovereignty, merely welcoming them home as lost kin. But he was Valheru, and all that meant in the fibre of any elf's being. He was one of their ancient enslavers, the pillagers of their labours and despoilers of their very bodies when the mood suited them. They were evil in every way imagined; yet Tomas was not like that.

Battling within himself, Tanderae hurried off on his own errand, to find the two brother elves and send them off to seek help in saving E'bar and all who lived there.

Hal stood silently, looking out over the ocean as the sun set. It had been decided he'd avail himself of Ruffio's means to travel to Rillanon, getting him there a day before the King's ship arrived. Tradition had the King lie in state three days before being sealed up in the vault of his ancestors, and then the Congress of Lords would meet, and the serious business of choosing a new king would be under way.

Ty had agreed to travel with him, and he was glad, for despite his sudden immersion in all things politic at the un-gentle hands of Jim Dasher Jamison, Ty was well practised in the ins and outs of court life and would be a valuable ally.

A soft sound from behind caused him to turn. Stephané had somehow stolen her way into his quarters and now stood regarding him with accusing eyes. 'You haven't come to see me,' she said as if it were a crime of the highest order.

'I've been very busy,' he said, and realized there were few worse things he could have said. He tried to clarify his state-ment. 'I mean, I wanted to see you, but with the Congress of Lords gathering in Rillanon to choose a new king, I have much to learn and . . .' He saw the amendment was getting him nowhere.

'You should stay here.' It wasn't a question or request, but a statement.

'I want to,' he said softly, 'or at least I want to be where you are.'

She took a step and suddenly was in his arms, squeezing him tightly. 'Mother told me about your "chat," and that she liked you very much as a result. Father saw how brave you were protecting everyone in the great hall. You are a duke, even if your duchy is full of Keshians, and my father would find you a place in court, I know it. Please, stay.'

His heart broke. 'I can't. I am related by blood to the crown of the Isles. It is my duty to go and elect the new king.'

'Will I ever see you again?'

He stepped back slightly, took her chin in his hand and said, 'That, Highness, is a certainty.' He kissed her and without another word she turned and fled, tears running down her face.

Hal stood still for a long time, the pain in his soul as deep and sharp as when he had learned of his father's death. At last, he crossed to a door and opened it, finding a servant waiting on the other side. 'Send for Lord Tyrone and the magician Ruffio,' he ordered. 'It's time to leave.'

21

DESTRUCTION

Pug probed.

'Be careful,' Miranda said for the umpteenth time.

'Yes, yes,' he said, annoyed and amused. With the knowledge that the Sven-ga'ri pre-dated the Valheru, they approached the problem of unlocking the matrix anew.

Nakor's thoughts came to them in the matrix. *It occurs to me that all those signatures of race that we found – demon, Valheru, elf – may be locks or guards enabling the matrix to tell the difference between friend and foe.*

To Pug this felt like stating the obvious.

Guards abound. They have a city of beings committed to guarding them on all sides. Why yet more locks?

Perhaps to keep the Pantathians out? answered Magnus.

Perhaps . . . echoed Pug.

They continued to study the matrix.

Krondor was in uproar when Martin and Brendan conDoin rode through the northern gate. They had been unable to find a ship heading south because the Duke of Yabon was sending every scrap of arms and armour back home, along with his army, to Ylith. So they rode until they were ready to sleep in the saddle and came to a city almost returned to normal.

Martin presented his orders to the gate captain who waved him through and they made straight for the palace. There they gave their mounts to the stable lackeys and hurried to the reception area. A frantic-looking guard captain read their orders then said, 'Well, you're too late. The Prince left days ago.'

'Left?' asked Martin.

'Haven't you heard? The King is dead. The Congress meets in a day to elect a new king. Of course the Prince of Krondor has to be there.'

Holding his orders as if they were so much scrap, Martin said, 'What am I to do with this?'

'Hold on to it, I suggest,' offered the captain. 'Find an inn: there should be plenty of rooms now that the Western Armies are marching home, and wait until someone comes for you.'

'What of the Duke?' asked Brendan.

'Duke of Krondor? He's with the Prince. As is Lord Sutherland, the Duke of Yabon, the Earl of LaMut, the Baron of Land's End, and every other titled noble in the west. You're a duke's son and brother: for all I know you may be the highest ranking noble left. We've got a squire or two hanging around, but if there's a real nobleman this side of Malac's Cross, I'll be surprised.'

Martin bade him thanks and turned away. Outside, they returned to the stables and saw their horses were about to be untacked. They waved away the lackeys and mounted up again. 'We'll give the horses a feedbag and water when we find an inn,' said Brendan.

One of the lackeys said, 'Try the Swan and Rook, down the road a bit on the right. Very nice place, I've been told.'

They thanked him and rode on. 'So what do we do now?' Brendan asked.

'Find an inn. Care for the horses. Eat our first decent meal in a week, and drink a lot of ale or wine or whatever the Armies of the West haven't consumed, and wait.'

'What are we waiting for?'

'Your guess is as good as mine,' said Martin.

Hal, Ty, Jim and Ruffio appeared in the courtyard of Jim's private apartment in Rillanon. A moment later Jim said, 'Something's wrong.'

'How do you know?' asked Hal.

'I know this city like the beat of my heart, as well as I know Krondor, and there's something very wrong. Come along.'

He moved into the main hall and found a palace page sleeping on the floor beside the door. With a gentle nudge of his toe, Jim awoke the boy. 'What's going on?'

'Your grandfather, sir, the Duke.' The boy tried not to yawn and failed. 'Sorry.'

'That's all right, boy,' said Jim. 'Now, what about my grandfather?'

'He said if you arrived here before the palace to come straight away. He doesn't care if you're covered in three days of road dirt, just come.'

Jim nodded and said, 'We'll be along straight away.'

'My lord,' said the boy. 'There's been a carriage outside since dawn and all night and dawn again, and I'm to tell you . . .' he cleared his voice, '"to get your arse into the coach and stop mucking about." That was what the Duke told me to say, sir. Not my idea.'

Jim smiled. 'All right. Let's go,' he motioned to the others, and they followed the boy outside.

The carriage that waited bore the ducal crest of Rillanon and the boy woke up the sleeping driver. From the mess beneath the team of horses it was clear they had been made to stand in traces for a full day, the driver and footman no doubt feeding and watering them where they stood.

As he climbed into the carriage, Jim said, 'We'll need a good rain to wash that lot.'

Once inside, Hal said, 'What could be so urgent that it can't wait another day? The King's funeral isn't until tomorrow and the Congress doesn't meet for four days.'

They rounded a circular roadway, then climbed a hillside towards the palace. It took them close to the city's outer wall and Ty said, 'I think I see why your grandfather wanted you here straight away.'

Just beyond the wall, hundreds of tents had been pitched and the smoke from campfires filled the afternoon sky. Sentries had been placed in picket lines across the length of the encampment, facing the wall, and dark blue banners flew from tall standards.

Jim sat back, looking as if he'd just eaten something very unpleasant. 'The Army of Maladon and Simrick. It looks like Prince Oliver arrived early and he's decided he won't take no for an answer.'

They rode the rest of the way to the palace in silence.

Pug pushed forward as gently as he could, his mind probing deeper into what he had come to think of as the 'red lock' that held together the matrix.

Magnus, Miranda, and Nakor all in their own way added

their magical ability to his own. But rather than any sort of brute force, they were attempting to prevent the triggering of a trap, setting off an alarm or otherwise doing damage to the structure.

Pug was attempting to 'draw' a map in his and their minds as they went. Nakor had observed some time earlier that the matrix was something like a maze, but in three dimensions. 'Even that's an illusion,' he had observed. 'We are dealing with a state of energy, the very fabric of reality.'

They continued their exploration.

The heavens exploded as Rider urged her mount down the Celestial Highway, oblivious to the splendour on all sides. Making the translation from the Bliss to the mortal realms took the fabrication of time, and for a while her thoughts were still tethered to the Bliss. As she sped farther from the Presence of the Source, she felt an identity emerging and her perceptions gathered inward, coalescing into a sense of self. At the end of the transition, the necessary shift from cosmic awareness to a limited sentience defined by her own physical perceptions, her identity returned. She was Rider, and her mission was vital.

Around her, star fields collided, releasing unimaginable furies of super-heated, illuminating heaven's arc with colours to confound the human eye. Great engines of energy pulsed beams billions of miles into the night, and in clouds of gas vast beyond measure, stars were born.

The vault of the sky was cluttered with the spinning orbs of universes birthing or dying. The procession of reality's evolution unfolded as time was warped and events ages apart appeared to her simultaneously. She did not pause to consider the magnificence of her surroundings as she raced downward, into the Rainbow Vortex. She was not equipped to appreciate the splendour, for she had no basis for comparison.

She had ridden this way countless times, yet could not

remember a single previous mission. Previous memories did not return when Rider was dispatched as Heaven's harbinger, and it was as if she were born anew. She did not question the why of it; she was content to know that when she had finished her task, she would once more return to the Presence and enter the Bliss.

A clattering of hooves told her she was no longer a thing of mind and spirit, but now a physical thing, and her mount was upon the Crystal Highway. The Crystal Highway appeared at the boundary of the realm of creation defined by thought, limitless in scope, and composed entirely of energy. Behind it lay perfect spiritual happiness, the state of oneness with all; beyond lay a transition from perfect harmony with the Source to becoming mortal once more.

She pressed on.

Hal entered the chamber with Jim, Ruffio and Ty, and found Lord Jamison waiting. 'We have a bit of a situation,' said the old man as the four found seats around a small table.

Jim said, 'If you mean the total armies of Maladon and Simrick sitting outside the city walls, yes, indeed we do.'

'No foreign army has set foot on this island in five hundred years,' said the Duke, smacking his hand down hard on the table.

Jim said, 'Well, as Oliver is King Gregory's nephew, and those are his armies to command . . .'

'When did you become a litigator?' asked his grandfather.

Jim shrugged.

'Do you think Oliver will move against the Congress if the vote goes against him?' asked Hal.

James sat back, looking every bit his seventy-plus years. 'I don't know. No noble has raised an army against the Crown since Jon the Pretender, to the everlasting infamy of his name. This may be no more than a reminder that Oliver has powerful allies to the east. The Queen of Roldem is his aunt from Maladon, and that counts for a lot.' James nodded. 'If he marries that girl from Roldem, that would give him a solid standing throughout the region.'

'But he's not Kingdom-born,' said Jim, noticing the distress on Hal's face at the mention of anyone marrying Stephané.

'That's always been the counter-argument,' said James.

There was a knock on the door and the Duke shouted, 'Come in!'

Servants arrived with wine and food, and quickly prepared the table. 'Thought you might be hungry,' he said after the servants left.

Jim poured wine and handed out the goblets. Another knock came and again the Duke bellowed for whoever was outside to come in. A messenger entered and handed him a parchment bearing a seal. Looking at Jim, the Duke said, 'You're not the only one with eyes out there.' His grin vanished as he read. 'Damn it to the seven hells!'

'What is it?' asked Jim.

'That damned fool Chadwick of Ran. He's landed his army to the south of the city.' He read on. 'And he's brought friends. Salador and Bas-Tyra are with him.'

Jim sat back. 'Are these fools starting a civil war before we've even buried the last king?'

Duke James shook his head in frustration and said, 'Give me that damn wine!'

Now Rider was fully-fleshed. Her form was human, but her face lacked the tiny imperfections of humanity, the creases and lines, spots and dimples. She had skin too smooth to be mortal, and her brown eyes, flecked with moats of ruby, were able to peer through realities. Her body was lithe and agile, as strong as tempered steel and as hard as diamond. Hair golden one moment, silver the next, flowed from under a black cap that was set at a rakish angle. From a shimmering brooch pin of alien make and unknown metal a long, flaming feather trailed, a rare phoenix plume. Only the powerful harmony of her magic kept it from vanishing into ash or setting her hair alight.

She rode a creature out of fable, a mare of golden hue, with hide that shimmered like metal and a mane and tail of copper sparkling with flashes of pure white light. Her breath was steam as she pounded across uncountable miles down through the Vortex into the Entropy Funnel, her hooves striking sparks on the perfect surface of the roadway. She was one of the most powerful of her kind, the Matriarch of the Heavenly Herd, the star-spanning mounts of angels. That she had been given the task of carrying the rider demonstrated the importance of this journey.

Rider focused on her mission: to reach the mortal realm and give orders to the awaiting host. It was time to assault an enemy seeking a foothold on a poor, sad little world. A strange place, it was a world of coincidence and destiny, a battleground in an ages-old struggle that was far greater than even the wisest among humanity could imagine, beyond even the understanding of the beings they called gods. All of reality as they knew it stood in peril and this one, tiny world, normally insignificant in the vast scheme of the universe, was where the struggle would soon commence. If this world fell, so would fall all of that sector of reality, and eventually all reality, even unto this realm.

As Rider raced along, primal matter leapt from orb to orb, massive surges of power to destroy star systems, causing the Golden Moons to thrum and vibrate, their pitch changing in a cacophony of sounds that were the highest music imaginable. Legends were told of lesser beings who had somehow found their way to the Sphere of the Golden Moons and died of thirst or starvation as they sat transfixed by a music so profound it immobilized the listener. It was the sound of everything.

Down through the higher realms she rode, feeling the falling energy states around her, as the abundance of creation, the immeasurable wealth of heaven's bounty cascaded down with her as she descended into the mortal realms. Vision became paramount as other senses faded, music and sound had to be heard rather than known, and the feel of her mount between her legs became a sensation that began to fatigue her. Separating from the Presence was painful at the end.

At the boundary of the Sphere and the Realm of Emergence, the road changed again, become the yellow-white road known as the Star Walk, the Gateway Path, or the Hall of Worlds. Time shifted as she entered the edge of the mortal realms, and she sensed its passing. Here was the boundary of reality as mortals knew it, where new matter entered their space and time. It was speculated about by many races, but none had come here, understood and returned to spread the word. The boundaries of mortal exploration were still vast distances down the Hall, lifetimes of exploration away.

At the edge of the Hall, near the boundary between the Sphere and the Hall, waited the Host. Immobile, they stood arrayed in battle rank, thousands of agents of Heaven, waiting for their orders. Ageless and patient beyond mortal comprehension, they were as alike as perfect statutes. Yes she knew them all, each and every one, for it was one of those things carried over from her time being in the Presence, being one with the Source. Before the arrayed ranks of the Host waited one alone, and she reined in her mount before him.

'Riakel,' she said in greeting.

'Rider,' he said in return. He was majestic in appearance, the personification of a human's vision of what an angel should look like: tall, broad of shoulder, features strong yet beautiful. Riakel's hair flowed to his shoulders and was ebony in colour, yet his skin shone pale yellow in the Hall's fey light. He wore a long flowing robe of white, and over it a battle harness. At his left hip was a massive sword in its scabbard, and she knew that once it was drawn it would burn with Heaven's fire.

Behind him stood silent rows of warrior angels, each displaying a slight difference in colour of skin, hair, eyes, yet all alike, ready to carry out their mission should the Celestial Rider fail in hers.

Riakel's black eyes fixed on her and he said nothing. There was no need for speech between them, for each had been sent on their missions with the full knowledge of what must be done.

Yet she felt the need to speak. 'How long?'

He inclined his head slightly to one side, as if cracking his neck, a very human gesture she knew meant the question was pointless. 'It is not known,' he answered. 'The Source always provides us with the knowledge we need.'

'But not until we need it,' she amended.

'Soon. Too long the demons have had free rein in the mortal realm while we have been confined here.' With a gesture towards the countless angels standing motionlessly behind him, the Master of the First Host repeated, 'Soon. Even now someone attempts to unlock the barrier, and should they succeed, we shall unleash Heaven's wrath as has never been known in mortal history.'

'I have your orders,' said Rider. 'The demons and their minions are to be obliterated, returned to the lower sphere. All except two. They have a role to play.'

'How will I know them?'

'You will know them.'

The Master of the First Host nodded. 'The balance must be restored.'

'But in the time specified, and not before.'

'You have another mission?'

She nodded. Knowledge manifested in her mind. 'Yes. I must be off.'

Without another word, the Rider turned her mount and moved back down the Hall of Worlds, passing the first pair of doors into the mortal realm.

She was now in what humans called the lowest heaven, a realm of wonderful, yet mortal beings. Most beings from the realms below would consider this realm ideal, for it combined the finest aspects of mortal experience with an apprehension of the wonders of the Higher Realms.

Time began to weigh on her, for now time was perceived

by her in the same way as it was by mortals. And time was short. The imbalances of the past needed to be corrected, and she was the last attempt by the Presence to correct that imbalance without there being utter destruction.

If she failed, and if he to whom she carried warning failed, then the Host would cease to merely battle Hell's minions; they would be fully unleashed to undertake a cleansing of the realm called the First Realm of Hell by those above it, and the First Realm of Heaven by those below it, and the Source would start anew.

It had happened before. Yet the Source was love and mystery and offered hope.

She sped past more doors as she plunged deeper into the mortal realms, into more populated space. The road twisted and turned and hundreds of doors were left behind. She would ride past ten thousand more before nearing the one through which she must travel, to the world called Midkemia.

A thrumming filled the air, harsh and discordant, jarring the senses like a physical blow. She reined in, for something was amiss. Suddenly Rider knew that the waiting host had not advanced far enough, did not know the waiting was not at the will of the Source! Something hobbled the mind here, limited perception, and robbed those from the higher realms of their usual strengths. As she pondered this realization, her mount reared up, stumbled, and fell back.

Rider pitched over the mare's haunches, striking the stones of the Hall with a force fit to break bones, but she was unhurt, for her body was still as hard as diamond. The oldest mare in the Heavenly Herd lay thrashing, and Rider turned to see her pain and hurried to inspect her injury.

This should not happen. It was impossible. No power in the mortal realm could harm the Matriarch of the Heavenly Herd or Rider. Yet the proof was before her, as the mare shuddered, then closed her eyes. Despite not belonging to the mortal realm, the celestial mount was confined in form and function by the limits of this reality. She faded into golden smoke, speeding back up the hall toward the Source, where she would re-form and once again take her place at the head of her herd.

But Rider now stood afoot, and knew that something profoundly wrong had intercepted her. She turned, her eyes blazing with anger. Drawing her sword, she advanced toward the cause of her fall. And walked into something invisible.

Pain shot through her body, her mind, and into her soul. This barrier was something so profoundly wrong that it tore at her. She fell back and felt the thrumming that came from the barrier grow more intense, rising up the scale to a pitch that hurt her now-mortal ears.

Still, she was Rider, and an agent of the Source. Even in the mortal realms her powers were unmatched by any who abided her. And there was nothing of fear in her being. 'Show yourself!' she demanded.

Something rose up before her on the other side of the barrier, roughly man-shaped but immense. It towered over her as a tree did a child.

Rider had lost her place in the Presence, was apart from the Source, but her knowledge was still considerable. Yet before her stood something unknown to her, something that was clearly powerful beyond compare in these mortal realms. 'What are you?' she demanded.

A tentacle reached out, passed effortlessly through the barrier and attempted to grapple with her. She swung down with her blade, which burned with Heaven's fire, and struck a blow that severed the tentacles. It withdrew, the severed section smoking. Then it vanished in a bright flash. From the other side of the barrier came a hollow sound, a distant chuckle that echoed like wind down a canyon. 'I am,' it said softly, yet the words were clear. 'I am that which was before.' Again the chuckle. 'I am that which was left behind.'

Rider knew fear then. She turned to flee, and as she did, the thing shot through the barrier to sweep over her, swallowing her in a darkness that was the antithesis of all she had ever known. It was a void so profound that her last, fleeting thought was despair, for she knew she would never again know the Presence, nor approach the Source. This was her end.

The black shape that had destroyed Rider vanished, leaving a chill wind to blow up the Hall. In time, the feathers of wings on the backs of a host of angels would rustle from that wind. And still they would wait, motionless and patient, though one or two among them might wonder when the call would come.

Rider's last conscious thought was hearing a loud click, as if tumblers in a lock were falling.

Pug probed further and they all heard the 'click' in their minds.

What's that? Miranda asked.

Nakor said, *A trap*—

Universes exploded.

Birds took to the sky as they sensed a pulse of energy gathering in the heart of the city. A Pantathian farmer transporting his crops to market noticed a mile away from the city that a massive flock had launched itself skyward. He paused to wonder what could have caused it.

Then his world ended.

The explosion was like nothing before experienced on this world. It was the tearing of the fundamental matter of existence, and the release was so destructive that the entire Pantathian city ceased to exist in the blink of an eye.

A blast of light was released, so bright that had any mortal eye looked at it, that creature would have been rendered blind at a distance of ten miles. A moment after the blast of light, a fireball was preceded by a wave of air moving at the speed of sound, so powerful that trees were knocked flat, animals were instantly killed by the impact, their bodies picked up and hurled for miles.

Then came the heat. Whatever it washed over was instantly turned to cinder.

On the mainland to the north, fishermen working the waters between the south coast of Kesh and the Isle of the Snake Men saw an unnatural flare in the south, climbing into the heavens as if someone had reached up to challenge the gods.

Outward the flames sped, and after two miles the heat dissipated and trees and plants were merely scorched and not set alight. After five miles, animals survived the sudden rise in heat, but saw a monstrous column of flame, dust, smoke, and ash climb into the skies and spread out in a mushroom shape.

From rabbits to eagles, elk to wolves, the animals on the island turned and galloped from the source of this calamity. All knew instinctively that nothing within that blast zone could live, and where once there had been a nation of gentle souls, now only death ruled.

ENTR'ACTE

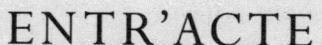

AWAKENINGS

Tomas sat up.

In the early morning hours he felt something rip through the fabric of this world in a way he had not known since he first donned the white-and-gold armour of the Dragon Lord. He looked around and saw that his wife was now awake, looking at him with wide eyes.

'Beloved,' she asked softly, 'what is it?'

He did not have any words for a moment, then at last he said, 'It's Pug . . . he's gone.'

She put her hand on his arm. 'Gone?'

'We have always had a bond and now it's severed.' He sat motionless a few seconds, then said, 'And there's something else.'

'What?' she asked as she saw his powerful back outlined in the faint moonlight coming in through the window of their quarters. He was moving to the chest in which he kept his armour. 'Tomas?'

He opened the chest and stared down at his legacy of Ashen-Shugar, the Valheru whose memories he shared. 'I feel something.'

'What?' she asked again.

Looking at the armour, then at his wife, he said, 'There is another.'

Draken-Korin slumbered on his ebony throne, the last vestiges of his mortal body stripped away. He stirred and saw that all had been returned as he had ordered it. Every inch of the chamber had been cleaned by his loyal tiger-men, and the torches lit. He stood and instantly those who were in the chamber fell to the floor in abject obeisance, touching their foreheads to the stone.

'I am hungry!' he roared. 'Bring me food. I must gather my strength.' He tilted his head, as if listening. 'There is another.'

Tanderae could feel the shift in the energy field of the planet. Something huge had just taken place. Whatever it was, it must be catastrophic to be felt at such a distance.

Then heaven tore open.

The blast knocked him off his feet as a massive pillar of ruby light exploded through the roof of the portal building and a wash of heat rolled over him. If there had been anyone inside the building when that explosion took place they were surely dead.

He got up on unsteady legs as the inhabitants of E'bar left

their homes to come outside and stare at the monstrous light. Egun found the Loremaster and said, 'What happened?'

'An explosion from the portal building.'

'Ancestors,' the captain of the Sentinels whispered. 'I was looking to find you. The Lord Regent was in there.'

'No longer,' said Tanderae. 'Find who you can of the Meet and ask them to assemble. Questions will be asked and we have no answers. Find the galasmancers and have them look in the portal room if they can do so safely, for we must know what is taking place.'

'What do you think this is?' asked the soldier.

'I fear it is a beacon,' said the Loremaster.

'A beacon?' The captain paused, then asked, 'For what?'

'What all beacons are for, Egun. To guide someone here.'

'Who?'

'That is what I fear to find out.'

In the wilds of western Kesh sprawls a massive lake, the Dragon Erye. Home to a peaceful people of Isalani descent – fishermen, farmers and hunters – the region has remained unchanged for centuries. A ring of mountains, the Watchmen, surrounds this lake, save for a river coursing north to the sea. In spring when the ice thaws in the peaks and the snows melt, the river floods and farmers rejoice as the farmland along its banks is renewed.

The mountains, the inaccessibility of the lake, the lack of riches have left this area neglected by conquerors, migratory invaders, bandits, or rogues. It may be the single most peaceful region on the entire world of Midkemia.

A potato farmer named Li Shun pushes his small cart along the road at dawn, taking his harvest to market. Winter potatoes are in short supply this year and he anticipates good trading.

Then comes the sound.

He stops. Turning his back on his cart, he moves down the road and as he takes each step, he wills his body to change.

High above the lake, in a meadow full of sheep, two brothers, Tai and Mak, sit near their campfire watching their flock. Their dog perks up his ears, listening. Then the two brothers stand, letting their crooks fall to the ground. They leave the whining dog behind as they move away from their camp, their bodies beginning to change with each step. Their forms flow and take on a much larger appearance.

In a nest high above the meadow, a dragon matriarch lies curled around a clutch of eggs. As is the nature of her kind, she will watch over them until they hatch. She is growing hungry, for she has not eaten in a month, but she has gorged herself on enough food to last for another month until the three eggs stir and then she will hunt on behalf of her hatchlings.

Then she hears the sound. She rises up and spreads her wings, throws back her head and lends her voice to that sound, amplifying and repeating it.

Around the world, dragons let go the illusion of human form, as hunters in the mountains throw aside their bows, a fisherman at sea lets his small boat sink as he becomes too massive for it to support him; a guard on a caravan leaves camp in the middle of the night and goes into the darkness never to be seen again by his companions.

Around the world dragon voices pick up the sound and repeat it, lending their power to the note.

The time has come.

It is the song they have not heard in the memory of the oldest living dragon in the world, but instinctively they know it.

In the darkness of western Novindus a massive black dragon launches itself into the starry night, the powerful snap of its wings cracking like thunder as it circles and climbs, seeking out a call so ancient it needs no words to know it.

In the noonday sun of Rillanon, on the highest southern peaks of that island, a massive white dragon cries out with emotions so profound it has no name for them; and it leaps into the sky, a massive cloud against the blue to a hunter who happens to look up.

Around the world the call repeats, and dragons in hiding among humans answer, and within minutes, it is echoed and answered and repeated. From distant mountains, and deep caverns, isolated beaches and lonely valleys, dragons rise.

In a vast cavern below an abandoned city, the greatest dragon of all lifts her head and listens. Around her robed figures wait, for this is the time of the nexus, the cusp of all things and now comes days of uncertainty.

Slowly she lowers her bejewelled head and closes her eyes, and her companions turn to guard the now slumbering Oracle of Aal, for she has come to the end of the future. This is when time itself will change, and even the most powerful seer in the history of the universe cannot see what tomorrow will bring.

And don't miss the final installment
of the Riftwar Cycle

MAGICIAN'S END
Book Three of the Chaoswar Saga

by Raymond E. Feist

Coming soon in hardcover
from Harper Voyager

LEGENDS OF THE RIFTWAR

HONORED ENEMY
978-0-06-079284-8

by Raymond E. Feist & William R. Forstchen

In the frozen northlands of the embattled realm of Midkemia, Dennis Hartraft's Marauders must band together with their bitter enemy, the Tsurani, to battle *moredhel,* a migrating horde of deadly dark elves.

MURDER IN LAMUT
978-0-06-079291-6

by Raymond E. Feist & Joel Rosenberg

For twenty years the mercenaries Durine, Kethol, and Pirojil have fought other people's battles, defeating numerous deadly enemies. Now the Three Swords find themselves trapped by a winter's storm inside a castle teeming with ambitious, plotting lords and ladies, and it falls on the mercenaries to solve a series of cold-blooded murders.

JIMMY THE HAND
978-0-06-079299-2

by Raymond E. Feist & S.M. Stirling

Forced to flee the only home he's ever known, Jimmy the Hand, boy thief of Krondor finds himself among the rural villagers of Land's End. But Land's End is home to a dark, dangerous presence even the local smugglers don't recognize. And suddenly Jimmy's youthful bravado is leading him into the maw of chaos . . . and, quite possibly, his doom.

HARPER VOYAGER
TRADE PAPERBACKS

HARPER Voyager
An Imprint of HarperCollins*Publishers*

www.harpervoyagerbooks.com

THE THACKERY T. LAMBSHEAD CABINET OF CURIOSITIES
Edited by Ann VanderMeer and Jeff VanderMeer
978-0-06-211683-3

HIDDEN THINGS
by Doyce Testerman
978-0-06-210811-1

ANGEL'S INK
by Jocelynn Drake
978-0-06-211785-4

ARCHON
by Sabrina Benulis
978-0-06-211690-1

THE DEVIL'S DIADEM
By Sara Douglass
978-0-06-220009-9

THE EXPLORER
by James Smythe
978-0-06-222941-0

HVT 1112